To Austin Cooper

JACK HOLMES AND HIS FRIEND

Forgetting Elena: A Novel
The Joy of Gay Sex (coauthored)
Nocturnes for the King of Naples: A Novel
States of Desire: Travels in Gay America
A Boy's Own Story: A Novel
The Beautiful Room Is Empty: A Novel
Caracole: A Novel
The Darker Proof: Stories from a Crisis
Genet: A Biography
The Burning Library: Essays
Our Paris: Sketches from Memory
Skinned Alive: Stories
The Farewell Symphony: A Novel
Marcel Proust
The Married Man: A Novel
The Flâneur: A Stroll Through the Paradoxes of Paris
Fanny: A Fiction
Arts and Letters: Essays
My Lives: A Memoir
Chaos: A Novella and Stories
Hotel de Dream: A New York Novel
Rimbaud: The Double Life of a Rebel
City Boy: My Life in New York During the 1960s and '70s
Sacred Monsters: New Essays on Literature and Art

JACK HOLMES AND HIS FRIEND

Edmund White

BLOOMSBURY
LONDON · BERLIN · NEW YORK · SYDNEY

First published in Great Britain 2012

Copyright © 2012 by Edmund White

The moral right of the author has been asserted

Bloomsbury Publishing Plc
50 Bedford Square
London
WC1B 3DP

www.bloomsbury.com

Bloomsbury Publishing, London, Berlin, New York and Sydney
A CIP catalogue record for this book is available from the British Library

ISBN 978 1 4088 0579 4 (hardback edition)
ISBN 978 1 4088 1517 5 (trade paperback edition)

10 9 8 7 6 5 4 3 2 1

Typeset by Westchester Book Group
Printed in Great Britain by Clays Ltd, St Ives plc

Part I

1.

JACK, WHO WAS from an eccentric Midwestern family, wasn't quite sure what a gentleman was other than someone who opened doors for ladies and didn't curse in mixed company. He'd gone to a boarding school, but one outside Detroit, which the sons of the "automobility" attended; they judged each other by their cars, not their manners or clothes. Although the schoolboys all had to wear coats and ties, their jackets were usually off the rack and were rumpled and styleless. Who would worry about clothes when he could tool around in a Corvette or Austin-Healey or Thunderbird up and down the leafy lanes of Bloomfield Hills or get into a drag race with an older businessman down Woodward Avenue?

Although Jack was bookish and refined after his own fashion, he was used to brash guys who lived in a loud, locker-banging, all-male world of muddy knees and broken noses and wolfed-down generic meals in the immense, pseudo-Gothic dining-hall they called the "cathedral of carbohydrates." In Detroit in the 1950s, no one earned extra points for reading, or for visiting Europe—well, okay, visiting it counted. Back then, it was still rare to travel abroad and cost a lot. The brainy daughter of rich Midwesterners might live with a French family for a semester in

Tours, which was supposed to have the best accent. By the end of six months, she could barely express herself in French, but she'd have lost that extra ten pounds and acquired dark, becoming clothes and a convincing French "r" (you could hear the returning American girls on the *Queen Mary* asking each other confidentially, "How's your 'r'?"). The boys didn't even consider doing anything so painful and embarrassing as tackling another language; they were all going to study automotive engineering in a normal Midwestern university.

Jack would have gone abroad, but his father, a chemical engineer, couldn't see the point. He sent his son to the University of Michigan because it was midway between his house in Cincinnati and his summer cottage on Walloon Lake, Michigan. Jack had been accepted at Harvard and had even won a merit scholarship there, but it turned out that Jack's father earned too much for Jack to receive anything other than a parchment for his pains. And Jack's father said he'd be damned if any son of his would attend a pinko school like Harvard.

Even at the University of Michigan, Jack managed to declare himself a socialist, while at the same time he joined his father's fraternity, a Southern one where they wore masks with eyeholes and held swords up during the initiation ceremony and pledged to protect the purity of Southern womanhood. They didn't have any black or even Jewish members (the handsome, dark-haired Jews all belonged to ZBT down the street), but Jack had plenty of Jewish friends and Chinese friends (he was majoring in Chinese art history), and he even knew a black poet whom all his bohemian friends admired intensely: Omar. When Omar talked to them about Rilke, they could hear the clack and rustle of angel wings.

Jack had feared that his father would oppose his studying

Chinese art history but no, he thought that China was the future and Jack was smart to be out ahead. What Jack didn't bother to tell his father was that he was studying mid-Ching painting and classical Chinese and that he had no interest in mastering contemporary conversational Mandarin. Nor did he much want to visit China; the land of his dreams lay entirely in the past. He took a few conversation classes to throw his father off his scent, but he was too embarrassed by the strange tonal sounds to be able to speak the language out loud. He did help one of his teachers translate a history of Buddhist art written in classical Chinese.

Jack was a tall, rangy guy with stomach muscles as hard as a turtle's shell. His straight hair was called dirty-blond, but in fact he kept it squeaky-clean with Breck shampoo, though he knew that product was for women. Girls who liked him said he had a "boy-next-door look," but if they really liked him, they said they could imagine him as the pitcher on a baseball team. Any hint of praise or interest in him made him perk up fool-ishly (which he instantly regretted). He wondered if he'd been undernoticed by his strange parents.

In boarding school, the boys had watched movies on Satur-day evenings with girls from their sister school. The boys, espe-cially the boarders, were as awkward as monks around women, and it was hard to convince them to talk to their guests during the cookie-and-cider reception after the projection. The day boys, who usually weren't around on weekends, were a lot more relaxed when they happened to attend. They treated women as if they were members of the same species at least, whereas the boarders gulped and turned funny colors and jabbed each other in the ribs, almost as if a girl were something like a newly pur-chased thoroughbred horse, valuable but hard to ride.

Jack got along with girls and boys because he was a classic "good guy." He had a way of addressing a total stranger with a highly specific, offbeat question. Standing in front of a student photo exhibit, he might say to a stranger, without any introduction, "You can tell all these pictures were taken by the same person, can't you? They all look like people in the 1930s." Odd as the approach might be, it required nothing from his interlocutor but an opinion. It suggested they'd known each other forever.

He never had to think about how far he'd go with a girl, since they were all so closely chaperoned. On an April Sunday he could walk hand in hand over the extensive grounds with his friend Annie, but she seemed as cool and chaste as he felt, and anyway she'd often invite another girl to tag along. They were ironic about the "pre-ruined" Greek temple with its columns that had been built fallen, since fallen columns were more picturesque than standing ones, or about the fat, murky goldfish in the Jonah pool, or about the heavily fringed Edwardian splendors of the Booth House with its silk lamp shades and handcarved oak breakfronts. Jack and his friends were always ironic, but often they didn't know if they were serious or not about any given subject. Irony was just a way of feeling superior instead of insecure.

In college in Ann Arbor, he had a brainy New Yorker for a roommate in the freshmen dorms. Howard was a slob who slept through most of his classes and never washed his clothes. In the evenings, when they were both awake and studying, they'd play a record of Prokofiev's sprightly *Classical* Symphony over and over again. The acidic variations on Mozart sounded as if a powdered wig had been given a lemon rinse. Howard was very thin, grinned all the time, and exposed his large and very pink upper gums and hunched his meager shoulders forward and shook with inaudible laughter. As actors said, he was "indicating" laughter. Howard was satirical but somehow kind at the same time.

Jack knew that Howard, as a New York Jew, was studying him with amusement as a type, a Midwestern WASP. Jack realized that each of them thought of himself as something usual, standard, and considered the other one to be exotic, a deviation. They got along very well. Jack had lived in boarding school for six years and could tolerate, even enjoy, almost anyone; he just drew a pink chalk line down the middle of the room and said to Howard that he should keep his filth on one side and never invade Jack's space. Howard raised his shoulders and shook all over with pretend laughter at this WASP "anality," as he labeled it. Jack chuckled when he thought how far he was from the conventional WASP of Howard's imagination. Jack felt that he was entirely self-invented, and that Howard conjured up images of tutors and Parcheesi tournaments, of trout fishing in cold-water private streams and fumblings with debs in the backs of Packard convertibles—when nothing could be farther from the grotesque chaos of his childhood.

Jack got good grades, and his fraternity prized him, especially since at least ten of his brothers were on probation. They were all lovable and hopeless—they were mediocre athletes, wretched scholars, bad even at organizing a float for the Homecoming Parade. They drank so much that they quite regularly barfed on their dates and blacked out nightly and had to be told the next morning about their latest excesses. They'd look sheepish and amused, almost as if they were subjects who'd walked out onto a ledge under hypnosis and couldn't remember anything. The fraternity did have a nice pseudo-Tudor house with half-timbering on the outside and a carved wood balcony on the inside where Caruso had once sung, but the whole place was falling apart.

The brothers talked a lot about pussy, but Jack wondered where they actually bedded their dates. At all "Greek" events there were chaperones, and almost no one had a car, though a few seniors rented private rooms just off campus. The girls, moreover, lived mostly in sororities, where there were curfews. Once the weather warmed up (the last two weeks of May), couples drifted off at night into the arboretum.

Then there were all the bohemian girls who joked and called themselves beatniks, but they despised the frat boys. The bohemians lived in dorms, too, but during the day or early evening they seemed to be available. You could tell the bohemian girls by their black stockings and black turtleneck sweaters and by their black boyfriends and regular presence in the middle room of the Student Union. Jack and the Greeks were in the first room, nerds and foreigners in the third; the bohemians were invariably in the middle room. Jack would get high on coffee and chatter endlessly to Wendy or Alice or Omar or Rebekkah in the middle room. He was supposed to be studying for biology or writing a paper on Buddhism, but when the talk got going, he was able to convince himself that this wit and fire, this laughter, and above all these theories about life and love—that all this was more important and original than mere "academics." At boarding school, every moment of the day had been regulated and measured by bells, but here the classes were few, and if a student skipped a lecture, no one was taking attendance. Maybe it was typical of Jack's excessively pliable nature that both the bohemians and the fraternity boys felt so at ease with him and counted him as one of them. He was a "nice" boy who knew how to please others; one of his friends thought he should become a diplomat. But in his heart Jack knew he wasn't a natural pleaser. At the end of an evening with friends he was always exhausted.

By the time he was a junior, he was living in a little room in the back of an old wood house. He shared a bathroom with two other guys, but that seemed no hardship to him, used to group living as he was. One of the guys on his floor was a painting student who never smiled, or if he did, it was out of sync and came long after everyone else had finished. Then he'd concede a pained smile with just half of his mouth, as if he'd figured out that that was what human beings did and he should join them and make an effort.

His name was Paul, and two or three times he invited Jack into his room for a cup of espresso, which he brewed in an Italian pot on his hot plate.

"Hey, neat," Jack said, intrigued by so much rumbling to produce the merest black sludge, and added, "I really like these big baseball players." He nodded toward a canvas so large it would take careful maneuvering to get it out the side entrance and down the fire escape. Some patches were detailed and realistic (a player's face, another's mitt), but the rest was in soft focus and drowned in circumambient color—a wash of green exceeding the stadium grounds and floating over into the surround, a blue sky leaking down onto the stands.

"Really?" Paul asked, lifting one eyebrow. But his delayed twitch of a smile showed he was pleased.

Paul's off-kilter responses made Jack uneasy. Jack didn't like complexity. Maybe because his childhood had been so stormy that now he longed for peaceful moral weather and the first hint of turbulence would cause him to flee south.

And yet he found Paul appealing—his long, hairless body, pale as pie dough, crimped here and there to bulge up as a big nose, a narrow, downturned mouth, an outsize, restless Adam's apple. He had no hair under his arms, which Jack knew because Paul painted bare-chested, often wearing nothing but his Jockey shorts, which looked two sizes too small, too tight and dubiously yellow; the elastic on one leg was broken and dangling down like some scary nodule formerly alive. His nipples were ridiculously small and dark: Nordic berries stunted by the cold. His ribs were as visible as hands around a cup. Wendy, his broad-hipped girlfriend, bursting out of her faded jeans and jiggling recklessly around in her University of Michigan sweatshirt, her glossy black ponytail perched on one shoulder like an expensive pet, was always smiling guiltily. She knew that her plentiful body amused, but might potentially offend, her austere lover. Everyone teased Wendy and everyone loved her, as if she were a prehistoric fertility symbol found one day among the tea things. But Paul often seemed pained, as much by Jack's calculated nice-guy blandness as by Wendy's alternating exuberance and sheepishness. Just by being quiet and staring at them hard, Paul could provoke self-conscious reactions in his friends.

Jack imagined that by the time Paul was forty he'd be sour and closed off, but since now he was just twenty he was still curious and still strangely underrehearsed for his life. He didn't know quite yet how he worked or what he wanted.

One day Paul invited Jack in for a cup of tea; he was painting in the nude. Jack was seated on a folding chair that Paul had cushioned with newspapers to protect Jack's clothes.

Jack felt uneasy, he couldn't say why. For chrissake, he hadn't set this deal up. Of course, maybe it was the way bohemians thought, or didn't think—it didn't mean a thing to them, clothes optional . . . he was certain his face was bright red. Paul would be sure to notice and laugh at him for being so square. Yes—that's what it was: a test for Jack that Jack was flunking.

Paul said, as he handed him the cup, "Maybe you'd pose for me one day. I couldn't pay you much—maybe two bucks an hour."

"Yeah. Maybe. My schedule—"

"Okay, okay," Paul said, smiling sarcastically as if Jack had admitted some sort of defeat.

That night, as he lay in his narrow bed, which was too short for his lanky body, Jack turned so often that eventually his feet were hanging out in the cold. Finally he had to sleep on his side with his knees drawn up to his chest. He slowly rubbed one foot against the other for warmth. He resented Paul for putting him in the same derisory category as big-ass Wendy. It would be so easy to fall into thinking that Paul was somehow superior with his stinting smiles, his cool arrogance, the cobalt blue diagonal of paint across his ribs, his loping walk, tucked-in buttocks, scrotum as red and veined as an autumn leaf in the rain, and the penis as big and dark as a bloodsucker when you suddenly notice it in horror and salt it and pull it off.

After that Jack avoided Paul, except he would sometimes hear Wendy laughing, mid-sex. Her laughter rang through two doors and her ecstasy aroused him. He could imagine her writhing on his own cot, spilling over the margins, her arms rising, turning her round melons into long gourds, full at the bottom and narrow at the top. Paul's hips were only half the breadth of Wendy's. Jack had noticed the difference. Jack became so horny that he ended up jerking off while picturing them, Paul's buttocks dimpling as he thrust, Wendy exulting as she held an invisible tambourine in each hand.

Jack found some respite from his erotic reveries in his work.

He enjoyed Chinese art history and was proud that he knew so many details about it, though admittedly only about a few selected moments in the full four thousand years. He knew a lot about ancient bronzes and how they had been cast using the lost wax technique, and about all those dragons and clouds and meanders. He knew all about "scholar painting" and how it had been done as a form of protest against the Mongol conquerors. The lightning-scarred tree was the heroic, resistant scholar himself. Jack was good on Sung landscape painting, and the use of "negative space," and the size relationship on three scales (heaven, mountain, man). He liked Ching academic painting, which appealed to no one else. What he didn't like was memorizing thousands of Chinese characters. But even that rote act drowned out the noise in his head. He'd made hundreds of flash cards (with the Chinese character and pronunciation on one side and the English meaning on the other), and he strummed through them at the Union when he was alone. People looked at him with curiosity when he "played solitaire" with his cards. Chinese art history enhanced his mystery, which suited Jack.

His father said he wouldn't let him graduate if he didn't take courses in typing and public speaking. Jack was a horrible public speaker, so shy that his teacher said he was "cold" and not likely to persuade anyone of anything. In their evaluations the other students said he was "snooty" or "aloof."

Wendy had a friend named Hillary, whom she introduced to Jack. They met in late April of Jack's senior year. Like Wendy, she was big-hipped and had long hair, and wore jeans and had precise, little-girl features emerging from her big, round face.

Jack liked it that she was hefty. She wasn't jiggly fat or cold-lard fat; she was firm and athletic, quick to climb over a fence and race down a meadow to the river. She loved to jump into her little red MG convertible with the bird's-eye maple dash-board and powerful motor, its tires spitting gravel out behind them. She was tough, with her clean-scrubbed face, black, un-plucked eyebrows, and hands rough from washing and polishing her roadster or currying her horse back home on weekends. But she could also open up like a tropical flower, a sticky-petaled pink hibiscus—at least that was how he pictured all this articu-lated floral wetness he was exploring with his fingers and couldn't see in the dark.

They were so happy rolling around at night in the long sweet-grass, heavy with dew and smelling of bush clover. Jack gloried in his own maleness when he was lying on top of Hillary. It sounded fatuous, but he liked his own broad rower's shoulders and narrow torero hips and princely waist—he was a prince when he sprawled above Hillary. Was that abnormal, he won-dered, to picture oneself, to glory in oneself? Did the average guy delight in the girl more than in himself? Most of the time he didn't have such a flattering image of himself. He saw himself rather as a friendly collie of a guy: big, toothy smile; trusting, warm eyes; a sort of abashed look when called on to do tricks—to shake hands, say. He called it his "good-guy look." (But then why did that teacher say he was a cold speaker? Had the teacher misinterpreted Jack's shyness?) Then again, some friends did com-plain that he was "reserved" and even "secretive."

Jack was just a little afraid of women, truth be told, unless they were pals or sisters and there was no physical deal beyond sitting back-to-back like bookends on a hay wagon, or sleeping in a two-person pile in the backseat of a dark car during the long trip back from a concert at Fisher Hall. Women liked him. He was often a little brother, sometimes a big brother; if there had been older women around, he would've been a good nephew type. He didn't talk to them about their hair or clothes, nothing beyond "You look really nice, Cindy." He wasn't a professional smoothie, though in the frat house he had a reputation as an "ass man," a seducer's standing based on nothing except rumors about his big cock and that time he'd been caught necking with Hillary in the back stairwell of the frat house, both of them seriously drunk on Drambuie.

With Hillary, though, he was completely at ease. She didn't want to go all the way, and she'd told him that. He remembered: They were walking along past all the sorority and fraternity mansions, but it was a Tuesday afternoon, and no other pedestrians were visible. Without looking at him, she said, "Jack, I've got something to tell you. Do you know what spasmophilia is?"

"I'm not sure I do."

"Well, I've got it. And that's what makes sex a problem for me."

"Really? Don't worry—"

"It's a panic attack, but it means the vagina clamps shut. My shrink says it's a form of hysteria, and when I say I feel perfectly calm, he says it's either the feeling of hysteria and panic *or* the actual spasms, not both. Your body is tightening up, he says, so you won't feel any panic, like conscious panic."

She scrutinized him calmly and said the word "conscious" as if it were a technical term, possibly beyond Jack's grasp.

"Gosh, that's fascinating. Isn't it amazing how—"

"My vagina clamps shut. My regular doctor, not my shrink, says it's a lack of calcium or sleep. He talks about"—and here she shrieked with laughter—"my neuro-vegetative functions! But it all comes down to a clamped vagina."

"Far be it from me—"

"Maybe I should take Miltown. Have you read that new Robert Lowell poem that begins, 'Tamed by Miltown, we lie on Mother's bed'? Very trendy, right? Is that your idea of poetry?"

"I'm afraid I haven't gotten much farther than Wallace Stevens. I'd never read him, and I took his poems to sit on the crapper and I couldn't get off it, I was so excited, and like a crazy person I kept saying out loud, 'This is it! Oh boy, this is it!'"

Hillary laughed so hard she had to stop right there on Washtenaw and hold on to Jack's shoulder. Someone driving past might have thought she was sobbing or having a panic attack.

"But the joke was on me," Jack said, "because at last I thought I had found pure poetry, poetry that didn't mean anything. I found it right there in the crapper, like 'Eureka!' Right? You could say it was abstract expressionist poetry, and I was sitting right there in my stall bouncing up and down—"

"Stop!" Hillary begged him. "You're killing me! Bouncing? No," she wailed.

"It wasn't until two days later that my English prof cleared up the confusion. That fuckin'"—and Jack lowered his voice to say the obscenity: he never swore—"that fuckin' Wallace Stevens, it turns out, means too much, all this metaphysical gobbledygook, though his language is as inscrutable as a nursery rhyme."

They both drew a deep breath and trudged along through the warm, humid day as the occasional car glided up and shimmered, and they felt they were walking in a glue trap and not making any progress. A huge squirrel ran up to them, then scuttled up a tree. Jack was somehow relieved that Hillary had a medical problem that prevented them from rushing into things. They felt very becalmed, almost extinguished. Jack was proud of how funny he'd been about Wallace Stevens.

After that, it was understood that when they were alone and had drunk a few beers, they could kiss and kiss, and Jack could pull up her shirt and unsnap her bra and fondle and lick Hillary's big, extremely sensitive breasts and lightly circle her nipples. Once in a while, if the chemistry was right, he might unbutton her jeans and pull aside her silky, lace-trimmed pan- ties and insert a finger into that liquid warmth, presumably so likely to clamp shut over his knuckles, though at the moment open and welcoming.

One time, she ran her hand wonderingly across his erection, which was safely shut in behind his Skivvies and khakis. She said, half reproachful and half admiring, "Jack, that's awfully big, you know. I mean, it's huge."

Jack suspected it was on the big end of the spectrum. Other guys stared at him in the showers sometimes, and he guessed they were slightly shocked or intrigued. His fraternity brothers had made it part of his myth. Now Hillary was saying, "Even without the spasmophilia, I'd be afraid to take all that. Maybe an older woman would like it, an experienced woman."

"C'mon," Jack complained, blushing in the dark, "moving right along . . ."

Later that night, when he was alone again, he turned on the lights while he was jacking off and actually looked at the damn thing. He could see that it was impressive in proportion to the rest of his body.

Hillary's comment drove him slightly batty. He'd been nice about her spasmophilia, even shrugged it off, as if it were fine by him. He'd started clowning about Wallace Stevens in the crapper just to change the subject, but later she'd treated him like some kind of freak. He decided he'd just keep it out of sight, like some smelly, overgrown truant forced to stand in the corner facing the wall. Or the retarded kid kept back a year in fifth grade. That's how he'd treat his dick.

With some graduation money an uncle had sent him, Jack bought a case of champagne and had a party in his minuscule room. Paul opened up his room as well, and Wendy made some "finger food," as she called the little crustless sandwiches. Though Paul pretended complete indifference to the opinion of other students, Jack noticed he'd propped up four huge canvases—the baseball images and a version of Larry Rivers's *Washington Crossing the Delaware*, which itself was a copy, wasn't it? Howard, his old roommate, came and shook all over with silent laughter and said satirical things so mild as to be good-natured. Hillary, who'd learned flamenco in Málaga the previous summer, snapped her fingers, drummed her boots, and looked stylishly angry until the downstairs neighbor complained and said that plaster dust was sifting down all over his furniture, and everyone quieted down immediately.

And then, from one day to the next, the campus was suddenly empty. Ann Arbor changed from a busy town into a sleepy village—and Jack had no plans. Some kids he knew said they were moving to New York, it would be a ball. He'd applied to Harvard again and been accepted again, into a Ph.D. program in oriental art. His favorite Michigan prof, a German named Max Loehr, had been hired away by Harvard and was urging Jack to follow him and do some "important work" on the evolution of the Buddha image, from Gandhara to Sui and Tang China. But Jack's father still refused to help out with the tuition to a communist university.

During the eerily quiet late-May days in Ann Arbor, Jack realized he didn't have any real friends. Sure, Hillary liked him, but she'd gone off to Kennebunkport for a summer of sailing, and she hadn't exactly invited him to join her. She'd never really trusted him (it sounded weird to say, but it was true) after she'd touched his dick. Jack was convinced that her fear of his size was behind her aversion; he wasn't just being paranoid. Paul had moved to New York for the summer to paint. He said he wanted to meet the older painters who still hung out at the Cedar Tavern—there'd even been an article about them in *Life*. Jack thought it sounded pretty cliché if it had made it all the way to *Life*. In the autumn, Paul was going to study painting at Yale, though he said he was ashamed to admit it, as though a real painter wouldn't take instruction. Paul said an authentic artist needed nothing but some scotch, hardship, solitude, and a good woman tiptoeing around cooking his meals. But Paul wasn't as sure of himself as he let on; he needed Yale's seal of approval.

"Besides," he said, "it's a really radical department now. The most radical in the country. Motherwell teaches there, I think, and Cy Twombly, and some other real bebop talents." Paul liked bebop jazz, and had extended the word to mean avant-garde and something as urban as traffic.

Then Paul was gone, with his mystery and pained, out-of-sync smile and his big paintings, which after much dithering he took off the stretchers and rolled up and shipped home in sturdy mailing tubes.

Jack wandered into Paul's empty room and sat on his bed

with the bare, stained mattress. Without Paul filling it up, without Wendy's apologetic smiles, her ripeness and shame, without the baseball players' blinding white uniforms burning over into the green grass, without the cooked smell of espresso, without the bar of cobalt blue slashed across Paul's ribs like a tribal marking, the room seemed small and lifeless and as dingy as the cast-aside torn underpants in the corner. Would Paul even bother with underpants at Yale?

2.

TWO GIRLS JACK knew from the middle room of the Student Union moved to New York and rented a big apartment on Cornelia Street in Greenwich Village. They said Jack could live with them for as long as he liked. He thought it was a disturbing sign of how "safe" they must imagine he was that it never occurred to them that his presence would hurt their reputations. Of course, they were bohemian girls and thought differently about these things.

One of them was Alice, who was from an old Southern family, though there was nothing of the debutante about her. She bit her nails and wore slacks and never put makeup on and drank a lot of scotch in the evenings. She did, however, like to hunt and fish, and she even owned a hunting lodge somewhere in Virginia. Her own family and its history fascinated her, and she spoke of making a documentary about it. She must have had an income because she never had a job, though she always seemed to have plenty to do. She sometimes helped out a well-known lesbian Broadway producer, maybe with money or finding investors. Strangers assumed that Alice was a lesbian but she wasn't; she slept with famous writers and jazz musicians, though she never discussed her partners and dreaded all publicity.

Jack was impressed that New York was a place where you could casually say that your boss was a lesbian and no one would blink or ask for more details.

Alice's friend and roommate, Rebekkah, had been conceived in the Village, as she liked to say, if raised in Brooklyn. She was the best writer to come out of the University of Michigan in recent years, but she preferred to be an actress. She and Alice rented a loft on Bleecker Street where they presented evenings of improvisational theater. They also had the idea of doing plays by some of Alice's famous writers, both the novelists and the poets. Rebekkah was wonderfully warm and kind and original; Jack could never predict what she was going to say next. She'd been raised by atheists and socialists, and she was an only child. Her mother was extremely girlish and as impulsive as Rebekkah, bubbling over with laughter so much that sometimes her words got lost in the hilarity. She wore her graying hair in a braid down one shoulder with Indian feathers stuck in it. Rebekkah was like that too, though her humor, unlike her mother's, was based on surprised indignation—about horrible right-wing politics and crazy American religious superstition and general bad taste in the arts. She'd widen her eyes as she talked about some new enormity.

When he arrived, Jack had only six hundred and fifty dollars, and after he'd given Alice seventy-five for his room, he was down in the five hundreds. He lived on waffles and sandwiches and the occasional banana. Sometimes the girls would cook up a big pot of spaghetti, which Jack didn't mind eating cold right out of the fridge. He didn't really think about food much, though sometimes he'd feel light-headed after walking too many hours without eating.

There was something about New York that made him want

to walk all the time, even if summer was hard upon him, and Jack
would sometimes come home to Cornelia Street soaked through
with sweat, which was odd since he rarely perspired. With its
tall buildings wavering in the heat and the blasts of dirty air
blown up through the grates by deafening subway trains, New
York sometimes felt like a rusting but still functioning factory
built by a giant. The streets were rough and patched, and even
late at night men in helmets and orange reflector vests drilled
under flimsy little tents or popped their heads up out of open
manholes like groundhogs.

Armies of shabby vagrants were on the march in the late afternoons, and the very old rooted through garbage cans and fished
out discarded newspapers, a supercilious expression on their faces,
as if this whole activity were beneath them and they weren't ac-
customed to it. It was a sort of snooty I-wonder-what-we-have-
here expression they were wearing. He'd never seen poor people
in such numbers before, especially not vagrants wearing shabby
jackets and torn ties, as if just a few weeks ago they'd been respectable office workers—or men like his father.

Jack thought maybe the whole idea of skyscrapers was a bad
one. At rush hour the stacked buildings dumped too many
people on the streets and into the subways. At night the buildings were empty, and block after block was deserted. Then he
felt like a lone cowboy riding through a deserted but dangerous
Monument Valley. The lights on all the floors were dark—or
occasionally they'd be left lit to form a giant cross. A few old
drunks would suddenly move and seem to smolder slightly in a
dark doorway like hot ash.

Sometimes Jack would wander through a pack of gays, all
sibilance and jingling and prancing, as if Santa's reindeer had
been watered with champagne and gone plunging off course.

Or he'd pass a solitary handsome stranger in jeans who stared at Jack—of course Jack would look away instantly. Most of the gays seemed to be over on Christopher Street.

Here on Cornelia, almost everyone was Italian or bohemian. At the end of the block, on Bleecker, there were pastry shops filled with soggy cannoli and hard, week-old butter cookies, or they had little newsstands selling pink sports papers from Italy, or there were dimly lit pizza parlors, or there was the looming somber bulk of Our Lady of Pompeii. At the other end of this block on Bleecker, at Seventh Avenue, was a butcher with un-skinned rabbits dangling on hooks in the window, or scalped goat heads, all teeth and eyes. And always, late at night, another drunk was hectoring the dark. More than once Jack saw a rat sneak across the street. If you stood in the right place, you could look over the crouched rooftops of Greenwich Village and see the spires of Midtown illuminated behind swirling clouds of pollution. As the summer wore on, New York seemed more and more deserted, dirty, tropical. He wondered if the city would pick up once the cold weather returned. Would there once again be people in suits and pale blue shirtdresses? Here, in the Village, all was quiet. But over on the avenues, muted cars were honking and fire engines were wailing. Jack never actually saw a fire, but it sounded as if some part of the city was always in flames.

He didn't think he could parlay Chinese art history into a job, though Max Loehr offered to get him an interview with a dealer, C. T. Loo, on Fifty-seventh Street. But Jack wanted to be a journalist; at least that sounded kind of cool. He went to an em-ployment agent, a woman who had half a dozen pencils piercing her bun and a little dirty office bathed in cigarette smoke. Her ashtray was the size of a dinner plate and nearly filled with stubs, crumpled or prostrate or still smoldering like an elite guard dying or dead on the battlefield, Zouave fatalities in their stained white tunics.

The agent, Shelly, sent him out on two appointments with magazines—one a men's soft-core porn monthly and the other a trade publication for the refrigeration industry. Until now most of the adults Jack had dealt with had been teachers, people paid to praise and nurture promising youngsters. Suddenly he was up against busy, dismissive men who weren't charmed by a candidate's brightness but were coolly sizing up the possibility of working him hard for very little pay. He was no longer a poodle, but a mule. Neither man hired him.

The haphazardness of the adult world shocked him. At school, if you put in some effort, you got good marks and the ascent was even and never too steep. But here in New York, nothing was systematic. Your chances of being hired were determined by who you knew, what kind of first impression you made, your looks, your accent, your timing (they had just fired someone that morning!)—even whether or not you reminded the boss of himself or of his younger self.

"Hey, kid, you're a go-getter, just like I was. I like that, kid," some man had actually said to Howard, who'd landed a job in hospital management. Of course, it helped that Howard's cousin attended the guy's temple in the Five Towns.

Jack had lunch with Howard, who was sweet and reassuring, so far from his usual mockery that it unnerved Jack—was his case so desperate that even Howard had put aside his mild form of perpetual satire?

They met in the Carnegie Deli, where Howard explained to him what a knish was and—"You never even heard of brisket before? Well, order a hot brisket sandwich on a kaiser roll with mayo. You'll like it, I guarantee it."

Eventually Howard made him eat sweet little cherry rugelach for dessert. The funny thing was that Jack knew that Howard ate this stuff regularly, but after Ann Arbor Howard surely had to recognize its folkloric status; he could no longer recommend it naturally, but rather had to do so with curatorial pride. It was as if Jack, in another world, would have been obliged to serve a bowl of Rice Krispies to a Belarusian, and even draw attention to its subtle snap, crackle, and pop. But with this difference: Midwesterners finally knew that their culture was expanding, was winning out, whereas every other ethnos was in retreat. Yeah, but not here. Not in New York. New York was Jewish; Jews felt great about being Jewish in New York. Their humor was funny, their melancholy was funny, their food was tasty and almost comic. It seemed a worldly, cozy, urban culture, and next to it WASPs were pretty bleak and uninitiated.

"But if you get really desperate, you can always ask your parents for money, right?"

Jack just smiled in response and tried to make his eyes go blank.

Howard searched deep into his eyes and said, "Wrong?"

Jack's smile grew broader.

"Okay, very wrong," Howard said. "I don't mean to go on about these differences, but really, you know, in Jewish families— okay, okay. I get it. WASP parents. No good. Bad. Very bad. Bad, bad WASPs." And Howard pretended to spank the air in front of him.

Jack nodded vaguely. He was so vague that Howard wondered if he was actually light-headed from hunger.

"Look, I'm going to give you a three-hundred-dollar loan. I know, you're too proud."

"No, I'm not, I'm not, I'm not," Jack said. Then, more

seriously, he said, "That would be a lifesaver, Howard. Are you sure you can afford it? I'll pay you back as soon—"

"Sh-sh-sh," Howard said, returning to his usual perkiness. "Just think of it as seed money."

Jack's main problem with job hunting was that the slightest rejection plunged him into three days of despair, followed by another two of apathy. He could lose a week if he didn't watch it. He had read a self-help book called *How to Land That Big Job* ("Getting yourself employed IS your new job. You must set about it with all the professionalism and eagerness you will be bringing to your actual position"), but it had only depressed him all the more.

Howard asked him, "What would you do if you could wave a magic wand and have any job in the world? Let's think big here."

"I don't know. I'd like to work on that hardcover quarterly, the *Northern Review*, the one with all the beautiful pictures."

"Isn't it a sort of history deal?"

And then, urged on by Howard, there he was on Sixth Avenue and Forty-eighth Street, on his way up to fill out an application form for the *Northern Review*, which had recently been bought by a publishing giant and moved from Boston to corporate headquarters here in Midtown. He always associated summer with shorts and T-shirts and lying on a beach in a swimsuit, but here he was walking in dress-up clothes across huge slabs of sunstruck sidewalk sparkling with mica and then being revolved into a cold, upended mausoleum and drawn up to the twenty-seventh-floor personnel office. He sat in the waiting room and checked off boxes and wrote a mini-essay about his broad interests and narrow expertise in Chinese art and his burning desire to communicate with readers who were intelligent but un-informed.

A week later he had a brief meeting with an old Austrian who had carefully brushed gray hair like wings under which the egg of his baldness was nesting, a crisp white shirt and a plain maroon silk tie, and a box of Dunhills beside him, which he was carefully working his way through. Karl Gephardt had been managing editor of *Look*—or was it *Life*—for years and now was heading up the *Northern Review* staff of twenty. He treated his present job as if it were a hobby, some sort of genteel reenactment on his lawn of a real battle he'd once conducted as a general. He glanced at Jack's résumé and said, "I called the great Max Loehr about you, and he said you were a nice enough boy, a bright boy, hardworking, with a good visual memory. A little recessive, easily forgotten."

Jack was stunned that his character, which felt like Play-Doh in his own hands, could be firmed up into such a tidy biscuit. He thought "nice enough" sounded dismissive, and Gephardt had said it in a singsong voice. And forgotten? Did people forget him as soon as he left the room? Or could they forget him even as he was sitting right there?

"He is a great man, Dr. Loehr," Jack said. He thought Gephardt's half-condescending reference to Loehr might be a trap and decided his own devotion would stand in attractive contrast to Gephardt's blasé attitude. But the whole idea that a fate—his fate—could be decided by a phone call disturbed him.

"You'll be hearing from us. Or rather"—and Gephardt let his half-moon glasses fall on their chain to his chest with dramatic donnishness—"I suppose you'll be evaluated by our two dear ladies in Personnel."

Jack realized he was being dismissed. He stood up awkwardly. "Very nice to meet you, Mr. Gephardt."

"No, no, call me Karl. We're all informal here" (a patent lie). "I'm not a professor." And suddenly Jack realized that these well-dressed, worldly editors scorned academics. He didn't know whether the news was good or bad. Maybe he'd just passed a stage, but there were probably many more to go.

The two dear ladies in Personnel were in their fifties and worked for the parent company, not the *Northern Review*. They'd been sitting in the same small office, with its dust and snake plants, for thirty years. Every surface was covered with files. They wore hats perched incongruously above their wide, bloated faces, like flowers taped to livestock. Their hair looked so processed that Jack suspected it was glued to the hats.

"Jack? Right. Jack. Now Jack, we're getting ourselves together. Where's my bag, Helen?" "Oh, for chrissake, I don't know where your bag is, Betty! Why would I know where yours is if I can't even find my own damn bag? Okay, let's get this show on the road. Pronto, pronto. Let's just get out the damn door." "Do you have your ciggies, Helen? Your company checkbook? Someone's got to pay for this goddamn meal, and it sure as hell isn't going to be me."

Jack felt invisible around these women. He was used to older women not really noticing him, though the other day a well-dressed woman in her forties had tried to pick him up in Riverside Park. He hadn't been interested, but he'd liked the signal that he was now an adult man. The lady had said, "Do you know anything about TV aerials? Oh, I wonder if you'd look at mine." He wasn't sure Helen and Betty even knew who he was exactly.

Pleasing them seemed like such an indirect way of landing a job, but he put on his best manners and held the door for them.

They had a taxi waiting for them on Forty-eighth Street, just west of Sixth, a very busy street. Amazingly, the cab conveyed them just two blocks, to a dim, old-fashioned Italian restaurant with a marble fountain playing feebly under red and blue spotlights, murals of Vesuvius on the wall, and a bald waiter with a dyed mustache and a much-laundered but still stained napkin draped over his arm. He showed them to their table. "The usual, signore?"

The usual turned out to be two double martinis, ice-cold and entirely ignorant of vermouth and served for some reason in Jack Daniels tumblers. Jack settled for a single martini. Within a matter of seconds, he felt his lips thickening and turning to rubber, his sense of balance lurching dramatically to the left, his thoughts coming loose and floating free. A chance word would trigger a joke in Jack's mind that would make him smile, even laugh—not that the dear ladies noticed.

"Okay, Jack, I guess you'll want a second martini and then some Chianti with your meal. That's red wine. It's what Italians drink. Good, though a little weak, and sour. Spaghetti or veal chop? A side of spaghetti comes with the chop if you're hungry. Helen and I just split a Caesar salad. Got a ciggy for me, Helen? I forgot mine. I'm not sure how you can smoke those Kents, but better than nothing, though that's what they taste like: nothing."

By the time he'd finished his second martini, his spaghetti and red sauce—a big staring pile of it served with hot garlic bread—seemed unapproachable, and Jack just stirred it with his fork and hoped that with enough stirring it would somehow lose volume.

"Oh Christ," said Betty, "you mean you don't eat either? Or is it not what you're used to eating back on the farm? You are a

Midwesterner, or Southerner, or something?" She pulled out Jack's dossier and put on reading glasses and studied it to no avail, tilting her head back until her expression resembled a turtle's, with bulging eyes, sad folds, and a small, dangerous mouth. She was obviously under the impression that all Midwesterners were right off the farm. After devoting some effort to paying, standing, and getting into the waiting taxi, the dear ladies headed back two blocks to their office. Jack wondered if they had cots somewhere under all those stacks and stacks of yellowing files; later he learned that they napped every afternoon at the infirmary before staggering out for a neighborhood happy hour and an early night of it in the smoke-soaked apartment they shared.

Just as he was about to close the taxi door on them, he heard his large, anesthetized mouth with a will of its own pronounce the words "Did I get the job?"

"Hold your horses, big boy, there are still a lot of forms to fill out and review," Betty said. "Get used to big-city bureaucracy. But yeah, we're going to take a chance on you. We like your . . . freshness. And you're a good egg. Good drinker. Now we have to get back to work. I don't know about you."

She looked forward, unsmiling, while Helen lit a Kent and blinked through a blowback of smoke.

Jack walked down through Times Square, patting his back pocket repeatedly to make sure his wallet was still there, jostling his way through a crowd of scared-looking tourists, accosted by men wearing sandwich boards and drunks mumbling for handouts. Time seemed at first molasses thick, then turpentine thin. He could scarcely stay on the sidewalk, and other pedestrians came hurtling at him gleefully like bumper cars—and then he was home. He'd walked forty blocks without noticing. Still dressed up and with his shoes on, he fell asleep in a cold sweat on the couch, smacking his dry lips and dreaming that a big woman out of Fellini was sitting on him, except he was a skinny nine-year-old boy.

He woke up when one of his roommates, Rebekkah, came home after her acting class. "You smell like a distillery, Jack Holmes." She always used both his names, because she argued that Jack was too short to be a proper name. "Are you going to seed, Jack Holmes, drinking in the middle of the day?" She said it in her low voice but with a laugh distorting the words.

He stood up, drank some water, adjusted his shockingly prominent erection in his trousers ("Zowie!" Rebekkah murmured, looking at it), and said, "I think I've landed a job just by drinking martinis with two elderly lesbians."

"What's the job?"

"I told you about the *Northern Review*, right?"

"That reactionary rag? That anti–*New Masses*?"

"Hold on, hold on." Jack raised his long, bony hands in the air and repressed Rebekkah's radicalism. "You're talking about my new place of employment."

Rebekkah, who was short and gap-toothed, with black glossy hair and a lovely, womanly body and a manner that alternated between torpor and exhilaration, looked delighted suddenly. Perhaps his announcement had sunk in only now. "Your what?" She slapped her thighs through her blue skirt and nearly shouted, "Your *what*? You got a job? By drinking old lesbians under the table?" Her laughter bubbled up out of her as her eyes bulged with surprise. "Wait a minute, Jack Holmes. Start at the beginning."

And he did. His personal style, cool and underplayed, was so at odds with Rebekkah's dramatic manner that it was hard to make much progress in telling her the tale. She exclaimed over every detail and found even the most ordinary things note-worthy or outrageous. "Two double martinis? Is that what you're telling me, Jack Holmes? They drank two double martinis? Not two single . . ." And then her voice would trail off, she would gaze blankly to the right as if distracted or bored—and suddenly she'd rebound to her hilarious lament over the drinks, the two-block taxi ride, the vague way of telling him that he was hired.

"Are you sure you're hired?"

"Well, no, I don't know anything for sure. It's as if the message was written in Braille and then half effaced."

As he spoke, she repeated words and then suddenly erupted, shouting. "Braille!" and slapping the tabletop. Then she said, "I have a half bottle of very good French champagne. A half bottle for a maybe job."

They drank it—it was still only three in the afternoon—and it occurred to Jack that it would be fun to lick Rebekkah's body all over, and before he knew it, he was doing it. This must be how rapists operate, Jack said to himself. They pass directly from the thought to the act.

Yet she was fully compliant—no spasmophilia here, just pure wet warmth and a reckless, unpredictable aggressiveness, as strange as her conversational alternation between glee and glum-ness. She sank a deep hickey into his neck—was that to mark her territory? She wriggled out of her skirt and lifted her blouse off without undoing the buttons except the top three. When she unclasped her brassiere, it liberated surprisingly mature breasts, with aubergine-colored aureoles and even a few pale hairs circling the nipples. She seemed to have some kind of harem-girl fantasy going on, because she danced two or three undulating steps before him, moving her pretty little feet with the high, smooth insteps and the bright red toenails. She lowered her eyes as if the display were private, internal. She even knelt on the floor between his legs and spread them, as he sat on a straight-backed chair, and she licked his scrotum, including the space between his anus and balls, and then she held his erection in both her small hands and started licking up the veiny, rigid column.

She looked up at him as she licked, and then she said, "I don't know about this giant, Jack Holmes. You're going to stretch me out of shape before I find and marry my normal-sized little Jewish husband, when and if I ever find him."

Jack could feel himself flushing with resentment and was aware of a snake of vexation coiling through his entrails.

"I know, I know," he said, thinking, I didn't start this. "I know it's a problem."

"A heavenly problem," Rebekkah sighed, and she straddled his lap and introduced his cock into her vagina and slowly sat on it. He could see it inching in, and he thought this was the best feeling in the world, this muscular glove grabbing every last microsurface of his greedy dick.

When it was all over, the daylight outside was dimming and Rebekkah continued to sit on his lap, squeezing his ribs with her knees. Jack wondered if she'd want him to marry her—a thought so crazy he didn't dare voice it, though that was what was circuiting through his mind. He'd been told that women always wanted to get married. When they heard Alice in the next room, Rebekkah led him by the hand to his own little room with the narrow bed, deftly gathering up their clothes from the floor in a single gesture.

They fell asleep, and when Jack woke up it was the next morning, and Rebekkah had written in lipstick on his mirror over the dresser, "What a guy!" and Jack, feeling priggish and ungrateful, wondered how he'd ever get it off. The phone rang in the kitchen in the empty apartment. Naked, Jack rushed to answer it. It was Gephardt's secretary asking in Briarcliff accents if he could wind up his affairs and start working the following Monday.

"Yes, I can. Uh—what time does the workday start?"

The secretary, Donna, laughed for a second as if the word "workday" shocked her or sounded a bit brutal. "Oh, ten or ten thirty, more or less. And by the way, Betty and Helen, the dear ladies, they want you to stop by sometime this week—sometime in the morning, I'd recommend—and fill out some more of their eternal forms."

Jack didn't have the vulgarity to ask how much he'd be paid. He was surprised to hear the dear ladies, who'd seemed to hold his fate in their hands, suddenly laughed off as the alcoholic fussbudgets they were.

3.

O<small>N J A C K ' S F I R S T</small> day at the *Northern Review* he was
overcaffeinated, overdressed, and under-instructed. He
was given a desk in a cubicle next to a woman in her late forties, who'd been with the magazine all of her working life;
until recently she and the whole operation had been in Boston.
He thought she was probably a secret drinker since, as he
quickly learned, she was irritable in the mornings and made a
meal of opening her mail and reading open-submission ideas or
even unsolicited articles sent in by unknown writers. She'd read
a few lines, mumble, "Oh brother," and then slap the offensive
submission into her overflowing out-box.

"Pardon?" Jack asked with a smile, wondering if "pardon"
sounded provincial.

"I said you never find a good story idea in the slush pile. I
don't know why that should be so. In twenty years of crawling
through this sludge, you'd think one gem, oh Lord, just one
gem. Is that too much to ask?"

Harriet wore baggy beige linen trousers and had teeth browned
by tobacco, coffee, and red wine. She might've been attractive
once, and she still had a hard-boiled elegance about her.
She'd cornered the market at the *Northern Review* on art and

architecture stories. She had "files" on all her pet projects: if
Jack brought her attention to an interesting art topic, she put
him in his place right away by showing him that she'd already
been maintaining a file for years on that and all related subjects.
Or she'd say, "You seriously prefer Michaels to Gwathmey?"
She had a way of wrinkling her nose to express a shade of doubt
or scorn. Or, in a more benign mood, she'd say, "I'm glad you're
interested in contemporary architecture. God knows no one
else around here is."

What flabbergasted Jack was that all the files so rarely led to
assigning a real writer to turn out a real article. Harriet just
kept building up her files. "Remember, Jack, we can all have
fun ideas—ideas are a dime a dozen—but you need the perfect
images. So if you don't have a good take—and I mean a striking take from an original photographer, quality pictures—then
the whole operation is pointless. The perfect take, the ideal writer,
a focused subject—that's what it requires to turn out a real *Northern Review* story."

He could tell by her phone conversations that she was very
deep into many potential projects, but none of them promised
to bear fruit anytime soon.

Nor did she want them to. Each Monday the staff had a
meeting, the "story conference," and if someone became excited about a show of Old Masters that had originated at the
Hermitage and was traveling to four North American muse-
ums, then Harriet lit up one cigarette after another and scrunched
in her chair until Gephardt said at last, "And what do you think,
Harriet?"

"Well, I can see why Jane is so enthusiastic, and that's certainly refreshing."

"But?" Gephardt asked with a touch of malice.

Harriet waved her hands in front of her like windshield wipers. "No buts. Just one tiny word of caution. All we have for these paintings are some pretty weird Kodachromes that the Soviets have sent us and everyone else, and the reds are all sort of orange, and the yellows are too gold, and the dark blues are shading off into black. If we publish these things without being able to correct the color, we're going to look like the biggest fools on earth. This show went to Belgium first, for some reason, and every color supplement I've seen from there is wildly different. I mean it's a goddamned joke!" After starting mildly enough out of deference, supposedly, to her colleague, Harriet had built up to a shout. "Everyone in town will be laughing at us," she added darkly, though Jack had a hard time picturing all these four-color-printing connoisseurs chortling together and mocking them.

"Maybe," Gephardt said, smiling slyly and looking out over his half-moon glasses, "we'll just have to send someone to Stalingrad with the reproductions in hand and correct them there."

"Oh no," Harriet said. "Un-unh, I've got way too much to do here. I could never just toss everything aside"—she made it sound like the acme of frivolity—"and go gaily gamboling over to Russia to work out the colors with some numbskull printer."

Gephardt rejoined with no pause. "I have in mind a very intelligent Swiss-German from Skia who would go with you. With Hans beside you, Harriet, you'd have no fears of being ridiculed for false colors throughout America."

Jack thought that Harriet looked sick—or maybe just a bit frightened. Her own color needed correcting. Was she afraid of planes? Of letting the whole office live happily without her for an entire week? Jack kept constructing scenarios and then revising them. Everyone around the table started warming to the idea.

"Okay," Gephardt said, "then it's settled. This will be our new cover story in the next issue: 'The Old Masters Come Toddling out of Red Russia.' That will be our headline."

"I don't think mumble mumble," Harriet mumbled.

"What?"

"I don't think you know what 'toddle' means in English."

Gephardt's eyes blazed. To punish Harriet, he said to Donna, his secretary, who was taking notes, "Book Harriet's flight for first thing next week. And help her with the cultural visa. And coordinate her trip with Hans Drucker. You have his number in Zurich, correct?"

"Yes," Donna said. "Yes, I do."

Gephardt added, "We have a bright young face here today, our neophyte staff member, Jack Holmes, who comes directly to us from Ann Arbor, Michigan, and who knows something about art."

"Send him mumble mumble," Harriet mumbled with a sick smile. Her hands were trembling when she lit up this time.

"What was that suggestion, Harriet?"

"I just said, Karl, that you could send young Jack here to Stalingrad."

"Of course now you are the one who's joking. Since only your expert eye can verify these vagrant colors."

Gephardt was obviously proud of his English and still offended by Harriet's objection to "toddling."

"Are you sure this piece can bear the weight of being a cover story?" Harriet asked skeptically.

Gephardt looked at her for three full beats, then smiled broadly as his glasses fell to his chest. "Very sure."

"In the mumble."

"What are you saying?"

"I'm saying that in the old days, we couldn't afford this sort of extravagant boondoggle. I hope we don't break the bank."

"I was hired, Harriet, to promote the highest possible quality no matter what it costs."

Jack was picking up that Gephardt had only come out of retirement two years ago to head up the *Northern Review*. The conflict, it seemed, was partly old guard versus new guard, but also partly distinguished New England intellectual review versus flashy, lavish picture magazine for a mass readership. But of course, for Gephardt it was mostly a question of everyone submitting to his superior taste and judgment and expertise.

"Phew! That was heavy, wasn't it?" a Southern guy from the art department whispered to Jack. "Wanna have some coffee?" When Jack glanced toward Harriet, the guy said, "Don't worry about her. She'll be out of here in about ten and gone for the rest of the day."

Jack smiled and said, "Well, in that case."

They went down to a coffee shop on the subway level of their building, a place that smelled of burned bagels and old bacon and bad coffee. After they'd ordered, Jack said, "What was all that?"

"Sugar, you've just seen the most recent installment of our daytime soap, *As the Turd Whirls*. I thought today's episode was pretty damn gripping. Old Gephardt really threw Missy Harriet a sidewinder. She's usually quick on her feet with the putdowns and nasty chuckles and superior airs, but today she didn't know what hit her. Maybe now Our Lady of the Thousand Obstructions will draw in her fangs just an itty-bit."

"Do you have names for everyone? I wonder what your name for me will be."

"My Next Husband, that's what I will call you." He said the "you" as if it had an umlaut over it. He was a sort of stage Southerner, Jack figured. He leered at Jack and licked his cherry red lips. His face was plain, but his small blue eyes never stopped boring through Jack. He had a ski jump nose and nearly invisible eyebrows much blonder than his straight, lusterless hair, cut military-short, a look that threw his permanently red ears into relief. His body was thin and flexible, his waist tiny, and his chest not much stouter. His shirt was bright red, as red as his lips, and a size too small for him. He wore black suspenders that fastened to his trouser tops with shiny gold clasps—they looked as if they were from a Paul Smith tuxedo set, whereas all his other clothes could have dressed a large doll from F. A. O. Schwarz.

"What's your name?" Jack asked. "Your real name."

"Herschel." He pronounced it on two crisp descending notes as if to say, "Wel-come."

When Jack looked puzzled, he said, "Herschel?"

Whereas the other members of the *Northern Review* staff seemed like sluggish etiolated fish who preferred to hide in their slimy miniature castles, Herschel was darting about, all blue neon.

Herschel filled him in on the office personalities. The man on crutches was sleeping with the woman playwright turned copyeditor. The mad, disheveled, but congenial older man in the back office with the missing teeth did nothing but put together anagrams based on *Alice in Wonderland*.

"Very Dickensian," Jack said.

"Oh no, not another egghead! Dickens who? Hey hon, we'll get along fine if you just think of me as the waitress in *The Most Happy Fella* who sings, 'Oh my feet, my poor, poor feet.'"

"Aren't you in the art department—do you do layout?"

"Yeah, what I call slinging hash."

Everything about Herschel felt dangerous. Jack didn't want to be pegged as a queer, and he knew he had to avoid Herschel's company, and yet there was something quick and amusing about this guy, and they were the only people under thirty in the office.

Jack realized every evening that the muscles in his cheeks ached from smiling so much. At the office he didn't want to disturb other people, but at the same time he wanted to look busy and useful. Impossible task—he felt as if he'd been apologizing all day every day for his existence. It was like one of those nightmares where all the other men are in evening clothes and you are big and pink and naked, squirming on a very small piano stool.

The man on crutches suggested he write captions for a picture story on the Via del Babuino in Rome. Jack remembered it vividly from a trip to Italy the summer of his junior year. Herschel, as it turned out, was doing the lavish layouts. There were just a few modest text blocks and one-line captions in very small type to think up. Like an idiot, Jack found himself reading the dummy type that Herschel had pasted in for size, as if it would give him a clue as to what he should write. It said over and over, "This is Baskerville 771," except for one line that read, "You're so damn cute. Looks like you've got a big one."

Jack could feel the coffee souring his stomach; he started hiccuping. It would seem as if hours and hours had already trudged around like shackled prisoners—but when he looked up it was still only eleven, and lunch wasn't until one. He was afraid of rushing through his captions and giving the impression that he wasn't serious. He found two guidebooks on Rome in the small company library and read them, but even so he was finished with his story a day later. He showed it to C. G., the man with the crutches, who had a handsome face and a poised, ironic manner.

They went over every word together. "These descriptions of the azalea pots are very good," C. G. said, smoking his pipe, "and I like the loafers as soft as chocolate bars left out in the sun. I suspect you have a real writing talent."

"Thanks," Jack said heartily.

"But you don't know how to make one thing follow another seamlessly. That's called 'tracking' in the business. We want everything to flow, to track. You'll see. Gephardt will write 'Huh?' in the margin if he doesn't get your point, or 'Make it track.' Or he'll think you need more facts or more 'color'; that's the lush descriptive prose you're so good at, but these old macho journalists like what they call 'nuts and bolts.' Sometimes they'll think you're long-winded and they'll say, 'Green 20 characters.' 'Greening' is cutting. Oh, and by the way, don't use words like 'therefore' and 'thus' and 'aforesaid' and 'latter'— sounds like school. I suppose the main thing is speed—saying the most in the fewest words. And be sure to identify every place name and foreign word without sounding pedantic, and don't ever be lofty and say, 'The well-known such and such,' because it may not be well known to the reader."

Every night Jack rushed home and switched into his jeans and loafers and faded blue cowboy shirt. One evening, just to tempt the devil, he didn't wear underwear; on Greenwich Avenue he got a lot of looks from men. One of them, a guy about forty who'd mastered the preppy look without having learned the manner, said to him, "Let me buy you a drink?" as he held open the door to a bar.

Jack laughed. "Sure."

A moment later he was sitting on a high stool next to his host, if that was what he should be called. "Do you live around here?" the man asked.

"Yes. On Cornelia. With two girls."

"Is one of them your girlfriend?"

"Sort of. Not really. I'm not sure, actually." He laughed, surprised at the truth of his statement.

"Are you usually that vague?" the guy asked. "I mean, about everything? I mean"—and the man gave him a charming smile—"that's probably good news for me, that you're not sure whether you're coming or going."

Jack smiled back. "I'm not that vague."

"Are you coming?" the man asked. When Jack looked embarrassed, the man said, "My name is Edward. Now, you can feel free to make up a name, but mine really is Edward. See?" He looked down at the monogram on his dress shirt: EGG. "Edward George Grant."

"That's a riot," Jack said.

They had many drinks together. Edward was buying. "No, come on," he protested. "I invited you." It was the sort of thing, Jack thought, that a European might say.

After the seventh highball, Edward said, "It looks like you're packing a big box there."

Jack said, "I guess most people are scared of it or think it's sort of . . ." He couldn't believe he was talking about this.

"Call me an old-fashioned size queen, but I like it. What would you say—eight inches? Nine?"

"I've never measured it. Where do you measure it from?"

"If you're gay you measure it from the asshole on up. That's why we say he's a gay eight, meaning six."

"And gay people"—Jack didn't want to sound too taxonomic—"actually like them big?"

"Leaping lizards," Edward said, swiveling on his barstool and looking the young man right in the eye. "Yes, Jack. We like them big. C'mon home with me for another drink. I just live on the corner of Eleventh and Fourth."

Jack said, "Okay," and he stepped down from his stool and looked astonished that he'd managed the feat. Edward gulped his drink down; he'd obviously not meant right away, but he liked Jack's enthusiasm.

The man gave Jack his eighth drink at home in his smart apartment, which had chocolate brown walls, gold griffon lamps on dimmers, forest green upholstery with brown piping, and hunting prints under hooded art lights. It was all very "masculine" and fitted with Edward's profession. He said he was a buyer for Barney's. They were chatting away when all of a sudden Edward reached across Jack and pulled out three magazines from a side table. "Like porn?" he asked.

"Sure," Jack said. "Who doesn't? It's so hard to get hold of." He noticed that Edward had offered him two magazines with all men in them and one with men and women. Jack, to show he was broad-minded (and perhaps available), picked up a gay one but looked at it with a supercilious expression.

Jack started getting hard as he studied these young men with their oiled biceps and posing straps, leaning on Greek columns. They all looked like they were sucking in their tummies, and their duck's ass haircuts didn't exactly go with the classical shields and spears.

"You're fabulous," Edward whispered as, fully clothed, he sank to the crawl space between the couch and the coffee table; the table was covered with dark green Morocco leather. Jack felt Edward tugging at his belt buckle and fly; he didn't know whether he, Jack, should scooch his pants down or just pretend to be asleep or unaware of this balding blond kneeling at his feet. Like everything in New York, it was a question of eti-

quette. Finally Jack compromised by closing his eyes and throwing his head back as if dozing but lifting his buttocks so Edward
could wriggle his trousers down to below his knees.

Yes, now that's more like it, Jack thought, as Edward went to
work. He felt it was incredibly kind and self-sacrificing that
Edward hadn't undressed and seemed to expect nothing in return. Hardly seemed fair. And frankly Jack was curious about
what was going on in Edward's pants.

In the end, Edward, who had a permanent tan, big, drooping
blue eyes, a chipped incisor, and very full lips, swallowed it all
and pulled himself together, then stood and said, "Holy moly."
He got up, sat back in a big wing chair, and lit a cigarette. Jack
looked around and Edward said, "Over there," indicating a small
door flush with the wall. The tiny bathroom was covered with
gold leaf wallpaper. On the toilet top was placed a wicker tray
holding twenty bottles of cologne, including one that had white
pebbles sunk in the pale brown liquid.

When Jack reemerged, Edward didn't get up. He extended a
hand and a white calling card. "Here's my number if you ever
want a repeat. I have to tell you, I was in heaven!" He was smoking, and the apartment smelled of Kools.

Jack put his jacket back on and mumbled, "Yeah, great," but
down on the street he threw the card away.

He was here in this vast city where the soft hand of anonymity effaced all individual difference. He was free to surrender his
nether half to Edward George Grant, EGG on his crotch, or to
sleep with Rebekkah, who had pecked him coolly on the cheek
just once since their champagne orgy the afternoon he landed the
job. The city swallowed every anecdote and digested it; nothing got remembered or even noticed. Not that Jack minded. He
thought he liked it that way. He decided he wasn't going to let

another man blow him; that was too easy, much simpler than seducing a woman and just as pleasurable. It could become addictive. Of course, with a woman you could have a real relationship conducted in the sunlight, whereas this homo thing was just slithering around in the shadows.

4.

AFTER SIX MONTHS in New York, Jack realized that most of the people he knew there were from the University of Michigan. He'd found a one-bedroom apartment of his own on Thirteenth Street, west of Eighth Avenue, but he still took most of his meals with Rebekkah and Alice. They shared expenses. Jack did the dishwashing since he really didn't know how to cook. For the first time in his life, he realized, he was putting on a bit of weight—they ate a lot of pasta and went to cheap Italian restaurants like Monte's on MacDougal Street. He decided to walk to work and cut out desserts, and he slimmed down quickly. If he made the slightest effort, the fat melted off him.

The beat movement was just winding down and the hippies were emerging, but Jack didn't feel connected to either group, though he liked his bohemian girls. They teased him for not being "hip," which was the new vogue word. Once he let himself in and heard Alice asking Rebekkah, "Isn't he a queer? Not that I care."

Rebekkah said, "Take it from me he's not queer. I mean, he wailed on my body." Jack thought it made him sound like a trumpet player. "But maybe he's bi."

"Oh, come *on*," Alice said. "Is anyone bi?"

"People think you are," Rebekkah blurted out.

Complete silence on Alice's side. Rebekkah had probably hurt her. Alice had a way of squinting as if not the light but the life around her was too strong and needed to be filtered. Yes, she had her way of squinting and frowning, slow to perceive the point of someone's conversation. Then she'd say, not loudly but emphatically, "Huh!" and pour herself another drink. She looked like a young, not particularly female version of one of the founding fathers—Jefferson or Washington, say. Rebekkah claimed she'd once had a long conversation on the phone with Alice before realizing that Alice was talking to her while being fucked by a famous older author.

Both girls pursued and collected celebrity writers. Back in Ann Arbor they'd attended readings as far away as Toledo. They counted their outing successful if one of them "bagged" a published writer. Alice, despite her horsey manner, had the most luck. She bagged the young author of a cult novel about a tiny horse with wings, which Jack thought was pretty fey, though most readers loved it, apparently. Everyone in Ann Arbor, including Jack, was impressed that a real writer with a movie option had moved in with Alice. One night the young author read a new story out loud to them. They all said it was excellent.

In New York, Alice also had a fling with a Nobel Prize–winning intellectual. She reported that he had a problem with premature ejaculation. Once Jack told her that he'd met someone who was writing a long biographical piece about the man; this person would love to talk to Alice. She cocked her head to one side and said with a frosty smile, "Over my dead body."

Their biggest catch was Charles Mingus. He was the one they both most respected, considering him a genius in every domain—as a jazz composer and a bassist and a bandleader.

They had met him back in Detroit one night after a concert. He liked the girls, he had said, because they were English-major cats and would know how to edit the shit out of his big sprawling memoir.

In New York they saw him frequently and sometimes worked with him deep into the night in his studio above the Bleecker Street Cinema. Jack had little to do with him and was surprised one night when Charlie recognized him on the street in front of the Bleecker Street Tavern and said, "Man, I wanna fuck you."

"What?" Jack asked.

"Man, I'm sick of chicks. Man, this chick just—" and he was off on a tirade about all the wrongs that had been done him by women.

Jack wasn't famous and didn't want to be. What would fame mean—that more people would single him out for unwanted attention? No, what Jack wanted, he decided, was a buddy. He'd never really had friends of either sex, though he imagined the two girls were as close as he'd come so far. Of course, they typecast him as super-WASP, even though Alice was much closer to the real thing than he'd ever be. Either you were off everyone's radar and flying solo, undetectable, or you registered with them and suffered the consequences—you became a character, a type, which was fine except it felt limiting. What he wanted and needed was a buddy, a guy his own age, a masculine guy who didn't look at you penetratingly and size you up. A buddy who would share with you his interest in books or old movies or fine sports writing. Yeah, you'd catch sight of your buddy out of the corner of your eye as the two of you headed out into the night, collars turned up against the cold and shoulders bumping. Someone who didn't stare at you and who could watch TV with you and make just the occasional wry comment while nursing a beer. Someone who made you feel like a minor adjective, not a major noun.

Jack went to Europe for ten days to work on a story on Dubrovnik. He was scouting for Gephardt despite Harriet's protests ("Okay, name me one great Yugoslav photographer, one, please, one who's living now"). Just before he left, he recommended to Gephardt that he hire this great guy, Will Wright, whom in fact he, Jack, didn't know. Will was Alice's next-door neighbor in Virginia and wanted a job in publishing. Alice said, "Oh, Will is great—tall, sort of handsome, ambitious. You'll like him. At least you won't be embarrassed you recommended him. He majored in English and wants to be a novelist."

When Jack came back from Dubrovnik, Will was already working at the *Northern Review.* He was in the next cubicle. The first things Jack noticed about him were his bad skin, his great height, his red nose and blue eyes, his light, joking manner, and his expensive shoes, which were beautifully polished like a fine old piece of furniture.

"Hey, Jack? Great to see you again," Will said, winking, shaking his hand but with a funny smile on his lips.

"Yeah, terrific to see you again, Will."

They decided to have lunch in the new little vest-pocket park east of Fifth. You could order a Coke and a hot dog there and sit on a stone bench and look at the other office workers.

After they got their hot dogs, Will said, "I can't thank you enough for getting me this job. They must like you a lot, since they took me on right away."

"Well, Princeton," Jack said. "You did go to—"

"You'd be surprised how little that counts."

"Seems to me everyone I meet in publishing went to Yale or Princeton."

"I guess there are some old-boy connections. Those schools should be good for something."

"I got accepted to Harvard twice and Princeton once and Haverford, but my dad was strapped for cash." Jack decided that sounded more plausible than the bitter truth.

"Michigan is supposed to be great," Will said agreeably.

"So tell me some things about you real quick so I can sound convincing when Gephardt questions me. By the way, what about those ladies in Personnel?" Suddenly Jack worried he was starting to sound gossipy and "fun" like Herschel.

"Original," Will said. "Highly original."

They shared a smile and a lifted eyebrow.

"Okay," Will said, suddenly planting his long, fine-boned hands on his knees. "My father is a lawyer. There are five kids in my family—I'm the second. We live in a big house, but we don't have any money. We're Catholics. I went to Portsmouth Abbey in Rhode Island. Benedictines. Lots of Latin and theology. I played lacrosse, rather clumsily. Then Princeton. I was in Ivy, my dad's eating club. I've never been engaged to be married."

Although Will seemed jokey-humble, almost apologetic, Jack thought it was a sign of how blue his blood was that he sort of as-sumed that Jack would catch his references. "My parents couldn't possibly afford all that," Will went on, "what with our big family, but two of my uncles helped out with tuition."

Suddenly it struck Jack that Will was confiding a lot of in-formation. Of course, most of it was to substantiate their alibi, but some, surely, was reckless considering they'd just met. Maybe Will needed a buddy too—not just in New York, where he was a newcomer, but in life. Will and Jack shared one eccentricity: they both liked to read new fiction. Even though their incomes were small, they would actually buy a new hardcover novel once a month. They would also go check out recent novels from the public library across from the Museum of Modern Art. Jack had simply gotten it into his head that he should be "civilized" and keep up with trends in most of the arts, whereas Will had a professional reason to read new novels. Jack remembered that Fitzgerald had gone to Princeton.

That night, as he was tossing on his bed, Jack wondered if old Gephardt had hired Will so quickly because he preferred him to Jack. Of course, Will had that foxhunting Princeton luster, and he was a bit taller (six feet two to Jack's six), and his shoes were expensive. Not that either Will or Jack was exactly an extrovert.

The next day at the office, when the coffee wagon came around in the afternoon, three or four of the nicer editors stood around in Will's cubicle. They were all talking, for some reason, about the plan to move the Whitney Museum uptown and whether it would draw as many people at that location, separated from the Museum of Modern Art. Will was sprawled on his chair, one leg thrown over its arm, his dress shirt looking so pale blue that it seemed transparent, the initials picked out in dark blue thread above his heart. He was positively glowing with interest and amusement, and he kept showing his perfect white teeth in deferential smiles. Jack wondered if he'd mistaken Will's affability for friendliness.

Jack decided that as a person Will was a host, if that meant he liked to receive people, listen to them, encourage them, though he maintained his cool distance. Of course, maybe Jack was wrong, but to him Will appeared to be more comfortable in a group than one-on-one.

That night Jack fell asleep on his new tan couch as soon as he got home. When he woke up at eleven he decided to go to a joint over on West Fourth where he could eat a burger and have a couple of beers. He'd slept through the dinner hour with his girls, and he decided he'd call them and explain to-morrow. Sitting at the crowded bar, he couldn't help listening to two puffy execs still in their suits; they'd clearly been drink-ing steadily since six. Most people seemed so inane, Jack thought, loudmouths with absolutely no idea that conversation should be interesting.

Will was obviously refined, careful, completely democratic, though not really, Jack wagered, not in his heart of hearts. He'd been raised to think he was superior but not show it. Jack thought of most Catholics as Irish or Italian immigrants, but of course there were those Catholic English aristocrats who had followed Lord Baltimore to America, though Will's family were Virginians. Was Will descended from English Catholics? He had the tall, narrow head and the eyes meant for a visor and the profile intended to be looked at against a gold banner. Jack sud-denly wondered if Will was wearing some of his father's dress shirts. They looked old, with their long, pointy collars; Jack would have to examine the initials more carefully.

The next day Jack and Will were drinking scotch together out of Will's flask. It was after hours and they were alone. It was a cold wintry night and below them the city was all lit up. Nei-ther of their cubicles had a window, but just across the hall was a big office with two windows, and Jack was drawn to the glit-tering glamour of the towers and streets outside. Black, Starr and Frost was the name of a jeweler on Fifth Avenue, and it rhymed in Jack's mind with this hard urban beauty, this motionless nocturnal amusement park, its rides all frozen and deserted but still lit up. Just for the conspicuous consumption of electricity, Manhattan couldn't be beat.

"Hey, boys," Herschel said in his syrupy Southern accent. "Don't you two look cozy? You're inseparable, aren't you? Not that I'm insinuating anything."

"Will Wright here. I don't think we've met." Will spoke in his heartiest manner and didn't stand up but stretched out a hand to Herschel, who produced a little boneless pullet of a hand and introduced himself nearly inaudibly. "Find a chair. Have a drink."

"Oh, now I remember," Herschel said, stirring his scotch and single cube with an index finger he kept licking. "Jack, you're the one who brought Will here, right? You're old friends, I gather."

"Well, old acquaintances," Jack said.

"Now you've hurt my feelings," Will said, clowning. "I thought we were best friends."

Even though it was a joke, the simple statement made Jack feel some sort of sunburst of joy inside, and he looked away lest his eyes betray the excess of feeling.

"I'll leave you girls to it," Herschel said, getting up. "This gal has to shake a leg. I've got a ticket to *She Loves Me*." He looked at Will. "I just love musicals. I identify with the waitress in *The Most Happy Fella*. Good night, Jacky babe." He hobbled out, singing, "Oh my feet, my poor, poor feet."

As soon as Herschel had vanished, Will said, "Wow! He's a live wire."

"Yes," Jack said, "he's in the Art Department," as if that explained everything.

"He's very funny," Will pronounced. "A live wire in a place of burned-out circuitry."

"Gee," Jack said, teasing him, "how eloquent! You must be a writer."

"Like you, like everyone here," Will said wearily.

"We're journalists. You're a writer. A novelist."

"I'm an unpublished writer. We're a dime a dozen in this city."

"Yeah," Jack protested, "but every published author was once an unpublished tyro." He could sense that his pulse was accelerating, which it sometimes did when he was trying out a bit of assuaging flattery. It never worked on his father, who remained superbly indifferent to the opinion of other people. Jack couldn't tell if it was working on Will.

A silence set in, and Will toasted Jack with a paper cup of scotch and an ironic smile. Jack worried that Will might assume he and that creepy Herschel were close, which was obviously what Herschel, the little troublemaker, had been trying to suggest. Jack said—not trusting his words since he felt the burning whiskey playing rope tricks behind his solar plexus—"I never spent five minutes with Herschel. He gives me the willies."

"Oh no," Will said, hearty again, "he's great fun. A real character."

Jack had heard other blue bloods seem to endorse but actually damn people they labeled as "characters." He knew how to read Will's comments. Of course, other rich people could be characters too, but that was different. They had their eccentricities, their rages and passions, the way the Greek gods did—human feelings writ large—but a character like Herschel was more of a zoological specimen: amusing, but not a candidate for friendship.

"I guess he wants us to think he's queer," Jack ventured.

"Oh no," Will said emphatically. "It's just an act, and a damn funny one too."

"You don't think he's sort of . . . perverted?" Jack asked. It was for some reason important to him that Will admit that Herschel was not like them, was in a class apart.

"You know him better than I do," Will said maddeningly.

One Friday in late November, Jack was heading out for an early lunch when suddenly people all around him began to cry and cling to each other. Nothing organized, and not involving everyone. But here and there people were looking up as if expecting an invasion. Or as if God had suddenly appeared in the sky in a gray swirl of robes and with a lifted hand like Michelangelo's deity. The isolation of all these thousands of strangers marching down the sidewalks had suddenly come to an end. Mourners grabbed each other and sobbed. "The president is dead," someone said in a quiet voice beside him. "See?" And the person pointed to a headline traveling in lights around the Time-Life Building. Yes, there it was. The president had been shot in Dallas. Damn fool Texans, Jack thought, and now what? Were they sure? Was it a Communist? Cuban? Or some damn Klansman? What will become of us all? he thought.

And people everywhere looked around as if they knew they'd all remember this exact moment forever. Jack had been only five when the war had come to an end. Now was the first adult moment in his life that felt historical. Yes, history was being made. He wanted to be with Will. He couldn't think of anyone closer to him, pathetic as that sounded. When Jack got back to the office, he was sure Will would be on the phone with his sister, with whom he lived, or with his parents, his father in his office or his mother at home. Family members were no doubt reaching out to each other "all across the land," as pundits were probably writing right now, but maybe Will hadn't heard yet, unlikely as that might seem in the media capital of the country, in a building full of journalists; Will could be oblivious to his surroundings.

Jack had no desire to call his parents. They'd be puzzled that he had made the effort and wonder what he wanted. He'd go over all this with his girls tonight at dinner, but he didn't need them to share this moment with him. They weren't witnesses to his life. He wouldn't be able to acknowledge the gravity of the occasion with them.

He wondered how he had let Will attain this hold over him so quickly, especially since Will had given no signs he wanted to be intimate.

He found Will at his desk, his head on his arms and his back shaking under his paper-thin pale blue shirt. Jack touched his shoulder and said, "Wanna go out for a drink?"

"I sure as hell do," Will said.

They never came back to the office that day. They got filthy drunk at the Irish pub downstairs, where some of the local cops were working up their conspiracy theories. Will and Jack kept saying, "Can you believe it?" Every once in a while the bartender would turn up the sound on the nonstop news.

Will said, "I know it's stupid to say, but as a Catholic . . . I mean, the guy was our first Catholic president." He got them two more boilermakers—beers with shots of whiskey on the side. "I just feel so shitty. Don't wanna sound melodramatic, but he was our first cool president, right? Maybe Lincoln was smart, but he was a nerd, right? Jack Kennedy was cool."

Jack felt mostly indifferent after the initial shock, but he decided to play along with Will's mood. Jack knew he was acting like a chick letting her man take the emotional lead, but it would be too brutal to declare how little he cared. What surprised him was how close Will obviously felt to the throne. Will acted as if he were that Texas governor who'd also been wounded. Or as if Kennedy were his cousin.

Late at night, when they weren't talking much and they both looked sleepy, Will suddenly said, "Wanna hear something weird?"

"Yeah."

"My dad was one of the guys in the hunt club to vote against the Kennedys joining us. Dad thinks they're kind of pushy. And the old man was a bootlegger. How snooty is that?"

"Yeah," Jack said leadenly, though somewhere in his innermost mind this information blazed like a vein of silver he could mine later.

"And here we are crying into our beers about a guy we wouldn't even let hunt with us."

"How fucked up is that?" Jack asked.

Will nodded in sodden agreement. "Pretty damn pathetic."

At home later that night (he'd barely managed to get in the door, he was so drunk, and he lost one of his contacts while trying to remove it), he was pissing when he thought, Damn! At first I felt Will was strange because he imagined he was as good as Jack Kennedy, but now I guess the Wrights think they're even better.

In bed, the room kept rising and falling like the horizon line seen from a ship in a storm. Up . . . it would go up! And then suddenly plunge down. Jack said to himself, I'm glad Kennedy died because it meant Will and I got to spend our first evening together.

He woke up at four in the morning feeling dehydrated and unbearably horny. Maybe it was the thirst joined to the horniness, but when he started jerking off, all he could think about was sucking Will's cock. He'd never sucked a cock. He wished he'd paid more attention to what that Edward guy had been doing to him. Maybe he should go back and take lessons. How sick is that, Jack said to himself over and over again. He had a fistful of come that he licked away like a cat—he was too tired to get up to find a tissue. He decided that the bizarre events of the day had pushed him too far, into this dangerous territory. He promised himself he'd never again jerk off over Will (or any other guy). New York was doing weird things to him.

5.

THE NEXT EVENING at dinner, Alice asked Jack how Will was doing at work.

"He's very bright, isn't he?" Jack said.

"Is he really?" Alice said. "He went to good schools and has read—well, not a lot but in a very selective way. He reads all the new novels, since that's what he wants to write. Of course, he's terribly competitive."

Jack nodded, but he hadn't thought of that. He wondered what else Alice had noticed. What else people back in Virginia said about Will. "Is he a big one for the women?" Jack asked, using a turn of phrase that sounded as unnatural to his own ears as his desire to elicit this sort of information.

"Oh, I think there were two or three fragile-looking debu-tantes," Alice said. She was smoking and drinking scotch. "But you know, with his bad skin he's always been shy."

"Do you think that's such a big deal?"

"You never had acne, I can see," Alice said. "But his was very bad, and he had it all over his back, big boils of it behind his ears and on his neck."

"Yeah," said Rebekkah, chiming in. "Jack Holmes has beau-tiful soft skin. Perfect skin any girl would envy." She said it with such kindness that there was nothing knowing or leering about her remark. She was the kindest girl in the world.

"Anyway," Alice said, narrowing her eyes, "why don't you invite Will to dinner with us? He must be lonely living with his sister Elaine and her two kids in that shabby town house. Tell him it won't be anything special, just our usual squat and gobble." Although Alice could be easily offended by other people's vulgarities (she often winced in conversations), she nevertheless enjoyed her own coarse expressions, not so much dirty as rustic.

"Tomorrow?" Jack asked a bit too eagerly.

"For instance," Alice drawled, looking away, even squinting at the little black-and-white television flickering in the next room.

"What is she like, this sister?"

"Elaine?" Alice drawled with a certain lofty amusement, as if it were absurd that someone didn't already know everything about her. "She's a beauty but has gotten rather broad in the beam. Where Will is timid, she is brash, really a heroine out of a swashbuckler. You will be impressed by how beautiful she is. And her little boy and girl are great kids. But she's penniless. Her handsome, do-nothing husband abandoned her for some trailer trash." Alice spit out the word "trash" and laughed, Jack imagined, not out of real vehemence but out of a schoolgirl defiance at saying such a thing at all. Her squinting eyes widened to reveal their fine Chippendale blue. "I suppose poor Ronald couldn't cope with the whole Wright clan, so he preferred Doreen from Hot Springs. Anyway, Elaine is penniless and she's come to New York and rented a run-down town house at a terribly impressive address in the East Sixties off Park, and her whole idea is to flirt and entertain like Scarlett O'Hara after the war and land a rich and social husband." Like all people in what they called "high society" back in Ann Arbor, Alice said "social" (and she very rarely pronounced the word) to mean someone of the right sort.

Jack drank in all these details about Will. "Has Elaine found anyone? Surely she wouldn't marry just for money."

"He would have to be presentable," Alice said matter-of-factly.

"Not a Jew," Rebekkah chimed in, pulling a comically long face.

"Hold on," Alice said, chortling and lifting a nearly transparent hand in protest. "There's a nice Mr. Shapiro in Virginia who goes everywhere, who keeps horses. That's the way in: horses!" She laughed as if she held the whole hunt world in contempt, but she didn't. "Of course, Harold Shapiro is well dressed and has a wonderful house near ours and a great trainer."

"Does he wear one of those red jackets? A Jew in a red hunting jacket?" Rebekkah asked, adding in a dramatic aside, "My poor people, so far from the shtetl."

"A red what?" Alice demanded, squinting even more fiercely. "Oh, a pink jacket. But yes, you're right, they're red. The first tailor of hunting garb was a Mr. Pink or something." Since she'd started working on her documentary, Alice had become more informed about her world, which in the past she'd always taken for granted.

That night, alone, Jack lay on his short, tan corduroy rep couch, hanging off both ends of it, and laughed at himself. He thought, I'm fascinated by all these details about the Wrights, but only because I have a crush on Will.

Will did come to dinner the next night, and he smoked two cigarettes (the first time Jack had ever seen him smoking). He held them fastidiously and a bit awkwardly, as if they were chopsticks. He sprawled with one long leg draped over the edge of the leather armchair bought from the Salvation Army and combined casualness with shyness. Jack was able to confirm that Will wore garters to hold up his long black lisle stockings. He and Alice sparred. "Okay, Will," she said, "you owe me one. I got you your job."

"Oh?" Will drawled. "For some reason I thought it was Jack."

"A mere technicality," she said. "You owe me."

"Then to be fair I should find you a job," he said, "but for some reason I don't think of you as a working girl."

"I'm going to make a documentary."

"I guess that counts as work. About what?"

"The hunt."

"Where?"

"Duh—our hunt."

"Hope you leave us out."

She laughed. "Of course I will. Movies are supposed to be interesting."

Rebekkah's eyes widened. She loved Alice, but found her hunting prints bizarre and her family stories even more exotic. Now she looked eagerly at Jack to make sure that he too was registering Alice's latest tossed-off effrontery.

Will seemed strangely vague or even evasive in responding to Alice's questions about Elaine. "Is she enjoying New York?" Alice asked. "I don't see how she can if you compare that thing, that disgusting town house, with that beautiful house your parents built her out behind their place."

"What's the little house called?" Rebekkah asked Alice while winking at Jack.

"Called?" Alice asked. "I keep forgetting none of you has ever been down to Virginia. Elaine's house is called the Rookery."

"Yeah, 'cause the builders really rooked Dad, har, har," Will said. "Well, she likes New York fine, but it's the children I worry about." Everyone assumed New York was bad for children.

Two days later Alice said, "There's something strange going on. Elaine is giving a big splashy man-trap party, and Will doesn't even seem to know about it. She told me he's not really living at her place."

Did this mean that Will had a lover? And was the lover male or female? Was that why Will had moved to New York, to lead a secret life? The scion of Charlottesville would never have any privacy back home.

Jack didn't know what to do with his new suspicions. Mythologizing Will's affair (if that's what it was) served the function of taming it, of making it less shocking to poor Jack (he thought of himself suddenly as poor, as bereft). He could see no way of tackling the subject directly with Will ("Hey, Will, who are you living with these days?"). Jack would have been willing to run the risk of seeming vulgar to Will if he'd thought a blunt question might work, but he was afraid Will would greet it with one of his thin-lipped smiles and total silence.

Was it a black woman? A married woman—a friend of the family? A beautiful young aunt? A retarded cousin? A common whore? A freckled teenage boy from Appalachia?

Fascinating to think about, but Jack felt . . . betrayed. Yes, he'd assumed that he and Will were both . . . bachelors. That they were both lonely and bereft. That they really had no one but each other, that they were buddies . . . almost exclusively.

For a day he avoided Will at the office and said that he

couldn't join him for lunch at Larré's, the French restaurant in
the East Fifties where Will liked to eat brains with capers and
where Jack would order sweetbreads with fries. It was a great
place, three big rooms crowded with smallish tables for two,
decked out in red-and-white-checked tablecloths and topped
with baskets of crusty bread, and the prix fixe was only $1.50 or
$1.75 if you took both a cheese course and a dessert. He and
Will ate there almost every day and then would check out an
art show on Fifty-seventh Street at Betty Parsons or Green's
(upstairs just west of Fifth Avenue) or across the street at Sidney
Janis. Or they'd grab a salad at the Museum of Modern Art
cafeteria and sit in the garden, looking at Matisse's female bathers
or the delicate, adipose bronze woman by Gaston Lachaise, standing on tiptoe. The sound of the fountain and the distant hum of
traffic through the latticework fence lulled them into a mood
both urban and bucolic. Soaring buildings on every side looked
down on the garden, but the trees were leafy and the lunch
crowd, mostly women, seemed unaware of all those voyeurs up
above looking down at them through leaves.

  Jack usually stayed out so late at night and drank so much
that the next day he felt exhausted and depressed—unless he
was with Will. His baseline was depression, best expressed by
his pale, drained complexion and the dark circles under his
eyes. He would come home from work and fall asleep, but soon
enough he'd wake up, beset by an irresistible desire to go out.
He was like Tristan, who can't die because the philter keeps
jolting him back into wakeful desire. Jack, what was Jack looking for as he walked the cold streets, felt the snow tattooing his
face, cruised people who were nothing but creeping, sexless
bundles of hoods, hats, coats, boots, slowly trudging across

piles of snow tossed back by snowplows? Even this Muscovite weather didn't dampen Jack's lust.

He was so tormented by the question of Will's lover that one night he decided he would follow him at an inconspicuous distance—but the next afternoon, just as he'd decided that Will was a bloodless monster, someone who'd probably not even noticed that Jack had been avoiding him, Will came into his office and said, bluntly, studying him with those blue eyes, "Are you avoiding me?"

"I heard you're living with someone and you never even told me about it."

"That's because you'd tell Alice, and she'd tell Elaine, who'd tell everyone in the whole wide world."

"Don't you know yet," Jack asked, "that I can keep a secret?"

"All right," Will said, touching his own chest, then his stomach, as if in such a critical moment he had to make sure he was still all there. "Let's go have a quiet drink someplace, if any place quiet exists in this wretched city."

Jack was frightened about what would ensue, but he was also grateful to Will for having said something direct. As they rode the elevator down, they stayed silent even though they were the only ones in it at this hour, listening to a Muzak version of "If I Knew You Were Comin' I'd've Baked a Cake," played by the Mantovani Strings, but so softly that the music sounded more like a memory than a melody. They smiled at each other nervously once when their glances crossed. On the way out on the ground floor Will's hand touched Jack's waist.

"Okay," Will said, after their drinks had come and they were seated at a highly polished wood table at the back of the Irish bar, which stank of cigarette smoke and spilled beer. "So what's wrong?"

Jack was looking at the black-and-white picture someone had put up of Kennedy with his sad eyes. "Okay, well, I heard from Alice, who heard from Elaine, that you're not really living with her."

Will laughed. "I've got an even bigger secret, one you'd never guess."

"Yes? I mean, I wouldn't?"

"I'm living alone. I found a little room without a kitchen, though it does have a sink and I can take a maid's bath in it. I'm writing, like a crazy man. I've almost finished the first draft and the Dial Press—not the whole press, a fellow over there—is interested, sort of, and—well, I should have told you, but it works for me having a secret. It feels very private. Maybe for men like us who've lived in dormitories for the last ten years, you know—"

"Of course I know," Jack said, "and I really like my little apartment," though in fact he didn't; his heart started pounding from the fear of being alone as soon as he came out of the subway each night and was a block away from his front door. "I know, or at least I can imagine, how exciting it must be to write your first book."

"Try my third. I've already written two novels that were so shitty agents and editors couldn't stay awake reading them, but now I'm really on to something."

"Great," Jack murmured, and he meant it, relieved that Will wasn't having an affair and that he was far more committed to his novel than to any woman. He'd met that young cult novelist in Ann Arbor, Alice's lover, the one who had written the "classic" about the tiny winged horse (already out of print), and he'd seen how seriously everyone had taken that guy, and how solemnly the novelist had taken himself when he'd read them his new story. Fiction was obviously the way to go, not quite as sacred as poetry but a damn sight more visible and profitable. Jack loved new novels and was glad Will was writing one.

"You've already been in contact with agents?"

"Yes," Will said, "a preppy lesbian Alice met playing tennis. Poor Alice, they all assume she's a dyke too, but she's really just a bossy straight girl." Jack was always surprised by the casual way the girls (and now Will) referred to dykes and fags, as if it were just a dubious variation of human sexuality rather than a vice and a mental illness (or a sin for a Catholic like Will). Jack felt that for all their joking around, they wouldn't want to spend time with a clearly identified homosexual (who would?); they simply liked to laugh about the disease, clowning that was apparently the height of sophistication. Of course, Jack, who'd let Edward suck his cock, was much more compromised than any of them. And it was all because his cock was so big that it seemed almost inevitable it would end up in some homosexual's mouth, just as a naturally fast runner would end up a track star. "Prey" wasn't quite the word, he knew. He hadn't resisted Edward in any way and, truth be told, he'd gone out that night without any underwear. But maybe he'd just been horny. Jack didn't like to think about it, though it was always shadowing his thoughts like a marauder.

"What's the idea behind your novel?" Jack asked, knowing he might be obtruding.

"The idea?" Will asked. Then he smiled. "I guess writers don't think like that. They stick pretty close to their inspiration like a divining rod over water. And then when it's all over they make up some bullshit to tell the press, or the curious, about the 'theme' or whatever."

Jack had never heard Will utter a single pretentious word

before, but perhaps only because the topics that had come up (the hunt, schools, jobs, friends) were all ones in which he'd been carefully drilled by his snobbish parents to sound as modest as possible. Writing fiction was an altogether new subject, his own, not a family theme, and while discussing it, Will was free to indulge a young male's egotism. Whereas Will usually sounded self-deprecating in the best aristocratic fashion, when it came to his "art" he was starting to sound pompous in the usual naïve American way.

"Is that all you're going to say for now?" Jack asked. He hoped that Will would see he was pulling his leg.

"I don't really know much more," Will said, "that's paraphrasable. I could say that my book is influenced by Thomas Pynchon's *V.* in that it has fantasy mixed in with classic storytelling, but my book is more tender, even sentimental, about love and beautiful young women in crisp summer dresses—maybe that's my Fitzgerald side. Oh god, I hope it adds up to more than Pynchon plus *Gatsby.*"

"Even those two elements," Jack said, "just those two elements sound great. That's what originality is. A slight variation or a new combination. At least that's what I think." Jack felt tears spring to his eyes as they did whenever he tried to sweet-talk someone.

"The minute it gets accepted, I'll let you read it," Will said. "You'll be my first reader."

Jack thought that sounded like a feeble consolation. In the next few weeks he came to think of Will's novel as a sort of rival and as one he couldn't compete with. Would Will become famous and drop all his old friends? Would he become a "catch" and attract rich and celebrated women? Would he quit the *Northern Review*?

Will was constantly taking notes in a small book that fit into an inside jacket pocket and was bound in red morocco with his name stamped inside in small gold type, the pages pale blue and Bible thin, the sort of "appointment book" that preppies always managed to have. Now that Jack knew about the novel-in-progress, Will didn't hesitate to scrawl things even in the midst of a conversation. Jack would wonder if something he'd said or done had been noteworthy.

Jack had no desire to write fiction. It meant taking yourself too seriously; there was no denying a novelist was some sort of indefatigable monologist. You had to believe that what you thought was worth saying; you had to possess the confidence to impose yourself on everyone, for hours and hours, even days.

He mentioned that once to Will on their way back from the Museum of Modern Art, or rather the library across the street, where they'd gone to renew their books. Will was reading a "nifty" novel by a young French writer their age called Le Clézio. Jack was reading a book about Ezra Pound and his circle. Jack said he didn't want to die stupid. It was a freakishly warm day for February, marked by turbulent gray clouds crossing and recrossing the sky, like a flotilla of warships on parade. A strangely warm wind smelling of ozone and clean rain (though no rain was in sight) eddied around them and disturbed Jack with its promise of elsewhere.

Will was embarrassed by this idea of novelist as monologist. "Christ, if I thought for a moment I had to hold forth like that before even one person in reality—no, Jack, my boy, it's a story. I'm a storyteller, and a story is always a kind of group effort, a manifestation of the Volk." That Will had such an elaborate ready-made response only proved Jack's point. Will thought of himself as a mouthpiece for the whole fucking race. He'd already worked up his acceptance speech.

Why not, Jack thought. Even James fucking Joyce had to start somewhere—didn't he declare himself to be the antennae of the race? Writing was definitely a form of pretentiousness, no way around that. But maybe Will had what it took.

Maybe. Just.

One wintry night, Will came over for dinner, not with the girls but at Jack's place. Jack had said that afternoon, "Hey, if you don't mind eating leftovers, I cooked my first real dinner last night." In fact, Will wasn't being given leftovers, but a beef stew Jack had made the previous night just for Will. "Maybe the girls will come by later," Jack said, but in fact he hadn't invited them. After dinner Jack produced a joint, and for the first time they got stoned together. They listened to Dionne Warwick singing, and they kept exchanging cryptic little smiles as if they were decoding secret messages in exactly the same way and at the same moment. Will was sprawling on the couch, and he leaned his head back and closed his eyes. One big hand, ropy with blue veins, the knuckles lightly dusted with gold hairs, rested on the cushion beside him.

Will looked so sexy and Jack wanted him so badly that it was hard to imagine the feeling wasn't mutual. What would happen if Jack slipped down onto the floor and put a hand on Will's crotch, just as Edward had done with him? It was like that afternoon he put the moves on Rebekkah when they were stoned and he felt like a rapist but it turned out that she too was eager to fuck. Or was it? Would Will sit up, alarmed, indignant, horrified? Maybe the situation was more like this music. It sounded so interesting and seductive that Jack was certain Will must be enjoying it too, and yet two weeks ago Will had stated flatly that he hated pop music of all sorts. "It's not really music. I don't even know what there is to listen to—loud, banal, rhythmically monotonous, predictable, too short to go anywhere. It doesn't develop. It's nothing. Nothing!"

It was so easy, stoned and looking at Will, to imagine that Dionne Warwick's slightly flat voice was bewitching him as it moved over those massed strings, just as it was compelling to imagine that Will was horny too, that he wouldn't mind a buddy's hot wet mouth engulfing him. Wasn't that fold in his crotch slowly thickening, ticking heartbeat by heartbeat into an erection? Will was pretending he was dozing, but he knew that Jack could smell his excitement, even from way over there.

But Jack did nothing and the moment froze like a smile on a chagrined face. Luckily. Because then Will stretched and sat up and spoke out of his severe Gothic face: "I fell asleep for a moment in spite of that treacly music. How can you listen to that garbage?"

"What music?" Jack asked, disingenuous. "Oh, that. I don't know who gave me that."

"Probably some misty-eyed, waxy-eared girl," Will said with a harsh little smile.

"Yeah, some girl," Jack repeated leadenly. He could see that the presumed erection didn't exist, that Will's crotch was as smooth and featureless as a doll's and the thickening fold had been a wishful invention.

"Well, Jack, my boy," Will said, standing and stretching, "it's time for the Old Masters to go toddling out of Russia." Jack had told Will about Gephardt's strange headline (which since appeared in the magazine and disappointingly elicited no response at all, certainly not the anticipated general derision).

"Maybe the dope wasn't a good idea," Jack said. "I'm zonked."

"But the beef stew definitely was a good idea," Will said, adding, "Yum-yum." He maintained the boarding school pose of licking his lips over any dish that wasn't actively repulsive.

Jack realized, lying in bed that night, that Will was guarded in ordinary conversation but more spontaneous and interesting when he talked about books. Suddenly he was no longer the deferential, almost shambling young gentleman, but rather a mind at work. The gentleman—armored in his good shoes and his father's monogrammed shirts with the turned collars—was a bag of old tricks, but the writer was someone vulnerable and egotistical, living in the moment, unprepared. At the same time, there was no denying that Will the author was pretentious. Sometimes Jack wondered if he'd like Will if he didn't love him.

Maybe because Jack had suspected Will of living with someone, he'd been forced to admit to himself how much he depended on the idea of Will's availability, his indeterminacy—the idea, since the reality was so elusive.

The next day Gephardt called them both in for a meeting. They sat in captain's chairs and felt like lieutenants and looked at Gephardt over the collection of obelisks that covered his desk, baby spires that seemed to have been hatched by the skyscrapers outside the window. Gephardt had shed his suit jacket and was showing an old pair of faded burgundy suspenders covered improbably with fading brown mallards.

"I just have a little idea I want to share with you," Gephardt said as he fiddled with a pipe cleaner, which came out of the detached pipe stem very brown and oily. "Or maybe it's more a question."

Although Gephardt raised one bushy white eyebrow, Will said nothing, producing a dog smile with a bit of protruding pink tongue between rows of white teeth. Jack didn't smile, but raised both eyebrows for a second above a mask, as if to indicate a general readiness and a resetting of all dials back to zero.

In a roundabout way that sounded almost devious, certainly loaded, Gephardt said, "Now I know both of you guys are very ambitious, and I don't want to be guilty of standing in your way. There are certain decisions higher-ups must make—or in English you say 'highers-up'? I think that would be better English, like 'walkers by.'"

Jack could feel his eyes drifting toward Will's, but he stopped their migration just in time, since he was afraid of dissolving into a great yawping laugh.

"In any e-went," Gephardt said, "I want you both to think of yourself as junior editors. I want you to think of ways you can take on more responsibility. Does that appeal to you, Jack?"

Jack had no idea what was being discussed, but he had the sickening feeling that whatever it was would lead to longer hours for no more money. He knew people were supposed to be ambitious and aggressive, but he almost wished time could be frozen and he could stay a simple staff writer forever, writing his picture captions and doing the odd bit of research.

"Yes," he said brightly, "immensely. I will do anything to—"

To what? His mind went blank.

"To become a real editor," he said, though he'd never thought about it for two seconds, and he hoped he didn't sound either delusional or dangerously grasping.

"And you, Will?"

"I'm not sure what's being discussed, concretely," Will said, "but five years from now I'd like to be assigning and editing stories for the magazine."

Jack thought that Will sounded much more mature than he did—and Will had obviously envisioned his future. Even in his readiness to say he wasn't sure what was under discussion, Will dealt with Gephardt more like an equal, more man-to-man. In his elegant way Will was manly.

Maybe because technically Jack had recommended Will, and had worked a few weeks longer for the *Northern Review*, he'd slipped into thinking he had a certain seniority on the job. And Jack assumed that because Will was so dedicated to writing fiction, he must see his "job-job" as nothing but a dull means to an exciting end. That's how the girls on Cornelia Street referred to their various salaried positions, as "job-jobs." They pretended they didn't even know what they were doing. Working was just a stopgap measure until they became full-time artists. They were quite clear that they didn't want jobs for the future, since their only real future would be in the arts, making documentaries or acting.

And then one night Jack's college girlfriend Hillary came to town and took Jack to a nice Spanish restaurant, El Faro, on West Fourth Street. At the next table were seated Will and a date and Herr and Frau Gephardt. Jack hadn't been paying attention when the headwaiter had led Hillary and him to the adjoining table. By the time he noticed, Gephardt had leapt out of his chair and was pumping Jack's hand heartily. "Oh, this is merry!" he exclaimed. "How gemütlich," he said. "You must meet my Helga. Liebchen. This is young Jack I've told you so much about." The handsome, gray-haired German woman, her broad face bare of makeup, wrapped Jack's nervous, bony hand in her well-padded one, its nails clipped short and unpainted. Her face could have been brutal except for the fine dusting of gold hair on her full cheeks, her mild blue eyes, and her general air of peace, as if she were a retired baker once famous for her cherry strudel.

"Hello, Jack, I am Helga," and she held onto his hand a second too long. Jack noticed they'd polished off a pitcher of sangria already and hadn't ordered yet. El Faro was such an old restaurant that the menus all looked tattered and stained.

Will was so embarrassed that he started braying. "Jack, my boy, who's your lovely date you've been keeping a secret from us?" Just like Will, Jack thought, to accuse me of keeping a secret when he's the sneaky one going off to dinner with our boss. And wasn't that clever of him to extend "me" into "us" ever so slyly, to place himself beside the Gephardts. Jack was shocked that Will was out for an evening with Gephardt, as if a student who passed for a regular guy had been seen brownnosing a prof.

And who was Will's girl with the short upper lip pulled back to reveal sparkling teeth and the incongruously low voice and the delicate knobby shoulders and the hair pushed up to uncover a ballerina's long neck. Lucy? Did Will say her name was Lucy something? She looked like someone's younger sister, a debutante with lots of smiles and no conversation, remarkable only for her breakable beauty.

Luckily Hillary had slimmed down a bit, and her hair was golden and shorter, and she was wearing an aquamarine linen dress that had a hundred tiny bone-white buttons running up the front. Not exactly stylish, except perhaps on Martha's Vineyard or in Maine. She said, in response to Will's question as they stood around awkwardly, "I live in Maine. Kennebunkport," and Jack was happy she hadn't mentioned Ann Arbor.

All these people he worked with at the *Northern Review* were Ivy League snobs. Though Jack had said straight out, "I am a Midwestern nobody," they never believed him. They thought he was one of them, and Jack found their misguided preconceptions rather flattering. He wondered what it was about him that misled them. It certainly wasn't his accent. He said "warsh" instead of "wash" and "melk" instead of "milk." And unlike all the Auchinclosses who worked around him, he didn't say "enuh-way" for "anyway" or describe people as "high-larious."

Hillary would only add to his myth; she was obviously the right sort. These snobbish ideas vaguely flitted through Jack's mind without nesting there. He toyed with them rather than embraced them. He felt there was something dangerously al-luring about social snobbism—dangerous to him. He was so accommodating to other people that he could easily become a successful social climber without even trying.

Jack noticed right away that Gephardt was more attracted to Hillary than to Will's Lucy. Looking at Helga you could see why: Gephardt preferred substantial women. Hillary had a mouth too wide for beauty but just large enough for love. She had a frank, open nature, and perhaps because she was hefty she never thought to play the girly-girly card. She was a guy among guys—and Jack in his ignorance thought that must be how Germans liked their women. A nice big hussar of a woman with a degree of elegance—that was the right combination.

Gephardt wanted them to pull up chairs to share another pitcher of sangria, but Jack begged off, saying he hadn't seen Hillary in a long while—"Oh, I see," Gephardt said with his

usual ham-fisted emphasis. "Little secrets to hide from the other."
Jack smiled weakly. He thought it wondrous that they were having a cozy little evening without him and they all accused him of
being secretive.

For Jack, the dinner was excruciating. Every second, he was
aware of his colleagues' proximity. He wanted to tell Hillary that
Will was his best friend, but he was afraid that Will would hear
and secretly snort with contempt or disagreement. He wanted to
tell her how much he liked his job. He wanted to find out what
Hillary was doing with her life, but he couldn't concentrate on
anything.

Out of the corner of his eye he was aware of everything Will
was doing. The way he was holding his cigarette between his
thumb and middle finger, as if smoking were an unfamiliar practice. The way he lowered his head, widened his eyes, and looked
up through his eyebrows each time Lucy said something, as if he
needed to demonstrate how charmed he was and how attentive
he was being, or maybe he thought he looked sexy that way. Will
was playing a bit "young" around Gephardt, laughing recklessly
and nodding frequently. With Jack, Will usually listened with a
poker face and a million-mile stare, though from time to time
he'd emit an unbidden chuckle. That was the look Jack had assumed was Will's natural one.

At last he and Hillary were out in the street. When she'd
threatened to order coffee, he'd insisted she would never sleep.

"You seemed awfully nervous in there," she said now as they
headed up West Fourth Street.

"I'm so sorry," Jack said. "Of all the places we could've chosen." He remembered that she'd chosen it. "It was wonderful
food, but that was torture sitting next to my boss."

Hillary seemed slightly miffed about the idea that the whole evening had been torture and said, "I thought your boss was a great guy."

"Did you think Will was handsome?"

"The young guy? Handsome? His girl was cute. Will . . . is that his name? He looked sort of shy and dim, no personality. You're a lot cuter."

They went back to Jack's apartment and made out on the corduroy couch, but to his surprise Jack didn't get hard, and he moved to a chair after he'd "freshened" Hillary's drink.

She looked offended and said, "What are you doing way over there?"

Jack laughed and said, "I can see you better from here."

"What's the real reason?"

He laughed some more. "Good ol' Ann Arbor honesty. Don't run up against that much here."

She gestured with both hands as if she were pulling it out of him.

"I wasn't—jeez, do I have to say?"

She nodded solemnly.

"I wasn't getting aroused," he said. "I was afraid of a fiasco. Even though you—you're more attractive than ever."

"Do you have a girlfriend?" she asked. "Feeling guilty?"

"No. No girlfriend."

"Maybe I put you off with all my talk about spasmophilia way back then, but I'm good at sex now."

"No, really, I liked your honesty. You were so frank. That made me feel closer to you. No, it's just—"

"Anyway, I'm over the ol' spaz," she said. "A Dr. Teitlebaum psychoanalyzed me out of it. It turns out it was all tied up with that charm bracelet I used to wear. It had been my mother's, and I thought—unconsciously, of course—that she was watching me. So I threw the bracelet into the Atlantic off Kennebunkport, and some twenty-two-pound lobster must be wearing it now as a very fetching necklace."

Jack laughed at the image, but when the laughter subsided he said, "But seriously, that cured you?"

"Yep. Hundred percent. Instantaneous." She patted the sofa beside her, but when Jack just raked his nails across his forehead and lowered his eyes (a tic he'd stolen from Will), she stood up. "Okay, I'm pushing off. I'm not desperate or anything."

"Hey," Jack said, standing up. "Come here," and he opened his arms.

But she ducked under them and said, "You take care, Jack."

"Want me to walk you over to Eighth to get you a taxi?"

"No," she said, "no need."

Jack felt a bit panicky when the door closed behind her. He didn't know whether it was because now he was alone and he was always afraid to be alone or because Hillary was a door he'd just closed—not Hillary in particular but her kind of good-natured girl, this kind of . . . "woman." Women. Was he through with women?

He often thought he'd get married some day. But to be honest, in the last few months whenever he thought of marriage, the woman, his wife, was pretty vague, more a smiling wraith than an actual sharp-featured person, and her main function seemed to be to accompany him on a double date with Will.

Jack drank two strong bourbons and went to bed and jacked off thinking about the double date, about glancing over his shoulder into the backseat, where Will had his old-fashioned baggy white boxer shorts down around his bony knees and his voluminous pale blue Egyptian-cotton dress shirt ballooning out around him, silk tie at half mast, but there, unmistakable in the dark, shone the hard pure white bone of his desire as his wife's hand with the big diamond ring held it in a fastidious grip. It was like looking down through the dark of the Forum on that fragment of white stone from which the Romans measured all distances on earth—the *milliarium aureum*, the golden milestone. All of Jack's thoughts radiated out from this white stone he'd never seen.

Jack was determined not to complain about Will's "date" with Gephardt or even razz him about trying to get ahead. He didn't want to annoy Will (that's what girls did), nor did he like to think of Will as grasping and ambitious. If that's what he was, Jack preferred not to know about it.

Suddenly Jack realized he was getting nowhere with his life. Will was writing a novel, he had a girl, he knew important people in New York through his family. He had designs on the *Northern Review*—and he was probably interviewing for better jobs elsewhere. Will was so damn secretive.

Jack had sleepwalked his way through boarding school and college, but here, in the working world, you had to grapple and climb or go peeling down the mountain. By nature he wanted to pass unnoticed, but that wasn't recommended. Jack loved anonymity—it allowed you to have your cake and eat it too. But in the working world, even to lead a little, private life, an inconspicuous life, you had to struggle and stick your elbows into other guys' ribs.

The next morning Will came into Jack's cubicle and sat on the floor hugging his knees. "How's it going?" he asked, looking at the frayed cuff of his khakis.

"Fine," Jack said.

"So who was the buhd?" Will asked, using the new Cockney import, "bird."

"Hillary? Oh, just an old friend. We used to date . . . before she filled out." The truth was she'd been forty pounds heavier back then.

"Fine piece of womanflesh," Will said, waxing the points of an invisible mustache.

"And your Lucy?"

"Her name is actually Luce. French. But she's not. Just a pal of my little sister. Pretty pathetic, huh? Raiding the Brownie pack?"

Jack thought he was the one who was pathetic, mooning over a secretive straight man who wasn't even all that attractive. Sometimes Jack thought that he and Will should live together, that he, Jack, should make Will dinner and suck his cock every night, that he should listen to Will's novel once a week and praise him every time, that he should keep a low profile at work and push Will ahead—and that he should recognize that at most he'd get two good years out of Will before the young author met the right girl: witty, nearly virginal, rich, fragile, feisty on the surface but essentially yielding.

Yes, just two years with Will, that's all he'd ever ask for from the gods. He knew he'd never be able to mention their affair to anyone, not even to Will. But if he could nurture Will's self-confidence, his talent, bring him pleasure, build him up, worship him! Yes, he'd worship Will's body, never expect anything more than an occasional hand tousling his hair . . . Just to know that Will would come bounding in the door, whistling, and sit down to dinner and eat with all the unquestioning sense of privilege of a real man, just as he'd stretch out on his bed and pretend to be asleep and let Jack measure all known distances from the *milliarium aureum*: that was Jack's dream.

It wasn't that he was queer; he just loved Will.

If that was Jack's fantasy, so deep and seductive that he could drift far, far away from shore on its current, his oars shipped, these days more often he jerked awake from it and its narcotic powers and realized he had to pull free of Will's spell, find someone new, someone loving and giving and sweet—a girl or, why not, even a boy. He'd botched things with Hillary and he was courting a straight guy—how pathetic was that?

Alice had a big party on a Saturday night in March, and Jack welcomed the occasion to meet someone new. He always thought that the natural result of a party would be encountering a new lover, though it had never happened yet. More than a hundred people came, even Mingus, even Will, who arrived with his beautiful sister Elaine. Alice had paid for three barrels of oysters to be trucked up from Delaware along with a professional oysterman, a shucker. She had also hired a bartender to make daiquiris, nothing but daiquiris. The guests, almost all under twenty-five, got drunk right away. They seemed flattered or at least stunned that Alice had gone to so much bother and expense for them; it wasn't the usual bring-your-own-bottle party on the cheap. The furniture was shoved to the walls, and soon dancers were stomping on the floor so hard it seemed to be buckling. Alice, who knew about parties, had invited the downstairs neighbors and promised them that such a rout would be only a once-a-decade affair.

Will stood along the sidelines clapping and encouraging the dancers, though Jack thought he must be hating every moment of it, especially the pop music. What had he done all those years at all those hundreds of debutante parties he'd attended? Then again, Will recognized socializing as a necessary if regrettable part of life and must have developed his own strategies for dealing with it. Anyway, the Lester Lanin music at deb parties was so bland as to be inoffensive. And maybe Will was hoping Alice would fix him up with some easygoing Greenwich Village babe. Will, like his father, no doubt, thought that all Village women were "loose."

Will waved at Jack exaggeratedly, crouching a bit and with a hand shading his eyes as if they were very far away from each other, hallooing across a valley, and not just ten or twelve feet apart. Maybe he wanted to mime an unbridgeable gulf and not have his chances for meeting a girl jinxed by a clingy office pal.

Alice had recently bought two ten-foot-long carved wooden spoons from Africa. When the crowd became so drunk that no one could stand up straight, Alice and a round-faced young man in a pink shirt with puffy pirate sleeves and with long sideburns that almost met at the chin began to do a "spoon dance." They held the long, heavy spoons at waist height and dueled each other. The music and chatter were so deafening that Jack could scarcely hear the hollow *chock-chock* of the colliding spoons. Alice was squinting fiercely. She took everything seriously, even the duel.

When the dance was over, Jack saw that Will had disappeared. Jack assumed he might have wandered off to the bathroom or for a daiquiri refill, but when Will didn't reappear after fifteen minutes, Jack made a tour of the whole apartment and even checked out the partygoers sitting in the stairwell. Jack was upset that he couldn't actually feel Will's precise location through some sort of heat detector; Jack thought of his whole being as attuned to his prey.

Alice never lost her impassivity, but as she came welling up through the crowd, Jack could see how pleased she was.

"Great party," he said.

She said, "It does seem okay. I've got someone here for you to meet," and only now did Jack see that she was followed by a small, smiley guy who looked to be no more than eighteen. "Jack, this is Peter. Peter's a famous ballet dancer." She then let herself be led away by the oyster shucker, who was exhausted and said he needed a break.

"Well, hello," Peter said in a deep voice as husky as an older actress's. He had an urchin's face with big eyes, sad beyond his years, pale afterimages of freckles scattered across his wide Tatar cheekbones, big, everted lips, a button nose, and bangs that he'd fashioned by pressing an uneven thatch down across his forehead—a haircut that if properly combed would be neat, classic, the anonymous helmet of a member of the corps.

Jack was puzzled as to why Alice thought they'd like each other. How could Jack find anything in common with a ballet dancer, a boy who could just as easily have been a girl if he hadn't had such heavily muscled legs—the very legs the word "thews" was invented to name, right?

"You're a very sexy man," the creature said to him, looking up at him and tilting his head to one side. "Very tall. I like tall men. Tall women dancers are the bane of my existence. That's why Mr. Joffrey has done so many solos for me. I can't dance with anyone because I'm so little." He laughed. "Not all over."

"What?"

"I said I'm not little all over."

Jack blushed and then was angry that he'd been made to feel awkward and said flat out, "I can see you have overdeveloped thews, for instance."

Peter blinked dramatically, dyed black eyelashes sweeping over enlarged pupils. "Oh. I'm sorry. I misunderstood. I thought you were gay."

"It's too loud in here," Jack said. "Wanna go down to the street and get some fresh air?"

Peter blinked again, the equivalent of inching open a fan and then snapping it shut. "Sure," he said huskily.

Fueled by a dozen daiquiris and three oysters, Jack flew down the stairs ahead of Peter, aware of the creature's eyes on his shoulders, making them broader and more muscular. Cornelia was dark and empty, though up at the corner West Fourth Street was streaming with light. Suddenly Jack grabbed Peter by his surprisingly small hot hand and yanked him into a doorway. Jack systematically undid the big buttons on Peter's peacoat, opened it, ran his hands over Peter's slender body, and pulled him in for a long, deep kiss. Their teeth, hard and wet, collided, and tongues took turns flowing into and out of each other's mouths. One of Jack's hands drifted down to Peter's butt, as prominent and horizontal as a shelf.

"What?" Peter gasped.

"I said—oh, nothing." He felt tongue-tied with urgency.

Peter ran his hand over Jack's erection through his trousers and said, "You should ensure this thing for two million."

For once Jack didn't resent the person commenting on his dick—maybe because Peter's own body was even more extraordinary. Jack had read in a review of *Viva Vivaldi!* in the *Times* about how Peter could kick the back of his head, how the ballet was a duel between him and another, bigger male dancer.

"You take my breath away," Peter growled. "I was afraid you were straight."

"I am, sort of," Jack said.

"That's okay," Peter said, "because I'm sort of a girl."

"Let's go back to my place. It's not too far."

"You sure move fast."

"C'mon," Jack said, pulling Peter along by the hand, "you're not that much of a girl. You've got a hard-on. I could feel it through your clothes. And my dad used to say that a hard dick has no conscience."

"Whoa! Wait a minute." Peter stopped short in the middle of West Fourth amid the flowing crowds. "I don't even know your name."

"Oh, Mr. Steinmetz," a teenage girl with turnout and a ponytail said, coming up to him. "I just want you to know how . . . magical you are. How you've changed my life and given me the courage to face all the challenges I'm having as a young dancer."

"Thank you," Peter said, patting her hand. "Thank you for telling me that. It means so much to me."

When they were alone again, Peter smiled faintly as they hurried across Sheridan Square, as if that stranger's praise had given him the necessary reassurance to run off with Jack.

"My name is Jack Holmes," Jack said, putting a hand on Peter's shoulder, "and I'm just a humble journalist and that's all I want to be. I think you're cute as hell, but I've only had sex with one other male—"

"Who said we're having sex?"

Jack stopped again and felt a drunk momentum continue to whirl him around. He looked down into Peter's face. "You know we're going to."

Peter shrugged and smiled and said, "Okay, Jack Holmes."

Maybe it was the daiquiris or just slipping free of the chains

of pointless love, but Jack felt more like an animal than ever
before. Once they were home, he found he liked biting Peter's
lips and putting a finger in his stinky little hole crushed between
those powerful buttocks. He liked weighing Peter's balls in his
right hand like dice. He liked branding Peter's hairless tummy
with the searing length of his penis. He liked sitting on the
edge of the bed and scooping Peter onto his lap, facing him, the
boy's head dreaming on his shoulder, Peter's calves grasping
Jack's waist, that little scabbard slowly expanding to swallow
the whole sword. Because he'd only ever dated women (and
not too many of them), Jack was used to saying he was in love
(to feeling he was in love) every time he kissed someone deeply
or undressed her. Now he started to whisper words of love, but
when he felt Peter squatting on his dick and bouncing up and
down on it, the whole flimsy bamboo scaffolding of sentiment
fell away to reveal the imposing dome of pure desire. If it would
turn out to be necessary to utter sweet nothings in order to re-
capture this moment, in order for them to sweat their way through
to another athletic orgasm, then Jack would say the needed words,
but he didn't feel them, he didn't want to love Peter, he just
wanted to fuck this perfect butt.

Later, they were lying in bed and smoking. "Why are we
smoking?" Jack asked. "Aren't you an athlete?"

"All dancers smoke," said Peter.

"Why?" Jack asked.

"Maybe to stay thin, it's partly that, but it's more to tempt
the devil on the same principle that a woman with a perfect face
might put a jewel in a nostril."

He drew on his cigarette and tapped its glowing ash into an
enameled dish. Jack stroked his back. Peter's skin was pale and
spongy, flesh that had been wrapped in sweat clothes year after

year. He started talking about how he was planning to have his sex changed.

Jack asked him why he wanted to do that.

"I'm too small to have all the juicy male roles, and anyway, 'Ballet is woman,' as Mr. Balanchine said. If I became a female, I'd be able to jump higher than any woman alive. I can already do toe work—I taught myself."

"Toe work?"

"Toe dancing. Men don't dance on their toes; only women do. And I'd be the right height as a woman."

"And what about sex?" Jack asked.

"You'd still like me if I were a girl? Maybe even more."

"But you'd probably get shyer and more delicate and want me to marry you if you were a girl. I wouldn't like that as much. Right now you're a wild man. I don't know much about men. Are all men like that, hell bound for pleasure, so frank and passionate?"

"Some men are big prisses. And a lot of gays would be afraid of your dick. If you went to a sauna they'd all follow you around, but then they wouldn't know what to do with it. They'd throw it over one shoulder and burp it and weep."

Jack laughed at the image.

Peter left at dawn because the company was taking a bus to Albany, where they'd be performing for three nights. At the door Peter said, "You're the universal ball, Jack Holmes. Everyone at that party wanted you."

"They did?"

"You really didn't notice, did you? That's nice." He put on his gloves. "Modesty is nice in a man."

"But you can't just go away like this."

"Catch a train up to Albany on Tuesday and spend the

night with me and ride in the company bus back to New York with us."

"Wouldn't you feel awkward?"

Peter stood on tiptoe and made Jack bend down and kissed him on the nose. "I'd be proud, Jack Holmes. Not everyone has a young, straight, handsome beau."

"I'm not sure about the straight or the handsome, but thanks."

Jack went back to bed and looked at the tube of body lotion for dry elbow he'd used as a lubricant; Peter had laughed at his amateurishness. It smelled of gardenias, like Jack's grandmother's soap. For all his talk of changing his sex, Peter's dick had been hard and energetic, pushing into Jack's chest. Jack felt exhilarated—the "universal ball." Did people really think of him like that? A man for everyone? He'd never felt so confident. Was it because Peter was as yielding and in need of protection as a girl but had all the boldness and strength of a boy?

Jack could imagine awakening sexually and becoming obsessed with Peter's ass, devoted to it and to him, but somehow he couldn't picture Peter caring for anything much beyond his own career.

Jack did take Tuesday afternoon off from work and flew up to Albany. During the intermission there were lots of girls aged eight to ten, all pacing the lobby and showing each other versions of new steps as they sipped their Cokes. Their mothers, standing off to one side, were dowdy and fat and dressed in aquamarine silk tops with sprays of glass and gold beads appliquéd across one breast; Jack thought they were probably more presentable in their ordinary work clothes. Albany felt very proletariat.

Jack was full of anticipation as he went back to his seat. Peter was about to dance in *Viva Vivaldi!,* and Jack had the jitters, almost as if he were a stage mother too.

He was astonished by Peter's performance. He was at varying moments a boy, a man, and a great lady—the grande dame came out when he took his bows, clutched the cellophane-wrapped roses to his breast, and pretended to search out individuals in the very top balcony. The Cuban dancer who shared the bill with him was so masculine he seemed to belong to another species.

Peter wasn't quite as happy to see him as Jack had expected, and over hamburgers at a diner, which was the only place still open at that hour (eleven), he seemed mildly curious about why Jack had come so far "for nothing," as he put it bitterly.

"Nothing? Man, that was one of the great performances."

"Get real, Jack," Peter said. "You know nothing about it. How many shows have you sat through?"

"Three. But I've seen tons on TV."

"Probably another three," Peter drawled, "so we're up to six—and anyway, you don't know what you're looking at."

Jack said, "You're really good at accepting compliments. Anyway, call me an idiot, but you don't have to be a lion to gasp over the lions at the circus."

Peter pretended to be vexed, but he couldn't keep from smiling. "The circus! I just knew it." After a silence he said, "I'm in a bad mood because Mr. Joffrey criticized me after the matinee for putting on feminine airs. He said the public doesn't go for that shit—that's exactly how he put it." Jack didn't know what to say. He thought, Peter is a paranoid prima donna.

Back at the hotel Peter said he was exhausted and sore all over, and they'd all have to pile in the bus at six A.M. to arrive in the city by two.

"I'm taking the seven o'clock train back," Jack said.

"You're not riding with us?"

"I've pushed myself on you enough," Jack said, feeling cool behind his politeness.

"Come over here." Peter patted the edge of the bed beside him. Jack complied. Peter said, "Why don't you kiss me?"

And again, this time without all those daiquiris and the exhilaration of Alice's spoon dance, Jack delved into all this hot, coiled muscularity; he even stood up and walked around the small room with his cock in Peter and Peter's powerful legs wrapped around his waist.

Later, as they were both dozing off, Jack said, "Call me an ignorant philistine, but it was terrific seeing you up there dancing tonight."

"For me," Peter whispered, "you've been nothing but a pain in the butt. Exactly what I like most in the world."

It seemed only half an hour later when the phone rang. The company manager told Peter to be downstairs in twenty-five minutes.

Jack took the train since he wasn't quite ready to brave the stares of all those dancers. He wasn't prepared to sit there while all those girls, those ballerinas, looked at him and saw Peter's lover, Peter's queer lover. The other boys, the company fags, might smirk and exchange looks. But the girls—that was a test Jack didn't want to subject himself to. Being with Peter alone and being with Peter in public were two different things.

Something told Jack that a nondancer could never fit into that world. Peter said they were all so competitive, and even as he was in front of the curtain receiving an ovation, he could hear a bitch in the chorus whispering, "Did you see how he started traveling downstage when he was doing his turns?" Another queen chimed in, "And what about that nelly port de bras? The broken wrist, the wilting fingertips, the shoulders like an anorectic *Vogue* model?"

The dancers were like members of holy orders—no outsider could ever breach the walls isolating them, their dedication, their single-mindedness. They'd chosen to deform their bodies and give up the world all in the name of a career that could last at best fifteen years. How could someone like Jack ever understand their sacrifices? For Jack, Peter was a problem not because he was effeminate but because he was a dancer.

6.

T HERE WAS A two-week period when Peter wasn't tour-
ing. The company was back in New York and, aside from
a class or two, Peter had nothing to do. He'd drop by Jack's
apartment in the early evening and lie down on the floor,
which was covered with tatami mats. Jack would undress him,
undo the elastic bandages around one knee and both feet. He'd
wash Peter's feet and legs in warm water and soap, then get him
to roll facedown on a towel. Jack had bought some patchouli-
scented oil, and he'd slowly, patiently massage the kinks out of
Peter's short, wide feet with the high insteps and blunt toes and
square-cut nails. His feet felt alert and sensitive, as if they were the
bodily organs that could see, read.

Jack then went to Peter's shoulders and sat astride his small,
muscular waist and rubbery buttocks. He worked his fingers into
Peter's shoulders and with his thumbs pushed the tension up his
spine toward his neck.

"Too hard, Jack Holmes," Peter complained. "That hurts."

When Jack relented and scribbled whispery, feathery cursive
letters across Peter's white, spongy skin, he said, "Too light, Jack
Holmes. That doesn't hurt enough."

Jack moved down to his lower back, which joined his tailbone in a more intricate way than usual, and dug deep with his thumbs. Then Jack's big, octave-and-a-half hands fanned out over Peter's high buttocks and molded them into Silly Putty shapes. But from time to time Jack was forced to stop and sit back and look at what God and the individual will and institutional discipline had wrought. He remembered that a philosophy professor in Ann Arbor had said that vision was the most spiritual sense and smelling the most animal; Jack went back and forth from gazing at Peter's ass with angelic indifference to spreading his cheeks and grazing his hole with his thumb and bringing it up to his nose with canine rapture. He thought that this blend of patchouli and boy mud was the most intoxicating scent, the true smell of modernity. Jack knew nothing about hippies, incense, or drugs, but he suspected that dozens of skinny, bearded guys on the Lower East Side were stretching out their male friends at this very moment, burning doss sticks and working their thumbs into unwashed curry-chutes. He could picture the imprint of an oily body on the bedticking thrown onto the floor . . . the smell of the sixties: ass and incense.

Jack told himself that he wasn't really gay. He was just lonely. Besides, Peter would be on tour at the end of this two-week period, and then they wouldn't see each other again for six months. Anyway, Jack was only catching up with all those hippie polymorphs out there on the Lower East Side, the free spirits he envied and feared. Anyway, it felt like being with a girl because Peter insisted on the role he was to play, and besides, he didn't want Jack to touch his dick. Truth be told, Peter was more feminine than Hillary and a more traditional woman than Rebekkah. And when Peter had his sex change, he'd be even more in character, wouldn't he? And Jack would find him/her even more alluring, wouldn't he?

"Hey!" Peter said. "Are you drifting off?"

"What?"

"Are you falling asleep on the job?"

In response Jack rolled Peter over to reveal the solid erection the boy had been hatching. Against Peter's protests, Jack applied an extra dollop of oil to the problem and worked with it for a long time.

Maybe things weren't so clear. Then again, maybe anyone, male or female, straight or gay, would want to play with this exquisite body.

But Jack resolved he'd start dating girls again.

By the fourth evening Jack was fed up with Peter. He complained all the time about Mr. Joffrey and Gerald Arpino, the resident choreographer. They weren't treating him with the requisite deference. They hadn't scheduled any new ballets for him during the next season. Even the two big ballets he'd starred in for several seasons were being programmed less frequently—an outrage, considering how much the public adored him. The two bosses both kept complaining that he, Peter, was too effeminate, not in his actual performances but in the way he took his bows, the way he exulted in the applause he inspired. Of course, it was ludicrous for the men to complain; it was obvious that they were jealous, they who were losing their hair and thickening in the waist no matter how many classes they gave or took. They were standing in Peter's way, and he wasn't going to tolerate it! A dancer had only so many good years, and he couldn't lose a single one. Mr. Joffrey had never found his own niche in the dance world. He wasn't Balanchine and he wasn't Robbins and he wasn't Cunningham—he wasn't anything distinctive, just an inept manager with a mildly talented choreographer. Even doddering old Martha Graham, gesturing from her couch as Phaedra—even she was more real than Joffrey. "She'll be remembered, mark my words," Peter exclaimed, "but Mr. Joffrey will be forgotten. He's done nothing original. Of course, if he'd build the company around me, he might have a chance at immortality."

Hour after hour, Peter raved about how invaluable he was and what a fool Joffrey was for not recognizing his genius. Jack was certain that Peter must be mistaken, that no dancer, no matter how talented, could be indispensable. Performers received that adulation, but they couldn't ensure the continuity—not even Nijinsky had turned out to be all that valuable, and he'd been the most famous dancer of the century.

Jack stopped listening. He wanted to get his hands on Peter to calm him down.

After Jack would massage Peter, he'd fuck him in six or seven different positions that Peter would suggest or even dictate. Peter treated the spurts of Jack's semen in the same way that he received applause—he threw his head back, lowered his eyelids, pursed his lips, and drank it all in as the homage of Jack's ardor. "Only you, Jack Holmes, only you," he'd murmur, as if only Jack owned the right size screwdriver to open this particular control box.

Jack would cook him a burger or make a chicken salad, serve him iced tea or orange juice, though there was always something wrong—the tea might overstimulate or constipate him, the juice was too acidic, the burger too carnivorous, the chicken choked with hormones. "I'll have to teach you to eat healthy," Peter said. "I eat lots of steamed vegetables and brown rice, and I arrange it all on the plate according to the principles of yang and yin."

"Oh sure," Jack said. "I'll run right out and do that. I went to a macrobiotic restaurant on Fifty-fifth off Sixth—the waitress was the biggest grouch in New York, and no wonder: she was starving!"

Peter laughed, like a child who's made a big dog bark. "Seriously," he said, "you'll feel a lot lighter, more airborne."

"I leave flying to you, Peter. I just want to stoke the old furnace."

Suddenly Jack realized he'd heard Will call eating "stoking the old furnace" more than once. Jack wondered if he was impersonating Will's mild heartiness with Peter in a parody of preppy masculinity. Did Peter bring out the manly in him? Or did Peter's diva combination of young woman and magic child demand an equal but opposite charade of understated macho wryness?

Or was Jack so in love with Will that when he missed him he became him?

This possibility made him turn away, disgusted, from Peter, who was sprawling naked on Jack's tatami mat. Suddenly everything about this man-boy-girl seemed obscene—his overdeveloped ass with its powerful grip, his drag queen delusions of grandeur, his skinny white torso punctuated by just a pair of black dots like a blank page inscribed with nothing but two periods, a double finality so at odds with so much potential. Peter's big, pouty lips, his husky voice, the slightly doctored color and wave of his hair, his unappeased narcissism—he was a walking, leaping, undulating formula for unhappiness.

Jack preferred Will's cold, uncaressed body, vague and pale and almost inert inside his baggy clothes. Surely Will hadn't connected with—or even visited—most of the corners of his body, as if it were a religious cult fallen into disuse, its shrines allowed to go to seed. One night, back in the fall, Will was joking about a girl who had wanted to go down on him. He had chided her out of it, saying, "I wouldn't if I were you. You never know what you're going to find down there." Will went on to compare his crotch to the floor of his workroom, with its sedimentation of food and food wrappers, dirty socks, abandoned underwear, old newspapers, and mud tracked in by his expensive shoes. Will had his three suits and his blazer (with the old gold fox-head buttons) dry-cleaned regularly, and his father's fragile, monogrammed shirts with the fraying collars washed and pressed by the French cleaners on Lexington near his sister Elaine's rented town house, and he polished his shoes himself and rinsed out his baggy boxer shorts and long lisle stockings. But otherwise, everything in his room, he said, was filthy, mostly organic, slowly decomposing into topsoil. The miracle was that Will could turn himself out so impeccably every morning.

Of course, when Will said, "You never know what you're going to find down there," Jack was soon obsessing about exactly what one would discover, the tangled pubic hair, a mousy brown, then the balls, the size of quail eggs, riding high and close in a sac matted with shorter, coarser hairs woven into a merkin so thick that no flesh could be seen through it, then a smallish, circumcised suburban penis, the kind he associated with the shower room at boarding school, and finally the hair running down his inner thighs and shading off into ordinary, sunbleached leg hair, again the very hair that reminded him of high school basketball players sitting on the sidelines, their silky shorts hiked up and their elbows resting on their knees. At the time, Jack figured, his fear of being caught staring had inhibited him;

he hadn't realized back in high school how he was glorying in all those long, hairy, muscled legs with the hair leading the eye up to their hidden treasure.

Jack preferred Will's inaccessibility to Peter's constant presence. Jack preferred daydreaming about the life he might lead with Will to having a real affair with Peter. He liked to imagine what Will's body would feel like and how it might respond rather than to know all too well how Peter's functioned. Real sex was too meaty, too medical, as if sex plunged you into all those pulsing, sweating systems, the nerves and valves and secretions, whereas imaginary sex remained speculative, spiritual, sepulchral.

He stopped answering Peter's calls and even, one evening, his exasperated ringing of the doorbell, and soon enough the Joffrey was off on another national tour. It occurred to Jack that it might have been kinder if he'd simply admitted to Peter that he was in love with another man, a real man, and that he, Jack, was just another fag. Such a confession would have shocked Peter, as if he'd been sleeping with a female. Jack had heard Peter explain that he couldn't possibly go to bed with another dancer ("And do what?" he'd demanded. "Bump pussies?"). Peter wasn't even sure he could accept macho men who didn't at least occasionally have sex with women.

Or maybe Jack had finally rid himself of homosexuality, and he was back to mooning over an unobtainable straight guy. Maybe Will's function was to be unobtainable, to allow Jack a bit of same-sex yearning without the danger of real cock-and-balls encounters. Jack had hated waking up with Peter. An empty bed every morning was Jack's proof that he hadn't chosen his sexuality yet, that he was a blank slate.

In his soul Jack had returned to Will. For him the silent reversion felt momentous, though he was sure Will hadn't even noticed it. That wasn't quite fair; Will was a novelist and observed, if not everything, at least whatever fell within his purview. For Will had once explained, in the pretentious way he adopted whenever he talked about his art, that novelists see no more than the man in the street unless it fits into the narrow range of their sensibilities: "It's as if a camera were rigged to click only at one particular intensity of light and no other."

Now Jack began to pretend he was behind in his work and to stay late at the office and wait for Will in order to grab a bite with him. Now he started quizzing Will about the novel and made him renew his promise that he, Jack, would be the first reader.

"And so you shall be, my boy," Will said. "The moment it's sold."

"From your lips to God's ears," Jack said, not sure what that expression meant; he hoped it solemnized a promise.

Will invited Jack to go down to Virginia for the point-to-point races. Jack started to make jokes about "dead pieces of animals glued to walls," but he noticed that those jokes were only funny if they came from an insider; all outsiders who dared to criticize the hunt were considered boorish at worst, irrelevant at least.

They arrived late. The yardman, Cicero, met Jack and Will and Elaine and her children at the train station and drove them out to Upperville in the family's decrepit, dark blue town car; the interior was carpeted with dog hairs and someone's cast-aside cashmere sweater worn through at the elbows. No one in the main house was still awake; Pinky, the black maid, was setting "Miz" Elaine's little house to rights. Pinky looked bone tired and merely mimed a welcome by slapping her knees and bending over to kiss Elaine's children, Teddy and Phoebe. "Give me some sugar," she murmured to Teddy, who pushed her aside. He was tired and irritable. Phoebe behaved with an eerie perfection. Her platinum blonde pageboy held back with a royal blue ribbon was impeccable, and she presented her pink cheek to be pecked by the maid.

In the big house only one dim lamp (a polychrome Chinese bull) was turned on under its café crème lamp shade, dangling fringe and scorched by a bulb on one side. A marble clock ticked expensively beside the capacious wing armchair Will had flopped down in; the clock showed a cherub, finger to his lips, just starting to draw a marble curtain across the clockface. It must have been made for a bedroom long ago, Jack figured. He didn't want to comment on the family's things. He'd once heard Will criticize someone who'd asked too many questions of that sort.

Jack took the matching chair, and they both sipped Johnny Walker from the bottle Jack had brought down as a "house gift." They didn't say much. Jack had to keep remembering that this was Will's childhood home, as familiar to him as the back of his hand. For Will there was nothing here that was challenging or unknown.

It was an early-nineteenth-century house painted white but peeling. It was at the end of a mile-long lane, straight as the part in Will's hair. There must have been fifteen or sixteen rooms, and as Jack strolled through the reception rooms, he saw they were full of hunting prints and images of foxes—everything from eighteenth-century fox heads cast in bronze to dime-store knickknacks of foxes trotting across crudely painted green grass. The value or quality didn't seem to matter, just the image of the totemic animal. The wallpaper in the library looked very old and hand-painted, like that in the White House; it showed scenes of the hunt, the women sidesaddle in full skirts, the men in red or black coats, and their mounts surrounded by twenty hounds or more. The paper was sun-faded in one corner.

In every room there were bouquets of wildflowers in silver vases. Big armchairs in worn chintz were drawn up to the cold fireplaces. The glass panes in the windows were tinted violet and were so old they'd warped. The glass was thinner at the top and thicker at the bottom, a reminder that glass is a slow liquid that flows downward over a century or two. In the dining room the big oval table and the ten spindly chairs and the inlaid sideboard resting on tapering legs were all an oxblood mahogany polished so often that you could see where the veneer was wearing thin. The whole house, it seemed, was maintained by Pinky (who cooked and cleaned) and her husband, Cicero. They were as black and shiny as eggplants and seldom spoke and never smiled. Will said that Pinky's great-grandparents had been slaves right here at Greenmount. He didn't seem ashamed of it, rather the contrary. Out back was Elaine's pretty little house, the Rookery, which her father had built her after her divorce. Jack helped her carry her bags in.

At the paddock the next morning Jack could feel small hands of tension digging into his shoulders. His neck was getting stiff, and he bobbed his head to limber it up. He was tense because he didn't know any of these people and they, of course, knew each other. He was tense because there were all sorts of rituals and uniforms that he didn't understand or possess, and that clearly counted a lot to the participants. Will put a hand on Jack's near shoulder and said, "I hope these people aren't boring you too much. They're real grind-asses, aren't they?"

They were walking back to the drinks table, which was set up near the paddock. "Boring? No, I just feel foolish because I'm not wearing the right clothes."

"I wouldn't worry about that. It's just a Virginia thing—no one from elsewhere would dream of owning these weird jackets. Why would they? They're ugly as shit." Will lit two cigarettes and handed one to Jack, something he'd never done before. In the strong overhead light Will's gunshot eyes were lost in shadow, but he was obviously looking closely at Jack. "I'm just grateful you came down here so we can look at the freak show together."

Jack felt a surge of joy race through his body, and he was afraid his cheeks might be turning red. "I don't think of it as a freak show. It's a noble old tradition. I'm only afraid of looking out of place."

"Don't worry about that. Remember, you're with me, and blood don't get any bluer than mine." Will laughed at his own absurdity, but Jack felt that Will's words were like a heavy wool cape draped over his shoulders protecting him from the cold.

Will had on the right plaid jacket, but a faded hand-me-down one, which suited him and seemed all the more traditional. He guided Jack around and introduced him not as a school friend nor as a friend from work; he'd just say, "Furlong, this is Jack," and he wouldn't give any further talking points to his friends.

That evening they had dinner with Will's family. They were nine at the table, and Pinky brought out a platter of sloppy joes but on a heavy nineteenth-century salver. There was also a

Rice-A-Roni pilaf served in a large silver bowl on which cherubs chased each other around the lip. Most of the conversation was about fetching the butter dish or the applesauce. Jack had no idea what sort of wine they were drinking, since it was presented in an amber glass ewer inserted into a silver sleeve, but he was sure it was a cheap one, maybe even a local one.

Will's father said grace before they began to eat. Something brief and impersonal, not at all like the long, improvised to-do lists Jack's Baptist relatives liked to impose on the deity ("And may little Billy be successful in his 4-H contest later today, O Lord"). Here the meal seemed like a giant jigsaw puzzle that had to be swiftly put together, then taken apart with no time at all to contemplate the final pattern. No, it was all just coming and going, this meal.

Jack kept thinking how lucky he'd been not to be born into a big, powerful family with traditions and expectations. He, Jack, had had nothing to rebel against except brute force and lunatic excess, whereas Will had to dodge through the minefield of his mother's strategic silences and his father's withering smiles. Will's mother, as she was dishing up the chocolate pudding, said, "Will, you should be a little nicer to Taffy. She's pining over you."

"Taffy Ladew? You can't be serious. That girl is an albino and has an IQ of 70."

Elaine said, "Mother, Will isn't interested in girls. At least not currently."

Will said, "Why, sure I am. And I have a lot to offer them with the five dollars I currently have in the bank, my eleven square feet of habitation ripe with old banana peels on the floor, my serious acne problem, my unpublished novel, a beginner's job in publishing, and no prospects. What girl wouldn't leap at the chance to date me?"

Will's mother said unsmilingly, "Not all girls are materialistic, Will. You have a fine mind and a sterling character."

Will made a face and said, "And those merits will get you a one-way subway ride in New York City."

Will's father said, rather primly, "You may have just put your finger on what's wrong with New York. Who wants an after-dinner drink? Thank you, dear, for the lovely meal," and Will Sr. stood up and sauntered off.

Neither of Will's parents treated Jack with any perceptible warmth. They didn't ask him questions or tease him or collude with him; they weren't seductive, as Jack's parents had been with his friends, behavior that had made it impossible for Jack to complain about his mother and father. Jack's parents used to systematically make conquests of the boys he brought home from school, though later, after the guests had departed, they ridiculed them in shockingly precise ways ("Such sensual little hands that Tommy has").

Will's parents, by contrast, were refreshingly cool and content to maintain their distance as parents and hosts. Jack thought that Will Sr. was more handsome than his son, more poised and elegant and sorted. If Will Jr. became more and more like his father over time, that would be all to the good.

Will's father now sat in the drawing room in front of a portrait of himself as a younger man.

Lying in his uncomfortable four-poster bed that night, Jack thought that with such a family baying behind him and nipping at his heels, Will could never vanish or throw the others off his scent. Jack had been surprised that Will's mother had been urging him to pursue Taffy Ladew, whose family was famous for gardens worthy of Versailles and nearly as extensive and varied. Her ambition to find Will a rich wife seemed out of character.

Of course Will couldn't ever experiment with homosex, even if he happened to belong to the 3 percent of the population who liked that sort of thing. No, Will would be reviled if he so much as married a delicate blonde heiress who was a Protestant, for chrissakes. Something Will Sr. had said had revealed that New York publishing was already considered daring enough, given that the young Will could have entered the failing family law practice.

Jack had always thought of himself as an extra in an opera, as an indistinguishable part of the crowd scene, but his passion for Will had singled him out, drawn him forward from the hooded ranks, shone a spotlight on his upraised face. In his own eyes, at least, he was now a lead if not a star, and he didn't like the attention.

But now he understood better than at any time previously how much pressure Will's family exerted on him. Jack placed all his own queer hopes of seducing Will on Will's destiny as a novelist. Because Will's art required him to study his world and himself, to map out his foibles and sound its shallows, he had every reason to be as original in his life as in his writing. Will's idol, Thomas Pynchon, had studied New York by looking up from its sewers, and he had mixed comic book riffs into the reasonable strains of urban realism. Wasn't Will under an obligation to be just as odd and original, just as strange?

But did Will have any talent? It was just a prejudice, but Jack thought that Will would be more forthright about his writing if he knew he was good, and if he were good, he'd know he was. Were there really any mute, unsung Miltons? Milton himself had become famous very young, hadn't he, as much for his beauty as for his Latin verses. Jack felt that both he and Will were betting everything on Will's talent. If his novel was a success,

Will would be free of his family. If he was free of his family and Virginia and Catholicism, Will might realize he loved Jack as much as Jack loved him.

In a dream, Jack floated up out of his bed and met Will in the bathroom between their rooms. They embraced—in fact Will was surprisingly the more ardent one, digging a sharp finger into Jack's back and streaking a slimy tongue, like a snail's pseudopod, down Jack's long neck.

He woke up to hear someone outside calling Will's name. When Jack went to the window, he could see it was Will's mother in jodhpurs and a tight jacket and a matching hat tied under her chin. Will threw open his window and called down, "What is it, Mother? I was sleeping."

"Leander wants to say hello," she said. It took a moment for Jack to realize that Leander was the horse.

"Well, hello to you, Leander. Now I'm going to grab a few more z's."

"You could ride the Puckster if you wanted."

"We'll see, Mother."

Jack realized he'd observed no other contact between mother and son except for the misguided prompt about Taffy. They were both shy and needed to move the horses as chessmen in their game.

Will went off to the hunt ball that evening, but Jack had said that he hated dances and didn't have a tux and preferred watching TV at home and relaxing with the children, who all cheered. They'd taken a liking to Jack, who played silly games with them and was even willing to be the fox they hunted. At one point Jack caught little Teddy streaking baby Phoebe's forehead with a bead of sweat that had fallen from Jack's face. "What are you doing?" Jack asked.

"I'm blooding her."

"Bleeding her?"

"No, silly. I'm blooding her."

When Jack looked up at Elaine, she sighed and said, "It's another grotesque ritual from the wonderful world of fox killing. The first time a child goes on a hunt, they daub him or her with the fox's blood, Lord knows why. It's called 'blooding.' Marks them for life as a moron." Elaine laughed. "People don't do it much anymore. It's dying out. You're going to tell everyone in New York about your weekend with the savages."

"Do you think foxhunting should be outlawed?" Jack asked her.

Before she could answer, Will came in wearing black tie, about to head out for the ball. "Oh, look at His Serene Elegantissimo," Elaine said.

"Yes," Will said, "I'll make the most elegant shadows in the darkest corner."

"Promise me," Elaine said, "that you'll ask Taffy to dance just once, just once, Will."

"I'm sorry," Will said, "but I don't socialize with albino feebs."

"She has thirty-seven million dollars," Elaine said. "If you add her millions to her IQ, it brings her nicely up into the normal range."

"Just because *you're* a fortune hunter, there's no reason to assume—" Will said, but Elaine beat the air with her hand and anxiously hushed him, glancing significantly at the children.

"Okay, I'm off," Will said. Framed by the wide doorway, he looked like a celebrity photo out of the past, a black-and-white Weegee of a Biddle or an Astor. Jack thought that this weekend had stolen Will from him, made him less of an individual and more of a personage, less a close-up and more just another face in a dynastic lineup.

After he'd gone and Jack had rough-housed with the children for half an hour, Elaine said, sipping on her cigarette, "You two boys are such good friends!"

"Well, we met at work."

"You got Will his job. He's so grateful to you."

"I didn't even know Will then; it was just a favor I was doing for Alice. Why didn't she come down for the races?" he asked, hoping to change the subject.

"Not her sort of thing. Alice is such a free spirit! Of course, she's making her documentary about us all. Maybe next year she'll get around to shooting the race. You must come back next year. I can see how close you and Will are."

"I'm devoted to Will," Jack said, as if to defend his friend's honor, "but I'm only one of Will's many acquaintances."

"Much more than that. Will is such a loner. He's one of the rare people I know who genuinely prefer their own company, but with you—"

"It's almost as if he's alone?" Jack asked, laughing at the revelation.

"Possibly," she conceded. "Because with true soul mates we experience no conflict. We're completely at peace."

Jack couldn't tell if she was mocking him by speaking in such a serious way. The whole discussion made him uneasy. Did she suspect they were both queers and feel that her duty as a sister and a Catholic was to intervene, to get her brother out of the clutches of this fiend-friend? Or did the queer option intrigue her? Perhaps now that, as a divorcée, she was a pariah (unless the pope could be bribed to annul her marriage), she was looking for allies in her rebellion against piety. After all, despite her efforts to protect her children's innocence, she was celebrated among her friends for her candor about seeking a rich second husband. Would she consider a homosexual to be a fellow rebel against conformity?

Jack didn't think he was a nonconformist; he simply loved Will. If he could have magically turned himself into a girl whom Will would want to marry, he'd have done it without hesitation. He'd have converted to Catholicism, become a woman, borne Will's many children, shopped for dresses at Peck and Peck, learned to cook Rice-A-Roni—where was the rebellion in any of that? Not that Jack was interested in being a woman. He'd never daydreamed about a sex change. He didn't secretly experiment with makeup or window-shop for dresses or fold his towel into a turban and study his steamy reflection in the mirror, the way Peter did. He liked women and had more female friends than male, but if the price of marrying Will had been banishing all other women from the face of the earth, he would gladly have paid it.

"Are you going to wait up for Will?" Elaine asked as she prepared to go back to the Rookery. She gave him a sweet, confiding smile.

"Wait up!?" Jack exclaimed, as if the very notion were absurd, though he'd been planning on it. "I'm off now to grab some z's." He realized as he said it how pathetic he was to deny Will with an expression right out of his mouth.

In bed Jack beat off thinking about Will's naked body. He thought about the scar from the boil on his neck and about his strong legs and deflated, charmless butt. Jack was careful not to get any come on Will's mother's sheets.

On the train back to New York the cars were steeped in cigarette smoke, and no one had washed the toilets in a century. Jack had to piss over lava layers of other people's shit ranging from yellow to black. Wet cigarette butts were crushed out in the sink. The paper doilies used as headrests on the seats were soiled and dangling lopsidedly. The train would creep into a field, then squeal to a stop and sit there for twenty minutes, creaking strangely before inching backward for another ten minutes.

The only way not to go crazy in a train is to treat it as a Christian penance, Will said. His eyes looked very small and poached through his wraparound sunglasses, which gave an incongruously contemporary look to his long Gothic face, more suited to a visor than to tinted plastic.

"And did you ever dance with the famous Taffy?" Jack asked. The violent lurching of the train had caused Jack's right knee to touch Will's left; neither of them pulled apart.

"You can't imagine what an abortion she is," Will said. "The whole ball was a collection of freaks—I tried to see it through your eyes, as if you'd gone. Reedy eighteen-year-old boys pushing matrons of eighty around the floor. Some of the extra men so immature they were playing tag in the cloakroom. And the food—as if all any dish required to be gourmet was a gooey white sauce."

Jack turned his body slightly toward Will's and put a hand on Will's thigh, then twisted his head away in an agony of laughter and said, "Stop! You're killing me."

Will levered his long body out of the seat and lurched off to the filthy toilet—surely, Jack thought, just an excuse to pull free, since he had peed only ten minutes before, and sure enough, on his return Will sprawled across the empty seats on the other side of the aisle and said he was going to try to sleep a bit. He rolled up his gabardine coat as a pillow.

Jack felt cruelly rebuffed and decided that soon he would

come clean with Will, but he wasn't quite sure how he would do it. At the next stop two old ladies got on. Their Southern voices sounded sweet and musical as they talked to each other in the seats just ahead. They spoke so softly that Jack couldn't distinguish words. They were so near that Jack wouldn't be able to talk privately with Will. He thought of his grandmother and her two sisters, whom he'd known just after the war when he was only six or seven, visiting out in East Texas. He could remember a room with the shades drawn, a room crowded by the big soft bed under its chenille bedspread. Little Jack sat on the bed in short pants and a carefully ironed white shirt, smiling and looking up at the three old ladies, all big and white and pillowy with huge naked breasts marked by veins.

He'd never seen his own mother naked, and he was surprised by these huge breasts. "Jack, aren't you too old to be looking at ladies' boozies?" his grandmother asked, laughing. One aunt ruffled his hair, and the other suggested he run out and play. He'd never thought of his grandmother as a woman before—more as a matron with a firm, molded mono-bosom and a diamond brooch and a low, Southern twang than as a woman with soft white breasts like warm dachshunds in constant motion, dogs with huge brown noses. The room where the three ladies were dressing smelled sweet from the clouds of powder they were dusting each other with. Half clothed, their bodies looked fat and pendent and puffy. He could see them, moving about on their stiff legs, reflected in the freestanding full-length mirror, the glass tilted slightly upward and held in a carved oak frame stained black. Their room felt secretive and girlish, and though his grandmother had always doted on him, he now saw her as a stranger, a member of a gleeful, secret sorority.

He liked these two old women ahead of him on the train and

thought he'd been too hasty in wanting to trade in the whole female race for a chance to marry Will. He looked out as the train passed a corrugated-metal shed, rusting in the weak sunlight, and his eyes filled with tears. He glanced quickly over at Will's sprawled body, his hands folded over his chest like those of a tomb effigy, but he was certain Will wasn't really sleeping.

The next day at the office he left promptly at five. Will said, "Where are you going in such a rush?"

Jack said, "I have an appointment with a psychotherapist."

"What? A what? I didn't know you were seeing a shrink."

"It's my first . . . session."

"Why on earth—was Virginia too much for you? Did we drive you around the bend?"

"Yes, in a sense," Jack said without a smile. From where he was standing, just outside Will's cubicle, Will looked as if he were a character in a play, a very realistic contemporary one about New York life. Jack felt so tired; he was middle-aged spiritually.

Will looked up at him through his eyebrows, the same seductive look he'd used on his pretty young date at El Faro. "Are you serious?"

"Yes," Jack said, looking away. "I realized I'm in love with you and that it's an illness and it's getting worse and our friendship isn't going anywhere."

Will crossed his legs protectively and glanced at the magazine on his desk. "What? Are you joking? What are you saying?" He drew a deep breath, as if absorbing bad news. Then he said, "I'm so sorry if I've done anything to cause you any pain or to lead you on, if that doesn't sound too high school." Will sketched in a nervous smile but immediately canceled it in deference to Jack's disease. Jack noticed Will didn't deny that their relationship wasn't going anywhere, whatever that meant.

"Well, I'm going to be late if I don't step on the gas," Jack said. "Maybe we can talk about all of this later." He noticed how Will's face froze. "If you want to. Maybe you don't want to."

Will waved imaginary bees away from his face and said, "No, no, I want to, I want to," which sounded sort of Jewish to Jack's ears. Jack thought, We're all so unused to expressing our feelings that we end up sounding like Woody Allen or Molly Goldberg. She's our only model for passionate utterance. He felt sorry for Will, so cornered, obviously wishing it would all just go away.

"Want to have dinner around eight, down in the Village? Maybe Monte's?" Jack asked. He was hurting inside. Somehow he'd expected a miracle, that Will would say, "I love you too, and we will live together our whole lives." Until now Jack had been able to nurse his illusions; now he had to deal with the facts. In his fantasies he'd been playing with clouds; now he had to pick up solid boxes with sharp corners. Reality felt like a pitiful comedown.

"Sounds like a plan," Will said, his eye feverishly scanning the article spread out before him, his hands tense on the arm-rests of his chair.

When Jack walked into the nearly empty restaurant, he saw that Will hadn't arrived yet, even though Jack himself was fifteen minutes late. Jack was starting his second manhattan when Will came flying in.

After he'd made his apologies and ordered a martini, Will said, "Well, how did it go? Did he make you lie down on the couch?"

"No, it's a woman, tall, with hooded eyes. She smokes Kents and has fat legs that are sort of served up to you by her Barcalounger."

"A Barcalounger!" Will exclaimed. "Upholstered in avocado green leatherette?"

"You got it in one."

"African art?"

"Bingo." Jack laughed. "I didn't realize you'd been psychoanalyzed."

"I dated a Jewish girl in Charlottesville whose mother was some sort of seedy Jungian who actually talked about the anima and the animus over dinner. I thought they were two different kinds of enema."

"The enemas are saved for the second date."

They both sighed at the same moment and consulted the menu, though they knew it by heart. Will ordered the fish and Jack the cannelloni.

Jack kept thinking that he could just as easily burst out laughing and shout, "April Fools!" and wheel in a giant cake from which girls in pasties and bikinis would pop out, that he could tap Will on the chest and say, "Fooled you! Man, you should've seen your face. You were practically sobbing with sympathy for the best friend turned cocksucker, but you were shitting bricks too, thinking, fuck! Am I going to have to go all pious for weeks on end nursing this lisping pansy out of his closet when I'd just as soon nail the bitch shut?"

Suddenly Jack had to admit how arbitrary (if violent) and changeable his feelings were, velvet robes with lots of Velcro that could be patted shut or ripped open.

"Sometimes," he said, "I think I'm just making all of this up."

Will was being very polite and respectful of the sickness, the

big fag sickness that had replaced his best buddy, his office side-
kick. "It's all new to me," Will said. "I even found myself comb-
ing my hair just before I walked in here tonight, wanting—but
not really!—wanting to make sure you still found me attractive.
I never felt like a sex object before. Now I know how girls must
feel. It seemed so crazy with all the handsome studs out there
that you'd go and pick shy, pimply Will. I question your taste!
But this"—and here Will looked at him steadily and let his smile
fade, fearing he was fishing for compliments—"is not about me
for once. It's about you, Jack." And a faint frown of sympathy
creased his forehead. He looked mortified by his own badinage
about such a grave subject. Or maybe he feared he'd made a
misstep by turning Jack's love into sexual desire; maybe Will
hoped it was all very ethereal and spiritual—no cocksucking,
just hand-holding.

"Dr. Adams—she's a Viennese Jew, but her name is Adams for
some reason—thinks the 'object choice problem'—that's you—is
just a symptom of a deeper problem."

"Which is what?" Will asked, a bit indignant. "Deeper
than me? How could that be? Like bed-wetting? Thumb-
sucking?"

"Boy, you really hate shrinks, don't you? Almost as much as
pop music."

"I just see them as con men and not based in science. What
they believe can't be verified or disproved."

"What would you do if you had a real problem? I guess you
have your priests for that."

Will's eyes widened with the slight shock of hearing his religion dismissed or even mentioned. He shrugged and said, "I
can't even imagine facing something like this."

Without thinking, Jack shot back, "Oh really? You can't

even imagine it? I thought novelists were good at imagining things."

Will closed his eyes and let thirty seconds trickle by. "There are plenty of freaky things in my life, but homosexuality—" He broke off as the waiter came by to replenish the breadbasket, which they'd nervously emptied as hungry young men will do.

"Plenty of freaky things?" Jack asked, surprised by his own sarcasm. "Like your preference for Ravel over Debussy?"

"That's funny," Will said, not smiling.

After the waiter brought their food, Jack said, "Isn't it nice that the waiters here are real lifetime waiters, not actors and singers and dancers? These guys have a certain dignity."

"Why is that nice?" Will asked. "You sound like my father. He'd agree with you that it was nice someone was trapped in a dead-end job."

A long silence settled over them. At last Will asked, "How do you want me to act?"

Several answers raced up to Jack's lips, but all of them implied that Will might someday love him. "No, you're fine," Jack said. "You've said nothing wrong. In fact you're being understanding."

"I should hope so!" Will said with mild indignation.

But then neither of them knew what form that understanding should take, and Jack, deciding to laugh it off, said, "What about your preference for Ravel? I was working up an article idea at the office, and I found out that Debussy had one of the first colostomies and Ravel wore face powder, rice powder in fact. Do you think he was a homo?"

Will winced at the word, recognizing that Jack had just flipped him a verbal bird. "Absolutely nothing is known about Ravel's sex life. He was tiny and lived in a doll's house and had a hun-

dred ties made by Proust's haberdasher and—'That's all, folks!' "
he called out, singing the cartoon tag.

"We're exhausted by our erudition," Jack said. "Are you any
good at thinking up story ideas?"

"There's the rub," Will said, neglecting his food as if Jack's
neuroses had killed his appetite. "The other day Gephardt said
that the only good story ideas come from the staff. That freelance writers never think of anything exciting or new, though
they can be led to water. But when we do come up with something, it gets killed. Harriet brings out her files and says we're
being precipitous. And didn't *Horizon* just do their own four-
page foldout on that very subject?"

"Frustrating," Jack said.

They stuck close to office gossip for the rest of the evening,
but as they chatted a terrible sadness rang inside Jack's head. He
realized that until now nothing had been spelled out. Until recently he and Will had never so much as mentioned the word
"homosexuality," and Jack had been able to make bargains with
a God he didn't believe in about an impossibility he couldn't
name. The idea that a month earlier he would have been satisfied with "just" two years of making meat loaf for Will and
sucking his cock every night now seemed not only pathetic but
close to insane. He'd built this fantasy out of air and set it on sand;
it was the wishing equivalent to paranoia, only yearning replaced
suspicion.

On his way home alone during this first balmy night of April,
Jack walked up West Fourth Street past Village apartments
glowing with lights in a delightful hodgepodge that looked like
the set for act two of *La Bohème*. Curtains billowed in third-
floor windows. Naked trees were beginning to think about getting ready for whatever was supposed to happen next. The street

curved on the diagonal and confusingly cut across other numbered streets (he was on the corner of West Fourth and West Eleventh). A few people in sweaters or windbreakers were sitting on stoops. Coffee shops and restaurants were open for business, but no one much seemed to care or to be around, the excited opening notes wouldn't be played for another three minutes and the chorus was still putting on costumes and makeup. The set was half lit with work lights but not yet dressed with people.

Jack's heart pounded as it usually did as he drew nearer his own apartment, but now it was worse, as if someone had taken away a holy medal he wore around his neck, his St. Will! A medal against the demon of loneliness and the dragon of self-hatred. He wondered what he'd think ten years from now. Was this just a foolish schoolboy crush, foolish because he was already twenty-two, an age when many guys were married and the father of a first kid? Would he now find a girl, affectionate and pretty? He knew that was what Will wished for him.

He pictured Herschel's knowing winks at work, the way he had once said of Will, "Your boyfriend's waiting for you down in the lobby."

Herschel had told him that half of the men and a third of the women on their floor, the eleventh, had made a pass at him. One day Herschel had arrived at work with a horrible black eye that was turning yellow at the edges and covered half his face; a bone in his cheek had been shattered as well. Herschel said, "Hubby don't like Baby sharing his dainty around."

"God, Herschel, you could lose your eye," Jack said. He hadn't even known until then that Herschel had a "hubby."

"Oh well, honey, I've still got another eye."

And Jack recognized that Herschel took himself no more seriously than that, that he thought of himself as an ephemeral fated to pivot gorgeously around for a season and then dry up and die. For his part, Jack didn't know what he was, what kind of plant or animal. When he was unhappy, sometimes he would contemplate suicide, but just as surely he would have jumped out of the path of a speeding car on his way to his death. He had his teeth cleaned twice a year, he went to the doctor for his annual checkup, his reflexes were hammered, his heart auscultated—and all for what? So that he could enjoy his misery in perfect health?

Now he felt more alone than ever. Now he knew that his feelings baffled and sickened Will. For months and months Jack had battened off hopes and dreams; now he had nothing to feed his imagination and he was truly solitary. No future; failed dreams in the past; and the present empty. At home he lay down on the corduroy couch. Everything in his apartment—the blue water jug, the heavy oak sideboard from the Salvation Army, the shiny, recently installed parquet floor and the Swedish area rug, the copy of an Eames chair that had cost him a month's salary—all these things nauseated him because they stank of his own personality, which he no longer liked. Everything represented a choice he'd made: the wrong choice. All his choices were wrong.

He'd never fainted in his life, but he wondered if this was the way it felt—a nerveless squalor and collapse, the last of your vital energies dripping from your feet and hands, your bones so soft they might tear like wet paper.

He lay there in the darkness for a long time. He looked at his watch, which required a major investment of energy, and saw that it was just midnight. He thought he should get up, clean his house, do push-ups, study Spanish from that new book that guaranteed mastery in twenty lessons—but then it came to him that his only reason for improving himself was to please Will, as if he were a Victorian girl who was acquiring all the polite accomplishments.

For the next week he made himself get to work on time, book up his evenings, do his jumping jacks and push-ups, keep his apartment tidy. He knew he couldn't indulge his despair even for an hour or the perpetual-motion machine would freeze; he'd never escape the stasis of depression.

The real challenge was seeing Will at the office. In the staff meeting, that Monday morning at ten, Jack cleverly drew Mary-Beth the copy editor into a conversation about the vacation in the Canaries she'd just returned from, so that it would seem only natural that he'd take the chair next to hers rather than his usual place beside Will. When his eyes grazed Will's during the meeting, he raised his palm and waved, but he suspected that his face gave him away—not its expression, which he was carefully regulating, but its age, after the weekend he'd endured. He was so sure that he was pale and hollowed out by all the thousands of square centimeters of duration he'd been subjected to that he wanted to run to the bathroom mirror to study the change wrought by passing time and somehow rub it off. He'd been put in a time machine, not one that had transported him to a different decade but one that had aged him. Jack had experienced everything, or at least much too much. His own suffering must be laughably obvious; Will must be saying to himself, "Look what the cat dragged in."

In fact, that afternoon Will came by his office cubicle during the three o'clock coffee break. Sal, with his coffee wagon, was doing his usual booming business, stationed beside the service elevator. Jack heard him ask, "Hey, Will, how come you never buy a coffee and a sweet roll in the morning anymore? Got some babe who's making you a champagne breakfast? You don't need to answer that one. That dreamy look in your eyes—the whole story's right there."

Will clearly realized that Jack must have heard Sal. He mumbled, "I'm back staying with my sister, the only dame who can put up with me. But sure, Sal, have it your way—a knock-out starlet is running out every morning to the bakery on the corner for me." The whole little scene with Sal was deeply embarrassing. To Sal, because he knew how to tease while keeping it light and general, and here things had taken a confessional nosedive. To Jack, because he didn't want to play the jealous lover, even if he was jealous and in love. To Will, because his tossed-off witticism had become such a clunker.

Now Will was here and he wanted to go out for a drink after work. Jack said sure. He almost added, "Like old times."

When they were settled in a booth at the Irish bar downstairs, they talked about today's story conference. Then Jack said, "I've been meeting such interesting people."

Will said, "Really? Like who?"

"Well, the girls have been inviting new people to dinner every night. We've decided we're already stale at age twenty-two. So the plan is to invite someone new every night to join us for our horrible spaghetti dinners. If they come back, we know it's not for the cuisine."

"But like who?" Will insisted.

"Well, Rebekkah is working at the *New York Review of Books*. She invited one of the debs from work. Most of the girls who work there are named Alexandra or Poppy, and their fathers own Squaw Valley or something, though you're never told that directly."

"So you met Alexandra Newton?"

"Yeah, do you know her?"

"I've seen her picture on the society page. What's she like?"

"She's a native New Yorker, but she'd never been on the subway before last night when I took her on one. I was taking her home. She lives on Sixty-fourth off Park."

"What else? Is she nice?"

"I'm tempted to say she's very well brought up, but I guess that's not something surprising that you people would notice about each other."

"You people!" Will growled.

"She's tall, very lean, wears what I'd call party clothes, all pale colors and taffeta that crackles when she moves. Her contacts don't fit her very well, and after we went up to her place for a drink, she eventually emerged from the bathroom in big black Steve Allen glasses."

Will clutched his chest as if the thought of a thin debutante in glasses was the ultimate arrow to his heart. "She had you up for drinks! You lucky SOB! How late did you stay?"

"Till midnight. She had a great bottle of scotch."

"What was her place like?"

"One bedroom. Everything matched. Light colors. Persian carpets—even they were light colors."

"You're practically engaged! Man, you know how to move."

But Jack wasn't ready to be hustled along into heterosexuality. "I told her I have homosexual . . . tendencies."

"You did? After how much booze?"

Was Will wounded that he, Jack, had confided during a first meeting with a total stranger the things he had taken a year to tell Will? Or did he fear that it could get around in smart circles that he, Will, had a queer crony? Knowing that someone was queer could place him at your mercy and, if you blabbed about it, could cost him his job. It was just as incriminating to be a fag's friend.

Jack realized that his own indiscretion could get him fired.

"How does that work?" Will asked.

"What?"

"If you tell a pretty girl you're queer, does she trust you more? Hey—good seduction technique, Holmes."

"Stiff price to pay, though, don't you think?" Jack asked, amused in a slightly disgusted way that Will's own longings had upstaged any compassion he might have felt for his best buddy.

"So this Alexandra—did she match stories with you?"

"You mean, one of her men for one of mine? If she did, I'm not at liberty to tell you. Everything we said was confidential. We trust each other."

"So there you are at midnight in a Park Avenue apartment drinking whiskey with a lovely bird, and she's telling you all about her sex life."

"She's not exactly a bird; she's really very human, Will, a bit of a lady, and just a bit brittle."

"And with one of those upper-class Brearley drawls, I bet."

"She did go to Brearley but later to Barnard, which was sort of a surprise to me. If you squeezed her too hard, you could break off a part."

"You mean she's bony?"

"She's slender, but she has a very nice figure. While I was there she slipped into a rose satin peignoir—what do you call them? A housecoat? No, that sounds frumpy."

"A hostess something-or-other."

"That sounds right. She wears her hair up off her neck. And she has a long, slender neck and beautiful features. I'm sure she puts her lipstick on with a brush. She just happened to have a lobster dip in the fridge, and she put it in a crystal bowl, the kind of bowl you'd receive at a bridal shower. You know, most of the people we know in New York, their apartments are dirty and cramped and smell funny and have rotting linoleum on the floor, and your aunt Wilma would be horrified. But Alexandra has a proper grown-up apartment on a high floor with a view, and I'm sure she has a maid."

"Did she sit very close to you?"

"As a matter of fact she did."

"You fucker," Will said, grinning, a word that was extremely uncharacteristic of Will but that Jack thought might come out when he was with other Princetonians. They were all terrible drinkers and very rough.

Suddenly Jack felt that his sad condition as a homosexual, which had quickly begun to pall, had taken a turn for Will toward something more amusing.

"It's not fair," Will said. "You and your girls are meeting all these superior people, and I'm stuck with my sister's B-list failures, her fallout from failing to land a husband."

"Maybe I'll introduce you to Alexandra."

"No, she sounds like a pill with her hostess gown and ill-fitting contacts and her highborn breakable bones. No, I like a nice horsey woman with a good seat and chilblains."

"I don't think we do chilblains in America," Jack observed. "I'm not even sure what they are."

Jack was so afraid of falling into the slovenliness of depression that at home he washed every dish with a lab technician's precision as soon as he used it. He ran the sweeper every day, as if he were living as a mannequin in a display, a store window, featuring home furnishings.

Sleep overcame him like a fatality. He could never remember his dreams because he was always awakened by an alarm clock, and the bother of turning it off banished his nocturnal thoughts. But he did walk around during the day certain that his dreams had been dense with incident, metallic and crowded, almost as if they were the plate that printers etched in ink to stamp out cartoons, those miniaturized panels hectic with action and dialogue bubbles.

Will kept finding reasons to see Jack. Every time they were together, they had to talk about Alexandra, though often as not Will was openly dismissive of her. "You and your rich girls," he would growl. "You are a snob, after all, Jack Holmes."

"*My* rich girls?"

"Yeah, what about the blonde from Kennebunkport you sloughed off?"

Jack resented this tactic. Will clearly wanted to pump Jack for information, but he pretended it was Jack who was seducing Alex, a subtle way of turning him back into a heterosexual while casting him as a libertine. Very flattering. After Will's little maneuver, Jack was no longer a spooky Liberace; no, he was back to being a regular guy but a dashing villain this time.

Jack wanted to talk to his shrink nonstop about Will, as one prospector might consult with another over the slightest gleam in the ground, even of fool's gold. But Dr. Adams seemed bored with Jack's "symptomatic acting-out," which she sneered at. Her attitude hurt his feelings. Whereas Jack thought of his love for Will as the one noble feeling of his life, Dr. Adams treated it as playpen stuff, as if two baby boys had thought it great fun to smear each other with their caca. Not only did she consider them to be dirty infants; she also conjured up the image of infantile egotism.

"I don't think you understand," Jack said. "I love Will."

She chuckled silently while exhaling smoke from her Kent. She even had the insolence to settle still farther back in the avocado Barcalounger, as if the tedium of Jack's "circular thinking" deserved nothing more than this horizontal position. Jack had read that Muslims feel that an insult is intended if one shows them the sole of one's foot; he suddenly sympathized with this premise. He resented the axonometric view of the soles on Dr. Adams's nearly orthopedic black shoes and of her overflowing ankles in their dark brown nylons. "You're right. I don't take too seriously this love of yours."

"Your contempt feels very castrating to me," Jack said. He wished she were a more traditional, noncommittal Freudian; he'd found her through Rebekkah, and now he thought she was too obviously opinionated.

"Oh, come on, Jack, don't use a technical term you don't understand. Why not just say you're pissed off at me for not playing along with your obsession?"

"Or pissed off that you label my finest feelings an obsession."

Dr. Adams let an expensive two-minute silence roll by; were it not for the continuing smoke signals, he might have thought she was dozing. Finally she said in a soft voice, "I think you have yet to discover your finest feelings."

Because she seemed to be beckoning him toward a happier future, Jack burst into tears. Dr. Adams came rising up to vertical in her chair for the occasion. She nudged a box of Kleenex toward him. He wondered bitterly if she ordered the Kleenex by the gross.

"I'm afraid our time is up," she said. She blinked in her prehistoric-saurian way, then actually stood, as if she feared he wouldn't make his exit quickly enough. That she could stand on her back two legs seemed to Jack like an important advance in evolution, one he admired.

The worst of it was that the natural person for him to complain to about Dr. Adams was Will himself, who considered all shrinks to be charlatans.

At the next session Jack told her about a long dream he'd had that had left his cortex feeling stained and flooded. "I'd come back to the *Northern Review* after many years away, and even the old people on the staff were too young to have ever known me, though two of them had heard of me. Someone—maybe it was me—had killed two young men, and they were locked into a beachside office. I mean, it was forty feet from the sea, but it was also somehow an office. There was a part of the dream where I was so happy because I was working on a slightly scandalous article about Alexander Graham Bell's granddaughter. Then I was back with the two dead bodies, both floating in sort of rubber layettes but beginning to stink anyway."

Dr. Adams lowered herself in her bathysphere, the better to be laved in the waters of the unconscious. When she reemerged, her mouth smoking, she said, "I think the two young dead men in this dream are you and Will. It's your younger, neurotic selves who are dying off to be replaced by—who knows? It's a hopeful dream."

"It is? It left me feeling guilty and scared."

"Those are screen feelings," Dr. Adams said, exhaling with authority. "They conceal the optimism you're feeling."

"Very effectively," Jack said. "Couldn't you just as easily say those are my homosexual feelings I want to kill off?"

Dr. Adams looked him in the eye. "That is what I am saying, Jack. I'm afraid our time is up."

Jack felt angry and said, "I'm afraid your time is up. I'm quitting."

Dr. Adams turned her mouth down in a circumflex of indifference and exposed her palms as if she could do nothing more about his foolishness.

"I suppose you think I'm resisting or something."

"You said the word, not I," said Dr. Adams, once again forced to stand, like an English monarch dismissing an African prince who hasn't quite grasped that his audience is over. Standing turned out to be the most dismissive act in her repertory of protocol.

Without Dr. Adams, Jack felt even lonelier, even crazy, though he had no respect for her. One night weeks ago he'd stuck his head into a gay bar in the West Village filled with horrible old men and their beers and cigarettes and show tunes; he headed there now. After six beers he sidled up to a chalky white young man with a Frankenstein haircut. He was dressed all wrong, like someone from Oshkosh, which Jack found endearing. His tragic approach to his own possibilities didn't include tenderness toward a fellow sufferer, but in spite of himself he was smiling at this guy's funny clothes and haircut. It helped that he had a farmworker's physique, which would have been attractive no matter how it was attired.

Jack began to pick up a different man almost every night. He'd come home from work and fall into a dreamless sleep, then wake up, grab a sandwich, and head out onto the streets. Sometimes he'd have dinner with the girls, especially if one of them had invited a new, interesting guest, but he'd always duck out early.

Two years ago the mayor had closed all but two of the bars in the Village, but that meant men were more likely to strike a deal with each other on Greenwich Avenue or Christopher Street or even one of the quiet, dark streets, like Bank or Charles. Jack could remember how thronged the West Village streets had been when he'd first arrived in the city; that had undoubtedly been one of the reasons.

Usually he was eager to get it all over with as quickly as possible. The minute he came, everything would seem so disgusting and unnatural—the hairy ass, the stubble on the chin, the penis that looked dark and shiny despite the white body, almost as if the penis belonged to a different race or was a vegetable rather than part of a mammal—and Jack would be sickened by how ashamed he felt. He longed for a trapdoor beside the bed into which he could push his trick.

Jack found something wrong with almost every man. The guy either lisped or had rules about not touching his hair or a crusty bottom or an undescended testicle or aureoles as big and dark as a slice of liverwurst or back and shoulder hair or neglected dental hygiene or a blue fear of being seen by someone he knew in the street . . . not one queer seemed normal or jolly.

It occurred to Jack that he was having all these adventures but they scarcely seemed credible even to him, since he had no one to share them with. He had no confidant and didn't know if he wanted one. Will would have been sickened by the details and seen their accumulation as proof that Jack was making no effort to get well. On the contrary, he was only sinking deeper into vice. Alexandra was sympathetic but only to the sole triste fact of his malady; she wouldn't want to know that he was exacerbating it, that his homosexuality was something he was practicing and not merely enduring.

The worst of it was that Jack never felt any affection for his so-called partners. He never wanted to crack a joke with one of them or cook him a midnight hamburger. He wouldn't have lent one ten dollars. He could afford to have chilly, inflexible principles where there was no affection.

Once at Alice's he was introduced to a young man he'd already slept with, but Jack and the guy were both expert in pretending they were meeting for the first time.

To his surprise, the guy was charming and funny and self-deprecating. Jack could remember almost nothing about him from their encounter, though they'd met just five or six weeks previously. In how many other cases had he poked a man for plumpness or doneness or scorned him for an ugly birthmark or failed to notice his wit or expertise about tapestries?

At least once a week Alexandra would invite Jack to dinner at her apartment. Always it was just the two of them. Jack suspected that she needed a friend and that, for her, friends (whom she didn't really understand) must be on as intimate a footing as lovers (whom she knew a lot about). She didn't feel comfortable around other women. They bored her just a bit and they envied her, which made them hard to tease, Alex's preferred manner. She could tease in a vigorous way so at odds with her delicate looks, or she could argue like a lawyer, one finger raised. She was smart and combative but always with a smile, even a readiness to laugh at herself when the words came spilling out of her too rapidly and, frustrated, she insisted, "You have no idea what you're talking about!" though she appeared to be the one who was confused.

Jack liked the dripless white candles screwed into the big wall sconces, which she'd bought as good copies of English antiques from James Robinson, the silversmith off Fifth Avenue. He liked the mother-of-pearl box of French cigarettes and the silver lighter with the green felt bottom as heavy as a curling stone. He liked the yellow and pale purple freesias smelling of oranges in the silver bowl and the expensive food from a caterer on the corner.

She smiled at him, her starry smile reminiscent of glamorous Hollywood studio portraits from the twenties. Her teeth were so white they were almost blue. She'd clap her hands and say, "What fun!" though he wasn't sure she was enjoying herself. Jack felt that by himself he wasn't sufficiently entertaining to carry a whole evening. He made a fine backup singer, but not a soloist. Alexandra had always wanted a brother, she said, but now that she had one she still seemed unfulfilled. Jack felt the same way; perhaps it was inevitable that Will would join them one evening soon, though Alexandra proclaimed stubbornly that she disliked nothing more than another eligible male on the make.

"That's what's so great about . . . us," she said, as if it had just occurred to her that to say "you" would have sounded too curatorial. "Us" sounded better, more polite. "We don't want anything from each other but insight and affection—we're like saints, entirely disinterested. Don't you think we're saintly, Jack?"

"I know you're a saint to feed me smoked salmon on toast points with sour cream on your best Spode."

She made him listen to a new record. She'd just learned the twist and wanted to teach it to him. But her specialty was sipping champagne in Waterford crystal filled from the iced bottle in the big bucket. Then she would curl up beside him and tell him about her latest love.

"He's a *Life* reporter—Jim Eisner?—a really big reporter. I'm surprised you've never heard of him. He's done some very dangerous assignments. One about organized crime in Philadelphia. They're already making a movie about it. And it's coming out as a book. Seriously, you've never heard of Jim Eisner?"

"No, and I bet you've never heard of my last forty-two boyfriends either."

"You're too funny," she said, insisting that his numerous exploits were comical exaggeration. "But have you ever been in love?" Here her beautiful brow wrinkled with kindly concern.

"Yes, I've told you—with Will. Hopeless love, since he'd sooner sleep with a polecat."

"Be serious." She curled her shoulder-length hair around her finger, which was freighted with enough diamonds to suggest polygamy. "Why can't this—this Will of yours—I hate the name Will. It sounds like the punch line in a cockney joke. But why can't this Will of yours be a little more considerate and show you some warmth, some tenderness? I mean, come on, for heaven's sake, would it matter so much to him to let you hold him for a moment?"

"I'd only want him to hold me if it did matter to him."

She lowered her pretty head in deference to his logic. "Yes," she nearly whispered, "I can see that." She thought about it for a moment.

"Could you hold another girl who was in love with you?" Jack asked.

Alexandra had been mistily contemplating a scene of brotherly love, a tableau right off the battlefield, but now, faced with heaving breasts and the moist warmth of another woman's body, she shuddered. "Hardly," she said. But then she thought about it and cocked her head to one side. "But I say why not? If it would mean so much to her, and if she were my dearest friend—I just hope I wouldn't get the giggles."

"The giggles would spoil everything."

Alexandra cleared away the dishes and the large old silver forks that had just three tines each and brought out a bowl of *mousse au chocolat*, which had probably started life in several minuscule white cartons from the caterer downstairs.

Now Alex had an objection: "But it's not the same thing, some big squishy woman with tears gumming her eyelashes— and a man in love. Men are . . . upright and forthright—"

"And right?" Jack looked at her intently.

"You're mocking me," Alexandra wailed.

"No, I happen to agree with you entirely." But he did not subscribe to her cult of noble, sensitive masculinity.

Taking a new approach, Alexandra said, "So what's so great about your Will?"

"He's a fine novelist, among other things," Jack lied.

"Gotcha!" Alexandra fluted, jumping up. "You told me your-self, Jack Holmes, that he's never shown you word one."

Jack rubbed his eyes, his lying eyes. "Pathetic, isn't it? I'm so in love I'm ready to attribute all the virtues to him." He felt he'd broken through a membrane he might better have left in-tact. He was acting as if he could lament how "pathetic" he was in a normal, jokey voice, rather than bemoaning it. He'd never before treated his sickness this conversationally.

Alexandra subsided into a small armchair upholstered in a

dull gold fabric. "It's always that way. We fall in love for no particular reason, certainly no good reason, and then we invent
sterling qualities that are supposed to justify our passion."

Jack liked this philosophical approach—it seemed so French
to insist on the irrationality of the passions in epigrams that
posited abstract truths.

Will quizzed him closely following every one of his evenings with Alexandra. "Man, she's in love with you! I'm going
to pretend to be homosexual—it drives the girls wild! It's like
that play by Wycherley where the guy pretends to be a eunuch
so that other men will trust their wives with him."

Jack smiled painfully. "Homosexual as capon? Is that the
flattering comparison you're searching for?"

Will frowned. "But you know what I mean. You've got to
admit that's a pretty neat explanation of your success."

"Not my beauty and natural charm?" Jack said. "I told her you
were a great novelist—now I have proof of your imagination."

"Speaking of proof—" Will pulled out of his desk drawer a
manila envelope containing what was obviously a slender volume.
"Look at this when you're alone. I don't want people around here
yammering about it."

When he was safely back in his cubicle, Jack opened the envelope. There it was—Will's novel. *The Truth About Sergeant Tavel*.
How typical of secretive Will to spring it on him this way. No
talk about an agent representing him or an editor buying it or
anything about those long lunches at the Algonquin, nothing
about the proposed cover, the cover copy, the sales campaign and
book tour plans—nothing. Jack could remember that on certain
days Will had worn a dark blue suit and tab shirt and an un-
stained silk tie and of course his London shoes, the black ones—
those must have been his book business days.

Jack resented Will's spiritual stinginess. Couldn't he have shared all or some of these steps? Alexandra had guessed the truth—she had said that Will was an emotional miser. Did he wish to keep things to himself as long as possible out of fear of failing? Or did he think that like Prince Hal he would soon be dropping all of his old, inferior friends?

Jack flipped through the book sacrilegiously and even read the last five pages first. He felt as unnatural in this first, terribly important encounter as someone being introduced to his future in-laws. He wanted to like the book, he needed to like it, he'd be expected to say he liked it, and any hesitation on his part would be detected and magnified. Jack's enthusiasm was guaranteed but not certain, and it certainly wouldn't be spontaneous.

Something about the manufacturing of the book felt flimsy, cheap; the paper would turn yellow and shatter in ten years. The cover was a cartoon, one of the first Jack had ever seen associated with a serious novel, which made it seem a bid for whatever was argotic and contemporary. But in fact it was poorly drawn, the colors dull, the printed letters toothless: no bite. Jack could already see the piles and piles of remainders in a store.

Jack wanted it to be good, the novel, because, as he thought, it emanates from my Will, my cold husband, my enigmatic friend. I need it to be good because Will must be talented, intelligent, to justify my devotion and his mysterious confidence in himself. I want it to be bad because Will has disappointed me and now he must pay.

Nor could Jack imagine anything written by someone he knew being good.

He was terrified he wouldn't be able to judge it. He dithered over it, turning it this way and that, unable to see the picture for the puzzle parts. He caught every third word, as if it were in a new language. As he read it, he saw people from real life materializing behind the shadowy characters like known faces popping into county fair cutouts, two smiling, freckled kids sticking their heads into the holes above the stern farmer and his wife in *American Gothic*. Or he overheard something he himself had once said, something that he'd gotten wrong—and that Will would have recycled because the error had caught in the filaments of his mind. *The Truth About Sergeant Tavel* was a patchwork of rehashed stories, filched readings from other books, speculations of the what-if sort, and improvisations in reverse. Then there were the fantasy elements. The young hero, named Hero, had a cat named Intrepid who hopped up into windows or descended into basements, slipped onto the subway and followed a villain through municipal sewers—and reported everything to Hero by typing it all out with his paws on Hero's new electric typewriter. Hero had learned to leave a blank page in the machine at night and the motor running. When Intrepid returned from his investigations, he could file his report instantly—and many of these hilarious feline screeds made their way into the novel.

Underlying everything was a pure, almost childlike love between Hero and Trumpetta. Yes, it must be Alexandra. He even caught several things that Alex had said to him that Will had copied verbatim. Gosh, Jack thought, I'm going to be in big trouble with her!

A large morning glory vine twined among the bars to their bedroom window and produced more and more blue blossoms that clamored full-throated in the first hours of the day and shriveled to sticky, umbilical sheaths in the afternoon—except that as Trumpetta became ill with some highly aesthetic wasting disease, the plant died. The desperate Hero saw his beloved condemned in the death of the morning glory. Intrepid wrote a final eulogy to Trumpetta, a letter that was strangely spelled but deeply felt, and then the cat vanished into the lower depths of the great, rustling city.

"But it's nothing," Jack said out loud to himself when he finished the book at four in the morning. "Sentimental horseshit." He got up and stretched and realized he'd missed the closing of the bars and only drunks would still be out cruising the streets. He was slightly panicked, but he dismissed the idea of an empty bed and a night without sex as a minor inconvenience. He made himself a meal of toast and scrambled eggs.

The book was tepid, gooey-sweet. Jack resented it and faintly scorned Will: To think I was in love with someone so insipid. I imagined that under all that reticence scalding seas of feeling were bubbling, that Will would be able to express in print all the passion he was too shy to show. At last the drab geode would be cracked open to expose its crystal teeth.

Damn! Jack thought. What would he say to Will? The problem was a social one, the challenge of how to hide his disappointment. If he faked enthusiasm, Will would detect the falseness right away. Nor would even the most outrageous praise come close to the ecstasy the poor young author was anticipating. Even if Jack had been genuinely delighted, some sort of problem would still have existed. And Will would have sniffed out the slightest hesitation, the smallest nuance of criticism. Nothing short of a Nobel Prize would satisfy Will. Jack had nothing genuine to go on.

Jack was sitting in his underpants on a dining room chair. He'd turned off his reading light, and now the only illumination in the room was the faint blue of the approaching dawn seeping through the filmy curtains. He had such conflicting thoughts. In one way he felt free at last of Will the Loser, the witless writer; it wasn't that Will had been unable to shape his feelings in the book, but rather that he didn't seem to have any feelings to draw on. A second later Will's flop made Jack feel protective toward him. Would Will be able to weather the failure of his book? Would he feel crushed and even bleaker than usual? Jack knew that Will had been talking about a second novel—would he go forward with it now? Would anyone want to publish it? Would Will's art have come and gone in a single night?

Of course Jack wondered if he might be wrong; maybe the book was good and sound—no, not brilliant, no one could say it was brilliant, it was a feeble thing, barely alive. Jack blamed Will's canniness, his way of playing with his cards close to his chest. Old Will thought he was so shrewd to hide in the margins of life, never to show a strong emotion, always to insist on his amateur status, to hold up his hands as he backed away. Will was the cunning loser with his bland caginess, his refusal to take a stand.

Jack was surprised by the anger pouring off him.

As it turned out, Will was satisfied by Jack's unconvincing enthusiasm since that very morning he had received a delirious Kirkus pre-pub review: "This charming fairy tale is as whimsical as a Boris Vian novel and as contemporary as Pynchon's latest. A morning glory becomes a startling symbol of the life force. A heroine, Trumpetta, faces a stylish death but languishes beautifully in her final moments—she is one of the finest and least forgettable female characters in recent memory. Love has never been as tender and childlike—or as grown-up. Good for all ages and library collections. No obscenity."

Will handed it to Jack and pretended to be annoyed with it. "I'm not sure I like a pastel word like 'whimsical,' but at least my character is unforgettable and the review is starred."

Jack made a nice recovery: "So few reviews are starred. Yours is the only starred novel in this issue, isn't it? Look, it is the only one. They should have said 'brilliant' ten times, all caps, but 'contemporary' and 'grown-up' aren't too shabby. Nor is 'least forgettable.'"

Jack wondered who could've written such a silly review— probably a girl, he thought. Definitely a female French major. Someone who liked Will's photo, heavily retouched to eliminate the acne scars. She was probably hoping for a date. Jack checked a Boris Vian novel out from the Donnelly library at lunchtime, but when Will saw it on his desk in the afternoon, he picked it up carelessly, thrummed it, and put it down. He said, "Never read the guy." Which couldn't have been true since, as Jack discovered, in the Vian novel there was also a flower that wilted in sympathy with the heroine.

Jack couldn't deny that he'd found Will's book trivial and thin, but he wondered if he'd failed to register its appeal. Whimsy wasn't something Jack could pick out in a lineup. It seemed as if *The Truth About Sergeant Tavel* might be a literary event, and now Jack couldn't help looking at Will as somebody up-and-coming. He wasn't the same Will. Some of the journalists who dropped by the offices of the *Northern Review* had published books of reportage, but no one recognized their names. Journalists weren't real writers. They had no aura. They weren't going to be picked out as signals from the background noise. But Will? He might become a contender, someone who would be singled out by the media to speak for a whole generation.

Maybe talent was simply a knack for stealing well, and Jack knew this thief too intimately.

"I'm going to give a copy of your book to Alexandra," Jack said.

Will put up an anguished hand and then let it drop, as if he recognized he could do nothing now to shape the career of his book. "Do you think that's wise?"

"She may blame my big mouth, since you've obviously taken a lot from her life, from what I've told you about her."

"She'll be flattered. Do you think she's intelligent enough to get it? But sure, we can't choose our readers."

Jack was slightly shocked by Will's use of "we." Not regal so much as a collective pronoun for all writers, the ones who counted.

"I think she'll be amused by how you've idealized her and made her into someone so innocent."

Will's lip actually curled. "She's not innocent?"

They were speaking nearly in whispers because the walls of Jack's office cubicle didn't go all the way to the ceiling. "I don't think I told you about her affairs—I'm so glad I didn't tell you."

With a trace of irritation Will said, "I wasn't exactly taking dictation from you, buddy. You have heard of the imagination?"

"Of course, I know you transformed everything." Jack looked to see how his ridiculous exaggeration was going over. Will had transformed very little about Alexandra, in fact. Many of the things he'd said, quoting her, he had obviously transcribed verbatim.

"But she's not innocent?" Will asked again. He was unusually impatient for the answer.

Oh, Jack thought. Her innocence . . .

"You can tell me now," Will said. "I'm not going to base another character on her. Has she had many lovers?"

"I should introduce you two. She's seen too much of life and you too little," Jack said. "You'd be perfect for each other. You're afraid of adventures and she's tired of hers."

"She is?" Will asked. "She told you that? Specifics! Okay, she's a big slut—really big?"

" 'Slut' is not a word in my vocabulary," Jack said. "At least not in discussing a woman."

Will frowned as a big faggy shadow suddenly flapped past overhead. "You're no fun," he said. He'd been sitting on the edge of Jack's desk, but now he pushed off and headed to the doorway. Since his good review this morning, he had become cooler and more elegant in his movements, as if he were just dropping in on the working world. He had a new way of tilting his head back as if a photographer had instructed him on how to catch the overhead light. Will was being someone else, a pianist in a 1930s *Vogue* photo, his mouth beautifully carved.

As soon as Jack was back home that evening, he stripped down to his boxer shorts, made a vodka and tonic, sprawled on the couch, and called Alexandra. While he talked to her, he reached into his shorts and cupped his balls. "Well, you'll never guess what happened today."

"I give up," she said.

"Will got a starred review in Kirkus."

"Is that the one critics read? That's terrific! Bravo, Will."

"It is terrific."

"But you don't really like the book much?"

"If you ever repeat that . . ."

Jack sipped his drink—the tonic and lime made him feel marooned in the tropics. The freedom to sprawl and grope himself while chatting with Alexandra was the best argument in favor of the telephone. In a face-to-face conversation he felt too monitored, but on the phone he could roll his eyes, stick out his tongue, nurse his penis into half an erection while his voice remained obediently sympathetic and encouraging.

"I have to admit I was surprised by the girl's enthusiasm—"

"The girl! Aren't those reviews unsigned? How do you know a girl wrote it?" Alex demanded.

"I don't."

"Aha! You just assumed that girls burble with absurd enthusiasm, especially over a young man's first novel."

"Well?"

"Jack Holmes, you've really gone too far this time." She laughed and pretended to be shocked. Half-humorous exasperation was her favorite mode.

"Are you wearing your dark red silk robe?" he asked.

"Yes, and I'm drinking tea from that beautiful cup you gave me and how dare you change the subject." But she inhaled a little laugh just to prove she was half-teasing him. "I won't ask what you're wearing—I'm easily shocked."

Jack said, "Will seemed happy and calmer than I've ever seen him. Alexandra, I have a terrible confession to make."

"Uh-oh," she said, her voice still merry and indignant. "What now?"

"I'm afraid you're going to recognize certain . . . elements of your life in Will's heroine."

"What!" A real indignation overtook the mock one. "Why would I—are you saying—how dare you, Jack Holmes! You mean to say that you fed that man all my secrets for his wretched book, that you ran from my side and seconds later started tattling to that iceberg about the most intimate details of my life that I entrusted you with in a sacred act of friendship, don't sweat it, I don't really care."

Jack swallowed and laughed a little laugh. "I'll bring it over right now."

He could hear her rustling around in the background. He

resented her—and then realized he resented anyone who made him feel guilty.

He could hear her breathing, then there was the sound of porcelain on porcelain. "You can leave the effing thing with the doorman." She hung up.

Alexandra had become one of his very closest friends (Fuckin' rich bitch! an angry, guilty part of his mind shouted), and he couldn't bear to think he'd betrayed her (East Side cunt!). Until this very moment he hadn't understood how thoroughly he'd pimped out her secrets to hungry Will—Will had used them both.

As he walked from the subway stop on Lexington over to Alexandra's building, he said out loud, "How oedipal!" and someone looked at him strangely. Were Will and Alex his parents?

All the time he'd been listening to Alex's confidences and been relaying them to an indifferent-seeming but actually greedy Will had felt as emotional as his childhood love for his impossible, elusive parents. A shrink would have a field day, he thought. Maybe I'm hoping to bring these attractive new parents together, but this time with me, the beloved son, as the crucial intermediary.

What if Alex liked the book and married Will and they adopted Jack as their sweet, exasperating son?

"It's not such a big deal," he said out loud. "Fuck them." Suddenly he had to face the possibility that he'd lose—he'd lost—her friendship and perhaps Will's. He still had Alice and Rebekkah as friends, his black-stockinged girls with their wit and talent. Suddenly he despised Alex's china and satin hostess gown, even her expensive thinness (only a diet of caviar and celery and daily dressage lessons could keep you that thin).

When he arrived at Alex's address, there she was sitting near

the front door looking minuscule and very white, like a sprig
of baby's breath. She had her hair pulled back in a ponytail to
reveal tiny marsupial ears and the blue veins visibly ticking at
her temples. She was wearing carefully ironed jeans and spool
heels. Jack pushed past the elderly doorman, dripping Rurita-
nian braid from his epaulets, and put the manila envelope in
her hands.

"Here he is," Alex said, "the traitor."

Jack thought of ten different things to say but finally muttered, "Call me when you've read it."

"I'll walk you to the corner," she said, and he thought that in
spite of it all she really was a nice girl.

Did the doorman think they were having a lovers' quarrel and
that's why she hadn't kissed him and they were both so solemn?
As they left the building, she took his hand and whispered,
"Louse!"

It was a cool, rainy night. "You'll get wet," Jack said.

"I don't care," Alex replied, "grouch, grouch."

"We're doing our own sound effects now?"

Their good-bye at the corner was almost shy; that she'd come
down to greet him already suggested a reconciliation.

As he walked along by himself, he decided he was glad he
didn't live up here on the East Side with its banks behind colonial
facades and its show windows full of evening dresses and over each
doorway a faded green canopy smelling of mildewed canvas. And
everyone seemed so sexless and grown-up. No sleazy Village homos; even the ones up here wore chinos and crew necks knotted
over their shoulders. And penny loafers without socks and beige
windbreakers.

Jack realized that the gay men in the Village with their black pegged pants and tight shirts excited him because he knew how easily they could be unwrapped.

It was too silly to subscribe to an uptown-downtown polarity, though. Both Will and Alex lived uptown—was it all right for heterosexuals to be more connubial than sexual?

Jack now came to see Will as untouchable. It was so clear from his book that he worshipped Woman—not a White Goddess but a debutante in a shirtdress. Will was no longer that guy sitting around with no date and bad skin; now he was a distinguished young author with a pedigree. *Town and Country* was planning a story on Will with a photo of him posing on a horse in front of the family house. Will still dropped by Jack's cubicle but kept consulting his watch. His schedule seemed very full. An uncle had just bought Will a membership at the Racquet and Tennis Club, and Will would amble over there three nights out of five to play squash with old prep school friends.

Alex called Jack the next morning at work. She'd stayed up all night reading and liked the book and wanted to meet Will. "Of course you misheard ten things out of twelve, Jack Holmes, but that's not Will's fault; old Will caught my essence. I think I come across as highly desirable and *racée,* half Holy Virgin and half mad deb." She laughed at herself and so did Jack, mostly out of relief.

"You really didn't mind being used?"

"Not at all," Alexandra said, musing. "I think he understood me—well, if not understood at least grasped me."

A distinction without a difference, Jack thought.

"I mean," she said, "he does seem to grasp the way my mind works—it's really extraordinary. He doesn't seem that perceptive about other women."

Jack was dying to mock her, but he didn't dare; he was so pleased she'd forgiven him.

"Of course," she said, her voice darkening, "a happy outcome doesn't pardon the appalling breach of confidentiality."

"You should be a lawyer," Jack said.

"Luckily for you I'm not."

They agreed that Jack would bring Will by for a drink. Alex started dithering: "Do you think we should meet in a public place?"

"Are you afraid he won't like your apartment?"

Alex was indignant. "No, Jack, I'm afraid I won't like him. If we meet in a bar, I can always slip away. I'll keep my hat on."

"Hat?" Jack asked, astounded.

"Yes, Jack, I have hats. Veils too."

Will seemed mildly contemptuous of a possible meeting. "Warn her I'm not going to write another book about her. And that *Tavel* is a work of fiction."

Jack hated the pretentious sound of "a work."

Will did agree reluctantly to a drink for the very next afternoon. Alex seemed equally annoyed at the prospect ("He's certainly keen," she said), but finally gave in.

That night Jack got rid of his adoring trick by saying, "I'm afraid I have a very jealous lover who's a violent Puerto Rican. If I tried to see you again, believe me, I wouldn't be doing you any favors. Pedro is coming back to town in the morning. Be sure you don't even say hi to me on the street if you see me with a big Latin ex-Marine."

Once the frightened trick had scurried off, Jack was free to worry himself sleepless over Will and Alexandra. As he tossed and turned, he kept playing out scenes between them. They snapped at each other, and Jack had to fill the silences. They stared at each other with entranced smiles, and Jack had to let himself out. Or they both made horrible brittle small talk.

Very, very late, after he'd drunk half a bottle of Jim Beam, Jack imagined them making love—Alexandra with her slender hips, nacreous collarbones, immaculate neck, breasts as small and high as those of a Lucas Cranach Eve; Will with his brown hair that turned auburn in the sunlight, his pale blue eyes so deeply set in their sockets that they looked black, his big nose and his rough skin, so at odds with his delicately modeled face that in the end he resembled an Adonis badly damaged by the elements.

Jack thought of Will's smile, so slow to dawn and so slow to fade that it always seemed unsettling.

How would they kiss? Would she abandon herself to desire, or would she have that slightly lost, even frightened look she sometimes wore when the conversation had outpaced her—until she could catch up by finding some new pretext for indignation? Will would be gallant, but how gentlemanly could you be pushing a stiff one between a girl's open legs? Or did Jack think that because he had already been corrupted by the brutality of gay life?

The next day Will canceled their drink; he was going to be interviewed by the *Roanoke Times*.

Alexandra laughed. "I just feel sorry for you, Jack. You've lost your little friend to fame." She didn't like the sound of that and added, "It will all die down soon, and he'll be back."

What amazed Jack was that a book as bad as *Tavel* could be such a success.

Suddenly free that evening, Jack went directly from work to Julius'. He knew he looked good in his suit. The padding made his shoulders immense. His legs in the dark wool looked endlessly long as he sat on the high barstool. His five o'clock shadow was dramatized by his white shirt collar, as he could see in the cracked mirror over the bar. He fell in with two men in their fifties who kept buying him gin and tonics but wanted him to try stingers (Jack knew how incapacitating they could be). Jack liked the attention, one man on each side, both of them interested in every word that fell from his lips. One of them, Hubert, had an iodine-colored tan and very white, very new teeth. Later, when he pictured Hubert, Jack wondered if his lips were that pink naturally. He had lots of short curly hairs springing up where his shirt collar opened. The hairs were both bronze and white but very thick, and around Hubert's lips Jack could see hair like bronze filings coming in—it would hurt to be kissed by him. The other man was taller and slender and had a disobedient comb-over that kept relaxing and pouring down his pale face. His name was Bud. They were Bud and Hubert—inseparable, apparently, but definitely not lovers. At least, they were leaning in too carnivorously over Jack to be lovers, weren't they, and anyway, could two men that old possibly love each other?

Bud and Hubert finally got Jack onto stingers, and this next part wasn't too clear, but Jack was stumbling through dark streets between them laughing so hard it hurt his spine and he wasn't sure he wouldn't vomit and then they were inside and Bud and Hubert were clawing at his belt and muttering to each other ("Easy does it, get the dick out") and Jack couldn't make the room stop turning but when he did both men were sprawled on the floor at his feet, sharing a big red dick that they were throttling.

When it was all over, they washed him down with a hot cloth, brewed him strong black coffee, and helped him buckle back up.

"So tell us, Bob—it's Bob, right?" Hubert asked.

"Yes, it's Bob," Jack said.

"What do you do in life?"

"Auto repairs."

"That's pretty macho stuff," Bud threw in. "We won't ask you where, don't worry."

Jack compressed his lips gratefully.

Hubert asked Jack if he was gay or bisexual or straight. Jack said he was bisexual, but unfortunately he'd fallen in love with a straight man.

Hubert wiped his bristling upper lip, as if he had a wet mustache. With a little smile he asked, "Where's the problem?" He looked as if he had a wonderful secret.

"The problem?" Jack exclaimed. "I'd say there's a big problem when you're in love with a straight guy."

Hubert said, "Depends."

"Depends on what?" Jack demanded.

"Would you suck his cock?"

"Night and day."

Hubert opened his hands to demonstrate the obviousness of his next words: "Then all you need to do is get him off somewhere on a vacation, ideally in a country where the women are heavily veiled. Then you get him very drunk and in a dark room, and you go down on him. I know a straight Italian lawyer who lives near here, and he gets horny—these straight guys do get horny, you know, and women are so slow and expensive. This lawyer stretches out on his bed, fully dressed, and we both get drunk. I sit on the bed near his feet. Never touch him. Then he pretends to fall asleep, quite a good actor, though he raises his ass so I can scoot his trousers down. Then I kneel on the floor beside him. And when it's over, I use the tissues he's thoughtfully put on the night table—what's wrong?"

Jack was afraid he'd be sick. "Nothing," he said.

Bud spoke up. "I agree with you, Bob. Straight men are the greatest. They're real men, for one thing, and it excites me to think I'm sucking dick that's been in pussy."

"Guess I'll be pushing off," Jack said. "Need to sleep before I go to work on all those cars. Got a real doozy—a Mercedes bent in half."

"You have damn smooth hands for a workingman," Bud said sourly. "But wait! Sit back down."

Jack was surprised by such vehemence. Until now Bud had seemed the softie.

"You see," Bud said, "I've been going down to the Dominican Republic for fifteen years. I own a successful janitorial-supply outfit in Westchester—it almost runs itself. So I've got the money and time to fly down to my house in the D.R." He took a breath. "I live there with my caretaker, Guillermo, whom I call my husband. We've been together for fifteen years. He lives next door to me with his wife and kids, and when I'm down there he spends one night with her and one night with me. And Chichita never makes any trouble."

"I guess," Jack said, "she knows which side her tortilla is oiled on."

Bud looked offended but then decided to laugh it off. He even slapped his leg and gasped, "Tortilla! That's a gem! I agree with you there's nothing like a big hard straight cock. I don't just suck my husband. He fucks me a lot. Chichita and I are both very happy senoritas with our husband's uncut penis."

"It's been great, fellows," Jack said, heading for the door.

"No repeats? Won't you give us your phone number?"

Jack had to hold one eye shut, but he wrote out his number

with the last two digits reversed. "It's been *real*," he said as he stumbled out.

At home he stood under the shower for a long time and made it hotter than was comfortable. He even washed out his mouth with soap.

At work the next day his face was clammy and his hands were cold. He nearly fell asleep on the toilet. When he came back to his desk, he put his head down.

That night he lay on his couch, drank a quart of water, and jerked off three times. Hangovers made him horny. And now he had new mental pictures to feed his imagination: Will sleeping but lifting his pelvis up obligingly for Jack to lower his trousers. Jack could feel the stiff blessedness between his lips, not that Jack ever got the chance to practice fellatio. The minute guys saw his dick, they jumped on it. If he ever sucked Will, he would have to remind himself that it wasn't the Holy Sacrament. He'd told Will that gay guys sucked dick much better than girls, who looked at cock warily, as if it were a dangerous fish bone. He'd have to make it pleasurable for Will. Fat chance.

Jack almost wished Bud and Hubert hadn't told him about their "straight trade" (that's what it was called). He'd sort of laid to rest the fantasy of living with and loving Will. God knew he'd never had the least encouragement from Will himself, and Will's novel revealed that he didn't have the slightest impulse of tenderness toward another man. In fiction, Will's love was chivalric and absolute.

When Jack complained to the girls about how difficult Will and Alex were being about meeting, Alice said, "Just give Will Alex's number. I'd get out of it if I were you."

Jack nodded solemnly, which hid the lost feeling her words

inspired in him. It almost hurt to think that Will and Alex could get along without him. Of course, he knew he would be dealt out right away.

Finally, the following Tuesday both Will and Alexandra were able to clear a moment in their schedules for each other. Jack walked with Will through the light drizzle to her building. They went up Fifth Avenue through the New York of nannies and doormen and well-dressed white men with raincoats and umbrellas that stylized them into the interchangeable figures in an architectural model scattered about for scale. The stoplights bled onto the uneven wet macadam, huge vowels of color pronounced out of the gathering darkness.

Alexandra wasn't wearing a hat, but she was in a black wool dress with red stripes across the shoulders and down the long sleeves all the way to her delicate wrists. No jewelry anywhere. No rings or bracelets. Just a touch of lipstick. Despite her going-to-concert dress, she'd put on her semi-humorous swashbuckling manner: "So, Will, tell me what you'll have to drink. I assume you drink—you are a Princeton man, right?" She was already halfway to the drinks cart.

Will had slumped to the couch without hesitation, no polite middle-class dithering for him. He said, "Got some scotch?"

"Sure," she said. She was being very jaunty. "Rocks? Soda?"

"Straight up," he said.

"And you, Jack?"

She'd put out some hors d'oeuvres. There was a stack of three small linen napkins. They'd been meticulously ironed. Will was fiddling with one now and looking at it. "Who gave you these?" he asked.

"No one," she said, still smiling but a bit defiantly. She gave them their drinks. "I bought them."

"Wait, wait!" Will said. He held the small napkin up taut between his hands as Exhibit A. "You actually set out one day and went to a . . . store and ordered gray . . . what is this—linen? Gray linen napkins with your own initials embroidered, right? Embroidered in red? You ordered the gray linen and red letters?"

"Don't be an idiot," Alex said cheerfully, sitting on an armchair holding her drink in one hand and tugging her skirt down with the other. "Of course I ordered them, who else would order them? My mother? I went to Saks and ordered them with all my other linens."

"Wait, wait!" Will exclaimed. "All your linens are gray and have your monogram in red? And you spend hours ironing them?"

"The maid irons them, Will. That's what maids do. Of course my linens aren't gray!" Alex said indignantly. Her cheeks flushed bright red. "My table linens are plain white—perhaps you'd like to see them? I suppose now that you're a novelist, you have this insatiable Balzacian curiosity about domestic details."

Jack admired the way she pronounced "Balzacian" to rhyme with "Alsatian." For a moment he hadn't recognized the word. He thought she was funny and impertinent to suggest that Will had only recently decided to set up shop as a novelist.

Jack noticed that his palms were sweating. He told himself that it was out of his hands now, that he should sit back and relax, and he tried to do just that. He crossed and recrossed his legs.

Will was still sprawling. He shook the little napkin. "How many of these do you have?"

"They're called cocktail napkins, and I have thirty."

"Thirty!" Will thundered. "You mean to say some nun—"

"Exactly, a nun, all that work is done by nuns. I see you're very au courant about the arts of the table."

Will pretended he hadn't heard her. He went on with his own inquisition and his own form of wry indignation. "Some nun spent thirty days monogramming this hoard of napkins—"

"Wait a minute," Alex said, jumping up and calling back from the kitchen. "It's called a job, Will Wright, not a penance. I forgot you're Catholic."

"Oh? How did you know?"

"It's all over your novel. No rational person could have written it." She came back in with a smile and a silver bowl of cashews that she placed on the coffee table at an equal distance between Will and Jack.

"Ouch!" Will exclaimed, pretending he'd just burned himself on something hot; he shook his hand to cool it off. "That really hurt, Alexandra."

"Of course your little friend Jack tells me everything about you. Remember, the information flow goes in both directions." She looked reproachfully at Jack. Then, by glancing down suddenly, she must have dislodged one of her troublesome contacts; for the next several moments she poked at her right eye and rolled it around behind a curtain of long hair.

At last it was back in place, but Will was still hammering on about the wretched cocktail napkins. "But why thirty of these things—is it part of a trousseau?"

Alex sat up very straight with her head held high. "Do you seriously imagine that women only do things in preparation for the great experience of their miserable lives: marriage?"

Will stared vacantly at her and then at some imaginary lint on his lapel, which he brushed off.

"Well?" Alex asked.

Will looked up as though he could barely focus on this topic. "You tell me," he said vaguely.

Jack felt sick—this was going so badly! He couldn't believe that neither of them was able to make more of an effort. For months Will had pumped Jack for information about Alex, and she'd seemed curious about him too, though in her much less insistent way. But now they were bickering like children. He'd assumed that at least they'd be civil.

When Alex started to refill their glasses, Jack pretended to be startled by how late it had become and rushed out, leaving a resentful-looking Will behind.

Later that night Alex phoned him. "That Will of yours!" she exclaimed, though there was also laughter in her tone.

"Oh god, I'm sorry," Jack said, his voice cracking like a kid's, "he's not usually that bad."

"I wonder," Alex said. "He seemed to be perfectly in his element."

Jack wasn't quite sure what that meant. After all, he didn't understand all their little turns of phrase and euphemisms. He was a false contender in their world of Auchinclosses and Astors, though they refused to believe him about his humble origins.

"By the way," Alex said, "he's a lot better-looking than you suggested."

"Oh please," Jack said, panicking, "please never say I described him as homely."

"I'd never hurt him," she said, quickly adding, "or any man. Men are so sensitive about their looks. It's their greatest virtue and their biggest failing."

"And their biggest—wow! You really know how to turn a phrase. How late did he stay?"

"Almost another hour. In the end he invited me out for

dinner, but I said I was otherwise engaged. I was a rag after he'd made so many gibes."

"You were holding your own," Jack said. He let out a big breath; he was feeling more sanguine.

"I do my best."

"Want to see that new movie tomorrow night, *Dr. Strangelove?*"

"Is it kind of political?"

"It's supposed to be funny."

Will was out of the office all the next day. That evening Alex didn't mention him, not even when they went for a late bite at Brasserie in the Seagram Building and sat at the counter; the combination of casualness and elegance there suited them both.

Jack walked her home and then, still wearing his suit from work, went to a bar he'd heard was a little bit gay. As soon as he stepped into the place on Second and Seventy-eighth, he realized it was just another straight pickup bar. He stayed for one drink and left, but on the sidewalk a guy in his late twenties cruised him hard. He even turned around and started following Jack. The guy wasn't in a suit but was wearing a powder blue crew neck sweater and carefully ironed chinos. They went back to his place, a studio crammed with color photos of his very blond parents and siblings. Strewn about were lots of nautical mementos, including a model of a big sailboat in a glass vitrine. When they kissed standing up and groped each other, the guy didn't seem unduly impressed with Jack's huge penis, and Jack felt relieved but also slightly confused, like a movie star who finally finds a Caribbean island where no one recognizes him.

The man lowered the lights, put on a Frank Sinatra LP, mixed them martinis, and sat in an armchair until he suddenly leapt up, joined Jack on the couch, held Jack's face between his hands as if it were a precious object and kissed him slowly with lots of tongue, and said, "You look wonderful in that dark suit. What do you do?"

"Corporate lawyer," Jack said.

"And your name, your first name? I know your last name is Heaven."

"It's Hal," Jack said. "Hal Heaven. And yours?"

"Billy Delight. I own IBM."

They both smiled, and soon they were undressing each other. The couch opened up into a bed with very clean sheets carefully ironed. Billy was romantic throughout and even afterward. He "freshened" Jack's drink when they were back in their underwear and told him about his childhood summers in Blue Hill, Maine. "The Commodore was the big cheese of the little Blue Hill yacht club." Jack wasn't sure whom he was talking about.

Jack was tempted to spend the night and actually fell asleep for a moment. He liked this guy—so much less of an egomaniac than Peter, more just a good-time Charlie. But then Jack pulled himself together and dressed and kissed Billy at the door. Billy had written out his telephone number on a deckled card. He was wearing a citrusy cologne.

Jack walked ten blocks before he hailed a cab. The streets were nearly deserted up here on the East Side—it was three o'clock in the morning.

At home he lay on his couch and thought about Billy. Admittedly Billy was a bit spinsterish with his ironed sheets and his ironed boxer shorts with the pearl compression buttons. But he was sweet and a good, appreciative kisser and not too carnivorous. For once Jack hadn't crumpled the number and thrown it away on the doorstep.

Jack thought about how he analyzed every small move either

Will or Alexandra made, how Olympian their lives had become for him, though neither of them was dramatic and they were both too discreet. While they were inching toward each other like snails, he was in full flight, beating his wings against the bars of his cage. But his flights were accomplished in the dark, and he never reported anything to them or to anyone else. Here was this nice Billy, with his family silver all polished on the sideboard next to a nautical brass-and-mahogany tambour clock. Jack had kissed him, and Billy, with his narrow hips only an octave wide, had sat on Jack's cock, and Jack had stood and carried him around the room like that and even pushed Billy's back against the cool wall next to the bathroom door; Billy was that light. His body was as small as Peter's but not as muscled. And no one would ever know of all these exploits or just the simple human pleasure of the story that began, "I met a blond boy on Second Avenue, and he invited me in, and soon enough his legs were wrapped around my waist."

Of course, there was nothing to suggest that Billy was a good conversationalist or that they shared any interests, but he did have a pretty body and he was a sophisticated East Side New Yorker.

Jack didn't want to call Billy from home or work, but the next day he did call him from a pay phone. Billy answered after three rings, and he asked Jack over for dinner on the next night. "Do you like polenta?"

"I'm not sure what it is," Jack said.

"It's like grits."

"Then sure, I'll like it plenty."

"Why don't you come over after work, and we'll have some drinks and I'll throw something together."

"Okay, but only if you'll cook in the nude."

Billy said in a natural low voice, "Mister, you got a deal."

Up to the very last moment Jack thought of not going to Billy's. He knew he was completely untraceable. Even on the Lexington Avenue subway he thought of getting off and heading back downtown.

Billy's apartment looked dusty in the last shreds of daylight coming through the single window that gave out onto an air shaft. But Billy, who was running late, pulled the heavy black-and-white tweed curtains shut, switched on the many atmospheric lamps, made them martinis with big green olives sweating in them, and then said, "I'm going to take a quick shower before I get into my regulation togs." He stood on his toes and kissed Jack coolly on the lips. Did "regulation togs" mean naked?

Jack sat down and wished there was a dog to play with. The martini turned like a trenching spade going down a narrow hole into his bowels. It cored him so quickly that by the time Billy emerged, riding on a puff of perfumed steam, Jack was tempted to doze off, but when he did so, his whole body revolved and he lurched up.

"Want me to freshen that?" Billy asked.

"I need black coffee and amphetamines, not another martini."

Billy was naked, and his body looked much more childlike than Jack remembered. He had a shower-pink butt, very prominent and cherubic but unwobbling, and a kid's little paunch with a tidy "inny" belly button and just a touch of blond pubic hair dusted around a small penis that curved snugly around his sac. His chest was hairless and flat and his arms slightly plump. Resting on top of so much childish inconsequence was a big, surprisingly adult head with horrible razor-cut hair, a geranium-red complexion, and heavy smoker's lines bracketing his mouth. Jack no longer found him appealing.

Fortunately Billy picked up on this mild distaste and did not cook in the nude but slipped on some faded jeans.

"You could have a shower too, while I make the polenta."

The nozzle was dialed to produce a wide spray that enveloped Jack's body. The bathroom was perfectly sterile, just as Jack liked it. No question mark pubes interrogating the tub, no nail clippings winking in the sink, no ghosts of old soap bars haunting the small plastic imitation-horn box next to the cologne bottles.

When he looked around, a white terry cloth robe (Jack's size, not Billy's) had been invisibly spirited in and laid on the closed toilet. Jack liked the attention, but he disliked it that Billy was such a practiced geisha.

They ate their polenta with a tomato-and-caper sauce and a salad and a store-bought dessert and drank two bottles of red wine. When the meal was over and Jack was leaning back, still in his robe but with his legs spread, Billy passed him a little bottle. Jack didn't quite know what it was, but he inhaled the stuff and a moment later Billy was kneeling under the table licking Jack's balls. When the rush died down, Jack pulled Billy up and said, "Come out of there. Here. Sit on my lap. Tell me something average. Talk to me. Let's take it slow."

"Sure, Hal. Anything you say. I do average very convincingly."

Jack liked having this warm boy sitting astride his legs, even though his face was disconcertingly mature. Jack decided to look not at his face but at his underarms, for Billy had laced his hands behind Jack's neck. A suspicion of pale silk floss floated away from paler silk skin. "And my name isn't Hal. It's really Jack. Sorry about that."

"Strangely enough, mine really is Billy."

"Yes, but your name is on the bell, Mr. William Haddington III."

Billy told him about his father, the Commodore, though he was quick to add that "commodore" was only an honorary title in the Navy. "It used to be above captain and below rear admiral, but now it means nothing, though Daddy likes us to call him that. He's a businessman, but in his dreams he's always sailing."

Jack pulled Billy tighter into his arms and squeezed him. He ran his hands over the small, elegant bumps of his spine, as evenly spaced as rosary beads. Then he relaxed him until he was almost reclining, and he kissed his small maroon nipples and his clavicle, which came swimming out of his shoulder like a spatula in batter.

The couch was opened into a bed, and before, during, and after making love, they talked and talked about New York and college and when did you know you were gay for sure. Jack even told Billy about his shrink.

Billy said, "I don't really care about getting well." He bit his cuticle. "I guess I should, but I don't. Can you picture me with a wife and children?"

Jack glanced automatically down to Billy's very small penis, then caught himself and looked away. "I'm not sure," he said.

"Well, I can't. Call me sick, but I like men. I guess I'm pretty passive."

"Thank god," Jack whispered as he kissed Billy's ear.

What Jack liked about Billy was how relaxed he was. He seemed to be shuffling through life, eyes half closed, humming a tune so broken up it couldn't be reconstructed. Jack was used to a supplicating look in men's eyes, which led him to feel nothing but stubborn resistance. With most guys Jack never had enough room to stretch out, but here was Billy letting him breathe and turn around—in fact, Jack wondered how many other gentlemen Billy was stringing along. He was so good at it and seemed so undesperate. So accommodating.

For Jack the most romantic moment occurred when he was heading home alone in the cab and thinking about the evening. He realized it was wrong to get too comfortable with another man. Next thing you knew, he'd be giving his hair a henna rinse and adding a little girly skip to his walk. Loving another man, a gay man, didn't make much sense. No other man (unless he was a real glandular case) would know how to fit his body or psyche to a male partner's.

And yet here was Billy, who knew, maybe because he was so super-casual, how to bend and snuggle right into the contours of Jack's body. It wasn't as if a woman was all that easy to get along with either. Let's face it, he thought: people are obstacle courses.

Over the next two weeks Jack saw Billy every other night. He finally even got up his courage and invited Billy to a restaurant. He could always say they worked together—unless they ran into someone from the office. Billy dressed well. He didn't lisp. Hell— Jack didn't owe anyone an explanation! If Billy had been just a few years younger, Jack could have said they'd gone to school together in Michigan. Jack regretted Billy's big, grown-up head. And yet Jack found himself smiling whenever he thought of Billy. Billy wasn't the kind of guy who could burrow into your heart—there was nothing elusive about him or even resistant. He was just an easy habit to acquire. He soothed the soul, but he didn't fire the imagination. Nor was there any future with him. Even with Will the most Jack had dared to hope for was two years. Now the thought of this foolish hope made Jack wince. His head hurt with the memory, and he massaged his temples.

Jack invited Billy down to his apartment and cooked him a chicken breast, which he'd learned from Rebekkah how to dip in egg and flour and then sauté. He even sprinkled it with chopped parsley and served it with frozen petits pois, which Alex had assured him always came out well.

Jack made martinis for them and had bought a bottle of white wine, which by mistake tasted sweet. Jack had decided that Billy was very "cool"—that was his word for him. As he'd look at Billy, the word "cool" would recycle like water in a diagram about precipitation. What a cool guy, he'd think. He has a beautiful slow smile, little feet that feel good when he presses back against my bare chest like a cat "kneading bread."

After Billy left, Jack said out loud, "I really gotta stop this dating—it's fuckin' faggy." He started taking his meals with his girls again. Alice asked him if Will and Alexandra had ever been introduced.

"It didn't really take," Jack said.

"What do you mean?"

"They kept spatting," Jack said. "I couldn't believe it."

Alice knocked back a jigger of whiskey and played with her spaghetti. "That can be a sign they're attracted to each other. It's called sex antagonism."

"I'd never fool around like that with sex antagonism!" Jack exclaimed.

Alice laughed a polite but noncommittal honk of "Huh!" and lit a cigarette.

"Are you going to smoke through the whole meal?" Jack asked.

Alice merely looked at him and blinked. "I heard it's called dining *à la russe*."

"What is?"

"Smoking through the meal."

"Nice name for a filthy habit," Jack said.

"Your manners could use a little work too. You've spattered tomato sauce all over your face."

Walking home, Jack realized that spending so much time with Billy, far from making him more effeminate, more homosexual and prissy, as he'd expected, had actually coarsened him. Billy was pushing him into a more manly role. With a girl, a guy had to tiptoe around not to offend her. Women wanted you to be gentle, but other men liked it rough.

When Jack called up a week later, Billy didn't question him or register any hurt. He certainly didn't come across as wounded. He talked about a trip he'd made to Boston to see some old friends from Colgate. Jack wondered if he'd even noticed that Jack had been missing in action.

The truth was that during the first half of their evenings, before Jack climaxed, he liked Billy and enjoyed himself. Billy was smart and could talk about politics and was pretty conservative. But the minute Jack came, he was sickened by their organs, their breath, the futile desire of one man to climb inside another. Billy was aware of Jack's darker postcoital moods and would get dressed quickly. It was as if Billy's mature head was the person who talked about the virtues of the Republican Party, and his boyish body was his other personality: generous, passionate, the liberal!

After sex Billy was perfect. He turned on the TV and talked

back to the announcer. No signs of affection. They could have been dorm-mates at Colgate.

One Sunday morning Jack was wandering around his apartment alone in his underpants and cooking a hamburger for breakfast (it was noon) when Alexandra phoned him. "So what do you think of the review?"

"What review?"

"In the Sunday *Times* book review? Of Will's book? Didn't you see it?"

"I've got it here—was it good?" Jack asked. Now he was sitting on his corduroy couch. His legs looked very long and meaty, surprisingly powerful thighs that could feed a family of four.

Alex laughed sadly. " 'Fraid not."

"Oh god," Jack said.

"It's very small, the review, on a page with . . . three . . . four! other reviews."

"But not good?"

"Mainly descriptive but no, a damning last line. And even the description makes it sound inoffensive."

"Not good," Jack said. He thought the soles of his feet looked yellow—was he eating too many carrots? Could carrots turn your soles yellow?

"Poor Will," Alexandra said.

"He'll be crushed. Can you hang on a second? I have to— one second—" He turned off the fire under the burger and went back to the couch and phone with a cold cup of coffee. "There. I thought the book was good, didn't you? Kind of good. Pretty good."

"Poor Will," Alex said. "You should call him up, Jack. Or maybe he has a girlfriend to look after him?"

"I don't think so," Jack said, "but who knows? He's so mysterious. Of course, he's got his sister."

"Oh, what's she like?" And they were off on a conversation about Elaine.

The review, only two paragraphs long, summarized the plot and then added, "The prose is at once shimmering and exact, the characters well observed and the story worth the telling. An unfortunately cloying feyness, however, hangs over everything, and some readers may break out in hives after such a prolonged exposure to whimsy. Nevertheless, Mr. Wright seems to have talent and his very next book could easily be a roaring (and not another treacly) success."

Jack called Will and Elaine's house several times but did not leave a message with the service. At last Elaine picked up. They talked for a while, and then she said in a low voice, "Will is absolutely devastated, but he's pretending to be very jaunty. He went out for a long walk and came back sort of drunk and said something sarcastic about his whimsy hives bothering him— obviously an allusion to . . ."

"Do you think he'd come here to dinner tonight if I invited him?"

"That's so sweet of you, Jack. Here, I'll go get him. Hang on."

After a while Will came to the phone. "What are you up to on this drizzly Sunday? What's happening, man?" He sounded tired but brave, or so Jack interpreted his tone of voice.

"Wanna come to dinner?" Jack asked. "I'm roasting a chicken and potatoes, and I've also got salad makings. I've also got a fifth of J&B."

"Now you're talking. Only one rule—"

"What *New York Times*? Never heard of that fuckin' rag. Used it once to wipe my ass, but it wasn't much good even for that."

"Okay, that's the kind of talk I like. I'll be down in an hour." It was only six. "Perfect," Jack said.

Will brought a bottle of very good Bordeaux that he said had been "floating around" his sister's house. He looked pale and hollow eyed and unshaved, and Jack suspected a direct question would make him shatter. Jack didn't touch him or look at him. He'd read that autistic children feel attacked by direct eye contact, and he decided to treat Will with therapeutic avoidance. He had also decided to take Rebekkah at her word and do nothing but stick a lemon in the chicken and pour some olive oil over it—and shove it in a medium oven for an hour. He was already sautéing the potatoes slowly in butter.

"That smells good," Will said, his lips almost blue, his long nose bluer, his eyes the dull, faded blue of old denim. He looked like someone on his first day up after surgery. Jack had hidden his copy of the Sunday *Times* in the bedroom closet and could think of no good reason Will would go in there.

Jack turned on the TV while he puttered around setting the table and looking after their drinks. "Try these potato chips, Will. They're amazingly good. Do you know Lay's?"

"Can't say I do, my boy," Will said with heroic chipperness.

"What is it with this 'my boy' stuff, Will?" Jack's instincts told him it would be bracing to challenge Will about something, but something completely trivial, certainly non-literary.

But everything led back to books. Will said, "I guess it's like Gatsby saying 'Old Boy' to everyone."

"No, no," Jack said with some urgency, "it's much better." He stopped short and realized he'd almost suggested that Will was a better writer than Fitzgerald.

They watched TV while they sipped their scotch and ate potato chips. Several times Will said, "Damn! These chips are really
good," and Jack nodded sagely. He was beginning to wonder if
he'd be able to get the dinner on the table, but he was sure Will
would just laugh if he dropped or burned it. He'd already burned
the potatoes, though they tasted good, and Will said, "They're
caramelized, Old Boy, caramelized," holding up a didactic finger, and for the rest of the evening he used Gatsby's irritating
"Old Boy" and managed to work "caramelized" into the conversation several times.

At last Jack got the chicken, which he split in half, onto a platter. Will looked at the charred carcass and the burned potatoes
and peas and said, "Are you sure you're not a heterosexual man?
This looks like a meal prepared by an incontestably heterosexual
man." He was having trouble enunciating "incontestably" and
"heterosexual" and had to back up and try them several times
over.

By the time they were finally seated, two thirds of the scotch
was gone and Jack had opened the wine. The TV was blaring in
the background (it was *What's My Line?*, and Bennett Cerf was
saying something droll and looking dapper in his tux). Will had
stabbed an incinerated chicken wing and was waving it in Jack's
face: "This is the best damn straight cock I've ever eaten."

"Have some more wine," Jack said. "You must never eat
straight coq without vin."

They both thought that was so funny that they laughed until
they were spraying bits of wine-soaked chicken.

"Unless it's caramelized," Will shouted, rising halfway up
out of his chair with such violence that it tipped over. "Unless
it's caramelized heterosex—historo—heterosexu—oh fuck! It's
inedible unless it's caramelized."

"Even gay cock has to be caramelized," Jack said solemnly, as he stood to fill their wineglasses.

Will clicked his heels and offered a toast: "To straight and gay cock, au vin or au caramel, may it always be juicy!"

Jack raised his glass, calling out, "Hear, hear, juicy!"

They both settled down heavily. They were looking very serious and formal.

By the time they finished pushing their burned "cock" around their plates, *What's My Line?* was coming to an end. Frank Sinatra was on, and he was supposed to identify the mystery guest, but he couldn't. Finally it was revealed that the guest was his new wife, the child bride Mia Farrow.

"Frankie!" Will shouted reproachfully. "It's your own fuckin' wife, Frankie, Old Boy! Your very own!" He stood up, as aggrieved as a baseball fan toward the umpire.

Jack wondered where all this would lead. He turned off the floor lamp and in the quaking bluish-white light projected by the television screen sat next to Will on the couch. Following his policy of no touching or eye contact, which he'd established a decade ago at the beginning of this evening, Jack stayed in his corner and looked at the screen. But then Bennett Cerf, who was the head of Random House, started to talk about a new best-selling book, and Will scooted way back and covered his eyes with his hand. Jack got up and switched the channel to the late news and sat back down beside Will. After a moment's silence, Will started groaning as if stung and turned his head away and shook silently. Jack sat forward and put a hand on Will's shoulder and said, "It's so damn unfair. It was probably some damn grad student who's never read anything but Spenser and Milton."

In a clotted voice trembling with anger, Will said, "I feel so humiliated. It's right there for everyone to read. And—sorry,

Jack—it sounds so faggy to be whimsical and fey—I mean, 'fey' is a way of saying fairyish, right?"

"Don't forget that it's just one person's opinion, a person you probably wouldn't even cross the room to speak to."

"Yeah, but people read the *Times* like it's holy writ," and he started to shake some more, his back shuddering with soundless sobs. Jack wasn't sure if he'd said "holy writ" or "as though it's," because his words were stifled by his hand.

Jack patted him in what he hoped was the least sexual and most veterinarian way possible. But maybe Will would interpret any touch—no, he was suffering, for god's sake, he needed succor, it was the least Jack could do. Jack put an arm around Will, who suddenly stood up and exposed a terrible face of pain. It was as if he'd slammed into a waffle iron—his face was mottled and pale but crisscrossed with red lines, and his blue eyes almost seemed to be leaking diluted blue tears. "Don't you see, Jack, how humiliating it is? No one in this fuckin' culture wants you to succeed. They want you to be as lame and pitiable as they are." He was chopping the air with both hands.

Will poured himself more whiskey and knocked it back. "If you make it, then they're all bowing and scraping around you, they can't wait to befriend you. But on your way up, if they can possibly knock you down, they will."

In one cold corner of his mind Jack hated all this talk about "them" and what "they" do or don't do to "you." He thought that everything, including fame, was a lot chancier than Will's theories suggested. But what he said was, "I think it's great you're feeling this so deeply, Will. It shows you're a real winner, a fighter. The average guy would just slink off, defeated. But you're really indignant. That's so healthy." He wondered how that would go down. He was practicing what an old teacher had called "moral sculpture," where you praise someone for virtues he hasn't yet secured.

Will looked at him with a glimmer of hope and said, "Maybe."

Jack decided to build on his success. "No, you're a champ, and when you've written another two or three books and won the fuckin' Pulitzer and become a household name, no one will remember this tiny setback."

Will looked at the TV with a strange interest, but he was just lost in thought. He said, without glancing at Jack, "Maybe. If I get that far. If I can survive this humiliation." Now Will slumped back on the couch; the word "humiliation" seemed to have undone him. He sagged under the weight of the word; it was twice his bulk, and it sat down on him and smothered him.

Now Jack had all the lights off, and he guided Will, holding on to his elbow, through the dark rooms to the big white bed, as if Will were an invalid. He put Will on the bed and unlaced his beautiful Church shoes and took them off. He had a hole in one black stocking, and a huge yellow-nailed toe was protruding, as lethal as an ostrich's spur.

Jack put Will's feet on his lap and massaged them. He worked vigorously, as if it were a well-known cure for a bad Sunday *Times* review. He pressed his thumbs into the insteps. He worked the inner side of each foot from the heel to the big toe. Without removing the delicate lisle stockings, he pulled and stretched and cracked and limbered up each toe. Will had thrown an arm back over his eyes. Jack couldn't help checking Will's crotch to see if the massage was exciting him, if not consciously at least autonomically, but no, nothing was stirring or stiffening there.

At last Will moved toward the center of the double bed and said, "Come here." When Jack was lying down beside him, Will pulled him into his arms and positioned Jack's head on his chest.

"There," Will said. Jack could smell the stuff Will used for his acne, and the burning-wood smell of scotch. "You're a good friend, Jack."

"Thanks," Jack said in such a small voice that he barely recognized it. Hearing it made him feel all the more childlike.

They lay there like that for five minutes, and then Will got up, went to the bathroom to pee, put his shoes and jacket back on, and then kissed Jack on the forehead and walked out the front door. Jack went into the bathroom and looked at the unflushed urine in the bowl. When he lay down, he didn't think this evening had been the start of something but rather the end.

7.

A LEX SAID OVER the phone, "I think Will likes that you're in love with him. Maybe it scares him too, but he's such a big neglected kid that he needs the attention."

"But how did you know?"

"You told me. Or at least it's always been obvious to me."

"Oh."

Then with friendly exasperation she said, "It's not a bad thing, Jack."

"It's not bad for one guy to like another?"

"Heavens, no. When is love ever a bad thing?"

"Let me think: between a man and a child? A mother and a son? A man and a sheep?"

"But that's perversion," she wailed.

"My point exactly," Jack said, and they shared a few more dry laughs before she hung up, saying she had somewhere to go.

Will seemed to be avoiding Jack at the office. Sometimes he'd sneak a little smile in his direction, but without stopping to talk to him.

When Jack spoke to her on the phone every day, more and more Alex seemed to be steering the conversation away from the subject of Will. One evening he called her from a pay phone and said, "I'm on the corner, Alex. I might just pop up."

"I can't see you."

"Okay."

"I'm in the shower."

"You're on the phone and in the shower? That could be fatal."

Of course, he was offended, and she could hear it in his voice. Finally she said, "I'm with someone right now."

"Really?"

"Yes, Will is here."

"What? What did you say? Will is . . . Most people don't answer the phone, Alex, when they're in flagrante delicto."

But she was already fluting "Bye" in that breathy little-girl voice that upper-class women affected only when signing off.

He wondered if they really were fucking. If so, he should be happy for them, especially since he'd brought them together.

Why had Alex said that Will liked it that Jack was in love with him? Had the two of them joked about it, with Alex curled up in Will's scrawny arms?

That night Billy cooked dinner for Jack, but Jack felt stifled and antagonistic the minute he walked through the door. He was wearing boots that were hard to remove, and he sat down and said, "Pull my boots off," and stuck a leg out.

With his back to Jack, Billy sat astride his extended leg and pulled at the boot until Jack, impatient, pushed Billy's back with his other foot, sending him toppling over with the boot in his hands. Billy got up with a very dark look on his face.

Refusing to apologize, Jack called out, "What about the other boot?"

"I'm going to get the meal on the table."

Jack knew that he was being disgusting, but bullying Billy

aroused him—and he hoped Billy would notice his tumescent crotch. He'd wrestled the other boot off on his own by the time Billy called him to the table.

He also knew that he was expected to say how good the meal was. Billy kept his eyes lowered and his face devoid of expression. He wouldn't forgive Jack until he apologized, but a black anger had taken hold of Jack, and he kept flashing on scenes of striking Billy, or kicking him, or pointing at his little-boy dick and laughing at it. Billy hadn't done anything wrong. All he'd done was to prepare another delicious dinner and serve a very good red wine. But even so Jack was mad at him, as he used to be as a child when forced to leave a kids' party and ride home in the backseat of the Cadillac with his drunken parents.

Part II

1.

Jack?" I said, stepping toward him, afraid I'd made a mistake. I stuck out my hand. We were both in front of the Museum of Modern Art. He'd just come out, and I was heading in.

"Hell, yes—Will! Will Wright!" and Jack lit up like a jack-o'-lantern with a crazy grin.

It was a cold, dark January day, and I calculated that eight or nine years had gone by. I said, "You must be thirty-two by now, right? Like me."

Jack grinned and put a warning finger to his lips, but he was still smiling all around his finger.

We laughed and he said, "Do you have time for a drink?"

I looked at my watch, pretending to be juggling important appointments in my head, then shrugged and said, "Sure, why not? We could walk up to the Plaza and have a drink at the Oak Room. But I only have time for a quickie."

Jack said that sounded good.

It seemed strange that he was so happy to see me, and I said so.

"You'd think we were long-lost brothers," I said.

"We are! How's Alex?"

"She's great. We live out in Larchmont now."

"And you're commuting?"

I shrugged my shoulders as if I knew I'd become a cliché, but I couldn't help adding, "We're happy out there," and even to my own ears my voice sounded serene.

"Hunting foxes out there?"

"No, never," I said. "Alex believes fervently in the prevention of cruelty to animals. We have twenty acres, even a stream and a pool, and the neighbors are pissed off because we refuse to do anything to control the so-called groundhog problem."

I looked at Jack and could see he was a bit perplexed but also impressed by the size of our property.

"You might think we were crazy people. We don't cut the grass or burn wasp hives or keep the pond from seeping or set traps for the raccoons or drive away stray dogs or kill ants or spray for mosquitoes. I guess most people would think that the house was abandoned, though of course inside Alex has decorated it with her wonderful taste, just as you'd suspect."

"What about termites?"

I laughed and said, "You caught us there. Alex and I had the whole house bagged and gassed, though we went through torments of self-reproach about it. But you don't want to hear about our . . ."

I left the sentence unfinished, and Jack rushed in with "You mean your Baha'i convictions?" and we both laughed in several ripples of hilarity. He'd always had a way of leaping ahead into a parallel world of fantasy.

Once we'd sat down at a table and ordered our drinks, I had an excuse to look him over more thoroughly. He'd definitely acquired a few lines. He'd also lost a few pounds, whereas I'd gained ten. He looked somehow shinier. His nose and jaw jut-

ted out fractionally further, and his glance was more complicated and worldly. He was wearing a burnt-lemon cologne—that
was new. He was sitting upright, but everything in him seemed
to be leaning toward me. I was happy to see him.

I said, "We've missed you."

"We? Do you have your feelings in a joint account?"

"Sort of," I said, irritated for a second. I was going to add,
"That's what being half of a couple means," but instead asked,
"What about you?"

"You mean, am I still going ahead with that funny queer
thing I do?"

I thought he was being too tart if he hoped to renew our
friendship.

"No," I said, deliberately not smiling, "I just wondered if you
were single or not."

Jack laughed and sat back in his chair. I'd seated him so that
he'd be looking out on the horses and carriages on the other
side of Central Park South.

"Sometimes I can make something last six or eight weeks,"
he said. "Eight weeks. That's my longest marriage."

I tried to look sympathetic. "But why is that?"

"But, Will," he said, "I like it that way." He smiled mysteri-
ously and added, "I'm a libertine."

That struck me as such a strange thing to say—he seemed
almost to glow with the announcement—that I looked around,
half hoping to see a friend whom I could call over in order to
change the subject. Still, while it was true that everyone assumed
that being half of a stable couple was a great thing, maybe it wasn't
always. Or for everyone. Jack didn't seem worried about being
alone for Christmas—wasn't that what everyone said, though
most people were miserable being with their families over the

holidays. Maybe he did worry and this was just bravado, pretending to be a libertine.

"Did you know this used to be a sort of gay bar?" Jack said.

"The Oak Room?"

"Originally it was a men-only bar, and even when women could come, they seldom did. It was for men in suits who wanted other men in suits. I used to come here by myself, and older men in suits would tell the bartender to offer me a drink." He laughed. "It was for men who liked sidecars."

"How the hell do you make a sidecar?" I said gamely.

"Brandy. Triple sec. Lemon juice."

"That's obscene."

"There's a really bad novel in which the hero wakes his wife every morning with a cocktail shaker full of sidecars. The book came out in 1929 just before the crash. The author never wrote another book."

"That was a piece of bad luck," I said.

I was hoping he wouldn't ask me about my own writing. Was that what Jack was working up to, by mentioning unsuccessful novels? Had he turned cruel? Of course, he was a big reader. He read a novel a week—or used to. That had been a point of pride for him. Just as he went to the latest art exhibits and attended concerts. That was his idea of a New Yorker. Or used to be.

"What are you working on these days?" he asked.

"Ah, that," I said, "we must save for another day."

After that *Times* review I became ill every time I thought of working on a new novel. I could feel my stomach start to sour, even to heave. I knew I'd get back to a novel at some point, but the next time, I thought, I'd do it in secret, under everyone else's radar. I'd do it for myself. This time I'd have a real experi-

ence to write about. And when I wrote something, I'd ask myself if I liked it, whether I could improve it in any way. And if I
was sure it met my standards after it sat in my drawer for a year
or two, I'd show it to Alex and Jack, and my old editor—if he was
still in business.

I stood up and looked at my watch. "I have seventeen minutes to get to the train station." I handed him my card and threw
down a ten-dollar bill.

"That's too much!" he said.

"Are you still at the *Northern Review*?" I asked, implying that
if so he might not be able to afford the Oak Room.

"No," he said, "*Newsweek*."

"Books?"

"Business."

"Big changes are afoot," I said. "Let's have lunch next week."

"And does Alex ever get into town?"

"Never. We have two kids—a girl and a little boy."

"That was fast!"

"But you'll have to come out to Larchmont and see the
crazy people and their overgrown estate," I said, immediately
regretting the word "estate" and making a face to indicate my
irony.

"Well. Who could say no to an invitation like that?"

I rushed off, although I could easily have taken the six forty-
seven and still made it home in time for dinner.

I drove my little battered station car back to the house as usual.
I'm sure the neighbors looked down on my ten-year-old Stude-
baker Hawk with the vestigial tail fins just as they abhorred our
weed-filled lawns, fetid pond, garbage mulch. Of course, I was a
hundred percent committed to letting nature engulf our grounds,

though I recognized the burden we'd placed on our children's frail shoulders. The neighbor kids shunned them as weirdos, and that cute, hateful Mary Beth next door would sing, "Shame, shame," while stroking one index finger on the other. My poor little Margaret came home in tears every time.

When I entered the front door, the kids made a rush for me, grabbing my legs and calling out, "Daddy, Daddy!" Baby Palmer didn't look too sure what a daddy might be, though he was enthusiastic about the idea. He was always shaking his pudgy hands in the air, stepping awkwardly and drooling. I felt like the hunter who's brought home a bloody Bambi to hack apart and parcel out to his greedy tribe. I loved their excitement, even if their mother had put them up to it.

Alex came up to me in her soft, distracted way and without a word presented me with her sculpted cheek. I put an arm around her waist—but gently, gently. Alex had become so fragile that I was afraid of breaking one of her ribs. I was proud of her slenderness when I compared her to the neighbors, women as plump and ponderous as Clydesdale mares, yet I feared the slightest wind could blow her away.

I doubted she even bothered to eat during the day. At night she drank two large vodka martinis straight up and well chilled, with a twist, then played with her dinner. Tonight it was vegetarian moussaka, extremely healthy like everything we ate. Alex's moussaka almost tasted like real food. In the city, I cheated at lunchtime. I ate a secret steak or, my favorite, liver and bacon with greasy onions.

Often Alex could taste the carnage on my lips and would say, "It's your life."

Our house had been built by a Finnish architect in the thirties, and the walls were curving horizontal blond boards, highly varnished, steamed and bent into nautical shapes, not a sharp corner anywhere, and lots of original Barcelona chairs, which all needed their leather straps tightened a notch. The windows were small rectangles placed high, like squashed portholes. Alex was playing an LP of *Finlandia*. I guess she was in a Finnish mood. Margaret was in a Marimekko dress.

The French au pair girl, Ghislaine, who was not supposed to smoke but always smelled of Gitanes, came in to scoop up her charges, a tilted smile scarcely rhyming with her sad eyes. I couldn't help looking at her firm, ample hips rolling under her dress, but I immediately glanced away. She refused to eat just Alex's vegetarian dishes. Every other dinner was some savory recipe she prepared for herself—shrimp curry or a chicken breast in a cream-and-calvados sauce.

"You'll never guess who I ran into today," I said.

"Herr Pogner?" Alex asked, naming her old piano teacher.

"No. Jack. Jack Holmes."

Alex broke into a big smile, but something guarded instantly came into her eyes, as if she were seeing a favorite dog that had once bitten her. "How did he look?"

"Very sleek," I said. "He's even thinner, and his clothes were very conservative and nice—believe it or not, even his shoes. He had on some Peel shoes."

"Copying you, I guess. Is he terribly prosperous?"

"I don't really know. He's working for *Newsweek* in the business section."

"I guess they get good investment tips," she said, looking skeptically at a dark bit of eggplant on the end of her fork. "Did he ask about me?"

"Yes, right away. I told him about Larchmont and the children. He seemed most impressed by the size of our property."

"I hope you didn't scare him off by talking about our reversion to nature."

"I did mention it. I was in search of neutral topics."

"Neutral! I'm afraid it makes us sound terribly controversial."
She smiled with her old love of combat. "He was my friend, but
I guess it was you he was in love with. Did you see more signs of
unrequited passion?"

"Oh Alex, I wouldn't notice something like that."

She rang the little bell next to her, and Emily, the cook, came in
to clear. Emily was a comfortable middle-aged woman who felt
like an aunt; she didn't wear a uniform, and she made no fuss over
how she served.

"You're too macho to recognize if another man loves you?"

Her saying that in front of staff made me wince.

I rubbed my forehead and brought my hand down over my
eyes and said, "Gosh, I'm tired."

I remembered always fearing that other people would see me
with Jack and think I was queer. We could have a quick lunch
together, and that was okay, but dinner—a quiet dinner between two men—was definitely wandering into the pink zone.
Maybe it had to do with the way I was raised, but I was always
afraid of lingering over a theater review or even admitting I wrote
fiction. I suppose if my third-form English master at Portsmouth
Abbey hadn't praised my writing, I would never have taken
fiction up. But he was also the football coach. I didn't want to
arouse suspicions of any sort; I didn't want to be "unusual." I
preferred to be invisible. I'm a born observer, or want to be, and
good observers are always invisible, in my opinion. Eventually
it had seemed elegantly masculine to be a writer, like Fitzgerald, though I laid off the booze. All those writers back then—
Hemingway and Dashiell Hammett—were drunks. And macho.

"So what else did he say?" Alex asked, drumming her fine hands on the tabletop. It was a game with her, this insistence, but I liked it. I preferred it to the recent bouts of melancholy that swept over her most evenings. Alex's melancholy, fleeting as it might be, took all her energy—hers and mine. I could see that if I invited Jack out here (but would he ever come?), it would give Alex something to focus on rather than treating a sick groundhog or exploring the moral dilemma of hurting basement mold.

We went into the living room, which had a Finnish couch designed by Saarinen and a thick woven rug, extended like a flap on the floor, that could be pulled up over one's knees against the polar cold. We sat on the couch together and left the rug on the floor. I made us each a sidecar, since Jack had mentioned it and I was curious. I found the recipe in my bar guide.

Alex said, "This could trigger a full-scale diabetic attack." We were looking up at the windows, against which leafless bushes were pressed like beggars outside a church. Alex drank her side-car, which astonished me, since she never had anything else beyond her two vodka martinis and one glass of wine. I poured out a second one for her. "Too watery?" I asked.

"No, perfect," she said. "It's the lemon I like."

We talked about Jack late into the night. She was unusually gleeful, almost as if she'd fallen asleep for a hundred years and awoken hungry. Alex was always available to me and the children, abundantly so, but too often she was afraid to go out. Emily, in fact, had started to order the groceries and have them delivered, though on weekends Alex would accompany me to the yacht club if I drove. She was still a beautiful woman with her lustrous hair and exquisite features and her dramatically slender body, but when older couples (most of our club's members were at least twenty years older than us) came by to exchange a few bibulous words, she had a tight, rat-a-tat way of gasping, "Yes, yes, really, absolutely, yes," in reply, and when they'd gone off she'd say to me, "Extraordinary what passes for conversation out here." It made her irritable and angry that other people would just naturally assume she wanted to talk about fertilizers and insecticides.

"Don't they know that I'm not in favor of anything that ends in "cide"? Fratricide? Herbicide? Fungicide?"

We'd gradually worked our way through most of the smart set in the vicinity. The problem was the women, who had a way of assuming aloud that we hadn't noticed what was happening to our garden. Mrs. Callisher would write out on a slip of paper the name of her gardener. If we tried to sit out in the gazebo with them and drink our cocktails, the ladies would slap mosquitoes and say, "Couldn't we at least put out a torch? Funny, we don't have mosquitoes." And once when we walked past the seething, scummy pond, Mrs. Erlich wrinkled her little nose and said, "No swans? But you know they just love to gobble down mosquitoes." Alex couldn't let such remarks slip by.

I might have been tempted to say something pacifying, but she was ever alert to the first sign of insult or betrayal on my part. Of course, she enjoyed making a great game of it, yet she was capable of calling out, "Traitor! Horrible traitor!" with an ambiguously icy smile.

Ghislaine brought in the children all fragrant and rosy from their bath.

Palmer was warm and smiling in his pajamas, and for the first time I saw a glint of red in his brown hair, and I wondered what genetic vagary had produced it.

"Da!" he said, glancing up, searching for words, but then, when we all looked at him, he lost his nerve and giggled and tried to

wriggle around in Ghislaine's arms. I thought what a lucky little bastard he was pressing his face into her breasts.

My Margaret, sober and reproachful, held a book she wanted
her mommy to read her, but I said to her, "You can read perfectly well, Peg. Mommy and Daddy are having an important
talk. Read your book for half an hour, then turn off your light
because you have a big day tomorrow, dressage—"

"And jazz dancing at two," Alex chimed in. "Angel, don't
plague Mummy now." And I thought that I'd have hated a mother
who called herself "Mummy."

When we were alone again, we ended by pulling the heavy
Saarinen rug over our knees. We drank a second batch of sidecars. Alex reminded me that we'd both have dreadful hangovers, though she seemed to have shed her melancholy. I'd heard
someone at the office say of a friend that he was "clinically depressed," and I sometimes wondered if this applied to Alex too.

I turned on the standing floor lamp made of thin cedar
slats, and the light it cast warmed the room up as if it were one
of those old tile corner stoves you find in Austria. Outside, a
feral cat, puffed up and suddenly four feet long, tiptoed to the
sliding glass door and looked in at us with tawny eyes and made
a horrible screech, leading Alex to say, like the headmistress of
a girls' school, "Language, ladies. Language!" and we laughed
harder than we had in months—and this unaccustomed sound
must have frightened Margaret, who came creeping up to the
threshold, sucking her thumb and asking, "Mummy? What's
wrong?"

Alex turned and looked at her in a stunned way. I wondered
if Peggy had ever seen her mother drunk before. "Nothing is
wrong, my angel," she said. "Mummy and Daddy are having a
playdate."

"Can grown-ups play?"

"They certainly can, can't they, Daddy?"

I mumbled in affectionate agreement. I hated it when my wife called me Daddy. In sex, all right, but not in front of the children.

Margaret lowered her head and looked up through her eyebrows at these two strangers, her parents.

At the mention of "playdate" I'd felt a stirring in my groin, and now I stood and turned my back to Alex and adjusted myself. Ever since little Palmer had started having asthma attacks in the middle of the night, we'd been keeping him in the room next to ours, and we were always listening for his gasps. When they came, violently and unpredictably, neither of us could ever fall back into very deep sleep. Of course, it was hell on our sex life, which I'd about given up on—though tonight, with sidecars and Alex's enthusiasm over our renewed contact with Jack, I sensed she was feeling expansive, maybe amorous.

Once Margaret had been sent off, still sucking her thumb (despite Ghislaine's warning that she'd get buckteeth, *dents de lapin*, that way), I said that we should go up to my study and listen to a new record I'd just bought. Alex nodded and put her arm around my waist.

Upstairs we sat on the long leather couch, and I served us each a glass of cold seltzer water from the little fridge. We made our way through the LP without talking, Alex rhythmically advancing her chin in some curious Watusi way, the deb's idea of how to get in the groove. It was some pop music that I despised but that I knew would please Alex.

I'd closed the heavy door to my study, blocking out the sounds from the rest of the house. Ghislaine was still awake monitoring Palmer's breathing. I'd succumbed to my usual resentment of

Alex's nature worship, since surely a dusty, wild garden full of plant pollen and animal dander wasn't recommended for an asthmatic child, but that last sidecar had helped me to bank the fires of irritation.

I'd turned on one dim light, and we began to kiss in earnest. I undid Alex's Corfam belt—never leather!—and tugged her shantung trousers open. There was a creaking up above—a raccoon? a man on the roof? We also had a rule that there would be no locks on doors anywhere in the house, but this time, determined, I jumped up and propped a chair against the door to ensure our privacy.

It had been so long since I'd made love to Alex, I wasn't entirely sure I wanted to. Of course, men, especially workingmen, the ones I'd known during summer jobs back in college, were constantly complaining that they didn't get enough pussy. They pretended that all they liked was to eat pussy. That was the running gag all summer as I was loading trucks in Raleigh. Blacks and whites—they had that one thing in common. "Will, you still pumping that ol' dick in that ol' cooze? The bitches don't like that shit, they think that's bogue. They want you to have some good eats. You got to get down there and eat out that pussy. Watch my tongue. They want it flickin'. Just think you's the devil-serpent himself, flickin' into Eve's sweet little pussy, that weren't no apple. Or think you're an eel sliding into a nice little clamshell. Just open it up—see, watch my tongue, flickin'-like." They would fall down with laughter at me and my queasy smile as they went into a chorus of "Sh-sh." They got out that first consonant sound, the susurrus both a general assent and a way for each man to declare his distance—"What's this shit? These guys are too. Fucking. Much."

Oddly, I wondered if Jack would have thought it was a

turn-on, all those real guys slapping each other on the back and bragging about their oral sex skills.

And I held Alex's face between my hands and kissed her lips gently, gently.

Over the years I'd learned how to curb my appetites and bathe every horny move in romance, as if it were a gear shifting in a reservoir of oil. I whispered her name in her ear. It had been so long, but I remembered she liked this, and she did breathe faster and she arched her back. Slowly, thoughtfully, I undid the buttons of her blouse as if patiently meditating on home truths. I lifted her blouse off and with a practiced hand squeezed together the hooks of her bra. Her lovely breasts, released from so much expensive uplift, tumbled warmly into my hands. I rubbed my grizzly face against them and she said, "Oh Will," and I knew I was home free.

We'd gone so long without sex that our reciprocal forms of timidity, I feared, had nearly paralyzed us. When, bored at work, I thought of Alex, I would remember her pain during childbirth, the guilt I'd felt about imposing that pain upon her, and I would remember our many vigils beside Palmer's bed as he gasped and turned blue and we reached for the inhaler and prayed. After that first attack we'd banned animals from the house and had an exterminator in to make sure there were no cockroaches, since research suggested they could trigger asthma somehow. But I'd found no way to convince Alex to control the garden; its wildness had taken on an Edenic significance for her.

Now I had her down to her panties with my finger inside her. Unhelpfully, the record had come to an end, and I was afraid the silence would sober her up or set her to listening for distant gasps.

I was fumbling around in my mind for some blessed isle, sun-swept and tropical, in the cold sea of so many calculations and fears and memories. I needed to meet her as one brown body to another on a white sand beach.

And then she opened her legs a fraction and closed her eyes and touched her breast, and I could feel myself getting harder.

When it was all over and we were back in our bedroom, Alex nibbled my ear and whispered that she was glad we'd fulfilled our conjugal duties. That was how she put it and we both laughed. We talked about taking a vacation, just the two of us, in the Bahamas, where she'd often traveled as a girl. Just as we were drifting off, Alex brought up Jack's name, and I asked, "Were you ever in love with him?"

"No, right away I found out he was homosexual," she said. "It was like he'd entered a whole new category."

"Sister?"

"There's nothing feminine about Jack . . . that I know of. No, he's more like a little brother who's unhappy. Or ill. An unhappy little brother who's convalescing."

"But before that, before you knew?"

Alex yawned and placed her warm cheek on my chest and an arm around my waist. "Will, how flattering. I do think you might be a little bit jealous."

"Answer!"

"He is sexy. But you—I found you so maddening that I knew right away I was falling for you. Besides, even though you're an old Catholic and a foxhunter, I figured out we were cast from the same mold. Not that Jack isn't perfectly *sortable*, but—"

"You're babbling," I said, impatient with her constant gallicisms. "Go to sleep."

And she did, still twitching with little social smiles and a deprecating lifting of her eyebrows.

The next morning she fluttered about the children, preparing my macrobiotic snack for work (seaweed, pickled radish, and a clump of cold brown rice), but suddenly she cast me a long mauve look and blushed, and I could see she was thinking of last night. Even Ghislaine looked a little less voluptuous moving about under her dress.

What struck me was that all of this sensuality had been declared under the banner of Jack's reentry into our life. Was he a lord of misrule capable of spreading vice and excitement as he rode his pard and smeared grapes across his face? Or was Alex just lonely, isolated in the ever-shrinking corner she was painting herself into, the lunatic of Laurel Lane?

I invited Jack out to Larchmont the following Saturday. I told him when and where the train departed from Grand Central, but I also offered to drive in and chauffeur him to and fro. I knew how cowardly New Yorkers could be about venturing into exurbia. But Jack accepted readily enough and asked if he could bring a woman friend along.

"Sure," I said, flummoxed for a second by this complication.

In a nice recovery I added, "Warn her that we're major back-to-nature loons and the house is foundering in its own ooze. And tell her that everything on her kiln-fired dish will be arranged according to its yangness."

Jack's friend was called Pia, and I guessed she was Italian, though she had no accent. She had long straight hair through which the tips of her pale ears peeped, and she smelled nicely of vanilla—almost as if she'd dabbed her wrists with pure vanilla extract, the way the maids would do back in Virginia before church. She had a small Cupid's bow mouth and dramatic blue eyes that seemed strangely flat and swimming. When she smiled, her lip would curl up at one corner to reveal her eyetooth, and her huge eyes would swim from one side to the other. She had a small, straight nose and a ready laugh, though usually she didn't seem to have quite caught the joke. Her breasts looked as if they'd been very small and high in adolescence but were filling out nicely in the fullness of time. I was taken by her, but I hid it by looking at Jack most of the time and treating Alex with extra attention, almost as if she were a convalescent.

We had two martinis each in the blond bentwood living room seated on the sagging Barcelona chairs. It was early February, so there was nothing to tempt us outside for long, though we did make a quick circuit around the dolphin fountain and the sundial and past the overgrown path down to the frozen pool. Luckily everything was dead for the winter, and we weren't confronted by anything too feral and scary. It was getting dark. I'd built a fire inside, and it looked good after the desolation of the garden.

Ghislaine brought in the children, who made the rounds and kissed the four adults on each cheek. "Enchanting," Pia whispered, smiling at Alex with complicity.

Of course, Pia was the enchantment I was staring at in the short bursts of attention I'd permit myself.

Alex was absorbed by Jack. She was leaping up and kissing him on the forehead every other minute, and I thought, Idea for story: a straight man pretends to be gay so husbands will trust him with their wives. Then I remembered I'd accused Jack of employing that strategy years ago, when he'd first met Alex. She held his hands and leaned back and said, "Let me look at you! You're thinner."

"So are you."

"You have more character in your face."

"Lines. I'm more lined. Whereas you—"

"Lines."

"Not at all. You look even younger. How amazing you've kept your figure after two babies."

She laughed and said, "Luckily for you I'm dressed. You wouldn't believe my battle-scarred body. A real horror show."

Pia said, "I love your house. It's enchanting."

The dinner wasn't too horrible. It was roasted root vegetables with a tahini sauce. There was lots of sugary California red wine, which Pia treated as a complete novelty, albeit an enchanting one. For dessert there was a compote of dried fruit cooked in sherry with a cinnamon stick.

"You guys are very back-to-nature, huh?" Jack asked boisterously. "You make me feel sooty and urban, like an old fluorescent light tube."

We all laughed. I wondered if they were planning to spend the night or take the late train back. If they stayed, would I get a chance to tuck Pia in? I sort of resented Jack for inadvertently casting this temptation in my path, or was he actively trying to test our marriage, which was complete with adorable children and conspicuous mosses on the old manse?

At a certain point Jack said, "How did you guys ever get the money together to buy this place? Twenty-five acres in Larchmont! That must have cost a cool million."

I sipped my iced Kahlua and said, "What's that Robert Frost poem, 'Provide, Provide'?"

But Jack couldn't hear my discreet warning, or in any event he refused to back off.

"No," he kept on, "I mean, who paid for this layout?"

Alex said with elegant simplicity, "My father. Didn't you know he was rich? Remember how I used to collect Ching vases?"

"Yeah. I do," Jack conceded. "So what?"

"Those things don't come cheap. How many girls do you know with a whole breakfront stuffed with Ch'ien-lung?"

"That was awfully nice of your dad," Jack said, but the conversation left me feeling bruised, and I wondered if that had been Jack's intention. Had Jack just assumed I couldn't have paid for the place? He wasn't done yet. "You never did say, Will, what you do for a living now."

"I write annual reports for corporations. They're too paralyzed by bureaucracy to write them for themselves, so I have a freelance business—"

"But what are they?" Pia asked, sounding fastidious, as if she'd found a mouse paw in the compote.

Before I could answer, Jack said, "They're these glossy pamphlets sent to the stockholders explaining why the company's losses are a good thing. I get them at *Newsweek* all the time. The law forces companies to make a full disclosure, but these four-color photos and carefully worded bromides are designed to throw dust in everyone's eyes."

Alex, the little traitor, laughed the loudest and said, "Is that what you do, Will? I never really understood till now. It's all a big deception?"

Still trying to be jaunty, I asked, "How else do you think I pay for all the dried apricots and cinnamon sticks we consume?"

Pia said, "No one in my family works and they never have, unless collecting rents can be called work. Oh: or making wine."

"Where is your family from?" Alex asked.

"Chianti," Pia said. "I love hearing about the jobs real people have in America."

"You have no accent," I said. "Were you educated in the States?"

"Yes," Pia said, "at Smith."

"Smith?" Alex exclaimed. "I wanted to go there, but I was too dumb to get in, so I went to Cornell."

They talked about their schools and then about Tuscany and how enchanting it was. Pia confessed that her mother was American and she'd grown up bilingual. I was dying to ask her what her enchanting little American forebears had done for money.

Alex grabbed Jack's hand and said, "But this is such fun! Can't you stay over? We can give you adjoining bedrooms and even new toothbrushes, and we can have a wonderful brunch in the morning and smoke Gitanes. Please say you will!"

I was still smarting from the revelation about who'd paid for our house and how mendacious and pointless my job was, but Pia looked ever more enchanting now that her little ears were standing completely clear of her straight hair and she was speaking a bit less guardedly with that rough alto cast to her voice. She was friendly and sweet, and she knew how to smile encouragingly at a man and nod him into affirmation.

Pia said, "But you must have a very charged day tomorrow with the children, I can imagine, and maybe it would be best, Jack . . ." But she didn't finish the sentence. She was too much of a real woman to impose her will on Jack. I thought it was such a phony foreignism to say "charged" instead of "full" or "crowded," but at the same time I didn't care. I was completely under Pia's spell. I almost pitied her for wanting to be interesting since we weren't.

"Yes, Will," Jack said, "if you could drive us to the station, we could make the eleven ten. Next time! We'll spend the night the next time." He looked at Alex fondly, saying, "Remember how you used to wear that red silk—what do you call them?—hostess gown? I thought you were the height of sophistication."

Alex socked him in the arm. "And now? You cad!"

When I came back from the station, Alex was very excited and running around the house. She was listening to a Mozart sonata LP very softly because she'd read that Mozart helped you digest.

"That was such fun!" she said, and she kissed me on the cheek timidly and awkwardly, since that was a demonstration she never made, not just like that, swooping down out of nowhere; a peck. She didn't peck. Though come to think of it, she'd been pecking Jack all evening.

"Yes. So do you think Jack has changed?" I asked.

I was wondering if she would want to have sex after our revelries of the week before; I was wondering whether I would. Part of me longed to sleep in a different room, pretend I had a cold, so I could jerk off thinking about Pia.

Alex said, "He's more sure of himself, don't you think? I wonder why he brought that girl out here with her not-quite-convincing continental ways—anyway, Jack doesn't like girls, does he? And Jack used to say he was just an ordinary Midwesterner, but why is he always escorting these social tarts around? I think secretly he's a snob."

"You sound jealous."

Alex started to protest. In fact, the vein on her forehead was throbbing visibly as it did when she was about to blow a gasket—but then she caught herself and smiled. That was her most endearing quality, this trick of catching herself in mid-mood.

"You're right," she said. "I guess I want to be his only friend."

In bed we talked more about Jack for a while.

"And Pia," she said. "Does that mean 'pious' in Italian? Isn't that Ingrid Bergman's daughter's name?"

I said, "I suppose it's just another Italian name, but it does sound awfully tacky and Sicilian."

"Yes," Alex said, "but Pia was Ingrid Bergman's legitimate child—the Swedish one."

I said, "I thought she was pleasant and pretty."

"Oh-ho!" Alex said, sitting up in bed then as if she were a detective and she'd just uncovered a clue. She subsided back and said, in a high voice, really the voice of Palmer, "Why did Jack drop you? All those years ago? I mean, I know you said it was because you rebuffed his advances, but was that—"

"Rebuffed his advances? God, Alex, you make me sound like a Victorian prude. Anyway, I dropped him."

She was in her white silk pajamas without a collar, and she looked as luminous as a sad Picasso child.

"You dropped him? Why? I never dared ask you for the details."

I laughed quietly and turned off the light.

"Keep the light on. I like to look at you when you're lying."

"Yes, my dear, but we're in bed to sleep."

"But you still haven't told me."

"After we'd talked it over again and again, his obsession with me, and I thought everything was settled, I was in the crapper at work reading the paper, and suddenly, for no reason, I looked up, which no one ever does, and there was Jack above the partition, looking down at me."

"How could he be—"

"He was obviously standing on the toilet seat in the adjoining stall and getting his jollies by looking down at my crotch."

"Astounding! He was masturbating? How did that make you feel?"

"Not good." And I thought about what I'd felt. "Like a

sex object. Feminists are always whimpering about being objectified—"

"Will, I'm a feminist."

"So am I," I said, deflating her objection. "I mean, you have a friend, and he's read your book and shared your shitty review and knows you're in love with Alex, and you've gotten drunk together, and talked about God, and death, and art—and then you catch him looking at your dick over the crapper-stall wall, and this guy is supposed to be your buddy . . ."

"Not very elegant, I admit."

"It's not just inelegant, it's a betrayal. It's why regular guys don't like fags—they're always trying to sneak a feel or stare at you in the locker room. I've never had that many buddies, not really close ones, but I can see the point of buddies—you're just two guys standing side by side looking out at the world. But if the other guy is on the make in whatever way, it doesn't matter which way—for instance, if he wants to get into your club or hobnob with your friends or get you to buy insurance—then the whole thing is off."

"Disinterested as the saints."

"What?"

Alex could be irritating with her cryptic remarks.

"You expect friends to be disinterested," she said. "To have no hidden motives."

"Don't you?"

"I suppose that's another way we're alike—I don't have many friends," she said.

"Men friends. You have men friends."

"Oh well, before my marriage. You're my friend. Our children are my friends. Animals are my friends."

"Anyway, you don't want to have your best buddy suddenly

leering at your privates in the middle of the day. At work. He didn't even have the good grace to tackle me drunk and late at night."

"But he didn't tackle you, Will. He was hoping you'd never notice." She sighed and turned on her side toward me and stroked my face with the back of her hand. "It's really rather sweet, Jack lusting after you, so hopeless since you like women."

"It's true I've always liked women, admired them. Men just don't interest me."

"But maybe," Alex said, yawning, "that's why you like Jack. Because he was always accommodating himself to you. Yearning for you, just as a woman might—I'm not saying he's effeminate. There's nothing effeminate about Jack Holmes."

"That makes it sound as if I only want to be adored."

"Then put it this way. An ordinary heterosexual man wouldn't make a huge, huge effort to become friends with you, and you certainly wouldn't try. When boys are teenagers it's easy, being on the same sports team or in the same eating club, but after that . . ."

"So you think I can only be friends with a fag?"

"I don't like that word, Will. It's like 'nigger' or 'Yid.' Really, it is. But yes, you need someone to make all the effort because you're off on your own cloud."

"I'm too shy." I could admit I was shy.

"So what happened that day? Did you shake your fist up at Jack?"

"The awful thing is that the crapper scene happened after I got my horrible *Times* review, after we got drunk together and I gave him a hug for a moment—"

"You what!"

"Remember how bummed out—"

"You held him?"

"Yes, he had me to dinner that night the review—"

"Well, then, of course he thinks he can take liberties with you, if you held him."

I was suddenly angry at Alex's screwy reasoning.

She said, "Stop smoldering, Will."

She rubbed her delicate fingertips into her temples, some sort of yoga trick she did when she was tensing up.

I started again, in such a low, soft voice that she glanced at me in puzzlement. "I was being nice to him, Alex. I knew that would make his day, and besides, he'd been very kind to me."

She got up and stuck a finger into the plant on the sill, I suppose to see if it needed water. Then she went into the bathroom to wash her hands and—yes, she was brushing her hair again in that maddeningly vigorous way of hers.

When she returned she said, "Anyway, tonight was a wonderful evening, and I'm glad we're friends with Jack again— and of course you were a giant sweetie to hold him that one time. I was just startled: it's so out of character. But it's to be encouraged, dear."

I just wanted to sleep now. Alex had this way of reacting priggishly at first to something, then doing an about-face and endorsing it, especially if doing so made her look broad-minded. She'd object to taking ghetto kids into our Larchmont Country Day, and then she'd campaign for it while quietly transferring our own children to the local Montessori, saying it was because she liked their "philosophy of education" more. She always wanted to look liberal, since in her own mind she was on the barricades as Miss Liberty, the bare-breasted one, in that French painting.

As I started to doze off, I thought about Pia, and for some

reason I pictured her very tan in Capri, wriggling out of her swimsuit and revealing two milk white globes fore and two aft.

I wondered again if Jack was up to some mischief, bringing that woman into our house. After all, he'd introduced me to Alex. Now did he think it was time for me to have a mistress? Would he be watching me and Pia over the partition of the crapper?

Idea for novel: queer finds mistress for beloved straight man.

I was tempted to get out of bed and jot it down at the risk of disturbing Alex's very light sleep. But then I realized I could never tackle that subject. A married man can't write autobiographical novels, not if they're based on the truth.

A WEEK LATER Jack called me at the office and invited me to dinner. He said Pia was coming and some Italian friends of hers—it was a last-minute thing for that very evening, otherwise he would have insisted that Alex come in. He was going to call her before long anyway and lure her into town for a leisurely lunch.

We talked long enough for a worry to hatch in my brain. I lowered my voice and said, "Jack? Do me a favor? When you talk to Alex, say it was just the two of us—would that be okay? She gets jealous so easily."

I called Alex and told her that I had to work late and that then, if possible, I might grab a bite with Jack——and that I was going to stay over at the Princeton Club.

"But you don't even have a toothbrush or a clean shirt," Alex objected.

"My girl has already run over to the Brothers," I said, warbling the "Brothers," as I always did to get a laugh out of her. But this time she didn't recall the witticism, if that's what it was. It was just a silly way of saying the name.

"The what?"

"Brooks Brothers. She bought me some hose and boxers and a shirt and picked up some toiletries at the drugstore."

"Well, all right, then," Alex said dubiously.

Was she envious or jealous? Was she reluctant to share Jack with me, or worried I might hold him again? Or did she fear that I might meet up with Pia and hold her?

"Have fun," she said with sudden briskness, "and if you think of it, call me before you go to sleep."

I promised I would. I knew calling her wasn't as optional as she made it sound.

Jack wanted to meet at a place in Midtown called the Monkey Bar and then eat a steak somewhere. While I was waiting for him, I listened to a new song, "Treat Her like a Lady," and it made me smile though I hated pop music. Then I thought about how half the fun of straight life, normal life, was the difference between men and women. It was fun to treat a woman like a lady, buy her things, pay for her, protect her—and women, if they were smart, treated a man like a man, and not necessarily like a gentleman. Poor gay men, who didn't have anything like those reciprocal roles. They didn't have partners who wore diamond earrings and bracelets and needed to be zipped up and led across the dance floor in a gown. Their partners didn't touch expensive perfume to pulse points or wear nylons and garter belts. When Jack arrived, I asked him what he thought about all this.

He said, "We idealize some men—the boy next door, the athlete, the golden boy—but we make them into something we wish we'd been, whereas you don't want to be a lady."

"No," I said, nodding and smiling, "we don't."

"Of course, there are gay transvestites," Jack said.

"Yeah," I said, "but you still have the problem of the hairy butthole. After I pulled off all of those silky nothings, if I was faced with an asshole black with hair—sorry! That would make me lose it." I told him how much I liked the song.

He said, "I'm not sure you understand that song."

"Really?"

"It's about how you can fuck lots of women if you treat them like ladies, if you open doors for them and pay for things. It's about seducing women, not about liking them."

I preferred my own interpretation even if it was wrong.

Jack smiled and said, "Do you like this bar?"

"I sure do. I never knew it was here. Look, there's Pia!"

I thought that even if her asshole were Armenian with hair, I'd want to lie down with her.

After we'd settled in and chitchatted about the pneumatic drills tearing up Fifty-sixth Street, Jack suddenly said, "Will thinks two gay men are too similar to have much fun."

I blushed—I could feel my face heating up—but I said, "I was listening to that song 'Treat Her like a Lady,' and I was thinking there'd be no thrill in treating a guy like a guy."

"Women like to treat a guy like a guy," Pia said, with a slow, sweet smile, looking ecumenically back and forth between Jack and me.

I thought, If we had an affair, what would be in it for her? I asked, "What is it that women like to do for guys, precisely?"

A man at the next table kept saying "fortunately" over and over again, and for some reason that made me remember choir practice and the priest striking a tuning fork and holding it up to give us our pitch. I held the fork once, and it felt cold and surprisingly heavy in my hand.

"I can't speak for all women," Pia said, "but my idea of feminism is that women should help men into their coats. Light their cigarettes. Not all the time but often, you know?"

I thought that sounded like a pretty dim idea of feminism. I could just hear Alex snorting with outrage. But who was I to question such mild militancy?

Jack had moved into a bigger apartment not far from the Monkey Bar, and he invited us over for a cold supper. He'd made a whole salmon with a dill mayonnaise, and he started us out with a vichyssoise soup, which Pia claimed was an American invention and not at all French, despite the name.

"Look at this goddamned terrace!" I said, walking out onto it.

"Yes," Jack said, "I was lucky to find this tiny penthouse. It's just two rooms. But it has the terrace, and I'm going to put trees in tubs out here in another two or three weeks, when it finally warms up."

"Did you have all these drawers and doors mirrored?" Pia asked. It seemed she'd never been here before. Which meant that Jack had invited her just for my sake.

"Yes," he said, "I found a real craftsman." Though he'd mentioned Italian friends of Pia's, I noticed there were just three place settings.

As Jack was warming up a baguette in the oven, Pia stepped out onto the terrace and I joined her; like me she was gripping the rail and bending over slightly to look down. There wasn't much to see except a car nosing down Sixty-sixth and over to the right a water tower positioned on top of a lower building. I was intensely aware of Pia's body, and I was tempted to scoot closer and touch hips. The more romantic thing would be to touch her hand. We could check in to a hotel together—the Plaza, maybe. Except we might see people we knew there. Better a smaller hotel with less traffic, more tourists.

Just then she turned and leaned with her back against the rail, crossing her arms. "Did you see the first forsythia today?"

"Yes, coming in on the train. A promise of spring, though a pretty feeble one." I thought, I'm supposed to be a writer and talk like that.

"Let's look at the other side of the terrace." And she started to walk toward it, turning her head to smile back at me. She's moving us out of Jack's view so I can kiss her, I thought. If we do go to a hotel, shall I use my real name and make it Mr. and Mrs. Wright? I might have to use a credit card—it would have to match.

As I looked at her in the softer light of the southern terrace, I thought, She really is beautiful! That small perfect nose like baked bisque and that low voice full of laughter though she's not a funny person and then those ears peeking out through her straight hair and those big flat eyes constantly moving. Her mouth seemed tiny—and suddenly it dawned on me that she was a Major Beauty, that she could be a movie star or a model, and I wondered why it had taken me so long to wake up to her star power. I'd seen right off in Larchmont that she was attractive, but that her beauty could be considered mythic had come to me slowly, almost as if I'd needed to talk myself into it or hear someone else exclaim over it and Jack hadn't. Jack had played everything very low-key.

Was Jack a sort of Iago hoping to make me—no, that didn't make sense. I wasn't any sort of Othello. Did he want Pia to sleep with me and then give him all the details later? Tell him if I was a good fuck? I wasn't sure if I was good in bed. We weren't like homos, learning technique from each other. And I was so inexperienced with women, and Alex was so romantic that she'd never wanted to break the spell by saying, "More to the left," or "Harder," or "Slower." I wasn't sure I could picture Pia telling Jack, "It's small to medium, gets nice and hard, like a blackjack, and he's better than most white guys at cunnilingus. His feet smell like an attic that's never been aired." Hell, she was too kind to tattle.

I touched her hand, and she looked at me with her slight avatar of a smile and her large, flat eyes, endlessly swimming. She had a trick of bowing her head so she could glance up at me. I was so afraid I'd mistaken her friendliness for flirtation that I scarcely knew what to do now, so I put my hands on her elbows and pulled her toward me and kissed her on the forehead. I said, "This terrace demands a kiss, even an avuncular one."

She said, with her slow, lopsided smile, and in her low voice, "It certainly does. Let's see if Jack needs any help." She took my hand and led me back in as if we were little friends.

As it turned out, I was at the Princeton Club by an early hour and able to call Alex with a clear conscience. The next day I phoned Jack from the office to thank him and to feel around about what Pia thought about me.

Jack said, "You like her."

"Why do you say that?" I swallowed. "Yes, very much."

"She's a great kid," he said, and I thought that for him she was probably nothing more than a kid, that he hadn't noticed her small mouth and her big, full breasts, that he'd not seen her hips sliding under that skirt as she walked ahead of us, hips that begged to be grabbed. To him she was like a car to a nondriver, but to me she promised the open road. But then I remembered Jack always noticed sexual details in both men and women.

"Yeah," I said, "a great kid." In his mouth the words had sounded breezy; in mine, tragic.

Then he said, "But wouldn't Alex be pissed if you flirted with her?" Was he taunting me or was he really innocent, the possibility of a flirtation only an afterthought for him instead of at the very heart of his dark design?

I laughed and said, "She would be, but luckily it was all just playful, just something to get the old blood flowing." Jack had once made fun of my "imperturbable jauntiness." I guessed this was a case in point. "I told her it was just the two of us. But did . . . Pia say anything about me?" I hated sounding pathetic.

"She thinks you're very nice," Jack said with maddening sunniness.

I waited for him to go on, then said in a low growl, "Details, details!"

"I don't think she said anything else."

I was so shocked that I blurted out, "What on earth do you two talk about?"

Jack laughed insultingly, then added after a pause, "Is that a serious question?"

"Yes," I gurgled nearly inaudibly.

"My apartment. She's helped me a lot, though last night was the first time she'd seen it. She was the one who got the Indian print pillows, and she has an expert framer, pricey."

"Okay, okay, very funny," I said. "When you invited us together, did you consult with her first? And wasn't she coming with friends?"

"I'm not a matchmaker, Will." He went very quiet, then said, as if it were a brand-new idea, "Do you want me to set you up with Pia?"

I should have just gasped "Yes," but I became pointlessly cagey: "How would you do that, Jack?"

"I could make a date with both of you and then call the

restaurant to say I couldn't make it, and then you'd be on your own with her."

"Not *too* swift," I said admiringly.

"So should I do it?" he asked.

I was grateful to him but also suspicious. And I resented the way he was pressuring me. "Let me think it over," I said.

He responded with a dubious, mocking little murmur, though I might have imagined the mockery.

On the way home that night I bought Alex a perfect white-jade Buddha at C. T. Loo's on Fifty-seventh Street, which set me back five hundred dollars. She was flabbergasted and oddly worried, since I hadn't given her anything that extravagant in years. "But Will," she said, standing so close that her eyes kept shifting back and forth from my right eye to my left. "What a dream angel you are," she said tonelessly.

"You're my dream angel," I whispered into her ear. "I was thinking about you all day," I lied, "and I remembered that Jack used to visit Loo and almost worked for him and that his gallery was on Fifty-seventh and Madison on some high-up floor, and I found it easily, and of course everything was out of my range, but this Buddha seemed so perfect and it's eighteenth century, which is kind of your period, isn't it?"

"It's ex-quisite," she said, with the emphasis on the "ex," which her mother had taught her.

She was happy now that she'd overcome her fear that something was seriously wrong. I could see that she'd been waiting for me to deliver the terrible news (I've gone bankrupt, I have cancer, the albatross is extinct), but when it hadn't materialized, she'd begun to weigh her gift fondly in her hand.

The following week she said she was taking the children to St. Barts with her mother. It was their spring vacation. Did I want to come along? I said that this was the exact moment when Union Carbide had scheduled photography of its Scranton plant for the annual report, and I'd have to be there—not that the photographer would regard me as anything but a nuisance. "It's the client who needs to see me—reassurance, feet on the ground," I said, as if I were citing overly familiar facts that only merited shorthand.

I called Jack and asked him if he could implement Plan A. "You know," I said, "where you stand us up, Pia and me, in a restaurant."

We chatted for a while about our work, then later (perhaps I was feeling an excess of Catholic guilt) I suddenly turned hostile. "Tell me something, Jack, m'boy, why are you doing all this?"

"Playing the pimp? I don't have the slightest idea. It can't possibly do me any good, and it could turn into a disaster in at least three ways."

I felt as if Jack and I were playing chess. He'd just taken my queen. He couldn't have come up with a quicker, surer way to puncture my suspicions and make me feel that he was the one doing me a favor. Suddenly I saw myself as an ingrate.

"Alex would never forgive me if she caught wind of this."

"Why would she ever know?" I asked. "I'd be the last person—"

"And then your own guilt might turn you against me. You'd either resent me because Pia wouldn't respond to you—"

"Did she say anything about not responding?"

"You'd resent me even more if it did work out. How can all this possibly end well?"

"When did you become so wise?" I asked bitterly. He just exhaled. "No, seriously," I said. I didn't want to say, it sounds as if you've had a lot of experience enabling adulterers.

What he said was, "I'm seeing a new shrink now, and she

pointed out to me that I have this neurotic way of getting involved with a certain straight couple."

"What does your shrink think it means?"

"She thinks it's oedipal, though she doesn't like that word."

I hoisted myself up above the conversation, rotated it fifteen degrees, and said, "How could a certain straight friend help you out—help to reduce your stress level?"

I could almost hear Jack blinking as he thought that one over. "I guess by not telling me what happens later between you and Pia. I'll set it up for you, but keep me out of it."

"I can't," I said. "I'll need keys to your apartment. I don't want to take her to a hotel—too sordid."

"Too dangerous, you mean," he said.

The whole conversation left me feeling exhausted, as if I'd been sleepwalking for hours across a girder twenty stories up. Now I awoke with a start, looked down, and panicked.

The next day I called Jack and gave him three free dates he could try out on Pia. He sounded dry and grimly efficient, as if he'd resolved to relieve himself of this painful duty as quickly as possible. Later in the day he phoned back to say that we all had a date at seven on the sixteenth at the Four Seasons. I calculated that a dinner with decent wine would set me back a small fortune. I was careful not to voice anything but the deepest gratitude. I was excited by the thought of sleeping with Pia, so much so that I couldn't even contemplate the possibility of saying, "Look, Jack, if it makes you feel awkward, then let's just drop the whole thing."

On the commuter train out of Grand Central that night, I sat next to two loudmouths who were eating greasy sausages and onions, and the smell overpowered me, but I kept slipping through an air lock into a private embrace with Pia, my hand inching up her skirt and feeling the tops of her nylons and the smoother, cooler texture of her skin above. Then, as my hand slid along the inside of her thighs . . .

Her perfumed, long-limbed presence in the train was my refuge. I didn't work up a whole scenario. It was just a deep kiss here and then a glance into her large eyes there and the feeling of her hands all over me as she ordered me to lie perfectly still and not respond in any way except with one part of my body, involuntarily. And then I started to doze off as the train lurched and stopped and even crawled backward for a few minutes, and I thought, It's a gift when something magical steps into actual time.

3.

ALTHOUGH I'D EATEN at Brasserie in the Seagram Building lots of times, I'd only once been to the other restaurant in the building, the Four Seasons, when a rich friend of my sister Elaine's was paying. I think it was Elaine's birthday.

I left my coat downstairs, on the street level, and hurried up the carpeted stairs to the big dining room on its two levels. The ceilings were high, the napery dazzling, the windows hung with long, fine gold chains echoed by the chandeliers, and I imagined that this sort of luminous spareness, this sort of muted splendor, could only be bought dear.

"You're the first to arrive," said the maître d'hôtel. "Would you prefer to wait at the bar or the table?"

"The table," I said. I started to offer an explanation, but I didn't have one. He led me down the hall to Siberia, I supposed, for social outcasts or unknowns, past the superb Picasso tapestry and into the Pool Room with its budding trees in tubs. It was still light outside. This might be exile, I thought, but it's attractive as hell. Jack had made the reservation—didn't he have the requisite clout to get us into the Grill Room? Or did he think a Pool Room table would be more romantic? Or more private? I wondered if Pia knew all these codes.

I sat for ten minutes feeling that anxious boredom I always experience when something exciting is about to happen. I remembered all the time growing up when I'd been underdressed and red with acne in places far less grand than this one. Now I felt half-sure of myself. No holes in my stockings. Brand-new button-down shirt, the collar unfrayed, the blue unfaded. My shoes were handmade and English. My nails clipped evenly and clean, my ears properly reamed, my face finally all one color and that a pale Norman white with only a few interesting acne scars.

And there she was in a candy-striped silk dress, red and beige, following the maître d' at a rapid pace, her feet in very high heels, also beige, and the look on her face slightly foolish, foolishly happy. I rose to greet her and then subsided as the maître d' pushed her chair in. She shone like an ingot in the banklike majesty of this room; the light outside had just faded, and the gold bead curtains came to life, strafed by the electric lights projected up onto them.

"It seems funny just to say hi in this room," I said. "It feels like we should be hammering out the Treaty of Versailles or something."

"Where is Jack?" she asked. "I thought I'd be late."

We ordered Gibsons, and they arrived in very large, pale, frosted glasses as if they were snowflowers flown in from the north pole. She looked around nervously; she must have known more people than I did, and soon I was sledding down a jealousy path faster and faster. I asked her what she did with her days.

"I am actually very busy with my hemophilia, my charity. We have a big dinner-dance we're planning for June, and I hope you and Alex will buy a table. It will be at the Pierre and very lovely, and I promise to put amusing people at your table. And then, you know I promised to help Jack with his apartment, and he decided the Indian prints we bought are too banal and he wants something more sumptuous, so I've ordered him some silk from Zurich—Zumsteg, the same factory that made the fabric in my dress."

"Let me feel it," I said, and looking her right in the eye, I rubbed her sleeve between my thumb and forefinger. Her jabbering dried like saliva on her lips, and she looked at me with eyes big with terror or maybe desire. Usually I was incapable of breaking through the social automatisms, but tonight I understood that I had to be direct.

"I'm a little afraid of you," she said, and I appreciated her gravity, even her courage to admit her fear.

"I'm a very nice man."

"Jack says you're cagey."

"Thanks for that, Jack."

"I don't want to stir up any trouble. What he said was that you play with your cards very close to your chest."

"What cards? You know everything there is to know about me—one wife, two children, a silly job, good shoes, a fascination with you. All my cards are on the table. But if I am holding a few to my chest you might as well put your head on it so you can see them." This line suddenly seemed so laborious that I almost burst out laughing. Everything verbal about seduction—the compliments, the sweet talk—seemed so stiff and absurd, though I knew that certain women (was Pia one of them?) considered this approach to be "romantic." What I preferred was the blunt honesty of the body, the way two different bodies took their time learning each other's ways. Wetness or hardness—no way to deny the body's interests.

At that moment a waiter came up and said I was wanted on the phone. I excused myself as Pia said, "It must be Jack."

I spoke with him from the bar in the Grill Room. "How's it going?" he asked.

"Fine. So what do I tell her?"

"That my car broke down in Narragansett as I was driving back from Providence."

"And listen. Just send me your hotel bill for tonight. And Jack?"

"Yes?"

"You're the greatest."

"That I already knew."

If Pia ever figured out the fast one we'd pulled on her, she'd have plenty of proof of my caginess.

"Narragansett?" Pia exclaimed. "You Americans have such funny place names."

"In honor of the Indians we stole the land from and killed. In Australia all the names are Aboriginal for the same reason— Wagga Wagga or Goonengerry. Are you disappointed he's not coming?"

"I see Jack all the time. But it does put us in a rather compromising position," she said with a laugh in her voice. She touched my knee under the table, and my cock broke its bonds and stood up, in spite of all the tight, dark good tailoring.

I kept wondering how I was going to introduce the subject of Jack's apartment. Could I say, "Jack is staying in Narragansett tonight while his Aston Martin is being repaired. You could show me the changes you're planning on making to his apartment. I have a bottomless appetite for home-decorating hints."

But it was too soon. First I wanted to get another bottle of Montrachet down her throat.

At a certain point Pia stopped eating and started chain-smoking. Cigarettes seemed to make her more discerning, if silence,

pursed lips, and narrowed eyes indicated discernment. In truth I
didn't understand any of her signals. I was flying blind.

I remembered a blunt Romanian girl I'd dated in college
who would say, "You've gotten fat," or "I no longer love you,"
or would slam a door I'd just opened for her. That Romanian
had completely shaken me; until then I'd always hidden behind
my good manners.

Pia was much closer to my world, but she had her own European approach, even if she was only half continental and on
the privileged edge of the spectrum. But she had touched me
under the table.

When I started to order the second bottle, she said, "I don't
think we really need that. We've already stopped eating," and I
remembered the strange European notion that wine was a food.

"Do you want dessert?" I asked.

And she went "Tsk-tsk" and window-wipered her index
finger from right to left—that irritating European way of saying no. I knew that they didn't mean anything by it, that to them
it didn't come across as pedantic or parental. But as a good American I was still ruffled by it.

"Check, please," I said to the waiter.

"No coffee?"

"Just a check."

When we were on the street, I said, "I have a key to Jack's place.
Why don't we stop by? I want to see the changes you're making."

"Will he be there?"

"Not until tomorrow afternoon."

"I can only picture him in Narragansett in a tepee with a peace
pipe eating buffalo meat." And she nattered on without ever
clearly saying she'd come with me or she wouldn't. When the

doorman saw us, he said, "Good evening. I'm not sure Mr. Holmes—"

"No, Henry," she said, "he won't be back until tomorrow, but I wanted to show something to this gentleman. We have keys."

The apartment was immaculate but had the slightly sour smell of ripening garbage left too long in the can. It also looked forlorn before all the little indirect lights were switched on and the terrace doors flung open.

I made us martinis. It took a moment for me to put my hands on all the ingredients and the shaker. When I came into the living room, there she was in that silk dress that had taken on a new life under all the cunning little lights she'd switched on.

I sat beside her and was very conscious of our clothes—of mine disguising the hairy beast underneath and my problematic testicles, one so much lower than the other that the boys in the locker room had dubbed me Won Hung Low; of hers lending such a lovely radiance to her cinched-in waist, mediating between her full, breathing breasts and her even fuller hips, which also seemed as if they were breathing invisibly.

I pictured Jack up here putting the moves on his boys, but they probably just tore each other's clothes off while standing in the doorway, undoing each other's familiar belts, pulling off each other's familiar shirts and underpants and socks, the easygoing camaraderie of undressing another man, but how dull. How lacking in mystery. Whereas here I was confronted with a woman, and me having known only a dozen in my whole life, compared to Jack's hundreds of men and where was the delight in a man? Nor could another man give you anything but low-level tedious companionship. I pictured two men sitting at a table facing out with a chair between them, looking for some entertainment, some third person: a woman.

As I sat next to Pia I was quickly enveloped by her wonderful light perfume. She was showing me the new Zumsteg silk covers for the pillows, now that the Indian prints had been banished—and our lips touched and I don't know, was it her touch and scent and warmth that made the room lurch slightly or was it the wine and martinis?

This is where I start all over, I thought. I thought that almost ten years of marital fidelity had been criminal and a mistake, a sacrifice to some pointless, cowardly ideal, and I appreciated Pia's roundness, her springiness, the richness of flesh compared to Alex's gauntness, Alex's punishing hip bones and the three horizontal bones like a military decoration between her small breasts, and I suddenly hated Catholicism. The coward's excuse. The lazy man's alibi. I could hear music, as if my life were now an old-fashioned Technicolor musical. As I swarmed over Pia and my hands bunched and smoothed the silk almost satin, I thought of Rodin's *The Kiss*, a man as hard as marble, a woman fluid as a wave. Idea for story: a man misses out on the one authentic moment of his life because he's too busy comparing it to old works of art, mostly kitsch. I chuckled at my own thought, and Pia pushed me gently away. "What? Were you laughing at me?"

"Just at myself. As for you, I marvel at you."

She said, "I'm so happy."

"Me too," I whispered. And I thought, The married man has every motive in the world to keep it simple. He's luckiest when there's little past, no future, an absolute and abundant present.

But then, maybe Pia is truly sophisticated, not longing for a one-and-only full-time relationship. Maybe she's a sybarite in search of wine, men, and song.

Or maybe she's a romantic who loves me in some humble, simple way and would never dream of demanding anything, of disturbing my marriage.

Or maybe she's Jack's puppet and will repeat back to him every insignificant detail about me. That idea made me shudder.

At last we were both out of our clothes. I had one black stocking dangling from my right foot, which made it look seriously white, like some appalling English potted meat newly pried out of the can. She had indentations in her smooth, soft skin where the waistband of her panties had been cinching her in. But otherwise she now looked less like a girl and more like a woman, almost as if in nudity she'd gone up a full size. Her shoulders were firm and sloping; her breasts sagged a bit under their own weight; her pubic hair was also longer and thicker than I'd anticipated. Sort of shaggy with age.

But her feet were superb, sensitive and fresh, her ankles fine, her legs wrapped around with long, sheathed muscles. Her breasts reminded me of anemones for some reason—maybe because the aureoles were big and dark, and the surrounding petals were soft and relaxed and drooping, radiating out from so much dark intensity.

I ran my hands over her, over every inch of her, as if I were blind and needed to memorize her body since I couldn't see it, though I could see it, and did. I wondered if her eyes would look more normal, less arresting, if they were seen upside down. Had her eyes been inverted? Was that the trick of their beauty?

When my hand gently entered her she was wet and warm, and that wetness seemed to me like a form of mercy, the

expression of generosity and goodness. Idea for story: men
make so many crude cunt jokes because they love it too much,
just as the worst English swear word used to be "bloody," which
means "by our lady," the holy person we most revere.

After it was all over we fell asleep, and then I woke up at three
in the morning, dry mouthed. I moved slightly away to be out of
the path of Pia's sour breath. Her breasts and her belly and even
her chin looked larger and too relaxed from this angle, as if she'd
gained yet another ten pounds in her sleep. I even resented that
she was here, presuming to share a mattress with me, and the
words "loose morals" drifted past the center of my mind, though
not for long enough to be introspected.

But when the alarm went off, she was already bathed and
dressed and scented and made up and mounted on her high heels
and brisk and affectionate. She left a cup of coffee (black, not
the way I liked it) beside the bed and kissed me on the forehead
and said, "Now I must vanish. I have to pack to go to Washington on the noon train, but I'll be back at the weekend. Here's
my private number." She put her card next to the cup. My mind
cantered satirically around the locution "at the weekend," which
I supposed must be an anglicism. Yet I was grateful because she
hadn't pressed me for a rematch.

After Pia had gone, I showered and shaved and put on the
fresh shirt I'd brought in my briefcase. I wrote Jack a note: "Mis-
sion accomplished. Thanks for the hospitality. You are a hell of
a good friend. The apartment is looking swell." Actually his
apartment looked garish and busy and dusty in the sunlight.

I tried to collect my thoughts: It's true that a gay friend is
different, maybe better, because he's not a rival. He's not part of
the whole dismal system. He's not one more pussy-whipped

churchgoer who's learned to keep his head, the big head and the little one, in check. Everyone thinks gay guys are sissies and mama's boys, but they're actually people who've chosen their sexuality over all the comforts of home. They're bravely obsessional—but at a price. This apartment, sure, it's impressive, but it's not comfortable and it's sort of dirty—it lacks a woman's touch. I'm sure Jack brings men back here in industrial quantities, and why not? He's still young, and he exudes a strong sensuality that is almost like body odor, though he has no smell. He reeks of sex—you can see it in his eyes. He never looks at people above the waist, nor can he follow the thread of the usual conversation about property values and the new school bill. Jack doesn't look at men or women as neighbors and colleagues or beleaguered fellow parents. For him, their suits or dresses are just the thinnest tissue to be lifted off or torn away like the clothes on paper dolls. Once he said to me that he thought it was ridiculous that some people were turned on by cowboy hats or motorcycle jackets or peasant blouses. "For me," he said, "clothes are erotic only when they're shed. I don't give a damn what people are wearing so long as they end up naked."

It's strange that his way, the sexual way, would be considered a secondary route; in Larchmont the high road is social, economic, stable, and if all the good couples had their way, we'd soon stop wriggling and oscillating altogether and condense into a single hard point of stasis.

Jack's not that way. He's a dirty boy, and he understands other dirty boys and girls. Is Pia a dirty girl? She was pretty extreme for a first date—but then, what do I know? She's definitely in the fast lane, and I'm in the parking lot. She licked my balls.

But what do these people do when they get older, old? We'll have our children and our grandchildren, but what will they have? Snapshots of former loves? Old party favors? Then again, is a grandchild really such a consolation? Doesn't a grandson by his very existence define his grandfather as a superfluous man?

4.

THAT DAY I commissioned an experienced commercial photographer to take large, almost abstract pictures of a chemical process at a client's plant in Lackawanna. I rushed up there on a puddle jumper, then rented a car. No one needed me, but my presence kept costs down. I'd worked out a successful formula for these annual reports—especially for ailing behemoths in the chemical industry. I wrote short, upbeat paragraphs of nearly cryptic generalities to be printed beside blazing out-of-focus photos of molten reds and rolled-out yellows. The disappointing actuarial report could be slipped in, in agate type, after a whole book of glossy photos and clichés about the future.

I called Alex that evening from my highway motel, which I preferred to the old hotel downtown, where the curtains smelled of coal.

She told me the children's news: Palmer had gotten a *mention très bien* in Kindergarten French, and Margaret was learning in ballet how to do a full curtsy, and she was now going around bowing to the dogs and staff.

I told Alex that these accomplishments seemed surreal in a Lackawanna motel where the outside traffic noise was punctuated only by the thumping of the ice machine.

"My poor angel," she said. "I hate to think of you up there alone. So bleak. Monsieur should have his comforts! Where did we go wrong in planning our lives? Should we sell our house, buy a little brownstone in Greenwich Village? I heard of one for just fifty thousand dollars, I guess because New York is so dangerous. But then you could retire and write your novels. Or we could live cheaply in Paris. That would be such a thrilling opportunity for the children. Margaret's already perfected her curtsy. And Palmer can say 'Bonjour, comment allez-vous?'"

"Let's not go overboard," I said. "I like my job, even if it is pointless. I've made it very profitable, and I'm the first Wright in two generations to earn any money. If I gave it up to write novels—"

"But who knows, you might earn money with your novels," she protested.

"Not likely," I said. "Anyway, I don't like living off your father's money."

"But if we sold the house—"

"You'd hate it, Alex. I know how important it is to you to live surrounded by nature."

A long silence ensued and then she said, "You're right," her voice very faint. I didn't want to admit it to myself, but I liked keeping Alex in the country so that I could get away from time to time.

That night, as I tried to get to sleep, I replayed in my mind everything I'd done with Pia. I'd been waiting all day for this moment. Idea for story: Sex is real for a man only when he can masturbate later and reclaim the images for his imagination. Develop into bigger point about the imagination and its dangers.

And it was true: I'd been carrying around with me the possibility of reliving last night as if it were a gift that someone had given me on an important occasion, but that I hadn't been allowed to open yet. I could taste her throat as she thrust her head back while my hands kneaded her plush buttocks. I inched deeper inside her, or I lay on my back and she sat on me, her hair curtaining her glittering smile, and she groaned with something between pleasure and pain, "God, that's so damn good!" Alex never admitted to any earthly pleasure, to anything that made her gasp; Alex was a mystic of love, whereas Pia was a blues singer of lust. Idea for story: naive white man thinks of all orgasmic women as Negro until he meets Italian heiress.

Since I didn't know where Pia was in Washington or how to reach her, I called Jack, and was amazed to find him at home.

"Where on earth are you?" he asked. "If I sound weird, it's because I'm drunk. Someone at the magazine roped me into a horrible drinks party—"

"How could that be so horrible?"

"But it was!" he insisted with a laugh.

Unsure of his degree of irony, I said, "Did you forget to eat?"

"Oh, I ate: four olives," he said. "Where are you?"

"In a Lackawanna Days Inn."

"Is this a cry for help? Did you think you were dialing the suicide hotline?"

He told me that he'd been to Albany the week before for his work and that it was surely just as appalling. We were both enjoying playing New Yorkers shocked by the provinces.

"So: that Pia of yours!" I said.

Jack laughed and said, "Was she good in the sack? Be advised: I'll be asking her the same question about you."

I said, "I'm sure she's the most passionate woman I've ever known."

"Maybe it's not her nature. Maybe you just turn her on."

"Tell me," I said, "when you're with another man, does your greatest pleasure come from exciting him?"

"I don't think we're that altruistic," he said. I could hear him reflecting. "Of course, it's nice to get good reviews, especially if the guy spreads the word to other possible victims. But no, I think we're more selfish."

"See," I said excitedly, "it's so damn thrilling to watch a lady become an animal in your arms, to hear her growling, to see her head whipping from side to side."

"Men don't lose control like that," Jack said, almost sourly, as if he were questioning my bragging. Or was he envious? Did he wish he could produce that effect? Or did he still dream of my fucking him? "But even if they did start growling, I think that would freak me out. I don't like them even to talk. Gay men say the dumbest things, all about hot balls and hungry holes."

I found myself wincing, not wanting the specifics. An embarrassing silence settled in like a sudden cold front ending a warm spring day.

Then, on a different note, he asked, "Are you going to continue seeing Pia?"

I almost wanted to tell him that I might not if I could find the time to jerk off three times a day but that otherwise I couldn't see how I would stop obsessing about her.

"I want to," I said. "She's a wonderful woman. By the way, you don't know how I could get in touch with her today, do you?"

"Try her at home."

"But she's in Washington."

"No, she's not. I just spoke with her."

"Oh."

"Maybe her trip was called off," he added quickly as if he'd made a faux pas.

"I wouldn't want to look as if I were testing what she'd told me. Or give her the feeling we'd been discussing her and that's how I knew she was at home."

"You're being complicated. Call her."

After work I'd eaten a hamburger steak and mashed potatoes under a blanket of gravy. I felt sick and wished I had a quart bottle of seltzer, but I was too tired to dress and drive to a 7-Eleven.

I sat on the toilet and leaned forward with my arms on my knees and strained, but nothing happened. I stood up and looked in the mirror. I supposed that no man in history had ever thought his own face looked dishonest. Maybe by definition that was impossible to think. But I wondered if someone studying me—a man? a woman? probably a man—would say I had a shifty face.

I went back to the bed and lay down, looking at the telephone as if it might ring.

I felt strange about having discussed sex with Jack. We'd never done that before. It seemed odd that he, a faggot, should be so much more experienced than a normal guy like me, but was it real experience? Men and women played for keeps, for babies, for money, and they let the law govern their union and disunion. God and nature had made their bodies fit together. But what permanence or public acknowledgment could two fairies count on? Two barren boys cornholing each other; must hurt like hell, I thought. They can't go anywhere as a couple unless they don't mind flaunting their fancy ways. I guess now they wouldn't get fired for being gay. Or would they? But people must still treat them as freaks; why are they so affected, with their sibilance and shrill laughter and swooping intonations, their clothes too tight, too bright?

Not that Jack was like that. I suspected that many female staffers at *Newsweek* must be pining over him. Was he perverse enough to fool them deliberately? How many more years could he get away with this masquerade before people demanded that he marry? Maybe he would come clean, but could he on the job?

I decided not to try Pia. It took all my resolve and sense of strategy; I kept looking at the neatly printed card she'd given me with what she called her "private number" on it. How many numbers did she have, for chrissake?

I called Jack again and told him he shouldn't mention to Pia that he'd told me she hadn't gone to D.C.

"You've got it bad," Jack drawled. "This is beginning to feel like high school."

"You can say that," I snapped, "because you don't care about anyone that much."

"Are you sure of that?" he asked, with a trace of asperity. Then he sighed and said, "Maybe you're right."

At last I got to sleep and had long dreams in which Pia or a near-Pia teased me, denied me sex while permitting me to touch her stomach. We were in an old-fashioned sleeping car with sooty dark green serge upholstery and soft blue night-lights beside the net hammock where I'd stowed my wool sweater and toiletries. When I awakened, I'd worked myself halfway out of my pajama bottoms and was pressing a hot, sticky erection into the bare mattress.

Back in New York I dropped into the office. The Lackawanna pictures had already been developed. I looked at the slides on the light table with a magnifying glass. They were exactly what I wanted.

When I called Pia at three, I didn't mention Washington at all, in case she was aware that I knew she hadn't been there. She asked me if I could come by for a quick drink.

Her apartment was just a studio in a white brick high-rise on Third Avenue in the Seventies, but she'd obviously decorated it with care so it could be photographed by shelter magazines. She was a "stylist," it turned out, someone who could locate and rent absolutely anything for professional photographers. She'd managed to hire an animal trainer and get two grown deer up slippery stairs to a photographer's studio on Fifth Avenue across from the Forty-second Street Library. She'd assembled on a single school playground the thirty-two prizes to be awarded in a contest—everything from a Cuisinart to a Piper Cub. She'd had to have the plane's wings removed to maneuver it on a truck bed through the streets.

Her apartment had a double bed that also served as a couch, piled high with thirty pillows in mink covers. There was a profusion of smelly, camera-ready cheeses and hothouse fruits artfully arranged on a round, blue-and-white Moroccan platter. There were two delicate white chairs with a blue Isis on the back folding a wing over her own standing body, arrayed in a gown with vertical pleats; the chairs looked as if they were remnants from a 1930s Cleopatra film. The sunlight created a wide, brilliant band hectic with dust motes.

I was put off by the mink, the cheese, the dust, and Pia's own ripeness in the harem pants she was wearing. Her bottom was big and jiggly, and the strip of bare flesh between the pants and her beaded bodice looked clammy.

Or that's what some other Will would have said, an imbecile invulnerable to her.

Did Jack look at women with the weary indifference of a eunuch? I couldn't, since even if Pia came across as so much less distinguished than my wife and even if I had contempt for her, that scorn was linked to my desire. I'd come to respect Alex too much to desire her.

It hadn't always been that way. When I'd first met Alex, I'd been passionate about her *and* revered her. I was a Charlottesville boy, spotty and naive, enflamed with dreams of glory. And she was a New York debutante, with her fragile beauty, her fine porcelain, her satin hostess gown, and a freezer full of crab claws. She had her adorable cross-eyed way of disputing everything I said, beating fragile fists against my chest while laughing at herself and insisting she was serious.

Pia and I sat on the couch-bed with its raw-silk spread, the lines of white silk alternating with beige wool stripes: the upscale bedouin look. We chattered about this and that, carefully avoiding any mention of Washington or Lackawanna, and sipped our cocktails. I couldn't stop nibbling on the cold lemon peel, relishing its bitterness. We were treating with airy indifference the fact that I had to catch the six forty and it was already five twenty.

"It's nice," I said, "that you can keep your big window uncurtained and no one can look in, you're so high up."

"Another drink?" she asked, and I stood up with her and put our glasses down on the sill and took her in my arms. Until now the distance between us had been a form of suffering, not that holding her eased the pain completely. On the margins I noted that she and her mink pelts were vulgar, but between the margins the wide column of reality that I was perusing was compelling—compelling me to pull her closer, to kiss her with a need that was

irredeemable. Talking about how "nice" her uncurtained window was sounded to my ears like a madman's little rhyme before
he threw himself off a bridge. The air was crackling with the big
banner of drama. My life had become dramatic.

We saw each other whenever we could snatch a free moment,
usually an hour at lunchtime, though I preferred to spend the night
with her after she'd elaborately stripped her bed of the mink pillows and stacked them in three neat piles on the parquet. I learned
that she liked caviar, and I'd bring it over in little jars from Cavi-
arteria on Madison Avenue, though she scolded me for being so
extravagant. She was a rich girl used to frugality. Once she prepared the caviar in what she called the "Russian manner," with
small boiled potatoes, sour cream, and melted butter. She showed
me how to make an incision in a peeled potato, then fill it with
the caviar and other ingredients and eat it in a single bite. We ended
up feeding these potatoes to each other.

I don't think she worked much as a stylist, though like every
rich lady in New York she felt obliged to have a job. Of course,
she also had her charities. She thought my indifference to these
was maddening, though she liked men too much to be a feminist about it. It seemed to be my fate to inspire mock feminist
indignation in unbelievably sweet women.

Pia told me that her mother, Toni, was a debutante from Sac-
ramento. I was surprised that the people out there bothered with
"society"—I thought of the women as riding around in convertibles the whole time with scarves tied over their hair. At St.
Moritz on a ski holiday Toni met an Italian *baronino* who'd rebelled against his family in Brescia and was working as a waiter
in Barcelona. Some of his rich childhood friends, it turned out,

were paying for his St. Moritz sojourn. Later Pia wondered if his friends hadn't been staking him on a bet that he'd meet someone precisely like Toni.

Toni and Alessandro were very happy for a while with her money and his hand-kissing charm. She'd been brought up in a very Protestant way, taught to keep her expenses down, live modestly, and contribute most of her income to disease-related causes, but Sandro, as a Catholic, felt no such scruples. He knew about pleasure and how to secure it for himself and confer it on Toni and several other women.

"So you see," Pia said, "I have a double heritage. The famous American puritanism and the voluptuousness of Italy. It's all rather fascinating, don't you think?"

I leaned over her to kiss her lips. "I'm afraid not much of the puritanism rubbed off."

Months went by like that—the whole summer and part of the fall.

I didn't know if Alex suspected. Luckily we'd had sex only rarely during the preceding two years, so in all likelihood she wouldn't notice any diminished desire on my part. What increased was my tenderness and gratitude toward her. I pretended to myself that she did know about my affair with Pia and that she countenanced it because it brought me pleasure. In a cockeyed way I thought of the excitement and unpredictability of my affair with Pia—its passion and the moodiness it inspired—as compensation for the novels I wasn't writing, a rough transcript of the feelings I might have summoned up as a solitary creator before the empty page.

Pia and I couldn't go out to restaurants often for fear of being seen, though I'd discovered a disgusting Indian place upstairs on Forty-ninth Street where no one we knew would dare to eat. We drank sweet pomegranate cocktails and ate crushed-kitty curries and oily puri and desserts of coiled doggie-do pastry dissolving in clouded honey. Usually we had the place to ourselves, and we'd recline on pillows and watch a cockroach investigate the corner of a dusty windowsill.

Slowly I learned bits and pieces about her life. She was older than me, drifting about somewhere in her mid-thirties. She'd studied international relations in D.C. (I don't think she ever told me the name of the school). I thought she'd told us she'd gone to Smith. Lying always surprised me but I didn't much care. She praised American campus life and hands-on teaching and preferred that to the big-city impersonality of European universities.

She said, "I tried the Sorbonne and La Sapienza in Rome, both laughable."

She seemed ashamed to admit it, but her mother had ended up buying off Alessandro.

"He pretended that as a Catholic he had scruples about divorce. He even has a genuine saint in his family, a 1920s doctor who saved the life of a Jewish child in Liverpool—one of his miracles—and instantly baptized him, which of course enraged the child's parents. Maybe he's just a Blessed. And we have another Blessed, Lucia Crocifissa—I love these names, aren't they delicious?"

So much conspicuous piety in his bloodlines, I gathered, made it difficult for Sandro to accept the sin and humiliation of divorce for less than two million dollars, a Maserati, and a modern villa near Borgo San Sepolcro.

"A scoundrel," I said, but Pia looked hurt and tears sprang to her eyes.

"I didn't tell you all that so that you could mock my father," she said.

"What am I supposed to say?" I asked in consternation. "Probably nothing, huh?"

"It's just that my father is a dear poetic man, a Don Juan, perhaps—but then, we of all people shouldn't be too quick to condemn him. Now he lives with a thoroughly elegant Italian mistress, a countess with a whole floor of a Renaissance palace on the most beautiful street in Europe, Via Garibaldi in Genoa. It's like the Grand Canal but straightened out and without the water. He's such a snob, Sandro, that he loves his countess and their Luca Giordano paintings and their two maids tiptoeing around and even the three corgis."

"Well, in that case," I said, as if I'd just been enlightened.

Her mother had a house in the South of France, in Menton, but she seemed to know almost no one there and spent most of her time in San Francisco, where she was still "Baronessa Toni." She attended the opera and was active in a charity devoted to rape victims all over the world. Pia admired her mother but found her frugality a bit ridiculous.

"She's the sort of woman who might serve ten lamb chops to ten people with a teaspoon each of commercial mint jelly, and this from a woman who's eaten at the best tables in Italy and France."

"But what about you?" I asked. "You interest me more than they do."

"I do?" she asked, and she blushed for the first and only time I'd ever observed. "What do you want to know? Ask me anything."

"Who was your first lover?"

I don't think that was the sort of question she'd had in mind, but she said, "It was a lifeguard at Laguna. I don't know who we were visiting down there. Nor can I imagine how I escaped everyone's supervision to run off with him."

"How old were you?"

"Fourteen. He must have been seventeen. He had a white stripe painted down his nose and a superbly tanned hairless body, a black Speedo with a white-and-red cross on the side, and— well, his attraction to me was obvious. Let's say he filled out his Speedo nicely."

She kissed me as if I might be jealous, whereas I was aroused, filling out my own boxer shorts more than adequately.

"Now that I think of it," she said, "he must have been kind of pervy, going after a girl so young. I still had braces on my teeth and no breasts."

"Where did he take you?"

"There was some sort of clubhouse. He asked me if I'd put lotion on his back. He was afraid of burning. I just shrugged and kept looking down. As I followed him, I thought everyone must know where I was going and why."

"He probably saw you staring at him on the beach."

"Possibly. I was trying to get rid of my virginity as if it were an annoying little brother. No one wanted me as long as it was tagging along. But the lifeguard asked me if I was a virgin, and when I made a sound of vexation and squeaked, 'Yeah, squeak-squeak' he said, 'Good.' He told me he liked to rack up cherries. 'And where do you put them,' I asked, and he swatted me on the butt with his sign-out sheet and said, 'Brat!'"

"Did it hurt?"

"Who's the perv now?" she asked. "Yes. He was efficient and had a washcloth for the blood, and he said, 'Now you'll remember me for the rest of your life,' and I have. I even remember his name. A ridiculous one: Forrest Green."

I found out she'd been married at twenty to a rich boy. She

knew from her mother's example to avoid fortune hunters, but she'd not been warned against dullards.

"He bored me with his golfing and Young Republicans, and he never liked to hear about our family rape charity, as if it were in bad taste."

"How long did that last?"

"Three years but the last two out of inertia. No children. I'm not sure I can have children."

I found this news reassuring, though I was careful to look sympathetic.

"And after that?" I was staring into her swimming, upside-down eyes.

"I met a younger man. I was staying with friends in Milan, and they said they had an unexpected guest and would I mind sharing a room with him—there were two small beds. He was so beautiful, ten years younger than I, tall and blond, from Bergamo. No, nothing interesting. Office work. He fell in love with me, and within a week he wanted to marry me. I said he should come live with me, in Sardinia for a year, and if he still wanted to marry me at the end of twelve months, I'd consider it."

"Did he and did you?"

"It was a sacrifice for him to leave his mother and his clerical job—I know that sounds funny—but he was happy in Sardinia. I'd bought a little house by the sea. He loved swimming, and we had a cat and a dog, and I cooked for him. He was quite the homebody. When I thought of a twenty-two-year-old lover, I thought, Oh dear, drugs and bad girls and discos and dark moods. But no, he just wanted to play with the dog, swim, do some of his gardening, and spend the whole morning between my breasts."

"And the marriage?"

"It broke his heart, but I said no, which I often regret. I gave him the house. He was sweet—"

"But another bore?"

"At least he was *un bon coup.*"

I felt reassured. I was neither a golf bore nor a clerk bore. I wasn't a hairless blond, but I was presentable enough. I was a published author with an enchanting wife whom it would be fun for Pia to wean me away from.

I wasn't sure I could trust Pia to be discreet. If she was deliberately "careless" and allowed Alex to find out about our affair, that might serve her purposes if she wanted me to herself. But if she was afraid of being considered a home wrecker—we had three friends in common—then she might have a stake in preserving our secret. Or maybe she liked the idea of an intrigue with me but prized her independence. Or maybe the thought of having a rival excited her. Or maybe she was just vamping with me until she located another young hairless blond, one with more money and conversation this time around.

One day she asked me, "Does most of your money come from Alex's family?"

The question didn't seem loaded, but I wondered if she was investigating how free I was to choose a new woman.

We were in Brooklyn, walking along the Promenade. The sky was dark and twisted and packed with clouds. The November rain had finally let up, and we'd emerged out of another obscure restaurant. It was Italian and had candles in Chianti bottles and black-and-white photos of mafiosi at christenings. We'd chosen Brooklyn Heights because no one we knew was likely to go there. No one ever went to Brooklyn; it might as well have been Akron.

"Her father bought the house," I said, "and is always settling

more money on her to avoid inheritance taxes. It doesn't amount
to much because you can only give up to five thousand a year.
And she does own income-producing property somewhere, the
usual cattle ranch or orange grove. But I earn money. I make a
decent amount from my boring annual reports business, not that
any salary is ever real money. I have no inheritance coming or
prospects like that. Nothing. No investments. I spend everything
I make on taxes and staff and the children—all those dance lessons add up."

Pia seemed even more passionate when we went back to her
studio that afternoon, as if my very averageness as a father and
salary man acted on her as an aphrodisiac. Or maybe she thought
we'd shared valuable secrets. Sometimes she accused me of being
cold and too reserved.

I'd figured out that my company nearly ran itself, especially
in the period before the earnings reports were released and the
disappointing results had to be disguised with palliative pictures
and words. I was free to spend almost half a day with Pia three
afternoons a week. Love likes to illustrate itself among friends and
strangers and to mark its festivals with ceremonies—and none of
that could we do. We were confined to bad curries and to hours
of sunlight on the bed beside the three neat piles of mink pillows
on the floor and the Moroccan platter of cheeses going steadily
off.

I wondered if Alex suspected anything. She complained that
she could never reach me at the office. I reminded her that I
called on clients most afternoons and even played squash with
them but was almost always at my desk in the morning. She
teased me for getting flabby despite the squash. When I missed
two events at Palmer's school, she was hurt, but it seemed to

make her happy when I encouraged her to plan for us to go on a Serengeti camera safari later in the winter.

Jack had come up with the inspired idea of inviting friends— all straight, I noticed—twice a month to cocktails at the bar in one of the big, cool, cavernous rooms in the Museum of Natural History. It wasn't a party he'd had to arrange with the museum. Anyone was free to drink in the early evening at the little bar next to the dioramas of tigers in the bush. There'd be as few as twelve or as many as twenty people looking unusually vulnerable in the dim light.

Twice Alex took the train in to attend these odd parties; on each occasion Jack invited her out to dinner at Ruskay's over on Columbus Avenue. She'd come home full of news and more animated than I'd seen her in weeks.

"He has such interesting friends," she told me at breakfast. "His old college roommate was there, Howard, who's self-mocking and shy, with eyes as startled looking as Charles Trenet's. He told me about how he'd been such a slob in college that Jack had drawn a line down the center of their room with pink chalk, and how they'd listen to Prokofiev day in and day out. Alice and Rebekkah were there but also lots of new friends, an old guy from the magazine with teeth missing and a red nose. He's publishing something about Mother Goose. And there were other people too, a girl with too much makeup, real thick pancake, who kept vanishing and coming back, and then I found out she was a go-go girl in a nearby bar, but actually a film major at NYU whose thesis is a twenty-minute movie of Jack in the altogether—so we'll finally get to see what his tushy looks like."

"And that interests you?"

"Oh, just try to tell me, Will Wright, that you're utterly in-different to it."

"I imagine he's hairless and has flat muscles."

"But he's going to the gym now and like all those gay men has giant shoulders but skinny legs."

"Any sign of a mustache yet?"

"He'll never be a clone, I fear. But I forgot to tell you, the go-go girl is hysterically in love with Jack, and he thinks the whole movie thing is just a ruse to get his pants off."

"Maybe she'll convert him. After all, he had sex with women in college."

"He told me that he likes the way women feel more than the way men feel but that visually he prefers men, and that he likes women more than men but can only fall in love with men."

I was struck by how proud Alex was to have secured this information, what she treasured as "specifics."

She said, almost wistfully, "But I wonder if he's ever been in love with anyone beside you. If he'd ask me, I could give him specifics about you that would break the spell right away."

"What would you say?" I was smiling, but I could feel a surge of adrenaline run through me.

"I'd say that you're very forgetful about the little things but positively regal about the big ones. That your nipples are more sensitive than mine—"

"Don't you dare tell him that."

"That you're really an old-fashioned man out of an Arrow shirt ad: noble and patriotic and pious and gentle as a lamb un-less provoked and then fierce as a lion."

"I'm not all that pious. Would you describe me as a home-body?" I asked her, thinking of Pia's companion from Bergamo.

"Yes, of course, and when my mother asked me how I managed to keep you despite all of my failings and eccentricities and the predatory babes prancing about New York, I said we were the perfect match and always had been."

I thought for a while and then said, "I wonder if any of us would know what we're living through if we didn't at some point have to describe our lives to our friends."

"Do you suspect Jack of influencing me?"

"No, no! Never! You're being so female. I was just speaking generally."

"As a novelist. Oh Will, I wish you'd start writing again."

"No one's exactly waiting for my next literary offering."

I attended Jack's next cocktail event and had dinner with him. Alex had some meeting in Larchmont to protect the deer even though they were destroying everyone's gardens. I met and chatted with the guy who was converting Mother Goose into French homonyms.

I thought, Here we all are paying taxes and raising our vulnerable children and submitting to erotic temptations that may ruin everything and hoping to end this wretched war in Vietnam—and this jackass is wasting all his waking energy on French spellings of English fairy tales. What world is he living in? I was polite and he was unstoppable.

I met the pole dancer too, and I asked her if she had other film projects in mind for after she finished with Jack, and I could see from her confusion that she was a true obsessive who'd never imagined even for one single tiny second anything after Jack.

I talked to a stylish English redhead who wrote about dance for a magazine and had, as I finally noticed, a glass eye, too blue and crystalline to be convincing, though she'd trained her long auburn hair to sweep over it. She had a short, dark lover, a novelist stymied in his career and festering with resentment; I didn't mention my own failed novel.

At last Jack and I were alone at Ruskay's. "So these are your friends now?" I asked, as if determined to be tolerant toward this new cheesy world we were inhabiting. "They're all interesting."

"Are they?" Jack asked. "To me it's a rather depressing choice between solitude, which I enjoy only if it's broken from time to time, and—what was I saying? Oh, right. Solitude—or all this totally predictable chatter. I'm not especially intelligent, but I think I recognize intelligence when I see it. It's mainly a matter of surprise. Smart people say surprising things. They're not always in character."

"Whereas the pole dancer—"

"Who? Oh yeah, her name is Sammy."

"Sammy," I said, "can be counted on to talk about nothing but you."

"Did she really do that?"

"She's cute, in good shape from all that pole dancing. You should give her a whirl."

"I don't think I could get it up. Our tastes become narrower and deeper with time, don't you think?"

"How so?"

"Narrower in that now I only like men, but deeper in that now I like Negroes and Orientals and up to forty and down to twenty and workingmen."

"Workingmen?"

"Firemen. Not that they're easy to bag."

"Is that how you think of seduction: as bagging?"

"It's just a word, Will. The truth is that I'm absurdly romantic. Each time I kiss a man, I wonder if this could be the one. On the subway I'll look at a stranger and wonder if he could be Mr. Right."

I said, "Then why are you single?"

I was looking around, and I realized that Ruskay's was a gay restaurant. The waiters were all gay, as were half of the customers. The mirror-topped tables were gay, and so was the ubiquitous smell of the Windex used to wipe them. The old-fashioned tile floors, the dramatic lighting, the whoops of laughter almost instantly suppressed into terribly amused hissing—it all seemed extremely gay, down to the men in formfitting T-shirts despite the cold outside, and I hoped none of my clients would see me.

"Why am I single?" Jack said. "I blame our whole cruising ritual. You pick up a guy at a bar and bring him home without saying much and then fuck him and light up a cigarette, then tell your coming-out story, exchange numbers, and that's that. For someone to catch my attention, I'd have to meet him at work and wonder if he was gay and only gradually get to know him, and all the confidences would be exchanged slowly and reluctantly, and then at last we'd have some sort of clumsy sex, and it would be his first time—well, you get the picture."

For a moment I feared he was talking about our early friendship.

I said, "Good luck with that," and realized how insipid I sounded, how clinically cheerful. Jack came across as so worldly, so blasé and thoroughly at home in gay life. When had this transition taken place? In the years we hadn't seen each other, I guessed. The whole world was becoming more tolerant and progressive, and even stodgy Jack had been caught up in the general drift toward the left.

What I wanted to talk about was Alex and Pia, but Jack beat me to it.

"I think Alex suspects something but probably not another woman. She just can't imagine another woman. She thinks of you as shy and true-blue."

"If not a woman, then what?" I asked, alarmed.

"Gambling debts? A failing business? Your spying for the Soviet Union?"

"Did you make all that up?"

Jack smiled. He was eating an avocado salad without much appetite. Too many museum cocktails, I suspected. "I just made it up," he said. "But she does think you're preoccupied. She says you wake up during the night and pad down to the kitchen and drink a glass of milk, which you never used to do."

"I'm not worried; my life seems too good to be true." I shifted gears. "Do you remember when you asked me how Pia was in bed? Did you ever ask her about me? What'd she say?"

"She said you were a high school sophomore in the best and worst senses of the word."

I opened my hands in what I thought of as a very funny Jewish way. "And? What's that supposed to mean?"

"That you're clumsy and—"

"No staying power?"

"She didn't say that." Jack pushed his uneaten avocado slivers under a lettuce leaf. "No, just that you're all over her in some sweet high school way, the lovemaking equivalent of saying, 'Oh boy! Oh boy!'"

"Is that bad?"

"Better than falling asleep," he said, playing it to the hilt.

"What's the bad part?"

"There isn't any," he said. "She adores you. Maybe that will prove to be the bad part."

"I wonder why she adores me."

"Why do we all? I hear everything about you from both women—Alex especially praises you for being so fidel, as she puts it."

I thought about the whole situation for a moment.

"The two women confide in you, and you can see all the discrepancies in their accounts." I felt trapped and irritated but couldn't justify my feelings. "I only get to sleep with them—and perhaps Alex tells you we don't make love very often."

"She would never confide anything like that," he said. "Anyway, she's very romantic and pretty paranoid."

"Then what's your take on all this?"

"The stakes are high," Jack said. "If it were two men, everyone would expect them to cheat and break up after six months. Two months is my maximum. Anyway, nobody much cares about men's affairs. There are no children, no car pools, no you–do–the–lawn–work–and–I'll–cook sort of thing."

"Jesus, why is heterosexuality so fucked up?" I asked.

"I read something about eggs being dear and sperm cheap that was supposed to explain everything, but I forget what it means."

"Wait, wait!" I said. "I think it means that since a woman produces so few eggs, and once one is fertilized she's out of commission for a year, say, whereas men produce schools of minnows—but that's just stating the obvious."

We both sank into a depressed silence. There was a television turned on over the bar, and I said, "If this were a straight place, there would be some game on the TV, not modern dance."

"If it were civilized," Jack said, "there'd be no TV at all."

"There are plenty of women here, but somehow you just know it's a queer place."

"The bad food is the giveaway."

We ordered dessert and then Jack said, "Straight life is fine if you're married. But since everyone gets tired of that sooner or later—aren't men programmed to spread their genes as far and wide as possible?—well, then men want to experiment, and it's so easy in gay life. Two guys just stare at each other and get boners and lock themselves in the bathroom. And with a woman—but you tell me. You're the expert."

I held my head in my hands and looked down into the blue-mirrored tabletop: scary view of monster nostrils. "The real problem," I said, "is that women always want to marry, and you can do that only once at a time. It sounds vain, but hundreds of women would like to be Mrs. Will L. Wright."

"What does the 'L' stand for?"

"Luckinbill, but few women want to have a one-night stand or even a one-year stand with Will Luckinbill."

"I think Pia is enjoying it."

"She is?"

"She likes how you lie with half your weight on her, almost in a trance, then like a lion spotting an eland spring into action and kiss her neck and face and almost bite her mouth."

"She said all that?"

"She likes those trances and unannounced attacks. No one ever did that before, she said."

"But what about you?" I asked Jack. "Both women ignore

your needs and your . . . reality as a man. Do you ever feel they're treating you like some eunuch?"

"A eunuch? Funny question."

I started meeting Jack for drinks more often, as if I hoped to justify my adultery in his eyes—which was pointless, since he didn't disapprove. I did. The more fascinated I became with Pia, the guiltier I felt.

I'd never really understood sex before. Of course I'd jerked off a lot, but I'd never looked at hard-core pornography, too fastidious to buy anything other than *Playboy*. And when I masturbated I wasn't creative. I didn't invent new scenes. I just replayed those special few experiences I'd known in real life. I didn't choose this method; it was my temperament—a curious lack of imagination in someone who still considered himself a novelist. Because I'd only ever rewound my own tapes, I'd never explored anything kinky or even purely sensual, stripped of sentiment.

Now, with Pia, the prologue and the coda might be romantic, but everything in between was complete perversion. She was permitted to hold my cock at the base like a throttled child, and to lick the head with thorough care, almost (to change the image) as if it were a doll's head that she was painting with her tongue, determined to cover every last centimeter. I was free to explore her anus with my tongue while fingering her vagina as she rocked her body back and forth feverishly against my mouth. Neither of us knew these movements in advance. They weren't consecrated by habit. They were invented on the spot as a way of scratching what itched.

But what was freest was the aftermath, when we'd lie athwart her big bed in the sunlight, feeling the warmed air rise from the vents, my head on her belly or between her breasts. She'd said that her young blond from Bergamo had liked to spend the mornings between her breasts, and I could understand his predilection. I'd often get hungry and poke at the photogenic cheeses and fruits on the Moroccan plate. Her mink pillows glistened; I wondered if she kept them oiled. I also wondered why she didn't trim her bush, she who shaved her legs and plucked her eyebrows. Maybe no one had ever advised her on bush length. Finally I trimmed it with fingernail scissors, pretending it was some kinky fetish that excited me. There was an essentialist in me that didn't like the idea that I'd intervened and altered her toward a look I preferred. I had to squint morally and pretend that nature had trimmed her that way.

I'd read in a book about monkeys that the primate nervous system was slow to be turned on and even slower to switch off. If so, Pia was a super-primate in that she took forever to respond but once aroused could never calm down. I'd get tired and want to sleep but she would still be rubbing against me and panting. The next day at my desk, I'd spring a boner thinking about her plunging her arm down between her full thighs and fucking her own wrist and I'd call her.

Once Alex asked me why I smelled so strongly of a flowery perfume.

"Jasmine," she said. "It smells like jasmine at night."

I said, "Beth"—the name of my girl—"is wearing that new trendy perfume Sympathy for the Devil, and we're all complaining. It's giving us all headaches."

After that I asked Pia not to wear her jasmine perfume. She became cross and wouldn't say anything over lunch. At last, when we were alone and I was kissing her mouth and her large nipples, she muttered, "Will, it's really too inhibiting, all these rules and restrictions."

Idea for story: The married man has nothing to gain by arguing his case with his mistress or arguing at all. The most he can hope for is a benign sidestepping of any controversy.

During the children's fall break Alex flew with them back to St. Barts. She said it would help Margaret get over her lingering cold. I said I was going to stay in New York at the Pierre for the ten days they were away, since it would be too much of a downer commuting to an empty house. That way the staff would have a little break as well. Ghislaine could return to France for a holiday. My life in town gave me more opportunities to be with Pia, which mollified her for a while. And enabled me to know her better; my feelings for her deepened. I wasn't sure they would, but they did.

We had dinner with her brother Alfredo, who was severely depressed. He'd been a broker addicted to work and amphetamines. One day he came to and was sitting at a booth in Rikers Coffee Shop on Sheridan Square, and he realized that it was Tuesday evening and he'd lost four days, including two workdays.

He talked about it freely with an assumed AA joviality.

"You're so funny about all this, Alfredo," I said.

"We're always laughing in AA," he said with a trace of an Italian accent. "Right across the hall are the people in Al-Anon, the wives and children of drunks. They're all crying and we're all laughing."

"That's terrible," said Pia merrily.

"Terrible," Alfredo concurred.

A long silence set in. I started asking him questions worthy of a Virginia hostess.

"So who's your favorite Italian pop singer?"

"Milva," he said, which didn't get us very far.

"What's your favorite kind of pasta?"

"Pesto Genovese. That's the kind with green beans, potatoes, and pesto, served on these little twisted pasta spirals called
trofie."

Another silence.

Then I asked, "If you could travel anywhere in the world,
where would it be?"

"They say Bali is nice," he said mournfully, adding, "though
too many Australians, I've heard."

I got up to go to the men's room; when I came back a moment
later, Pia and Alfredo were in the middle of a vigorous conversation and I realized that my hostessy questions had had a chilling
effect. I subsided into silence and studied Alfredo, who had what
I took to be the patient earnestness of an addict on the mend.
I'd never met anyone in recovery, though plenty of my relatives
in Virginia were slaves to what an old aunt of mine had called
John Barleycorn. Part of me thought it could all be done with
willpower. I was surprised that an Italian would espouse AA,
which was so American in its belief in the group and in re-
demption.

He was a coarser version of Pia, with lower eyebrows, a much
bigger nose, and dumpling ears that made me think he'd been a
wrestler in school—his left ear was particularly swollen. He had
glimmers of Pia's charm, but sobriety had chastened him, nearly
extinguishing his vivacity.

"That will come back," Pia said when we were alone. "You
were wonderful, pure genius asking about Milva. He's usually
so shy; you got him to talk, and it was absolutely extraordinary.

I guess I hadn't realized how kind you are. You must be a wonderful father."

Her comment about my role as a father made her sad, which rubbed up against her appreciation of my kindness. She took my arm.

We spent an evening with Alfredo and a friend of his from Venice, Francesco. I surmised from sad stories about his defeats with women that Alfredo wasn't gay, but this Francesco was flamboyantly so. We went to a good Italian restaurant in the East Fifties, and Francesco laughed and joked and talked dirty for hours, like a professional entertainer. At one point he threw breadsticks at us all. The American diners looked horrified, but the Italian waiters laughed.

"Do you admire my figure, Will?" he asked, standing up. He pulled his shirt out of his trousers, exposing his midriff, and pointed to the right side and the left.

"Do you find it lovely?" he asked. "Touch. You have the right to touch it."

Alfredo said, "You exaggerate, Francesco. The poor man doesn't like men; he likes women."

"You all say that, but the gentleman is a novelist."

"Yes," Alfredo conceded.

"So that means he likes everything beautiful. He's an artist who admires beauty? I am correct?"

I caved in and touched his stomach, murmuring, "Lovely."

"There!" Francesco said. "You see, Alfredo? Pia? You are terrible, your disdain for my beauty. But you are not artists. Will is an artist."

He turned his chair toward me to exclude them, put his hand on his jaw, and propped his elbow up on the table. He said in a confidential voice, "Let's ignore them. They are philistines. I'm sad to say it, I've known them all my life, but I've been unable to improve them. They are rich and aristocrats but not very cultured, while I am a poor teacher living in just one room, but I exercise and take the sun and keep my hairs very blond and iron my own clothes and I know how to pose beautifully, no?"

He struck an absurd pose, standing and wrapping one arm around his chest. He squeezed his legs together and pursed his lips and crossed his eyes.

He said, "Do you admire my *plastique*, Will? Do you understand its beauty? I've based it on a basso-rilievo by Luini. My idea is to base my *plastique* on the sculpture of the *Rinascimento*. You're sensitive, you are too good for these terrible people. Tell me, is Pia a good lover? I mean, in the bed? Or is she like one of our Italian tagliatelle: no flavor, no sauce?"

He was thrilled with his own question, and he turned to Pia, jabbed a finger at her, stuck out his tongue, and said, "No sauce!"

Turning back to me, he declared in a low voice, "No sauce she has no sauce at all."

Now he returned to his main project: me.

"Will, you have tried the limp tagliatello, you have seen the beauty of my *plastique* in the Luini style"—and again he pursed his lips and crossed his eyes—"and now you should choose the lovely Venetian blond over the dull woman of Brescia. Yes, Pia is from Brescia, where the very poorest, dullest peasants live, very, very sad, they have no folk songs, no dances, no pretty costumes, they just—how you say?—ploe?"

"Plow," said Pia.

"Thank you, darling. They just ploe and look at the earth and wear terrible dark clothes, whereas we Venetians are dancing on our beautiful gondolas wearing rich tissues—"

"Fabrics," coached Alfredo helpfully.

"I am a professor of English!" Francesco announced indignantly. "How dare you correct me? 'Tissue' is perfectly correct, Mr. Native Speaker, no?"

"Well," I said, "it depends."

"But we are losing the points!" Francesco exclaimed. "We were talking of my beauty and my *plastique*"—again the pursed mouth and this time a hand frozen in midair—"and our cheerful gondolas and lovely folk songs and it's a question, Will, if you choose my beauty or this dull woman with no culture."

Shit, I thought, is this going to go on all evening?

But I realized that Europeans, at least the aristocrats, saw gays as entertaining and funny, and certainly Pia and Alfredo were urging Francesco on.

He'd just arrived from the Veneto, and he left us early because he was jet-lagged.

They said, "Isn't he adorable? We love our Francesco. He always keeps us laughing. How dull our Septembers in Venice would have been without him."

"Yeah, he's funny," I said, "if a bit extreme."

"Extreme?" Pia asked, suddenly hostile.

Alfredo said, "That's what we love about him."

"Yes, Francesco is adorable," Pia insisted. "We really should introduce him to Jack."

"I don't think so," I said.

"But why ever not?"

"Jack doesn't like flaming queens," I said.

"Queen!" Pia exclaimed. "How boorish. Francesco isn't a type any more than you are a public schoolboy. I'm sure Jack would find him amusing, but let's not squabble."

She changed the subject and, perhaps for the sake of Alfredo's morale, for the rest of the evening seemed genuinely cheerful. But she didn't invite me back home with her.

I'd assumed she was enamored of me, and somehow I hadn't imagined she might choose or not choose to be with me. I headed back to the Pierre.

Though my room was small, it was on a high floor looking down Fifth Avenue, with its lights starting and stopping traffic. Wounded by Pia's rejection, I tore the back of my trousers lurching past an overly ornate chair. I kicked the chair over. How dare she banish me after I said something obvious about her effeminate friend? Of course he's a screaming queen, I fumed—I'd learned that one from Jack. Judging from Jack's museum cocktail parties, he didn't have any gay friends. In all these years, I'd never met another gay man through Jack.

I thought, He's right. He just uses them for sex, which is what I should do—sleep with women, then toss them aside. Why have dangerous, family-threatening affairs with fleshy women who never say an interesting word, who've never read a book beyond Simone de Beauvoir's *The Second Sex*, the sole source of her ideas? If I make her listen to a Ravel piano concerto, she says, "It's dreamy." She misses all the wit and dynamism and asperity.

She's a moron and promiscuous out of boredom; just watch, one day she'll toss my way a cute little venereal disease to take home to my wife! I know it's the cheese going off—the Pont-l'Évêque—but I can't help associating the smell with her body, some yeast infection. Look at the company she keeps—a skinny, peroxided faggot probably nursing his own dose of the clap in that "beautiful" anus of his.

I took a deep breath and got ready for bed. I had Thomas

Pynchon's *Gravity's Rainbow*. I'd been putting off reading it for ages. I was afraid it would make me so jittery with envy (reviews had all been ecstatic) that I wouldn't be able to sleep, but I wanted something elevated in my life, something beyond my sexual obsession with this dunce and her court jester and depressed brother.

I would have called Alex down in St. Barts, but it was too late; she'd said they were living by the sun, the only sensible thing to do. I missed her and a sense of decency in my life. I missed Palmer and Peg. I felt so tenderly toward them and could picture them sleeping peacefully beside the beach and the water.

I wrestled with my sheets and I thought, No matter how luxurious a hotel is, there's no getting around the fact that other people have slept on these mattresses and rubbed themselves with these towels. I hated the dirt and expense of a hotel and longed for my nature-nut wife and our impeccable linens and health food meals.

I strummed my way through a few pages of Pynchon. Here was something about bananas—everyone making drinks and meals out of nothing but bananas. This Pynchon was wild! So intelligent and funny and original. Not in a million years would I have chosen someone like Francesco to spend an evening with. Then again, it seemed these Europeans loved to be amused more than anything else, as if boredom were stalking them night and day, the dreaded ennui. For them a gay man was as amusing as a dwarf was for a king. Francesco, despite his protestations of poverty, was probably a *baronino* like all the rest of them. He could be funny and outrageous, being one of them. He was probably always inventing some new bit of comedy. Tonight it was his "beauty" and his "*plastique*." And my sensitivity to those because

I was an "artist." That must have meant that Pia had told him I was a writer. Guess that counts more over there than it does here, I thought. Authors. Aristocratic faggots. All a way of staying amused in this dull world while advertising one's own exclusivity in taste and rank. Those people will never read Pynchon, even if he's translated. Too much work . . .

I asked myself, do I despise Pia?

I wished she weren't so vapid, so certain she was fascinating.

I turned over and over in my bed and finally made myself a scotch on the rocks from the minibar and smoked a Kent while watching part of a western on TV.

The phone rang.

"Hi," she said. "It's me. I'm down in the lobby. Can I come up?"

"Sure. It's room 1142."

"I don't have any panties on."

"Oh yeah?" I asked, afraid someone might hear—was the house phone next to the main desk? "Good, very good," I said. "Come on up."

I rushed to brush my teeth and hair. A moment later she was rolling her knuckles against my door in a muted knock. When I opened it, she had on a raincoat though it wasn't raining, and she was wearing a subdued smile.

I pulled her in, closed the door, embraced her for a long time, and then, still kissing her, pulled up the raincoat and placed a hand on her bare, firm ass and rubbed a finger against her asshole. I was so excited. I wanted to sodomize her, though I hadn't done that to anyone more than two or three times in my life. Two times.

She knew what I wanted and apparently wasn't afraid of it. She pulled my penis out of the opening in my pajama bottoms and turned around and rubbed her ass against it. We clawed our clothes off, and she knelt on all fours athwart the bed, saying, "A little lubricant might help."

I could think of nothing beyond a miniature bottle of magnolia body oil that the hotel provided, and I rushed into the bathroom to get it.

"Now go slow," she said.

I slathered some oil on her hole and worked a finger in. With my other hand I reached around and played with the nipple on that side.

"Yes," she said.

I was afraid that if getting in her became hard going or fecal I'd wilt, but the whole situation excited me. After I was in about an inch, she gasped and reached back and waved a blind hand in alarm. In a moment, though, the crisis had passed and she pushed back, saying, "Oh Will," and I went in nicely.

It didn't feel like the warm glove of the cunt. It was tighter at the entrance but loose and balloony inside, once past the ring (wasn't *anus* the Latin word for "ring"?). I loved that she was giving me this other orifice; now I'd had all three. Maybe it was bringing her pleasure only in the form of submission. She'd submitted her asshole to me; I was in the hole that gave birth every day to a turd. Now everything was dirtier, grittier, far from the rose water of romantic sex that Alex concocted and purveyed. Nor was Pia just enduring it; she was shoving her ass back on my dick, eager for more.

We lay beside each other and shared a Kent. "Don't you want to come?"

"No," she said, laughing, "I'm like a Greek girl who preserves her virginity by offering her croup to men." She excused herself, and I imagined her sitting on the toilet shitting out my babies. It was repulsive and thrilling and I felt a new intimacy between us. I wasn't sure exactly what I was feeling, but it included exhilaration.

We saw Francesco twice more over the next two weeks before he returned to Venice, and now that I understood how and why he was funny, I laughed like hell over his antics. He decided that all men, as they got older, resembled lesbians with their cropped hair and fat faces and sagging tits, and so he was going to prepare for that inevitable role by studying lesbians and doing dykeish things like making scenes in public, drinking beer, and buddying up to workingmen in positions of authority—cops, train conductors. He was also going to buy a cat and exchange cat pictures with lesbians. I had no idea whether they really did those things, but I went along with the joke.

We invited Jack on one of the evenings, and the way he responded astonished me.

We were in Little Italy, which Francesco called the Attic of Naples. He loved the souvenir stores and even picked up a Mussolini ashtray. "*Un tesoro*," he said, "a great treasure!"

He loved the sugary zeppole a vendor was selling and the "ancient Roman" decor of a restaurant complete with plastic busts of emperors and plastic Doric columns pressed against a printed vinyl mural of Vesuvius erupting.

"This was the way Naples was right after the war," said Francesco. "Oh, how they fleeced the conquering American soldiers, especially the sweet, trusting Negroes, who brought everyone such joy with their burnt honey skin and huge pink hands and their dancing—their dancing! It is so cruel, the American racism—why do you mistreat the poor Negro? The Negro loves Italy and the Italian boys and women. But Little Italy, even the espresso with its zest of lemon! No one has drunk coffee like this in Italy since 1900 in Palermo. Little Italy is like Pompeii, all of the Italian past so frozen in time."

As we sat in a café and ate creamy pastries, Jack laughed with real delight at everything Francesco said. Sitting next to Francesco, I could see him sweating and clenching his hands and licking his lips, and I thought about how much work it must be to be the life of the party, even if the party was just three or four friends. I was reminded of the time in church choir back in Charlottesville when I was standing next to a professional opera singer, a baritone, who'd been hired for Easter mass. At least a gallon of sweat poured off him, and his lungs filled audibly like the bellows of the pipe organ beside us.

Jack didn't need to distance himself. He and Francesco might have belonged to different species, though I was sure that Francesco, like Jack, had only straight friends—but then again, what did I know of Jack's nocturnal life? All I knew was that he never arrived at the office before eleven, which meant that he could go to bed at two A.M. and still get enough sleep. What did he do during those hours from eleven to two? He didn't watch television, though he was a reader.

What most impressed me was Jack's ease with the Italians, all three of them. He even knew a few expressions in Italian, including *magari* ("Would that it might be so"), so much more efficient than its English translation. I'd only just now learned that one from Pia, who used it all the time, even when she was speaking English.

I could see that Francesco didn't much like Jack. One clown doesn't like another unless they've worked out a routine together. Though really, Jack wasn't a clown. He never talked about his homosexuality in a group. He could tell jokes, and he certainly was pleasant and "light" in the way these people prized—Pia had even told me once that "lightness" was a patrician trait. But Jack didn't indulge in self-parody or confession. His "material" was never autobiographical. Nor did he prepare a whole "act" for each evening the way Francesco did. And unlike Francesco, he was never willing to appear grotesque. Jack did not seem to feel any affinity with other gay men unless he desired them.

In that way he was different from me. I liked women, all women. Certainly more than men. I'd always preferred my sisters to my brothers. I had never liked other men to touch me, and a sport like wrestling, a month's worth of it in high school gym class, gave me the creeps.

I realized that all women charmed me, even the stupid or loud ones. Even lesbians. I once saw a lesbian couple at a Greenwich Village party, and I found them touching—the way the more masculine one hovered over the more feminine one, who was a splashier dresser. There they were: The "butch," as Jack called them, wore a baggy black turtleneck and green corduroy trousers and had cropped hair but also simple gold hoops through her pretty ears, to prove she had a right to the ladies' room. She was bringing a drink to her "femme," who was considerably older, with blond hair and bangle bracelets and a low-cut blouse to reveal a scrawny chest. They were sweet. There was so much love circulating between them. Jack told me that this was common—a baby butch and an aging femme. I wanted to watch them making love, the chubby butch's buttocks ruched with cellulite, the femme rickety and skeletal and playing shy. Their physical flaws made them all the more beautiful in my eyes, especially the calm radiating from the butch's face. I felt that I understood them, that I could help them out even as I acknowledged that their relationship was designed to keep me and all other men away.

Jack didn't dote on gay—or even straight—men in the way that I doted on women. Nor did he seem indifferent or even cool to women, as I thought gay men must be. I guessed I had gotten that wrong. But wouldn't a gay man see a woman as a rival? Or try to tame her by turning her into a sister, the way competitive women did with each other? Yet there wasn't a trace of any of that in Jack. He was clear about his lack of sexual desire for women, but he was fully alive to their physical appeal. He'd say, "Catch the rack on that one," or "Her butt wiggles faster than a hummingbird's wings." Once I asked him how it was that he noticed those attractions, and he said, "It's my vice. I look for the sexual possibilities in everyone I meet, young or old, male or female."

Pia told me that she always felt very close to Jack physically, that he often took her hand at the movies or walked with an arm around her waist or a hand on her shoulder, almost like a proprietary Latin who is proud to lay even the slightest claim on a beautiful woman in public.

"We once slept together," she said. "It was late. We'd watched a movie on TV together, and we'd drunk two bottles of wine. I said he might as well stay over, and he nodded and stripped down to his underwear and held me all night, but it was just brother-sister."

"Was this—recently? Since I've known you?"

"*Geloso!*" she laughed, tapping the end of my nose with a playful fingertip. "No," she went on vaguely, "it was long ago. But in the middle of the night I woke up to feel him poking my hip with his huge *cazzo*; even though he was asleep, he probably imagined I was a handsome *ragazzo*."

"Hey," I said feebly, "that rhymes. *Cazzo, ragazzo.*" I was wondering why she was suddenly being so Italian . . .

So Jack's got a big dick, I thought, and she noticed it. Women say they don't care about dick size, but that's obviously rubbish.

"Oh, what the hey," she said.

Seeing Jack among the Europeans forced me to reevaluate him. He clearly felt completely at ease with "social" people now. In the early sixties, when I'd met him, I'd thought of his queerness as a deformity, a scandal, something akin to a heroin addiction or pedophilia or membership in the Communist Party. I'd liked Jack in spite of this, but since I'd known it could get him fired, I'd been determined to keep it a secret. I covered for him if anyone at the office quizzed me about who he was dating. Almost no one did, because Jack was extremely discreet. I thought I was a generous soul for taking on board a fag friend, obviously a liability to me and a permanent danger to himself.

Now everything had changed. Jack was no longer a faggot; he was gay. European aristocrats found him and his kind amusing. Befriending a gay was like knowing a Negro—you didn't want too many, but one was chic. Jack had become so confident, and he'd become even more polished. He was so attentive; he laughed so merrily, though he was never sycophantic. Most of all he had the relentless energy I'd always associated with "social" people. He'll end up as the president of the Bachelors' Cotillion, I thought.

On our Little Italy night we all went back to Pia's place and got drunk. We were nearly sick drinking bourbon and began to talk about sex. Someone had said that Americans talk about money so they won't have to talk about sex, and Europeans talk about sex so they won't have to talk about money. That night everyone's money secrets were safe. We kept passing the bottle, and Francesco began describing his "affair" with his older brother when Francesco was eleven and his brother was fifteen.

"Giacchino? You had sex with him?" said Pia. "I did too but much later."

"Now he's boringly straight," Francesco said, "and would kill me if he knew I was telling you this. When we were kids he loved to fuck me, and with no emotion. But I loved him. I was so hurt when I was thirteen and Giacchino came home from school and I tried to start something with him and he called me a *froscio*." He clarified for me: "A faggot."

"Wait a minute," I said, sitting on the floor between two towers of mink pillows. I had to put a hand over one eye to see. "Does anyone sheerish—sheerioushly believe in bisexuality?"

"Yes, of course," Pia said. She was lying across her bed on her stomach. She'd changed into a silk burnoose. "Everyone is bisexual. That was established by Freud."

"Established! What would he know?" Jack said. He was seated in a proper straight-back chair but appeared, in his dignified way, to be listing to one side. "Anyway, women are always flirting with lesbianism, and no one holds it against them. Straight men find it a turn-on, right, Will?"

"Yes," I conceded.

Pia said, "You can always tell the lesbian porn that's meant for men. At the last moment a man steps in and saves the day with his big penis and screws the women."

"It's true that straight men fantasize about lesbians," I said.

"That's why men like lesbian porn," Jack said.

I'd noticed before that Jack often said "men" when he meant straight men.

Toward dawn I stumbled back to the Pierre, realizing that the others were going to continue drinking. When I got up to my room, the lights were on and Alex, still fully dressed, was asleep in my bed, looking very tan.

5.

I RAN INTO the bathroom and gargled mouthwash and brushed my hair and splashed cold water on my face, but by then she was awake.

"Where have you been?" she asked. She was still half asleep. "I was going to surprise you. We came back a day early."

I sat on the edge of the bed and touched her face. "Oh, I must smell disgusting. I got drunk with Jack. If I'd only known—"

"But not at his place, right? Because he didn't pick up when I phoned."

"No, you're right. We were with some friends of his."

"The hotel was nice about letting me in. They said you aren't here very often."

"That's because I sneak past them and don't eat the chocolates they put on the pillow and make my own bed—"

"You do?" She was sitting up now. "Why would you make your own bed?" She yawned and politely covered her mouth.

"You know I have a phobia about hotels. I don't like the idea of sleeping on beds that other people have touched."

"We should get a little apartment of our own." Alex stretched. "I was so worried. Are you really that drunk?"

"I must smell like a distillery. Hey, welcome back! I know,

why don't we both get cleaned up and go over to the Edwardian Room for eggs Benedict?"

"That's a good idea." Looking around, she said, "I fell asleep
with all the lights on. I kept thinking you'd come back and it
would be such a lovely surprise. Or at least a surprise."

She stood and looked at herself in the full-length mirror to
see how badly her skirt was creased.

"It is, it's a wonderful surprise," I said.

She smiled a pinched little smile. She had a perfect tan, but
her crow's-feet looked deeper, though I was sure that she'd been
wearing her sunglasses every day in St. Barts, and that every
night she'd been applying hundred-dollar creams to her face.

When I took my shower after Alex, I glanced down at my
body, which looked scrawnier than before, though I was acquiring a roll of booze fat around the middle. As a teen I'd learned
to stop touching my testicles lest I lower the one all the more,
but now I found myself washing my genitals thoroughly. I gargled in the shower stream. A melody flitted through my brain,
but I couldn't summon up the words. I felt so confused. I just
stood there after I got out of the shower, not drying myself.

I was at a crossroads without a map. I checked the mirror but
could hardly meet my own eye. My cheekbones were pushing
their way out of my face, as if they were knuckles—two fists!—
under a white sheet, a very thin sheet that could easily be torn.

Once we were seated in sturdy upholstered chairs in the Edwardian Room, I began to feel decent again. I wondered if anyone looking at us envied us: a fine young couple, obviously
well-heeled, in love but in a kindly, almost unconscious way.

How far from the truth! I watched Alex as she talked, her
manner alternating between shyness and pugnaciousness, with
an accent drilled into her so many years ago by Brearley, clipped

but never loud or irritating, her vowels in the process of swimming away from American nasal tones, bound for the elegant farther shores of English "Received Pronunciation," the sacred "RP" coveted by her mother and her friends, though never so thoroughly adopted as to seem un-American. She had on fake pearl earrings as large and shiny as her eyes, as if a surrealist had added extra eyes to her ears.

She was telling me vacation tales about the adorable things Margaret and Palmer had done. Palmer had admired a black swimming instructor at the club, with his powerful chest, blinding smile, and close-cropped head. Margaret had said that she couldn't understand him and had asked Alex if he was speaking English.

"I assured her he was—are you listening to me? I know how a mother's stories can be tedious."

"Not to the father," I said. "The father is just so happy to see his wife and hear about his brood." It sounded strangely distancing for me to call myself "the father."

"Will," she said. She looked apologetic but also almost defiant—it was a complex look that I couldn't quite decipher. "Tell me. Are you and Jack lovers?"

I laughed in surprise, and I think that, literally, for the first time in my life, my jaw dropped. "Jack? And me?"

She lowered her lids and looked through her lashes with a sort of pained sympathy.

"You can tell me anything, you know. I just need to know."

"Are you crazy, Alex? I've never had sex with a man, not even when I was twelve. You don't honestly think—why would you think something like that? You know that I can't even bear for a man to touch me."

"You did hold him that time."

"You think you're so understanding, but you keep harping on that. It was . . . an act of generosity on my part! Against all my inclinations. I should never have—"

"Then you're not having an affair?"

"No," I said, signaling the waiter for more coffee. Suddenly a strategy occurred to me. "Are you?"

"Me? With whom, pray tell?"

"Does that mean you would if you could?"

"No, it just means you've lost your mind, Will."

"That's how I feel about your questions. I mean, I could suspect the young black swimming teacher if I wanted to. You were just now praising his body and smile and skills . . ."

She pressed her fingertips to her temples, and I saw tears come to her eyes.

"I'm sorry, Alex," I said. "I must still be sort of drunk, and this screwdriver isn't helping."

She said, "Have I been foolish to trust you? There's something so . . . tacky about infidelity. I was never happy with any other man before you, Will, but now I'm afraid I've let my guard down. We've been so happy these ten years, and now I feel like I'm going to be hurt. How could I have been so foolish?"

She asked it as a genuine question.

I didn't know what to say. Finally I said, "Did you drive in?"

She stared at me with tears still in her eyes and said, "Yes. Why?"

"Let's go home," I said. "I'll check out of the hotel and cancel my appointments at the office. I want to be with you and the children."

"You see, I believed you when you said that you adored me, that I was too good for you, that you never dreamed you could get a beauty like me. What a joke! Now I see what a complacent idiot I was."

She turned her spoon over on its stomach and looked critically at her bloated reflection in its humped back.

"Have I lost my looks? Men don't really like superior women anyway, do they? They prefer cheap girls. Have you found a cheap little slut who gets drunk with you and squeals with delight—a little pig?"

I looked at her in partially feigned bewilderment and wondered how good I was at lying.

"Alex!"

She dabbed her eyes with a tissue. I scrawled a signature in the air, calling for the check.

We walked in silence the short distance to the Pierre. Even at this early hour the streets were thronged. It was a gray, chilly day. "Not much of a homecoming for you," I said.

"Why do you—"

"The weather," I said impatiently, to push aside a more serious interpretation of my words. I thought this terrible tension in my shoulders would not go away until we talked it out.

In the car, once we were out of Manhattan and over the Brooklyn Bridge, we began to talk. I was glad I was driving; my wife's little Triumph was a stick shift, which gave me something to do and feel competent about. In the suburbs the leafless treetops slid past overhead like hands flayed to reveal their veins in an anatomy class. Alex kept fiddling with the heater.

"So, what's she like?" she asked jauntily.

"Who?" I asked.

"Your mistress."

"Love the old-fashioned word," I said, "but sorry, I don't have a mistress."

"A girlfriend, then. Let me guess: mid-twenties, an office worker, pretty, a bit overweight, a touch vulgar, but that's what makes her sexy."

"Stop this, Alex. Seriously. Stop it. No such woman exists."

"If it's not Jack and not a vulgar younger woman, then who—"

I looked at Alex, a second too long for her taste, and she begged me to return my eyes to the road.

Finally she said, "Remember, my father is a lawyer, a highly successful lawyer, and I grew up in a household used to arguments and counterarguments."

She seemed satisfied with herself, as if I'd been about to question her father's competence.

"Alex," I said, feeling her watching me, "I hate it when you get paranoid. Is this honestly how you want to pursue this?"

She shrugged and, after a pause, said in a little voice, "No. No. I want our perfect life back. Maybe you didn't think it was so perfect."

"Of course I thought—I think—it's perfect. I love you." I paused. "You love me." I risked a glance. "We love each other."

"For pity's sake, Will, keep looking at the road. This road is dangerous; it curves so much."

We sank into a silence that lasted until we pulled into our own long, long driveway, which Alex had designed to resemble a country road, with a grassy strip down the center. In this light, so weak but clear, our place seemed even more rustic, untamed. The long, dry grasses brushed against the bottom of the car. It began to rain.

"Look, Will—pheasants!"

And four big startled birds flapped noisily out of some high weeds a hundred yards ahead. We both gasped and looked happily at each other and simultaneously lowered our windows, as if we needed to breathe in our cold native air. That sudden gasp breaking through her mournful, prickly silence promised a reconciliation, if not today, then soon. At least it was feasible.

When we pulled up to the house, Alex said, "Ghislaine is turning out to be anorectic. Don't stare at her."

"Of course I won't stare."

"No, no, I know you won't. Perhaps I shouldn't have mentioned it, but she just got back from Normandy, and her fiancé laughed at her for all the weight she'd put on in America, and now she's taken draconian measures."

"It is true that sugar is added to everything Americans eat," I said blandly, grateful for this distraction.

"Not what we eat," Alex said. "Maybe in our house the strawberries are sandier, but at least it's all good honest organic produce. If Ghislaine would eat what we eat, she'd be slender but not skeletal."

"Yes," I said, smiling, taking her hand in mine, "you do look after us."

Secretly I was relieved that Ghislaine would no longer be such a voluptuous temptation inside her loose-fitting dark dresses.

I'd forgotten that the children would be at school. The house seemed bizarrely quiet except for the drum of rain.

"It's really raining now," I said, "and I can hear that that gutter needs cleaning."

"Yes," Alex said with a smile, "your city slicker days are over. By the way, I ordered lots of groceries yesterday when we came back, including some lovely trout, which I can sauté, and Ghislaine is making some purée de pommes de terre with celeriac.

You know how she does that. Shall we eat in an hour? Emily is off today. I even have some nice Riesling."

"Oh no," I said, "no wine. I'm off booze for a week."

"As you wish."

Ghislaine emerged briefly to say hello on the way to the pharmacy. She'd become dramatically thinner within two weeks. Had she swallowed a tapeworm? She was bundled up in two layers of bulky sweaters. "We have a certain pill in France, an alterna—" she began.

"Alternative?" I asked.

"Yes—one of those—kind of medicine in France. *Homéopathique.* Do you have them? Twenty little pills you put under your tongue for a grippe?"

"No, I don't think so," I said irritably, thinking, how could they be so superstitious?

"They're called Oscillococcinum."

"No," I said, laughing, "I'm sure we have nothing like that."

When Ghislaine came back from her fruitless search at the drugstore, we sat down to a salad, the fish, and the mashed potatoes. The neighbors were burning leaves, despite the damp, which had Alex in a rage because she'd given them a pamphlet and a lecture about the advantages of rot and mulch.

After lunch I went up for a nap, but I couldn't sleep. I thought about how safe and secure I felt here, despite the sound of an animal scrabbling on the roof and the mournful hooting of not one but two owls in the garden, if such a wasteland could be called a garden. I got up and looked out at it in all of its frowsiness, its dun and sere and wild devastation. And I thought about how hard it would be to sell this place. It would take at least a year of plowing and replanting to make it look normal—and the deaths of hundreds of woodland creatures.

I lay down again. Now that I was home I felt vacant, as empty as I had as a child when I'd been kept home with a fever, the sheets tucked in too tight, the jello disgusting, with a browning slice of banana entombed within. I had nothing to do, and my body missed all the stimulation it had been receiving. I could feel Pia's hand judging my balls or her tongue excavating my crack with small licks or my penis being coaxed into greater and greater greed. I felt as if my hard brown nipples, just vestigial bumps, were now pulsing with pleasure, as if they were emitting radio signals. In marriage I'd had a mouth for kissing and a penis for intercourse and ears to be whispered into, but now in concubinage my whole body had come alive and was glowing and yearning for more.

I wished I could collapse back into marital torpor. Alex's father might be a dynamic lawyer, but he obviously had a body that was 90 percent numb below the neck. I could tell how insensitive it was; I'd seen him at the Larchmont Yacht Club in a swimsuit. He could have lost a leg to a shark and felt nothing. Body armoring. A Charlottesville friend of mine, Edith, who was seeing a shrink, a follower of Wilhelm Reich, talked about "body armoring" all the time. The theory was that you hid your feelings and they got lodged in your muscles—which must have been why my shoulders ached. Edith had said that when her shrink manipulated her muscles, he would release the pain stored in them and she would sob. Pia never made me cry, but she did awaken me, unlock all those emotions—and now what was I supposed to do with these alerted, proliferating feelings?

Around five Alex came in with some smoky Lapsang tea and her oldest, most transparent china. The children lurked shyly behind her, clinging to her skirts, their faces brown as tupelo honey. They were looking at me as if they weren't quite sure what they'd find.

"Peggy," I called out. "Palmer. The two P's in the pod."

I extended my arms to them. Margaret ran to me, but Palmer turned away coyly in some silly game of his own, saying, "We're not peas."

He squeezed his eyes shut and pursed his lips into a smile and rubbed his face against his out-flung arms as if he were pretending—happily—to be indignant.

"Silly Daddy," he said, still rubbing his face, as if he'd walked into a sticky web and were trying to get it off. Then he became fascinated with a winter fly hobbling along a floorboard, and finally, magnetized against his will, he glided toward me while looking elsewhere and ended up in my arms. I thought, He's my son. He's my son.

Ghislaine, heavy with sweaters, came in and said indulgently, "*Les enfants! Allons-y! Vite, vite!*" and then they were all gone except Alex, who sat down in a slipper chair upholstered in a dull tan and muted pink peonies. I was sitting barefoot on the edge of our bed in khakis and a faded blue shirt. Outside, the daylight was draining away, and I was filled with suburban dread. Jack had once told me that he couldn't bear to live more than a hundred feet away from a subway hole. Neighborhood dogs were baying.

Alex had obviously decided we'd drawn too close to the edge of the abyss, and now she introduced a new "serious" subject, New York's disastrous finances and the rising crime rate. She liked Mayor Beame and his fiscal know-how. I wasn't so sure, but at least it was a good safe topic for us. When at last we were called to dinner, an early supper and one we could share with the children, I think we were both reassured, as if we'd been able to put some ordinary conversational plank beneath our feet and display our deft balancing skills.

Apropos of nothing I thought, Jack used to be the one who was close to being a criminal with his homosexuality, but now he's the toast of the town and I'm the one—if anyone could lift my lid and look in, they'd think I was the evildoer. I'm the adulterer.

At the bedroom doorway I kissed Alex and said, "I missed you," saying it experimentally to see if I could instill a feeling in myself simply by voicing it.

Alex held my face and kissed me all over and said, "I've missed you, terribly," which was more emotion than I'd bargained for. My soul flinched and ran off to hide. Idea for story: a couple play emotional hide-and-seek with each other over the years.

During supper I was called to the phone.

It was Pia. "What happened to you?" she asked.

"Alex came home. We're eating now."

"So early?"

"Children. It's when children eat."

"I wouldn't know."

"I'll call you tomorrow." I lowered my voice. "Don't call here."

"Another rule? I may not call you at all, anywhere. Let's just stop seeing each other."

"Fine," I said.

She hung up. When I went back to the dining room, Margaret started telling me excitedly about her scuba diving classes and the beautiful fish she'd seen.

Then Palmer chimed in. "And I—I—I saw some . . . bootiful . . . fish too, Daddy, in the boat, the bottom—" His face twisted right and left with the effort of formulating his thought for the person who hadn't been there. He was looking at the ceiling in concentration.

Margaret spoke up in her maddening way. "He means,

Daddy, that we went out in a glass-bottom boat one day to the coral reef, where we saw some lovely tropical fish." She sounded just as pedantic as her mother. Had Alex been so sure of herself even as a little girl?

I stroked the back of Palmer's neck and brushed my fingers through his long silky hair.

"It tickles, Daddy," he said, revealing his perfect white teeth. Usually his long upper lip covered his teeth, but now that he was laughing and pushing his head back into my hand I could see them, as distinct as notes played slowly on a piano without pedal.

I could tell from Alex's frozen smile that she had lots to say about the phone call, but I also knew I wouldn't hear about it till the meal was over and we were alone. I dreaded having to invent a lie—one that would hold up. Alex didn't let the children eat sweets; dessert was an apple each. After I bit into my apple, I saw traces of blood on the woody white flesh. I had two cold sores coming on, one on my tongue and one on the inside of my right cheek. Had Pia given me herpes? Or was I just run-down from all the late-night carousing?

When we were alone again, Alex asked, "Who was that on the phone?"

"It was Pia, that friend of Jack's."

"Yes?"

"She wanted us to come to lunch tomorrow, but I said I had to work. Sometimes these people . . ."

"Yes?"

"They don't realize that some people work."

"I'm sure she does realize it and counts herself lucky not to be one of them."

"I shouldn't have answered for both of us. Maybe you'd like to go."

"Do you see her often?"

"No," I said. I looked her right in the eye. I'm sure that at that moment I could have fooled a lie detector test—that's how cool I felt. I was speaking the truth for a world I wanted to inhabit in the future. A lie was a misleading report about a sin in the past, but I was predicting, not retelling.

Alex had made me cross a line. Up till now I hadn't had to lie outright. I'd omitted a few—quite a few—details. But this time my deception was wearing a bold face.

I took an early train to New York in the morning, and as soon as I was at my desk I phoned Jack. "You've got to help me," I said.

I explained to him about Alex's early return, how she'd been waiting for me at the Pierre and how Pia had called me at home.

"Alex is certain I have a mistress. Her word. At first she thought you and I were having an affair."

I immediately regretted saying that, only because people can never skip over any reference to themselves. It seemed urgent to me that Jack should understand the lies I'd told Alex and that he'd substantiate them, but he couldn't get past the flattering notion that Alex had believed he and I were lovers.

At last his curiosity was appeased, and I was able to run him through every part of his drill.

He said, "You're putting me in an awkward position."

"How so?"

"Basically you're telling me to choose you over her. If I lie to her, I'll never feel comfortable with her again."

I thought about it. My girl, Helen, was waving at me from the doorway—something was urgent—but I pointed at my watch and held up five fingers, pleading for that many minutes more. She cringed and covered her head with her arms—the roof was crashing in on us—but she walked away.

"Okay," I said, "then I'm asking you to choose me over her. I'm the one you love—surely that counts for something."

He was silent—with indignation, I was sure.

Then I said, "My marriage is at stake. Alex is so romantic and idealistic. If she learns about Pia, she'll walk out on me and take the children with her."

He said, "Does that mean you're willing to give Pia up?"

"No," I blurted out. Then I said, "Should I? Do you think I should?"

"Let me put it this way. What's keeping your marriage together? Why do you stay with Alex?"

"I'm a Catholic," I said. "Catholics don't get divorced."

His voice softened with weariness. "I thought you were going to tell me you still love Alex."

"She's very dear to me."

"That's what people say about an annoying aunt. A woman's white lie. So I'm supposed to lie a black lie because you have religious scruples about divorce and because I was once in love with you, feelings that you abhorred at the time and that I've worked long and hard to bury?"

"Bury alive," I said.

Helen came in and put a note in front of me: "Mr. Norris is on hold and is furious. He's threatening to ditch the account."

I nodded.

"Okay, look, Jack: my biggest account is about to bust a gut. Just do it, Jack. Choose me."

As I hung up, I wondered what Helen was making of my end of the conversation.

She filled me in quickly and I picked up. "Herb!" I said. "Forgive me. A little family crisis. No, no, it's all fine now. So you hated the pictures?"

I smiled at Helen, and she shook her hand in an it's-too-hot-to-handle gesture and shrugged and walked away.

"Hated, I see, is an understatement. Well, Herb, we can send out a new, more traditional photographer today. Or better yet, let me bring him over now. He's a great guy. Rick, Rick's his name. We'll have a drink, and you can explain to him what you want. Yeah, we can be there by five. Sure, Herb, sure. He can go up to Rochester tomorrow. We can have the whole thing in the can by Monday. No extra charge—are you kidding, fella? Old friends like us? I want to get this thing right, just as much as you do—more! More than you! Okay, then, let's say five. Don't worry about that. We can wait for you in the boardroom just as long as it takes for you to get free. And Rick will bring his portfolio—no, no, I agree. That other guy, Salvatore, he's a little far out, as they say. Yeah. Italian. You'll like Rick—a good Ohio guy. But talented! You'll see. The Norman Rockwell of photography."

An hour later, after I'd reached Rick and promised to double his usual fee, Jack called back. "Did you put out the fire?" he asked.

"Yeah, and you?" I asked.

"I talked to Alex. I told her we were with some college friends of mine last night getting pleasantly stewed and arguing about Gerry Ford. She wanted details, so I said we were with Bob and Becky Rogers—write this down—he's in roofing, a contractor, and she's a hands-on mom, they live on Third and Seventieth, all the kids at Chapin."

"You're a prince. They sound so boring I'm sure Alex won't remember a thing about them. Even I've already forgotten—hey! Did you make all that up?"

"Yep. But I do know a Bob Rogers at that address if she tries to check him out in the phone book. Alex asked me about Pia, and I said you'd not seen her since that time I'd brought her out to Larchmont, but that she'd called you because she was giving a big lunch for some Italian aristocrats, and two guests had dropped out, and I'd suggested you and Alex."

"You did good, my friend, real good."

I called Alex and told her about the emergency meeting at Norris Inc. and asked her to come in and meet me there.

"Darling," she said, "tonight? I just can't. Palmer's had another asthma attack."

"Poor little guy."

"And he didn't have a single attack during our vacation, but today he got really sick at school. The teacher called me in a panic, and Ghislaine and I rushed over there. He was blue."

"Where's he now?"

"He's here. He's okay. I brought him home."

"You did the right thing," I said. "I think we have to order all new rugs for his room. I was reading about dust motes and asthma. Call Bloomingdale's and order—"

"I know," she said. "I read the same article. And I've turned off the central heating and built a fire in his room."

"You've got your hands full. I'll have Helen call Bloomingdale's and order all that stuff. And sweetheart?"

"Yes?"

"I'll be home as soon as possible tonight."

"Will," she said. Then I think she didn't dare risk saying

anything else for a bit. After a pause she said, "It was really bad, Will. I'd forgotten how the problem, during an attack, is not breathing in but breathing out. He'd gasp and then just not release it. People die from asthma, you know. He fell asleep on my lap, and I just sat there with first one mask on his face for forty minutes and then the other for an hour. Now he's all right, but it scared him. It scared me. I've got a nebulizer ready to go right beside his bed. Dr. Baggy's been here."

That was what the children called the family physician, because he carried a big doctor's bag and made house calls. "Good," I said. "What did he tell you?"

"He said he'll outgrow it by age twelve. That most children do."

Palmer's attack tapped me on the shoulder and awakened me from the spell Pia had cast over me. The next day I went into a church near my office and confessed for the first time in two years. From the sound of his voice, the priest was old and frail. I was confessing to adultery, but I didn't think he was hearing me properly. All he told me to say, before sending me on my way, was four Our Fathers. Afterward I knelt in a side chapel and prayed. I said the Our Fathers.

I couldn't think what to say to the Holy Mother, but I asked her to intercede for me and for Palmer, and then I said the rosary without having any beads in my hand. I just said the words, and though my mind wandered, I felt satisfied that I'd performed a genuine act of contrition.

It all felt absurdly medieval as I came out onto Fifth Avenue and was suddenly studying the display windows at Saks, full of winter vacation fashions. I remembered that the Hindus—or was it the Buddhists?—taught that a man should lead an ordinary life as a merchant and a father, but that as old age approached he should become a monk and meditate and fast and give up the world and even his family and sex. I thought that sounded better than golfing, watching TV, and square-dancing in a retirement community or indulging in octogenarian dating, but would I have the courage to give up everything?

Father Bernard had never thought I had a real vocation back in second form when I was toying with the idea of becoming a priest. My father urged me to pursue it. No doubt Dad was attracted to the idea of a free education for me, poor man, overwhelmed as he must have been with the expenses of educating us all, though he was also pious enough. He probably wanted to give one child to the church.

It was a gray, rainy day, but the parading flotillas of umbrellas simplified the human landscape into great abstract shapes. I feared, though, that one umbrella would tip back to reveal Pia's restless eyes, slate blue in the lowering weather. I felt that the Holy Mother might just grant me the courage not to phone Pia, at least for a while (I was already temporizing with my vow). But I doubted I could resist Pia if I actually saw her. The fact that an ugly boil had just erupted at the base of my neck, above my shoulder but mercifully hidden by my shirt collar, also made me want to conceal my body from Pia's view, from any woman's except Alex's. I almost said to myself, I have nothing to hide from Alex, but I knew that wasn't true. I had nothing to hide from her but my sins.

That night Palmer had another attack despite the changes we'd made to his room and the substitution of a log fire for central heating. Ghislaine seemed especially distraught. Almost as if she were responsible. I suspected that her nerves were on edge from fasting. I even said to her, as if her emaciated face weren't dramatically obvious, "Aren't you losing a bit of weight, Ghislaine?"

She smiled happily and nodded.

"I mean, too much weight?"

"Oh, you Americans have such different ideas about . . . *le poids idéal.*"

I said, "I'd let up on the dieting for now if I were you."

She sniffed a contemptuous laugh at my suggestion.

Little Palmer slept in my arms in the dark while I held first one mask and then the other to his face. I could hear the faint hiss from the tank. Peggy was off in her room, but I caught the sound of her post-homework radio mumbling to itself. She was probably getting in a long phone call to one of the two girls she confided in. Alex had thrown something medicinal on the logs; it smelled like sage and made me think of a ranch outside Santa Fe where I'd camped for a month as a kid. A dude ranch. Such a happy period! I had been intimidated by the other boys until it turned out that I was one of the few who really knew how to ride.

I said a little silent prayer to St. Jude that Palmer would grow out of his asthma soon and that he could have a normal, athletic boy's life. Alex had said a month ago that she thought he might be gay, which had infuriated me. She was always saying irresponsible shit like that.

"He's six years old, Alex. No one's gay at six."

"That's not what Jack says. He claims he was attracted to a waiter when he was five. He can remember it distinctly."

"Jack's weird," I said. "Anyway, don't even think something like that—you'll make it come true."

"I don't believe in censoring my thoughts," she said. "Palmer wears my clothes. He's very sensitive, a loner, a poetic child—"

"You've got everything backward, dear. Palmer is sensitive because he's sick, he's had to cope with a terrible affliction. And yet the minute he outgrows it—"

"If he outgrows it," Alex chimed in. "Proust was asthmatic. And gay."

"How can you be so sure Proust was gay? Christ, I hate that word. Anyway, there's no connection."

Alex said, "It's all right for your best friend to be gay but not your son."

"Why wish that on the poor little mutt?" I asked. "Seriously, isn't life hard enough?"

I wondered if with a woman's instinct she'd picked up on something I had overlooked. Mothers know things about their own children. Was I hastening him toward homosexuality by holding him so tenderly? Yet it was impossible to get tough with the poor little bugger. Her clothes? He was wearing his mother's clothes. All kids played dress-up.

There was no way to predict what sort of world he'd inherit. Would the Russians rule supreme? Was America on the wane? This comfortable life that Alex's money had provided for us, would it be swept away by some new cataclysm like the Cuban Revolution? Would my son Palmer outgrow his asthma, or be a sickly little czarevitch slaughtered by the brutes of his generation and the next?

I was determined to conserve and increase Alex's fortune, not for us but for our children. We wouldn't spoil them or extinguish their spirit of enterprise. We wouldn't tell them that they were rich now. But I'd buy them properties in Canada, in Australia, in France, so that no matter where a revolution broke out, they'd still have some place to go.

Oddly, a tremendous lassitude came over me as I thought that there was no way to protect a child from every eventuality.

Once again I was seeing Jack constantly and talking to him on the phone once or twice a day. I'd never really had a close male friend before Jack. With other men, straight men, I knew I had to rib them about their jobs, their drinking, their women, and any little eccentricity or vanity. One guy at work started lifting weights and wearing his shirts tapered. We never let up on him. He admitted that he was expecting women to flirt with him now that he'd gotten in shape, but as he told us red-faced a month later, after many drinks, his only true admirers were homos at the gym. He couldn't change into his shorts in the locker room without first wrapping a towel around his waist because these two persistent fairies kept buzzing around him, hoping for a peep at his peter.

"Let 'em see it," we drunkenly shouted. "Then they'll lose interest!"

"Fuck you!" he bellowed. "I'd never shake them. Not after they saw what a real man was made of."

It didn't end there. We started calling him Real Man or Peter Peep, even in front of the girls in the office, which of course only infuriated him.

With Jack there was nothing of that heavy teasing. He never wore a cool smirk while I spoke to him, nor, when I confessed a weakness or doubt, did he hitch up his pants and say, "Oh yeah?" He wasn't competitive. He said that baseball was the most boring game known to man and that he preferred soccer, where the men were cuter and more scantily clad, though the scores were disappointingly low. There were so few safe ritual male topics available to us that we ended up saying things that were real and personal.

Jack never brought up Pia's name, but one day at last I mentioned her.

He said, "I had her on the phone all morning. She's very, very unhappy. I'm afraid she doesn't say very flattering things about you—she thinks you're cold and cagey and an emotional pygmy. But she did admit she's hopelessly in love with you."

"An emotional pygmy," I said. "And this is the person I opened myself up to? She knows more about me than anyone on earth—my confessor, my wife, you—and I'm still an emotional pygmy? What does she think you are—a sentimental giant?"

"Don't get mad at me," said Jack. "I didn't say it."

"Did you back me up?"

"I didn't have to. Her tongue may lash at you, but her heart defends you."

I thought about it and said, "I feel so sorry for her. And I miss her."

"Oh? I imagined your marriage was going through a rebirth."

"It never needed to be reborn," I said irritably. "Well, Alex needed to be reassured. And now I'm always, always with her."

"And your sex life?"

I felt I could either draw the usual veil over my marriage and its secrets or divulge them, so that my friendship with Jack could move to a newer, deeper level. I told him we should meet for a drink at the Shamrock, the Irish bar downstairs from my office.

As we sat there in our booth and drank our draft beers, an old fat guy in a dirty apron removed an aluminum tray of corned beef and gray cabbage from its bath of heated water. Everything stank of cabbage, which made me think of boarding school.

"Alex and I don't really have much of a sex life," I said. "The day she and the kids came back from St. Barts, we had great, intense sex, nothing fancy, just intense and full of feeling. It was like having the best conversation imaginable with no effort, no performance anxiety—isn't that what they call your fears of squirting too soon or not getting it up? But no, nothing like that. It was like giving her my heart and having her take it and put it inside her chest. That simple."

I sipped my beer and looked at the perpetual waterfall of the Miller High Life sign on the wall. The mirror over the bar was losing its silver backing in patches that resembled countries—on the right was France, and that downward smudge over there was England. The melancholy morality of place that discouraged rather than invited travel—that was the phrase that bubbled through my brain.

"But then?" Jack said.

"First," I said, "I want you to understand how . . . great our sex was, and I hate that word 'sex.' It makes it sound like some other form of activity, like dancing, whereas actually it's . . . a form of communication, like talking, though you're not quite sure what she's trying to tell you." I'd just said that; I was repeating myself like an idiot.

"Unless he tells you," Jack said, "in so many words."

"But then it's just talking dirty, the way Pia does."

"Oh, she does, does she? The naughty girl."

I regretted that I'd said anything. Now it was all going to be turned into gossip. We were all about to become "amusing." Idea for story: great love affair is turned into a smutty anecdote.

"Anyway," I said, not smiling, soldiering on as we started

our second beer, "as soon as they were back, Palmer had an asthma attack at school."

"How horrible," Jack said.

"It is horrible. It's like this." And I wheezed slowly for him and bugged my eyes out. The bartender looked over, blinked a couple of times, then looked away.

"At school they had him put a towel over his head and lean over a sink and inhale steam, which does sometimes help. We got him to the hospital, and they gave him oxygen. Steroids help a lot too. We have a nebulizer with cortisone. It's a new treatment. But steroids can also stunt a child's growth. Of course, we have a humidifier in every room Palmer uses."

"I see what you're driving at," Jack said with real sympathy. "It takes over your whole life." I knew he was making an effort to understand a parent's anxiety. He was free of anything like that.

"It ruins your sex life."

"I see." Jack reached across and patted my hand. I realized we hadn't touched since we'd become friends again. I appreciated his warmth—it was spontaneous. He told me about Alice and Rebekkah. Alice seemed to be spending more and more time in her fishing cabin drinking, though when she came to town she was still the best company.

"No one in Charlottesville liked her documentary about the hunt, but those people are impossible—they crave publicity and denounce it at the same time."

"And Rebekkah?"

"She's married to a man who seldom speaks and is virtually a hermit. But she's sweeter and smarter than ever."

The next day we met for lunch, sitting outside in the small park between our offices.

Jack said, "I've been reading Hemingway's *The Sun Also Rises*. Do you like him?"

"Very much."

"What surprised me," Jack said, "was how refined it all is. From his reputation you'd think he'd write like a thug, but instead he's a sort of dandy."

"Yes," I said.

"But what's all this stuff about physical courage? Is that a straight-guy thing?"

I thought about it for a second. "Guess so. If a thief broke into our house, I'd want to be able to protect Alex and the kids."

"Do you really think about that?"

"It's not an obsession. But you don't?"

"I got held up in the street once, and my apartment's been burgled twice, and I just shrugged. I guess that's another real difference. We're not too violent. I know some gay men who are taking karate classes because they're sick of being harassed in the streets. But that's not my style. I'd rather just take a taxi to the door of wherever I'm going."

I went into Scribner's one afternoon and bought a copy of *The Sun Also Rises*. While there, I also bought a book of isometric exercises, a routine I could do in my office without having to buy dumbbells or work up a sweat. I started doing them every day.

I'd lean against the wall and press into it or place my palms on my desk and push. I did facial isometrics, making grotesque faces like hooking my index fingers into the corners of my mouth and stretching it wide while trying to squeeze it shut at the same time. Or I placed the back of my tongue against the roof of my mouth and tilted my head back as far as it would go to stretch the neck muscles. It dawned on me that I was getting ready to see Pia again.

One day at lunch I said, "How's Pia doing? Is she still in the country?"

A little exasperated, Jack replied, "She lives here, Will. She's a New Yorker."

"But she is very jet-set. She thinks nothing of going to Venice or Capri or Saint-Tropez for a birthday party."

"But she lives here. She's an American citizen. She pays taxes here."

I nodded. "Has she found someone new?"

"She says you were never her type. That you're an American puritan without feelings and that her next love she hopes will be Jewish and have feelings."

I rubbed my forehead and muttered, "Christ." I smiled, since this meant that she was still thinking about me. "I'm Catholic and I have plenty of feelings."

"She says you're not a hairy-chested, sweaty, suffering Italian Catholic but some kind of cold Northern—"

"Puritan? Puritan Catholic? How fucked up is that?" I wondered if I sounded like a tough Hemingway guy.

I called her the next day. She was cool but cordial and said she could have lunch with me two days hence, but only for an hour between other appointments, and it might have to be in that little pasta joint on the corner of Seventy-third and Second. I gladly accepted her conditions.

When we finally saw each other, the restaurant was mercifully empty, the waiter sleepy, the sun shining, and neither of us could stop smiling. We were sitting in a glassed-in café on the sidewalk that had been tacked onto the gloomy main room. We had tortellini alla nonna, a dish with peas and mushrooms in a heavy cream sauce. If we'd been prudent, we would have asked for a table in back, but I didn't want to start off on the wrong foot. She had on a white blouse cinched in by a thick black belt and a long denim skirt. I knew she must be wearing a bra, but her breasts seemed to follow fully every movement she made, no matter how slight.

I did mentally rehearse an excuse I could use with a friend: "Look who I ran into!"

I asked Pia about her brother and for any news of Francesco. She seemed touched by my asking after both men and lit up, saying, "Alfredo is okay. And Francesco—well, you know, he's so delightfully crazy. But Jack is really the one I'm worried about."

"Oh? Why?"

"You haven't noticed anything?"

"No, but I'm not terribly observant."

"He's so lonely. Why doesn't he have a lover?"

"If you ask me, he enjoys being a free spirit. He loves sexual adventures."

"Then he could find a boyfriend who is equally . . . adventurous. Promiscuous. But he needs the human warmth. A constant companion. The intimacy, no?"

I said, "I guess we all do."

"Really?" She pushed her hair back almost defiantly behind one ear.

"I do," I said. "Do you?"

"Of course," she said. Then, distancing herself, she added, "In principle we all need warmth."

I looked at her so intensely that she lowered her eyes.

"But you know Jack so much better than I do," I said.

She said, "Have you ever noticed how he never talks about

his parents or his childhood? Americans always talk about their childhood. They find little stupid traumas to complain about. Europeans never do that—we're much too private, and why bore other people? Everyone had a bad childhood, anyway. Everyone except dull normals, who are to be pitied. Americans aren't really friends until they've exchanged incest confessions or a dramatic story of Papa's refusal to come to the horse show the day you won your first blue ribbon."

I laughed, happy merely to listen to her voice, to watch her as she rattled on. I felt that her breasts were performing under her blouse just for me.

"But Jack never talks about anything that happened before boarding school. And he loved his school, unlike most rich American boys, who complain that they were banished to boarding school by selfish, superficial parents."

"You're absolutely right," I said. "He's never volunteered a word about his childhood."

"And have you actually ever asked him anything about it?" she said, looking over the tops of imaginary glasses, though I refused to be scolded.

"I didn't dare," I said.

"You can be cold, Will."

"How so?"

"I've learned the hard way."

"I can also be very affectionate. Once I have my priorities straight."

"Are they straight now?"

I nodded and looked at her, pouring as much warmth as I could into my eyes. But they were so deep-set that I wondered if she could read them.

On our way out she glanced at my crotch and saw my erection. She looked uncomfortable and confused, but then she caught my eye and smiled—a startled smile of embarrassment, pure reaction, and then she melted into a conspiratorial little grin.

"Oh, what the hey," she said half grudgingly.

She took my hand and led me back to her apartment building. We went in silence. I didn't remind her of the afternoon appointment she'd pretended to have.

Once I was inside her, I felt my brain unscrambling. I was so happy to be with her—I'd really thought it would never happen again—that I kept standing aside mentally and trying to memorize everything we were doing. I observed my right hand on her left breast and my left hand circling her waist and cinching her up more tightly against me. I was glorying in her full, wet mouth, which still tasted of the creamy pasta and bitter espresso. We'd thrown ourselves across the bed, and she'd swept the thirty little pillows to the floor. The sunlight was hot, and we both stretched and untangled in it in a slow photosynthesis of pleasure and desire.

She had her orgasm first, and her contralto moans and tear-filled eyes made me widen and tighten into a band of gleaming steel above her—I could feel my whole body taking on bulk and sheen. Her pelvic thrusts seemed involuntary and completely unstoppable, whereas I was poised above her in a hot, milled point of pure will. She was fucking my cock with her cunt. I wasn't doing anything, just holding still. And then I finally collapsed beside her, my body jerking in the aftershocks. She'd never seen me twitch like that before. She half sat up in delight at the effect she'd produced and trailed her hand across my pelvis, which made me jackknife and wince.

Two minutes after it was all over, I started worrying—she was wearing that damn jasmine perfume again, and I realized I'd have to go to a barber shop in Grand Central and get the man to douse me in some cheap hair tonic, that clear blue stuff, which would disguise her perfume.

She'd bitten me on the neck, and when I looked at myself in the bathroom mirror, I realized it would turn into a blue-brown hickey—luckily it was just below the shirt-collar level, but for the next four days I'd have to undress in the dark.

How childish, I thought. Does that mean she wants to lay a bigger, louder, more obvious claim on me?

To hell with her.

Before I left, she could see that I was angry. I looked at my watch and actually slapped my forehead and went rushing out with kisses and promises to be in touch soon and thanks for taking me back—"into the fold." I literally said that. We both looked shocked and then laughed. Into the fold. Thank god we laughed.

I had the station barber give me a Mafia-style razor cut and drench me in cheap toilet water. Even he, looking at my hickey, winced, though he was an unflappable old man who held up the mirror for inspection without any sort of expression on his face. He gently powdered my neck and ears with a cloud of talc.

"That's the worst haircut you've ever had, Will Wright," Alex exclaimed, standing on tiptoe to kiss me. "You look like a corrections officer. And you smell like a cheap whorehouse."

I held her face between my hands and said pensively, "Oh, I thought you only knew about the expensive kind."

"Touché," she whispered.

Her lips, unlike Pia's, were thin, and her tongue made dart-

ing motions that somehow years ago she'd decided I adored,
just as I'd decided Alex loved glass paperweights with snow scenes
inside them. I'd been bringing them home to her after every
business trip when one day she came out with, "Actually I detest
snow scenes." I'd been hurt for a moment—and then laughed at
the whole misunderstanding. I'd never had the courage to tell
her I hated her little darting tongue motions.

During the next few days I'd be sitting in my office around
three in the afternoon, usually after a two-martini lunch, and I'd
reach down under my desk to rearrange my half-erection, and a
black wheel of dots would start to turn before my eyes, and my
mouth would fill up with saliva. I could see myself standing beside the bed Pia was lying on, where she was naked except for her
pearls, one pearl in her mouth, her nails small and dark red. The
minute the mood turned sexual, Pia would switch off her social
smiles. She became heavy, logy, even sullen with sluttishness,
unlike Alex, who, when she wasn't grinning like a mother at
her child's piano recital, was narrowing her eyes and compress-
ing her lips in what she imagined was a dreamy, romantic expression.

As I was phoning Pia to see if I could drop by, I thought,
This could all work out. With any luck I could get a good ten
years of sluttishness out of Pia, Alex none the wiser. After a decade of service I would renegotiate—by then Pia would be too
old and fat and irritating. She certainly wasn't becoming finer
or less predictable, nor was she slimming down or toning up.

My own cynicism disgusted me. Even when I'd been at my
horniest as a teenager, I'd never dreamed of mechanizing my
pleasures. Maybe that was why I could never cook up new jerk-
off fantasies, but could only replay the few exciting moments
I'd already tasted in real life.

There was nothing systematic or abstract about my desires; they were linked to particular girls and particular moments, repeatable only in my memory. And maybe that's why I treasured a woman's responses to my ministrations, her writhing and thrashing about. Since I couldn't dream up new delights, I had to dwell on those that experience had already afforded me.

I'd always been an idealist. I'd never been practical about guaranteeing myself a regular regimen of sex. To me each encounter was a miracle, a one-time thing. A unique and perfect surprise. To keep a sex partner on the side, ready and receptive, was like keeping a milk cow in the barn for the children's meals, too heartless a convenience.

Again I blamed the Catholic church. It had taught me that sin was a regular part of my life, that sex was a sin I had best contain. Now I contested everything about the Catholic solution, starting with the idea that "sex" was an identifiable unit of human and animal activity, rather than an abstract word flung over disparate feelings and motions with only a spurious unity, like a tarp thrown over junk in a rummage sale. That was "sex." Every bit as unreal as "sin," a linguistic or theological convenience.

I longed to be pagan, to intuit a god in every mountain, a nymph in every tree. I wanted my gods to be schemers, temperamental bullies ready to ignite and go up in flames. No better or wiser than human beings, just immortal and bigger and more powerful.

I despised Catholicism, but I'd been so thoroughly catechized that I still half crossed myself when I passed a church. I still felt abashed when Christmas came and went without my attending mass. When we traveled to Mexico one winter, I felt half envious and half ashamed as I watched the Aztec pilgrims crawl on their knees up the countless steps leading to a cathedral. Behind the altar hung hundreds and hundreds of ex-votos—tin replicas of eyes, a leg, a soldier—to testify to the miraculous protection or cures attributed to the Virgin of Guadalupe.

My mother never reproached me for losing my faith, but her own piety filled me with a melancholy regret. She'd never defend or even discuss her religion, but she lived it, and nothing more needed to be said. I thought of all the pointless debates I'd heard over the years about God, the authority of the Bible, the likelihood of the afterlife. My mother's inarguable faith trumped all those words. She had a good sense of humor and could see how greedy our local priest was for extra sweets. When someone brought up the question of purgatory and how many days one might be sentenced to spend in it, she would make the charming little gesture of brushing cobwebs out of her face. In fact, my mother's smiling approbation of the foibles of our local priest and her tacit impatience with the fine points of dogma rendered her more benign in my eyes. "Your mother is a very good woman," my father would say threateningly with a strange emphasis, as if he feared that her piety was too subtle and refined for me to grasp. My mother was so kind that once she said that she believed in hell because it was doctrinal, but she thought no one was in it.

Pia was Catholic, or rather papist. She saw the church as a political entity to be reckoned with, and she liked to say that there was no church in the world less spiritual or more imperial than St. Peter's. When Jack asked her what she thought of the Pope's policies on abortion and birth control and a celibate clergy and homosexuality, she just shrugged and said, "Don't look at me like that. I didn't think up all that crap. They're traditions. I thought you liked traditions, Jack. Aren't you a traditional man?"

In response Jack widened his eyes and touched his chest and whispered stagily to an unseen observer, "Traditional? Me?"

Pia ran into a Roman friend, Beatrice, who was working as a New York correspondent for a communist newspaper. Beatrice was a duchess and a communist, the Red Duchess, they called her, but she lived grandly with a tall, polished Texan who Pia assured me spoke good Italian. He was named Wyatt, and he was a rich trader in commodities.

Pia said, "Beatrice and Wyatt are the perfect couple. They have her title and his money, and they're both communists. Him not so much, but what the hey. I know you Americans can be alarmist about communism, but it's really very chic, especially if the people are of the intelligentsia and chic."

"What complete bullshit, Pia," I said. She really was moronic sometimes. "So it's 'you Americans' now, huh?" I asked.

"I'm happy for Beatrice," Pia said, ignoring me. "She's way up in her thirties, and I'm sure she thought she'd never find anyone. She had an affair with Angela's assistant, a black boy much younger than her named Jake, and she even had a little girl with him called Aïda. But he was a real nobody and unreliable, ten years younger and poor. Wyatt loves Aïda, though he's a Texan and you'd think he wouldn't—they're racist, right?"

I didn't want to discuss it. I shrugged and shook my head.

"Yes, I'm sure they are," she said. "But Wyatt's not. He's adorable and very enlightened and chic—a communist, as I said, not so frequent in Texas."

"You're right. Not so frequent in Texas."

"I hope you're not being sarcastic. Anyway, Wyatt is going to marry Beatrice, and I'm so happy for her and Aïda. She needs some stability in her life, and with such an attractive man!"

In Pia's private language, "attractive" usually meant rich.

I said, "I wonder if he's going to invite Aïda back to Texas to meet his folks."

Pia rolled her eyes, but my question was half serious.

"Aïda's going to be the flower girl," she said. "The wedding will be up here. Actually, in Bar Harbor. That's where they're holding the wedding."

We spent an evening with them. Beatrice was less scatter-brained than Pia, and I couldn't tell if she much liked Pia. She knew a lot about politics and had an eight-track of "Bella Ciao" that she'd turn up and sing along to—in that hoarse voice of hers, I imagined, even in her car as she sped through the city. Singing the communist partisan song without a trace of a smile.

Wyatt didn't have a Texas accent, though he did wear the most beautifully tooled boots I'd ever seen and jeans and a Saville Row dark blue blazer. He was light and cheerful in the regulation high-society manner and made no shadows, unlike me. He was extremely polite, almost as if he were the duke, and insisted that I go through a door first—and he touched my shoulder frequently with his huge hand as he guided me around and asked me lots of questions but not nosy ones. Maybe because I hoped to impress Wyatt, I told him I'd published a novel. "That's terrific," he said. "I'd like to write something someday."

Unlike most people, he didn't ask me if I'd had a bestseller or a movie sale. He was too sophisticated for that, I supposed. And I was impressed when he went on to confide in me by saying, "But I don't have the courage to write. Or the talent. That's the biggest problem—no talent."

"You should write about the life you live," I said. "Most writers are schoolteachers living in little provincial towns. You live with a duchess in New York."

"I'm just a simple boy from Lubbock."

He looked up with a grin from the cocktails he was mixing.

"Sure," I said, "but you also know about Tuscany and Wall Street."

"People don't want to read about privileged lives," he said and sighed.

I thought of a new reason to hate Catholicism. It had robbed me of sophisticated, sensual adventures I might have written about. Wyatt was probably a Baptist, such a stupid religion that it must have been all too easy for him to shed. There were no Baptist Dantes or Michelangelos or Palestrinas. Catholicism retained all the authority of its great art, even the contemporary work of Graham Greene and Evelyn Waugh and Flannery O'Connor, of Gerard Manley Hopkins. It was hard to throw over a religion that had been defined by such geniuses.

Later I asked Pia if Wyatt and Beatrice disapproved of my being a married man, and she replied, "Since there is no divorce in Italy, everyone is married to the wrong person. It's a fact of life."

But even though she said that, I felt that something had changed for her. Maybe after seeing Beatrice's happiness, she could imagine getting married herself to some big, "attractive" man. I felt she was on the lookout for someone more suitable than me. Maybe she'd thought she was too old to marry, yet Beatrice had proved that a woman in her late thirties was still viable. Pia was fond of me, even still in love with me, but she was no longer picturing a future with me.

When we said good-bye as I headed off for several days with

Alex and the children, she still got tears in her eyes, but now she looked away and tried to hide them, no longer using them as emotional blackmail. Before, she had liked it when I'd talked dirty to her on the phone. She'd giggle, and I could hear her breathing more heavily. Now she changed the subject, as if she found my obscenities obscene.

Nor did she respond as she once had to my silly love-talk. If I called her Honey Bunch or Puddnin' Pie or La Mia Pizza Margherita, she seemed exasperated. One day I said to her, "You don't like me to sweet-talk you anymore or to dirty-talk you."

And she said, "Are you only now realizing that things have changed between us?"

I didn't dare ask her how they'd changed, or if she'd found someone new, because I was afraid of the answer. I couldn't offer her marriage or even a sleepover date. I gave her an old jade necklace, but she looked embarrassed and begged me to take it back, to give it to someone more "suitable." For once she didn't even sound bitter at this allusion to Alex. If she had found someone new, how long would it take her to tell me? Maybe the new man had to extricate himself from another marriage. There were no eligible bachelors—straight ones—in their late thirties or older. There were a few widowers, but they were an actuarial rarity and were snapped up instantly. Some men her age got divorced, but usually only for younger women. A real hard-core bachelor of forty was obviously suffering from a dangerous personality disorder.

I felt that my days with Pia were numbered, I who had been so confident just a few weeks previously, so sure that she might last me for a good decade.

We continued to make love two or three times a week, but

we were both less excited, which made the act seem tiresome and vaguely sordid. Twice she said she had a headache, and once she pleaded her period, though surely it wasn't the right time of the month for that. (I was highly aware of the timetable for her periods because they were always so painful and copious, and she often took to her bed looking sallow and exhausted.) Once she winced when I licked her nipples, and I wondered if "he" had been working them over the night before.

One day she said, "This is embarrassing, and please don't think I'd be angry, I'm much too realistic for that"—realism she considered to be a supreme European virtue—"but do you have those . . . little bugs? *Pidocchi?*"

We looked up the word in the dictionary to make sure she meant "crabs." I told her I wasn't sleeping with anyone else, and if we had them, she must have given them to me.

"Let's not hand out blame," she said. "That is childish. We must be realistic and . . . scientific about this. You can get them from a public toilet seat. There are many ways to get them."

"I hope I haven't infected Alex," I said. "Do I have to shave all my pubic hair off? Burn our underclothes and sheets?"

Pia laughed. She tried to stifle her laugh and clapped a hand over her mouth, but it was as if a dysentery of merriment had doubled her up, and suddenly she excreted a big laugh that left her weak and twisting in her chair. "A bonfire in Larchmont," she screamed, "and you hairless as a newborn." And I hated her then and never wanted to see her again. She'd brought this infestation into our household.

I went to a gay doctor in the East Sixties whom Jack recommended, who handled gays and their horrors. The waiting room was filled with men whose hair color owed nothing to nature. Their clothes were designed to make them look twenty years younger if seen from a distance and from behind. Two guys were chatting about their Fire Island houses, which they were about to "open" (these guys obviously thought of their beach shacks as manors where the chandeliers were bagged and the furniture was draped in Holland cloth). The others were all quiet, leafing through homo magazines like *After Dark*, with their pictures of young male dancers and the latest "brilliant" clothes designer who'd combined black leather and black lace. For the most part the patients didn't talk to each other or even look at each other. It reminded me of the one time I'd gone to a Virginia cathouse. Everyone there was embarrassed and had silently agreed not to acknowledge the others.

The doctor, a beefy man with muscles and a Jewish name and a handlebar mustache and a lisp though his voice was pitched low, listened to my spiel and then said, "Come into the other room, undress down to your underwear, sit there."

He put on a headband with a mirror and a light, and he looked in my ears and throat and had me cough while he fingered my balls. He then knelt and rooted around in my pubic bush, especially at the beltline and then in the area where my balls and cock emerged out of my pelvis ("Blood-rich," he murmured). Finally he stood up and threw away his gloves.

"Yep, you've got 'em."

He disposed of the paper covering on the examination table.

"Here's a prescription for A-200. You put it on every hair from your neck down to your toes, including your toes if they're hairy. Get it into your crack too. Leave it on for two hours, then wash it off with soap and water."

"What about my wife?"

"Were you intimate with her recently?"

"No."

"What?"

"No," I said, "but we do sleep in the same bed."

"You might just get away with saying nothing," he said. "Tell her the sheets feel scratchy to you for some reason and ask her if you can change them, pillowcases too. And put on fresh under-wear and socks and shirt—everything!—and wash the old ones normally but in extra-hot water if possible."

"Is that it?"

"The eggs take a week to hatch, so do it again in seven days, the A-200. That should do it. If you see your wife scratching, then you've got to tell her."

"Is there any lie I could tell her?"

"Were you in a crummy motel recently?"

"Yes! That's perfect," I said, surprised at how perspicacious he was. I even forgave him the gratuitous testicle-grope-and-cough.

The next evening Alex went to the Metropolitan Opera with her mother to see *Tosca* and stayed over in Manhattan. I took advantage of her absence to spill some coffee on our sheets as an alibi and strip our bed and make it up fresh myself. I did the treatment and sat on the toilet seat naked the entire two hours, reading, then showered and scrubbed the toilet seat down with a cleaning spray. I threw my underclothes in with the regular dirty clothes.

The next day at the office I talked to Jack on the phone.

"All gone?" he asked.

"Yep! I can't thank you enough."

"Don't forget the second treatment."

"Are you kidding? Of course I won't."

"I talked to Dr. Siegal, and he thought you were sexy."

"Yeah, he made me cough for crabs."

"He said, 'A real man at last.' He was ready to go down on you, though he said one of your balls—"

"He told you that?"

"So it's true. Not much confidentiality on the gay circuit."

Despite Dr. Siegal's big mouth I was still glad I hadn't seen my regular physician.

"Hey, Jack?"

"Yes?"

"This is between us, but I don't really want to have sex with Pia again."

"Why? Because of the cootie-bugs?"

"Yeah."

"Didn't she do the treatment too?"

"She claims she did, but what if she gets reinfected by her paramour?"

"Her what?"

"By whoever infected her the last time."

Jack was silent.

I said, "Do you know who the guy is?"

"Don't do this to me," Jack said.

"Well? Do you?"

When he didn't say anything, I said, "I promise I won't mention it to her." I thought about it while he paused, and I added, "I guess I don't really have to know. Is it anyone we know?"

"No."

"Does he love Pia? Will he take care of her?"

"He's living with a woman he's been with for the last six years, but he promises to leave her. Apparently, though, the other woman is very fragile, even suicidal."

"Most married men say that," I mumbled ruefully, then spoke more loudly and distinctly. "I never said anything like that. I never said I'd leave Alex for her."

A moment ticked by.

Then I said, "Is he American? Italian?"

"He's English but lives in Rome."

"Is he rich?"

"No. Average. He teaches English to Italian businessmen."

Disappointed that my rival was so ordinary, I said, "What age?"

"I don't know him. Fifties, I think."

"Can they still keep it up at age fifty?" I asked, hostile but also genuinely curious.

"I don't have much experience with men in that age range. But yes, they can. Sort of."

"Sort of?"

"It's not real hard."

"Poor Pia," I said. "And the guy obviously keeps very elegant company."

"Because of the crabs?"

"Yeah," I said, then added, "Even the elite can get cootie-bugs."

And when that got a laugh out of him, I laughed—and there we were, laughing like kids, egging each other on. I felt a strange relief, and finally I wiped my eyes and blew my nose.

"He teaches English to Italian businessmen," I said matter-of-factly, "and around his crotch he's got a regular conga line of insects going, tiny marimbas in their paws and espadrilles drumming through his pubes. Is that correct?"

"Essentially correct," Jack said. "You've sussed that one out."

Americans had just started using that anglicism, "sussing out" one thing or the other.

"Hey, Jack, you know what all this makes me think of?"

"What?"

"When I was a teenager," I said, "I brought a girl home for the weekend. Tina. I remember her name was Tina. That was a very big deal for me, to invite a girl home. I hadn't slept with her yet, but I was hoping to. She was put in her own room—one of my sisters doubled up with another one of my sisters and let Tina use her room. Then in the morning my mother came in and sat on the edge of my bed and said, 'Will, that girl isn't clean. I looked at her panties, and they were stained. She has a venereal disease.'

"'Mother!' I said, whispering my indignation.

"'Trust me. I know about these things. I am not that naive. I can see she has gonorrhea. She's not clean, Will.' Of course, after that I didn't touch her."

"Do you think she really could tell?" Jack asked. "Do girls get a drip that would stain their panties?"

"I haven't a clue," I said.

"Do you think your mother just wanted to scare you off premarital sex?"

"No," I said and chuckled, "I think she really believed there was a danger."

Jack said, "Now, guys secrete something. The front of your underpants gets stiff from it, and it stings like hell to piss."

"This is the grossest conversation we've ever had," I said. "Anyway, I have now become completely turned off by Pia."

A week went by before Pia called to say she was going to Rome.

"For long?"

"I'm not sure," she said, then added, "Yes, for a long time. I like America, but I'm fed up with Americans."

"Can I ask you a question, Pia?"

"Yes, ask me anything you want."

"Do you have a new lover?"

"Yes."

"How long has he been . . . in your life?"

"I met him four months ago, but we've only been together for two months. I started loving him two months ago."

"I take it he's not American."

"English. He's English. But he lives in Rome, and we speak in Italian. Mostly."

"He must be an exceptional person."

"Average," she said. "He's average. Though not to me."

"So he's average," I said. "That's nice."

"He's exceptional in the way he loves me," she said bitterly. "He loves me passionately."

She said that word forcefully since she knew I'd mock it in my mind.

"A passionate Englishman? Now there's something new. And is he the one who gave us crabs?"

I could hear Pia making an exasperated sound, and then she hung up on me.

I knew that if I went over there with tears in my eyes, she'd go to bed with me again. Then I could go check in to a hotel right away, do the second A-200 treatment, wait two hours, wash it off, and go home.

I called Jack back and talked it over with him. He said, "Would you want her back? If she agreed to drop Oliver and come back to you like before, would you want her back?"

"If she'd agree to be faithful to me. If there'd be no syphilitic panties or crab lice."

"She was planning to shadow you on your Serengeti photo safari."

"What?" I asked.

I couldn't grasp what Jack had just said, no matter how slowly I replayed his words.

"She'd already signed up for that safari through the Serengeti that you and Alex are planning to take in January. She was going to pretend it was just a wonderful coincidence."

"That would have ruined the whole trip for me," I said. "Not to mention for Alex."

"I think that was the idea," Jack said. "She was jealous you were inviting Alex on such a glamorous trip. She used to ask me if you were still sleeping with Alex. I said I didn't know but yes, probably, once in a while."

"You said that?"

"Honestly I don't know what you do with Alex. But Pia was indignant that you might be having sex with her. She said, 'Is there anything more revolting than married men who still sleep with their wives?'"

"That sounds like Evelyn Waugh dialogue," I said, and I thought that if I'd kept a notebook, I would have written that one down.

I was angry. At Pia for hanging up on me. For taking a new lover, Oliver Average. And I was angry with Jack because he'd known Oliver's name all along, though at first he'd pretended not to. He'd obviously been Pia's confidant through every twist and turn. Did he encourage her to drop me? And how long was he going to wait before telling me about her utterly moronic little Serengeti scheme?

I felt ridiculously petty, worrying about Pia's affair with an average Englishman who was about as "cultured" as a petri dish. Bringing crabs back to the marriage bed. Yes, Pia was a woman and I, a man, but we might as well have been gay men for all the bitchiness and shallowness and venereal filth we were wallowing in.

I took the train back to Larchmont and sat next to a workman eating a hot dog reeking of near-meat and mustard.

6.

P IA MOVED BACK to Rome, and we never once spoke to each other before she left.

Jack said, "That shows what bad heterosexual values you both have."

"How so?"

"Straight people, as soon as they've broken up, it's off with their heads."

"And gays?"

"We stay friends. Why invest so much energy and time in another person and then just cut him out of your life forever? That's the nasty, brutish way straights behave."

"But it doesn't mean anything to you gay guys—it's all just a joke for you."

"Not a joke," Jack insisted. "We've invested so much—"

"Invested! But you're defending your investments like a dry goods merchant."

"And why do you straights gladly throw over everything you've achieved?"

"Love," I said, "isn't an achievement. It's like a sonata. Once you've finished playing it, nothing remains. Not even sounds in the air."

"There are marks on the page someone else can follow," he said.

My words made me feel melancholy. I recognized how insubstantial my love for Pia had been. Maybe it hadn't even been love, since it had contained a large admixture of scorn and lust. But we had made love so many times. She'd cooked pasta dishes for me. We'd showered together; she'd told me about her grandfather and his dog in Brescia. She'd described Baronessa Toni's little house in San Francisco on Russian Hill. I still remembered the younger man from Bergamo whom she'd installed in Sardinia. As a novelist I had ingested every detail with real zest. I told myself that perhaps she'd never known a novelist up close before; Pia had mistaken my professional curiosity for loving interest. Silly and snobbish as she was, nevertheless she'd fired my imagination as no one had ever done before.

When I thought of her in Rome with the half-hard average Brit and his parasite hordes, I found myself tossing and turning like St. Lawrence on his grill.

When I was honest with myself, I admitted that if I could have her back only on the condition that I marry her, I no longer wanted her, not at that price. I loved my children and my wife, even our funny Finnish house and the gardens gone wild. I admired Alex, her physical fragility and her moral strength. I loved Alex as the mother of my children. I loved her as this famous rich beauty I'd somehow captured . . .

But then I thought of the sunlight flooding Pia's big room like honey filling a comb and I felt deprived—of her body, her physical generosity—and I wondered if I'd ever find such a sensual woman again. Here I was, getting on in my thirties, and my best years as a man, as a body, were slipping by. I hadn't succeeded as a novelist. I wasn't a church or community leader. I was a faithless husband. I had no real friends except Jack. I only skimmed the latest novels, and then only those by writers I judged to be my rivals, which was absurd, since my novel had sold only 952 copies and had long been out of print. I'd detected a look of pity on Wyatt's face when I'd told him I was a novelist, though he'd pretended to be envious. His imagination and intellectual energy were going into making him richer, searching out new areas of investment, discovering which corporations had resourceful leaders—god, I sounded like one of my own brochures. Fiction, obviously, no longer attracted first-rate minds except Pynchon or Woiwode or that Frenchman, Le Clézio. The best minds, I supposed, were going into physics or math or business.

And then, returning like the piano solo in a concerto after a vigorous tutti, came the thought of Pia wriggling out of her harem pants, which made her look so hippy, her big, firm breasts with their large black aureoles already swinging free, and I wondered if I were the sort of weak, confused man who couldn't recognize a good thing when he had it. Would Wyatt have realized right away that with Pia (or Beatrice, still better, since she was more intelligent) he had his thumb on the very pulse of life, that this was the heartbeat, steady and strong, that would sustain him for years, and that he'd be foolish and in a sense lazy not to throw everything and everyone over for her? Were cock and cunt the most important things in life? The big, red, slippery heart of a couple? Should everything else be sacrificed to keep a well-suited pussy and penis happily throbbing together? If this genital couple, huge and smoking, sat happily on a throne, didn't it dwarf and overshadow everything else—house, children, money, marriage, friendship, even love?

The very physicality of her white body thrown back on

those gleaming, oiled mink pillows, that fur so alive and pagan and luxurious all around her, now seemed to me as appealing as it had once been intermittently disgusting. I thought of my long-limbed, pale body with the scanty patch of sandy hair on my hard chest, my big hip bones jutting up above my hard, blue-white stomach, a desolate moonlit mesa ringing a desert, my aristocratic feet with the big toe shorter than its neighbors; I could see the shambling, underloved, boarding school body, this quixotic sadness next to the ripe loveliness of my Dulcinea's curves and clefts.

I jerked off, and then as I wiped up I thought that Pia wasn't so special.

Suddenly I had a lot of extra time. I was more attentive to Alex, and she and I planned our safari carefully. Of course, most of the arrangements were handled by the travel company, but there were a few options left for us to dither over. Alex always chose the more expensive accommodations. It was just a reflex with her, though she wasn't extravagant by nature and was anything but showy in her tastes.

My parents were coming up to Larchmont to stay with the children while we were away. My mother had learned not to criticize the wildness that surrounded us. Like any old person, if seventy-two was old, she had her own ideas, and when she heard the raccoons marching about on the roof and tearing up the shingles, she was alarmed. She'd spent most of her life as a gardener taming the very excesses Alex indulged. Nor, as a horsewoman, did she believe that giving in to animals was kind. Children and horses longed for a tight rein, she assured me, but there was nothing she could say to Alex. She loved Peggy and Palmer, and after their fashion they loved her. Though they'd picked up from Alex that my mother was sweet but old-fashioned (considered a bad thing).

Alex could tell I was disheartened, and she was very patient and thoughtful with me. She had Ghislaine prepare a steak au poivre for my father though no red meat had ever been cooked in our house before and very little chicken or fish.

I wondered how Alex explained my moodiness to herself until the day when she heard me sigh and she grabbed my hand and said, with sympathy, "I can just imagine, Will, how difficult it must be to write fiction. I read somewhere that it's a pure act of speculation."

I thought, She imagines I've started a new novel. I realized right away that the symptoms of artistic frustration mimicked those of unhappiness in love, and I lowered my head and smiled as if she were right and it was all too painful to discuss. It occurred to me that I'd learned so much about sex and love and Europe from Pia—maybe I could start a new novel soon. But then I worried that Alex would recognize Pia in my pages. Christ! A novelist shouldn't have to worry about domestic suspicions.

Alex was a perfect traveler. Unlike most beautiful women, every morning she was ready to go in a few minutes, she applied no makeup except a trace of lipstick and sunscreen, and her clothes were few and functional and wash-and-wear. Of course, she always looked impeccable. Neither of us was much of a photographer. Alex said, "I'd rather come back with a few transcendent memories than an album of snapshots," and I had to agree with her. She was awed by the first herd of elands we saw coursing through the tall grasses. She grabbed my hand, and when at last she looked at me, she had tears in her eyes and a dazzled smile on her lips.

The other travelers were at least twenty years older than us, and they made a fuss over us. We were once again the enviable young couple, the American aristocrats with our soft voices, good manners, and slender bodies, and not those Larchmont crazies who'd let their grounds go to seed. I allowed as to how I'd published a novel, and the people from Cleveland I'd confided in told the others, and soon their nicknames for us were Scott and Zelda. We tried to ignore the warnings those names suggested of alcoholic defeat and madness and to enjoy their more glamorous associations.

The trip was just what I needed. I stopped expecting Pia's phone calls or letters. Every day was a mild challenge and a distraction and left me no time to brood over my faithless mistress. Nor were the stiff-jointed, big-butted ladies in our safari possible objects of desire.

Alex and I became much, much closer. We were no longer Czar Nicholas and Alexandra, the anxious parents hovering over our sickly son. Now we were playful; we got into a pillow fight. We even had a wrestling-tickling match that ended excitingly. Maybe because the other members of the safari saw us as so princely, so adorable, we tried to live up to their perceptions. Alex looked smart in her dark safari suit with the long-waisted, carefully tailored jacket sporting huge external pockets she was careful to keep empty and flat. She bought an absurdly colonial pith helmet that everyone admired, though its associations made the progressive Cleveland lady uneasy. Alex was relaxed and warm with the black servants and remembered their names and little things they confided in her. And at the end of the safari she made me take photos of her and everyone else, white and black, and we tipped the staff handsomely.

"Who do you miss the most?" Alex asked as we were driven to the airport.

"The children," I said. "And Jack."

"Jack? Really?"

"Yes," I said. "He and I have gotten way beyond his old infatuation with me. After all, neither of us is exactly a boy anymore. We're middle-aged men. But I think all that passion Jack once felt for me helped. It got me to overcome my usual reserve—I am reserved, right?"

"Check," she said with a smile.

"And it brought us closer. Who do you miss the most?"

"The children," she said. "My mother, though she drives me bats. Ghislaine a little bit. The house. I miss the house almost as if it were a person. But it all feels like a burden. I mean, a real responsibility. I feel ridiculous saying that to you, Mr. Sweetie, you work so hard, but—"

"No, no," I hastened to say, "you're the one with the real responsibilities."

During the long plane trip back to New York after our transfer in London, I thought about Jack. The truth was, the pangs I'd felt after Pia had dropped me had made me sympathize with what he'd probably gone through over me. I thought about how every person obsesseed over the moments in his life when he was the rejected one, but could scarcely remember when he had done the rejecting.

I also thought about Alex. We'd had great sex that one time after the pillow fight, since a little sweat and laughter and adolescent grabbing had sufficed to move Alex out of the moon-light of romantic love and into the knockabout afternoon of adolescent pleasure.

But even those romantic nights were more tolerable in Africa than they'd been for years. When I held Alex or ran my hands over her exquisite body, I thought, My girl, my girl. With Pia every expression of affection had been trailed by guilt and shame, like those sumptuous colors that painters use that are composed of coffee grounds and soot. Now with Alex, once again, I felt I was doing what I was supposed to do, make love to my wife. It was a pleasure that was also a duty.

My girl, I thought.

Once I even said, "My girl," and Alex winked at me. I hadn't remembered she knew how to wink. In Africa we had to be very quiet about our lovemaking since our cabins on stilts in the sa-vanna had such thin walls, which we shared with several other couples. That need for silence made the long naked sessions in the lamplight all the more thrilling, as if someone had turned off the audio.

Once we were home, I expected to feel rejuvenated and pur-poseful and, well, not resigned but committed to my real life. Alex and I had figured out a new marriage enhancement. She would come into the city once a week, and we'd have dinner with someone or just each other and catch a play or a concert or a performance of the New York City Ballet.

We liked the ballet so much that some "social" friends Alex had known since her debutante days, Max and Sofia Phipps, persuaded us to become Friends of the Ballet at the rate of two thousand dollars a year. In return we were allowed to attend re-hearsals and opening night parties.

Jack was duly impressed. "Max Phipps! He's the grandson of

the museum Phipps, and they have a ten-room apartment on Fifth Avenue across from the Metropolitan Museum."

I said, "If I ever lose my standing with you, Jack, I see how I can regain it. A big apartment at a good address. But seriously, they're very nice, quiet people, passionate about the arts. He's tall and broad shouldered and has a red bottlebrush mustache, and she's beautiful and fun and very animated. They have a real love match of a marriage."

"What sort of work does he do?"

"He runs the family foundation."

"See?"

Jack kept pumping me for details about Max and Sofia, and it occurred to me that after a certain age homosexuals replaced sex with social ambitions.

Part III

1.

JACK HAD NEVER been in love with anyone except Will. He felt embarrassed about his passion for Will and winced when he remembered it. It seemed so self-hating and childish. Although Jack had no interest in gay liberation, which struck him as raucous and led by shaggy-haired leftists with smelly feet, nevertheless the movement had made him see how "unliberated" he'd been to fall for a straight man.

Jack started seeing yet another woman shrink. She thought his homosexuality was just a "symptom" of a deeper conflict. She wouldn't discuss his sex life at all, but once she said it was his "unsuccessful" attempt to administer therapy to himself. She said it might be more "fruitful" if he stopped "acting out" altogether.

"You mean you want me to stop having sex?"

"It's only a suggestion. But do you understand my logic?"

"I understand it, but I don't accept it," Jack said grimly.

"It's true," she said upon reflection, "compulsive behavior is hard to give up. Then again, you might have a few feelings if you stopped administering your own therapy to yourself."

"You don't think I have any feelings?"

The possibility of emotional sterility haunted Jack for weeks to come. He thought it was cruel of Dr. Sauer to have hinted at that, especially since she'd resorted to it only as a way to make her point.

He couldn't argue against her "logic" since he had no alternative theory of the personality on tap. But he knew he didn't want a fifty-year-old woman to tell him to become celibate.

At the same time he had to admit that sex for him was more an addiction than an art. In the late afternoon, as his workday started to wind down, he'd plot out that evening's activities.

He had several fuck buddies he could line up at short notice—if one wasn't available, then another would be. They were all good, reliable sex partners and nice guys he took an interest in. If they got the sex out of the way first, they could have a chatty little dinner somewhere and call it an early evening. The only drawback was that Jack liked to have a few drinks and smoke a joint and even take a quaalude before having sex, especially with someone who was a bit dull because overly familiar, and those preparations made it hard for him to sit up straight at the table and hold a conversation.

Marijuana really was his favorite aphrodisiac. He never smoked it for fun, in order to groove on a television program or song or to go for a walk. In fact, he never went for a walk with no goal, any more than he ever watched a movie alone, stoned or not. Marijuana sensitized his whole body and especially his lips and nipples. Without pot he scarcely felt someone's kisses or embraces, and his mind wandered. With it he heard soaring mental music, his skin was a snare drum, and every other part of his body resonated when touched like a skylight under a pelting rain.

But more important, the drug made him fantasize about covering someone, penetrating him, treasuring him. Jack's cranium cracked open, and the airborne seeds of these desires sprouted and overflowed. A second later, without any decision on his part, he'd passed over from desire to act. His inhibitions melted away. He stopped trying to read his partner's desires and simply imposed his own. If it occurred to him to turn around and park his anus on the guy's mouth, he did so without hesitating—and rarely did the guy push him away.

Most men fed off the violence and specificity of Jack's desires. Jack realized he'd never experienced anything quite as exciting as what they were going through.

Sometimes men would ask him if he was ever the passive partner, but he would say, "With a cock like mine nobody wants to fuck me."

He knew that at the local gay bar, where he played pool, he had a reputation for being hung. With an asset in gold like his dick, it was hard for him to get serious about bodybuilding. He still wore the same size jeans and T-shirts that he had in high school. People didn't much care, especially if they'd been tipped off about the dimensions of his penis. In the steam room men stared and sometimes, as they leaned forward on the tile bench and gaped, literally drooled.

He'd lied to Will once when he'd said that he blamed the unvarying rituals of cruising for his failure to develop a relationship that was lasting. What he hadn't admitted was that he'd designed it that way, worked out these terms of impermanence with great care.

He'd had so many men fall in love with him that he'd had to become cautious. It wasn't just that he was well-endowed. After all, he was a journalist at a famous national newsweekly, and he had a nice apartment and was good-looking and wore clothes well. He was soft-spoken and quick to laugh. He'd taught himself to cook a few simple meals. Of course he read or at least consulted all the new business books, but he also read at least one ambitious novel a month.

He had three big green plants on an étagère near his front window and remembered to water them. Once a week a cleaning lady came in for half a day. She told him he was unusually tidy for a man.

Because he wrote about business, friends assumed that he cultivated his own portfolio, but being without a partner and children left him with little motivation to build wealth. He set aside a small part of his monthly salary in a retirement fund, though thinking about retirement when he was only in his late thirties depressed him. He needed nearly his whole salary to live comfortably in New York. He ate out five nights a week and spent a small fortune on vodka tonics at the pickup bars.

He was always expecting his real life to begin in another year or two. He hadn't worked out the details, but he vaguely hoped that suddenly he'd be doing different, better work and living in another city far away with new, superior people, even a perfect lover. Strangely enough, when he pictured that lover, he was an older man, not his type at all but someone who might be a lively companion. When he wasn't in heat or bored or afraid to be alone, he deplored his relentless sex drive. He started to do volunteer work for St. Luke's in the Village; they provided free shelter for the local bums, but they needed someone to stay awake and supervise the men lest they steal from one another. One night every two weeks Jack would sit on top of a ladder and survey the loud, sleeping men, or he'd patrol the aisles between the beds. He thought he was no better than they were, except that his addiction was more or less compatible with holding down a job.

He liked the idea of volunteering and doing charity work. He enjoyed going to benefits for the church. He recognized that he had a natural gift for getting along with old rich ladies. He thought they were cute, and even a very grand doyenne of society never intimidated him. He started beaming the minute they began talking together, and he would touch her elbow or even her waist. A few drew back in horror, but most of them liked his physical warmth. He could be very soothing. No one quite knew who he was, but he fell into that vague category of "extra men," those creatures with good manners, nice clothes, respectable jobs, and no obvious moral flaws. They could be counted on to fill out a table or cut in at a dance. Husbands trusted their wives to them for a night out at the opera or an outing to the Village in search of antiques. Everyone assumed that most of the extra men above a certain age were gay or pathologically single, but no one wanted to talk about these drawbacks too openly. For one thing, it was very agreeable for a sexagenarian lady to have a handsome, well-groomed younger man flirt with her—why dispel that pleasant mystery?

Jack felt safe in society. One charity led to others. He liked the way evening clothes stylized his presence; dressed like that he looked neither rich nor poor, neither East Coast nor Midwest, neither scion nor employee. Social people were mainly interested in one another and more narrowly in one another's schedules. Where were they going next? Where had they just been? Venice in September, Gstaad in December, New York in the spring, Maine in the summer—it was a constant circulation through the world's veins and always a safe topic of conversation. The movies were the other safe topic.

Jack made no effort to keep up. He was quick to admit he was just a journalist—but that was interesting too, wasn't it? the older women wanted to know. He'd always appealed to social people; they'd always assumed he was one of them. Some critics said that friendships with them never went anywhere, never grew deeper and stronger, but Jack welcomed this very blandness, or rather formality. He supposed that if picture researchers at a magazine twenty years from now tried to identify the guests in a group shot of a charity event, he'd be labeled "unknown man." He liked it like that.

Little old ladies actually excited a curiosity and tenderness and affection in him. When he saw one at the opera bravely mounting the red-carpeted stairs, he'd break out into a smile. His other youngish male friends would think he was nuts when he whispered, "Isn't she a cute little lady?" They'd draw loony circles in the air next to their ears.

He liked to go to bed in the nude, and before he fell asleep he would run his hands over his body, all the parts that other men neglected in their feverish fixation on his cock. He'd stroke his buttocks and the insides of his thighs and his stomach. Since he had so many partners, he seldom felt the urge to masturbate, but if he did he would pull down his shades and seal his curtains shut and turn on a bright light and slather himself in baby oil and look at his erect penis in a mirror as if it belonged to someone else or was someone else. He'd stop along the way to fondle his testicles.

Once in a while he'd turn off the lights, lie down, throw his head back, and surrender to a long reverie about an ideal youngster he'd never met except in previous sessions. This person had a sense of humor. Jack always began with hearing the low, warm laugh in his imagination. He was smaller than Jack, his body temperature half a degree higher—and, yes, he was blond, that was right, with a beautiful nape and a long tan back. He wore glasses, but they were a prop as disposable as a starlet's in a 1940s film. The kid felt comfortable lying just to one side and half on top of Jack.

Jack would call Will during the day from time to time, but they had an unspoken agreement to hang up quickly if they had too much work to do or a conference looming. Jack almost never phoned Will at home, but he was glad when Will called him in the evening. Of course, Will, who for so long was obsessed with Pia, couldn't discuss her when he was in Larchmont, so he found little reason to telephone Jack.

Jack felt that he lived in a rough-and-ready world of men, these piggy men who pushed each other aside to get what they wanted, whereas Will, like all straight men, had been half femi-nized by his participation in the world of women. Women were hurt easily. They wanted romance and believed in fidelity, even lifelong fidelity. When women cried, straight men backed down right away and did what they wanted. If a gay man cried, his partner laughed and walked away in disgust. Straight men were easily intimidated by women's moods and whims, whereas gay guys thought emotional women were annoying and emotional men silly. Put that way, it seemed as if Jack believed that gay men were tougher and more masculine than their housebroken straight counterparts. That wasn't exactly accurate. In straight life, since women were so busy round the clock playing them-selves, men were nudged into opposite and reciprocal male roles. The more women wept, the more their husbands resembled In-dian braves in their silence and stoicism. The only gender gay men dealt with was the same, not the opposite, and if gay men sounded shriller or more hysterical or more voluble than heterosexual braves, it was because gay guys played squaws, braves, and berdaches all at once. Gays shunned women, but the feminine came back in their gestures and intonations, the return of the repressed. Nevertheless, Jack never doubted that gay life was more bruising than straight life and that men did not coddle or play up to one another the way women (when they weren't having a fit) had been trained to indulge straight men.

Jack thought of Will as an amateur at living.

From little things Will said, Jack picked up that Will suspected he was milking Pia and even Alex for details about Will's anatomy and amatory style, but it wasn't true. Mooning over Will had cost him so dear ten years earlier that Jack instinctively steered clear. Anyway, Pia volunteered much too much information, completely unprompted.

"He's so stuffy. I finally got him to let me lick his bottom, which he loved once he unclenched his buttocks and I had a little access. He wriggled and moaned like a girl when you tongue her labia, but he's so squeamish he wouldn't kiss me after my mouth had been down there. He's gentle, too gentle, but it must be said, he has great staying power, though his verge is only half the length of yours, Jack—I remember it perfectly well, your monster, the night you assaulted me in your sleep. You've made the silly choice to pursue boys in order to show how interesting you can be, but the minute you're off guard and fall asleep, you start dry humping the girls. The oddest thing is that Will has no smell at all! I've never encountered that before."

"And me?" Jack asked. "Do I have a smell?"

"Yes, you smell like, how do you say, *muscade*?"

"I smell like nutmeg?"

Pia nodded gravely, as if it were an unpleasant odor.

When Pia met Oliver, her Englishman in Rome, she told Jack all about him.

"He's an average man," she said, "but he adores me and is willing to leave his partner for me, even though that woman is very fragile."

"Suicidal?" Jack asked merrily.

"Probably," Pia said.

They both whooped with incredulous laughter, and Jack said, "We're terrible people."

"Yes," Pia concurred with a shiver of delight. "What the hey! I look at Beatrice and Wyatt, and I think it's not fair Will won't let me wear my perfume or spend a whole night with him, and he's still sleeping with that back-to-nature bitch with her skinny body, and now he's going to take her to the Serengeti."

Jack kept saying, "Don't look to me for an answer!"

"Why not?"

"He's my best friend, and Alex is an old friend, and—"

"Old?" Pia said. "Yes, she admits to being two years older than Will, but I'm sure she must be at least a decade older."

"Oh Pia."

"No, look at her crow's-feet and the what-do-you-call-them? The marionette lines beside her mouth. That is an old, old woman."

When the crab lice entered the picture, Pia chortled.

"Good!" she said to Jack over the phone. "Now his old lady will have a whole new herd of wild animals to feel compassionate about. I wonder if she will go against her own philosophy and terminate the poor louses."

"Lice. Did Oliver give them to you?"

"Heavens, no. Poor Oliver, he's so terribly British. He'd die with shame. No, I must have got them from that black delivery boy from Bloomie's."

"Do you just go to bed with everybody?"

"Yes, I do. I have very long days. And I'm not an American puritan. Besides, he was a charming young man. Very creative. Very."

"No doubt." Then Jack added, "I'm the same way. I go to bed with almost everyone."

After Will returned from Africa, Pia phoned Jack one morning so early that he was still in bed.

"It's three in the afternoon here in Rome," she said, "and I'm about to have a siesta. It's time you woke up."

She asked him if Will and Alex had fought in the Serengeti. "I'm sure," she said, "by the end of those two weeks they were swinging from branches and hurling coconuts and caca at each other and devouring each other's louses."

"Lice," Jack said. "No, it seems to have gone well. How's Rome?"

"Jack, I'm so much in love. No, not with poor Oliver, who's never had the gumption to leave his unhappy woman. No, I've met a very gallant Sicilian prince whose title goes back to the Normans and who's a culture counselor for his village, though he lives in Rome, and he plays the saxophone like a Negro and he's extremely gallant."

"Married?"

"Everyone's married in Italy, but his wife is a tiny little black raisin who lives in Sicily and was almost destroyed by the earthquake but is somehow hanging on. He even has a Breton name, Gaetano."

She kept probing to find out how much Will missed her and how deeply he'd suffered over her defection.

"Don't tell him it's over with Oliver. Better to let him think I'm flourishing with one man than surviving with two. Do you think Will wants me back?"

"Now? I'm not sure. But he certainly missed you at first, and his ego took quite a battering."

"Good! My ego too."

Jack wondered how long it would be before Pia was back in New York stalking Will. He decided to say nothing to him about her call. Jack got a big raise and rented a two-bedroom apartment two floors down in the same building. He was giving up the terrace but gaining much more space at an only slightly higher rent. Will asked him why he needed the extra bedroom.

"For you," Jack said. "In case you get drunk and want to stay over. You've told me about your hotel phobia, your horror of sleeping on a bed soaked through with—"

"Stop!" Will exclaimed, trying to laugh off his genuine fear. "It makes me queasy just to think of those dirty beds and sheets and towels dripping microbes, all that stained luxury."

Jack said, "I am buying a new bed and sheets and towels and consecrating them to you. No one will ever share them."

They were drinking at Jack's new place.

"You're so thoughtful. Am I thoughtful?"

"You're observant," Jack said, "which is even rarer."

"I'm not sure. I didn't see Pia's change of heart coming at all. I think as soon as she started hanging out with Beatrice and Wyatt, she envied them. She suddenly didn't want to be a back-street wife. Did she seriously think I'd leave Alex for her?"

"Didn't you ever consider it? I can imagine that it at least crossed your mind."

"Why would I do that to poor Alex or little Palmer? Or prissy old Margaret? And my mother would have a cow. She can almost accept that I don't go to mass and that the children are practically pagans, but she could never tolerate another divorce in the family."

Will had taken off his shoes and was getting drunk. Jack liked it that Will was opening up so much and scratching his leg and smiling foolishly. Sometimes when Jack came home from work to this new apartment, he would wonder if he should buy a cat to take the chill off his solitude.

Now he had Will here sprawling on the couch and talking freely. In moving, Jack had gotten rid of most of Pia's pillows and fabrics and other decorative touches; Will felt more comfortable, free of all reminders of her presence.

One sleety Tuesday evening in February Will called and asked if he could come by.

"Of course," Jack said. "You can even stay over. I wish you would. I had your sheets and towels washed so they wouldn't be stiff."

"Okay," Will said simply. "I'll be there in fifteen minutes."

After he hung up, Jack dashed about adjusting the lights and slipping into jeans and a sweater and carrying his dishes to the sink and setting out a new bottle of Scotch.

Will looked very handsome when he came in, with his hair black and wet and curling over his forehead. He wasn't wearing a tie, and he'd turned his overcoat collar up. His long nose looked almost blue. Jack, who bullied his tricks, knew that he became practically servile around Will. Not that Will noticed. And not that Jack was quick to agree with Will, though he did stick close to Will's interests. When they had settled in, Jack said, "What's up?"

"You must promise not to tell anyone else. It's a top secret deal, even if it will be very hard to conceal from other people, it's that juicy."

"You know I'm discreet."

Will raised an eyebrow, which Jack duly noted.

"I had dinner with Beatrice and Wyatt at their apartment. They know this great soul food place in Harlem for barbecue takeout with greens and corn bread and creamy potato salad."

"Who else was with you?"

"It was just the three of us. They were very attentive and friendly."

"I wonder what they want."

"Wait, wait," Will said. "They were both very casually dressed. She in dark slacks and a white halter top, he in jeans and a polo shirt, even though it's so cold out. They were both barefoot. Their apartment is very toasty, plus they'd made a fire."

"Were they trying to seduce you?"

"Wait, wait. Wyatt had found a copy of my novel and read it, and he told me it was exactly the sort of thing he'd write if he had the imagination and intelligence. Then the duchess said she was going to send the book to Einaudi in Italy. She knows an editor there, and she's convinced that my sort of 'existential fantasy,' as she called it, would appeal to sophisticated Italians."

"I'm glad they're taking you so seriously," Jack said.

"Wait, wait," Will said, "you were right the first time. They asked me if I'd like to attend an orgy they're . . . throwing next Friday."

"An orgy?"

"Yes, this will be their third one. The first two were great successes, they said. They said a 'sex party,' actually. They've been recruiting people very, very carefully."

"Did you accept?"

"You can imagine I wanted to know about the cocks-and-balls problem. But Wyatt assured me that the men didn't play with each other, that only one of the seven men swings both ways. That's how they put it. I said, 'Call me square, but I don't want to swing on any condition.' They appeared to be surprised and even disappointed. That bitch Pia had told them you and I were sometime lovers."

"And are you tempted to go?" Jack asked.

"The idea of several women including Beatrice all naked and available at the same time seems irresistible." Will suddenly became lost in thought and then said, as if he'd had a revelation, "Huh. It just occurred to me that Wyatt might be the one bisexual. I guess they would've tried me out tonight if I hadn't brought up the cocks-and-balls problem. Even so, Beatrice held me tight at the door the way a guy might hold a girl, and she kissed me for a long time with lots of tongue."

"While Wyatt looked on?"

"He seemed pretty cool about it all."

A silence installed itself in the room. Finally Will gulped some more whiskey and said, "I guess I'll go to the sex party. As Pia the moron would say, 'What the hey.'"

"I'm jealous!" Jack announced. "You're going to be screwing all those people."

"Hold on now, you're always bragging about those saunas and backroom bars you go to and how that one time you lured five people back to your place. And we straight men—we don't have that sort of luck. We have to buy women drinks and date them and tell them how lovely they are, and how they're our true soul mate."

Jack said, "Do you think women really like sex?"

"Some do," Will said. "Black women do, I think."

"And white women?"

"I think their motors are slow to turn over. They need drinks and kisses and kindness and a totally safe environment . . ."

"And then?"

"And then they get so much more excited than we do. Once the motor is roaring along, they can't turn it off. One woman told me that they need all that buildup because it's so hard to open yourself up, to be penetrated by another person—but maybe you know something about that?"

Jack laughed. "Don't look so embarrassed. This is a really interesting conversation, don't you agree?"

"I guess."

"I don't know much about being penetrated. I've only been fucked five times in my life."

"But why? Aren't you guys supposed to like that?"

"I don't want to get used to it. Now it just hurts. I guess it's like smoking. After you stop hating it, you become addicted to it."

Will crossed his legs. Obviously he'd just imagined it happening to him. He made a face. He said, "I fucked Pia in the ass once. She liked the degradation, but she said it made her feel like she had to go poopy."

"She was lying," Jack said. "She loved it."

"Really? I wonder why she was afraid to tell me that."

"She was always afraid you'd think she was too kinky."

"I hate the way Europeans think that puritanism explains everything about America. Anyway, what they mean is prudish, not puritanical. There's no reason to imagine that the puritans were that prudish. I'd like to write a pamphlet in praise of puritanism that would be handed out on every plane bound for America and would explain that it was the puritans who thought up universal free and compulsory education and prison reform and abolitionism." He subsided, then added, "So she thought she was too kinky for me?"

Jack said, "She was afraid of scaring you off."

"I was more turned off by her brain, which was the size of a golf ball."

"Maybe I'm stupid too, but I've always found her original and entertaining."

"Soon you'll be praising her for being amusing. That's what these bored Europeans like—so-called amusing people."

"Back to sex," Jack said. "Ever get tired of being the aggressor? I mean, straight men have to be aggressive their whole lives with no letup, don't they? It sounds so fatiguing."

"You are naive, Jack. Women can be aggressive. I may not have much experience, but I know three women who like to be on top. Pia liked to tie me up and sit on my dick. And I was powerless to resist. I knew a guy in college who claimed that his girlfriend would strap on a dildo and fuck him in the ass."

"I wonder if that guy is still straight. So you think women are just as sexual as men, even more so?"

"They can have multiple orgasms—can guys have multiple orgasms?"

"If they wait a while in between. Do you really believe in female orgasms?" Jack asked.

"Hell, yes, I believe in them." A big laugh erupted out of him.

"Do you think highly sexed women are more masculine? After all, the sex hormone is the male hormone, right?"

"You mean women with mustaches are hornier? That doesn't sound right," Will said.

"Older women look more like men," Jack said, "and they're the really horny ones."

"Yeah, the randy old bitches."

"Gay men hate baby-doll women in short nighties with pig-tails and lollipops and high squeaky voices."

"Straight guys think they're stupid as shit but get an automatic hard-on around them."

"Why?"

Will got up and strode around the room impatiently.

"Why? You'd think you were an anthropologist and I was a Zulu. After all, we straight people have nature on our side. Pro-creation."

"God?"

"Why not? God, too, since I believe in Him."

"So you think Goldie Hawn's appeal is God-given?"

"You can make anything sound ridiculous, Jack. But yes, the whole point is making babies, so that's why heterosexual men are more attracted to baby-dolls than to old cows. Young women are more fertile; their babies come out healthier."

Jack asked him what time he had to be up in the morning for work and set his own alarm for eight. In Will's bathroom he laid out a new toothbrush and a tube of toothpaste he'd bought just for this emergency. He was careful not to lurk around to watch him undress. He said, "Sleep well," and closed his bedroom door.

He put on pajamas, which he never did. Was it in case Will barged into his room?

Jack went to the window, pulled back the curtain, and sat looking out for a moment. The sleet had stopped. The clouds were very low and burning from underneath; they were like huge helium-filled silver balloons nosing their way around corners and bumping into dark buildings in which only every tenth or twentieth window was lit. No bare windows—they were all curtained. He wondered how many lonely people were in those closed rooms.

He felt fussed by his drunken, seemingly breezy conversation with Will. He leaned forward and pressed his forehead against the cold windowpane. When he shut his eyes, time and space flowed around him.

Something about Will's presence in the other room confused him. For a night they were playing house. Tomorrow Jack would get up an hour earlier than usual and prepare coffee and toast and scrambled eggs and even set the table with dishes and silverware that he hoped would be up to Will's standards of cleanliness. Will would rush off to work, and they wouldn't even shake hands good-bye because they didn't do that.

And Jack would—what? Sit and listen to the furniture creak? Jerk off while whispering Will's name? Will was such an unlikely object of affection, so chaste and cagey and . . . opaque, really.

It was like falling in love with Grover Cleveland.

Was he letting himself fall in love with Will all over again? Why? Because Will was unobtainable? Or because Will was a real man, if masculine reality was measured by a refusal to touch half the human race? Will was a bad habit it seemed he'd never get over. Jack felt like one of those courtiers who back up when leaving the king's presence.

He could see from the way Will talked about Pia that he could be cold and vengeful. He felt that he and Will had to do something big and decisive before long, or else they'd just fritter the rest of their lives away. The gods had been good to them: they still had their health and young faces and lusty bodies; Will was rich and Jack was comfortable. But if they didn't watch out, they'd become dim and devious in their desires, mediocre in their accomplishments. He laughed at himself and stood up, sheathed in his unfamiliar pajamas. He went to the kitchen for a glass of water.

As he was going to sleep, he remembered asking Will if there was nothing about Pia he recalled fondly.

Will had become irate against the poor woman all over again. But then he'd caught himself, slumped, thought it over, and smiled. He said, "She was a good egg. She never once refused me. She gave me complete access to her pussy, even during those painful periods of hers."

"That didn't put you off: the blood?"

"No."

2.

JACK MET A gay trainee at work so close to his ideal—
young, blond, Canadian, preppy, intelligent—that he
couldn't resist breaking his rule never to date a colleague. He
asked Rupert out to dinner.

Rupert was a curious combination of intellectual nerd and
little sex god. He did a hundred sit-ups and a hundred push-ups
every morning. His stomach was as segmented as a bar of white
chocolate. He had flossy blond hair under his arms. His lips were
full and, endearingly, he wore braces, which made him self-
conscious. He had straight pale hair. He had a hooked nose.

His body was as slippery and cool as water and, like water, it
flowed all around Jack. Rupert's feet were unblemished, with
anklebones so snug and unobtrusive that Jack could imagine an
entire Japanese religious cult based on their worship.

His buttocks could have served as flotation devices. They were
"buoyant with youth," as Jack described them to Will, whose
face froze when he was forced to take on board this unwelcome
information, though Jack could see that Will liked Rupert well
enough. Around Will, Rupert had a surprisingly deep voice and
a less surprisingly ingratiating manner.

In the bedroom Rupert was not so masculine. If Jack praised

his buns, Rupert would half faint and put one hand behind his head and languidly point his elbow to the ceiling like a Michelangelo slave. "Really? You really like them?" he'd ask and touch his ass; now his deep tones sounded more like Marlene Dietrich's. He wasn't being droll or parodying a beautiful woman but glorying in this role that Jack was conferring on him and that corresponded neatly to his inner girl. It was no more playacting than learning to be a boy was for a boy.

He was a trainee in the book-reviewing department, which meant he looked through the dozens of galleys that flooded into the office every day and came up with a list of six or seven every week for the three staff reviewers to consider. Rupert would write a short, savvy account.

"Another incantatory, meaningless piece of dreck by Mlle. Duras. A book that takes longer to read than it took her to write. It appears to be about a sailboat in the Atlantic and the usual adultery on the high seas, but who could tell what's really happening under the layers of alcoholic prose?"

At first Rupert, fresh from his Humanities 6 course at Harvard, had tended to compare everything to *Samson Agonistes*, but right away he caught on that that wasn't cool. The writers of reference should be Oates, Roth, Bellow, and Updike, not Euripides and Milton.

When Rupert responded to a question, he would pause for so long that Jack would fear he hadn't heard it. At last Rupert would say, "So . . ."

He'd studied philosophy and now kept making pronouncements with what Jack considered to be an adorable sententiousness. The boy was quite an original.

Jack broke his rule and gave Rupert a key to the apartment. Once Jack came in and found a little old crone with thick glasses and a hooked nose bent over a book, her nose almost touching the page. Jack drew back in alarm—but the crone turned out to be Rupert without his contacts in and without his head thrown back in his usual triumphant posture.

The transformation from butt-boy to witch was so dramatic that ever after Jack found something factitious about Rupert's beauty.

Rupert was polite and wanted to talk over Jack's business stories, especially the ones he was writing just then. Did the Republicans have a point in calling for more deregulation? Were Carter's economics shaped by his agrarian past? Was Japan really going to outstrip the United States in GNP? How soon? Would the Japanese soon rule the world?

Rupert, so entirely naked and pneumatic in his twenty-second year, would lie with his head resting on his open hand, which was pressed palm down on Jack's chest. Jack would wind up his economic explanation and listen for Rupert's light emery board snore, but no, Rupert was awake, blinking against Jack's chest, and at last would say, "So . . .," and give a good summary of Jack's points and throw in a fresh question.

If his conversational style was grave when treating real subjects, it was silly when the topic was gay life. Rupert had just discovered how to camp, and in a giggly voice that would crack from baritone to soprano, he'd refer to Will as Miss Will or Wilhemina, then fall about laughing. Or he'd switch the genders of their colleagues at work. Once he even referred to himself as Miss Me. He talked wildly about throwing over his *Newsweek* job and becoming a go-go boy in a gay bar and even bought silver Mylar panties that he modeled for Jack, who got an erection, though he thought they were in deplorable taste. Suddenly Jack had a new insight into how straight guys could find baby-dolls both grating and exciting.

Ever since he'd seen Rupert as a crone, Jack had been less enthralled by the boy's beauty. Nevertheless, one evening Rupert pulled on a tight pair of black briefs and marched bare-chested out of the bedroom to the kitchen for a glass of milk, and Jack registered how perfect he was, starting with his feet. Jack remembered from his study of the Buddha image that in the very beginning it had been forbidden to show the Buddha, so he had been represented by an empty seat under the bo tree or by footprints. Yes, these feet could be made to stand in for a deity, and Jack liked to feel them pressed against his chest while he looked down into the boy's face and fucked him. But why did Rupert playact the "sublime" so much during sex?

Once he overheard Rupert giggling on the phone as he rumbled along in his unlikely bass voice, gossiping with his roommate (a girl) back in Brooklyn about how exciting it was to date an older man and be "penetrated" by him—which he said with donnish humor. Jack thought that the role he played with Rupert was as easy to put on as old loafers, whereas the one he'd have to assume with Will if he could seduce him would be as precarious and deforming as high heels.

Rupert was at a loss about how to be gay, and his alternating outbursts of camp and gravity, of "Whee!" and "So . . . ," did nothing to work toward the excluded middle: feeling natural as a man who loved a man. Maybe introspective straight guys, and he'd have to ask Will, were just as confused about how to love a woman, how to knead their sentiments into their sexuality and roll it all out into a continuous surface that didn't tear apart.

But no matter how confused Rupert might be about identity,

he was very competent on presentation. He looked like an Olympic diver in his black briefs as he crossed the living room and headed for the kitchen. Jack could hear Will talking to Rupert—he must have let himself in. Oh god, Rupert was being polite and Canadian standing there half naked, his speech slushy because of his braces. He could hear Rupert saying, "Pardon? Oh! I see! So . . ." And Jack could imagine him bobbing forward like a weather bird, his superb body so active even in its poise. He was at once so goofy and so formal.

Jack was proud of having Rupert out there, rare as a silver rose, interrogating Will about his evening. Then suddenly he leapt up out of bed in his boxer shorts and ran out and said, "Did I hear the word 'orgy'?"

Will smiled, his mouth blurry and red from kissing. "Yep. I had me some good orgy."

"Will, you're completely stoned," Jack said. "Come into my room and let's debrief!"

Ordinarily, Jack knew, Will would have resisted an invitation to sit on a bed with two homosexuals in their underpants, but stoned as he was, he staggered off to Jack's room grinning.

"So how many people were there?" Jack asked calmly, as if the orgy had been an office mixer.

"Eleven. Six women and five men. Everyone was between thirty and forty-five except for one woman, Amy, who was twenty-two, and she's coming over later."

"Here?" Jack asked.

"Yes, here."

"My age," Rupert gurgled approvingly as he removed a microscopic pillow feather from his gleaming shoulder and smiled at it.

"And how did it all . . . happen?" Jack asked.

Will lay back on the bed with his hands behind his head, and from Jack's angle all he could see was Will's pointed chin sawing up and down as he spoke.

"When I got there, they were all sitting around in that huge living room in front of the fire, talking. Two or three people arrived after me. Nothing indicated what was to come—no salacious remarks, no touching or naughty lip-licking. Nothing. The drinks were very strong, and enormous doobies were constantly circling the room. I'm sure they were sprayed with horse tranquilizer. The lights were low. Beatrice may be a communist, but she remains true to her aristocratic roots, and she had a very relaxed, natural way of introducing everyone by first name and giving us each an identifying tag. I was 'Will, the novelist and publicist,' which is correct enough."

"So everything was comme il faut," Rupert said sententiously, though perhaps French came to his lips more naturally since he was Canadian, or so Jack preferred to think.

When Rupert rested his hand on Jack's leg, Jack made a face and waved him away—none of which was observed by Will, who was still staring at the ceiling and talking.

It was strange, unprecedented, for Will to let down his guard this way and sprawl on a bed with two men—one in love with him. The whole tense, larger-than-life moment only worked if treated as a lighthearted improvisation, an after-hours dorm meeting in someone's room with contraband chocolates and filched glasses of milk. Rupert was coolly lighting and passing funny cigarettes of his own devising. Now they were all three implicated in this midwinter mischief.

"And what about your problem with cocks and balls?" Jack asked Will.

"Oh, the good old cocks-and-balls problem."

"Where's the problem?" Rupert shrugged prettily.

"Beatrice and Wyatt slipped off to the bedroom, leaving the door open, and we could all see they were undressing each other right away and getting down to it. Another woman, a pretty Asian chick, was in there in a flash, inserting herself between them. Then one of the guys got up and began kneeling between Kim Chee's legs and eating her out—"

"That was her name?" Rupert asked.

"No real names have been used in this article," Will said. "Some guy who did seem a little light in the loafers started kissing Beatrice while fondling Wyatt's humongous penis. Wyatt liked it and pushed the guy down to the floor, and Loafer Lite and Kim Chee took turns servicing him, but that was the only male-male funny business I witnessed."

"Bummer," Rupert said.

Will sat up and grinned at Rupert. "This is one greedy little guy you got here, Jack."

"And what did you do?" Jack said.

"Of course, I was the most uptight, but I was so high I was staring in through the doorway as if the others were little mechanical Santa's helpers in a Christmas window at Lord and Taylor. And I was still trying to make conversation with Amy, who's this senior at Sarah Lawrence. We were actually talking about Günter Grass—"

"Major author," Rupert allowed.

"And then, Will?"

"She made the first move. She slumped to the floor and put

her hand on my leg, and I took that for an invitation. She pulled me into the other room, though I could feel my erection melting. I was spooked by Loafer Lite and Wyatt."

"So," Rupert intoned, "you're homophobic?"

"And how are you, Rupert, at eating out pussy?" Will blithely asked him.

Rupert made a face as if he'd bitten into a lemon.

"Stick to the story," Jack said.

"Listen to you, Miss Boss," Rupert said, which made Jack frown mightily.

"Did you . . . interact with any of the other women?" Jack asked.

"I couldn't resist Beatrice, and she did seem receptive—she was receptive, lying back on the bed with her legs spread. But Amy's the one I really like."

The doorbell rang, and Will slipped out and closed Jack's door behind him. Jack and Rupert could hear a girl's voice in the hallway, and then before long she and Will must have gone into Will's room because everything was silent.

"So we should give Will a demonstration of the delightful things two men can do together," Rupert said.

"He'd love that," Jack said, and he folded this silly, serious young man into his arms.

During the next two weeks Jack's apartment was transformed. He who was used to solitude and to taking his meals alone now never knew who would be there—Rupert or Will or Amy or all of them at once. It felt like college. Jack brought home twice as many groceries as usual and had the cleaning woman in an extra time each week. His heart no longer pounded from loneliness as he approached his own door in the evening; if the apartment was empty, it wouldn't be for long.

Sometimes he was annoyed if dirty dishes were left in the sink or if an ashtray hadn't been emptied. But Will was good about buying bottles of whiskey and champagne and bags of potato chips; Amy kept two bouquets of fresh flowers going. Rupert did nothing but push-ups, or "press-ups," as he called them. Maybe that was enough as his contribution to his host's happiness.

At first Amy was elusive and no more than a laugh tinkling behind a door or a slender shade streaking into the bathroom, a hand pouring a glass of orange juice by the light of the open fridge. By the third day, though, Will had introduced her properly. Amy was tall and extremely warm. She touched Jack and Rupert on the arm or shoulder when she talked to them—a nice change, Jack thought, from those women who were wary of gay men or convinced that gay men hated them.

Rupert wanted to know right away what she was majoring in (French) and who her favorite French author was (Gide). "Wasn't he a bit of a homo himself?" Rupert asked.

"Was he ever! And the one time he slept with a woman— and it wasn't his wife—he sired a child, a daughter. His wife was furious. His wife was his cousin. When he ran off with his best friend's teenage son, his wife was so ticked off she burned all of Gide's letters to her, the perfect revenge, since he considered those hundreds of letters to be his finest writing."

Rupert was more beautiful than Amy, Jack thought. Did Will see Rupert as an older version of Palmer?

Amy had a large mouth, appealing at age twenty-one, but one that Jack thought would be grotesque by age forty. She had a straightforward relish in telling her Gidean tale that frightened Jack. He wondered if she could be capable of great unconscious cruelty, or rather unable to see it as anything other than a pretext for a spicy anecdote.

And what had happened to Will's wife? Was Alex burning all his letters now? He was changing his shirt every day—had he bought new ones?

The first time Jack and Will were alone, Jack asked him.

"I called Alex," Will said, "and told her that I was having a midlife crisis early and that I was staying with you in town for the next few weeks. By the way, I should be paying half your rent."

"Okay," Jack said automatically. "But how did Alex react?"

"She pretended to be understanding, then called me at work in tears and asked me if I wanted a divorce."

"Do you?"

"For Chrissake, I just want a holiday from my life."

"Would you ever consent to inviting Alex along to one of your wife-swapping parties?"

"Are you crazy?" Will asked. "I'm never going to another one. I'm just happy I met Amy."

"And is Amy happy?"

"Doesn't she seem happy to you?"

Jack noticed that Will and Amy went through a lot of scotch. Rupert reported that he'd had a long, cozy chat with Amy, and she'd admitted that she'd just dropped out of Sarah Lawrence for the semester. She had gone to the dean the previous week, told him she was having emotional problems, and shown him the letter her psychiatrist had written for the occasion.

"So she thinks she's learning a lot about life and literature from Will, more than she'd ever learn at school."

"Life and literature," Jack exclaimed, "two things Will knows nothing about! He never reads except to thrum through a novel by someone he conceives of as the competition."

Rupert said, "Isn't it strange how heterosexuals see competition and rivals everywhere? Meanwhile, gays never play team sports, although we're good at running, tennis, swimming."

Jack said, "Gays don't understand competition. They're either giving up in advance or devious and murderous."

Rupert would burst into Jack's office at work and sit on the desk and sift through Jack's drafts with idle curiosity, until Jack had to tell him in whispered fury that he must not visit him again during office hours.

Rupert blinked hard and stood up as if stunned. "Why are you being so uptight?"

"I'm uptight because journalists are a conservative, macho bunch, and the business slot is the most conservative of them all after sports. You can find other arty jobs all over town in the media, but there are very few business posts. I've worked hard for this one, and I don't want to lose it because a cute little bitch parks her million-dollar ass on my desk."

Rupert went to the door with a grin at once flirtatious and humiliated and hurried away, tears in his eyes.

When Jack left the apartment at ten in the morning, Will wasn't usually even awake.

One day Alex called Jack at the office. "Do I disturb you?" she said.

Jack thought of saying he had a meeting, but he considered this conversation inevitable.

"No. I'll close my door. There. I'm all yours."

"Don't worry. I'm not going to make a scene. I just want to

know how Will is, in your opinion, and what you think is mo-
tivating him."

Jack looked at the paper in his typewriter. He'd already filled
half a page with copy about Chrysler's new boss.

"Will says he wants a holiday from his life."

"Do you think his life, his life with me and the children and
the house, feels like work to him?"

"I don't think Will would ever let those words cross his
mind, much less say them."

"I know, I know," Alex conceded with a sigh. "He's so Catholic and devoted, but maybe that's the problem. Does he ever groan
and sigh—but that's not a fruitful line of inquiry—"

The copyboy opened the door and, without even looking at
Jack, slipped a page into his in-box.

"We could meet for lunch tomorrow."

"Let's do that too," Alex said, "but I have to get this out over
the phone because I'll feel such a bore saying it all in person. I
feel like a bore now."

"Nothing could be less boring," Jack said in a serious tone.
He looked at the page in his in-box. The editor was asking him
to cut ten lines.

"Does he have a new girlfriend?"

Jack asked, "Haven't you talked to him about this?"

"I know you want to be loyal to Will, but you must be loyal
to me too. We're friends too."

"Yes, he is seeing a girl, but she's only a college student, very
sweet and—well, I don't see how he could be in love with her.
I don't think he even takes her seriously."

"What's her name?"

"Amy."

"And her family name?"

"I don't know. He only met her ten days ago. I think she's only a small part of his smoke-pot-and-drop-out hippie days."

"You know he's not going into work?"

"I suspected as much."

"Suspected? Doesn't he talk all this over with you?"

"No, not at all."

"I thought you were best friends."

"Two very reserved men, even if they're best friends . . . besides, I have the feeling Will doesn't want to put too fine a point on anything, not even his thoughts, as if by not choosing, not declaring his intentions, he can have everything he wants and not be stuck with anything definite."

"Has he mentioned how long he intends to stay with you?"

"He said something about a month."

"A month more?"

"Alex?"

"Yes?"

"How are you holding up?"

"You know me, Jack. I always want to do the noble thing but not give in too easily. I see other women whose husbands are straying—Larchmont is full of them—and they make a terrible stink, call up the other woman and denounce her as a home-wrecking cunt, sob to their husband and call their mother-in-law and get drunk and barge into the office shrieking. Not my style."

"No. I can't see you doing that."

They both laughed politely.

"But on the other hand I don't want to be a wimp and give up too easily."

"You really love him?"

"Yes. He's lovable. As you know better than anyone. Does it bother you to see him with Amy?"

"No. No, I don't think so. Let me think this out. I owe you the truth. Okay: I like having him close at hand, under my roof. I'm not jealous when I see him with Amy, maybe just because she could be his daughter and he doesn't pay attention when she talks. I have a sort of beau these days too, cute and young, and he sleeps over."

"All four of you! Very cozy."

"I think I took up with Rupert because I felt I was falling in love with Will all over again, and I couldn't bear that."

"Will is such a professional charmer."

Jack said, "I don't blame him. It was just my own . . . neediness, I guess."

"He's not the easiest person to be in love with, is he?" Alex said. "I mean, he's not terribly giving."

"Though he tries," Jack said.

"He tries."

They met the next day for lunch way east at a little French restaurant. It had a sloping skylight half covered with dirty snow. The restaurant was packed, but the maître d', forewarned by Jack, seated them at a table with no neighbors and not in a banquette. Alex ordered a cheese quiche and a green salad—the only vegetarian dishes on the menu.

"It's very hard lying to the children," she said. "They think their father is off on a long business trip. But this absence after the safari—ça fait beaucoup."

"Do you talk to him?"

"Every other day, I suppose. He's very hail-fellow-well-met, of course: very Princeton. I try to have some perspective. I've

been working for a charity for children in Cambodia, and compared to what they face—malnutrition, prostitution, physical
mutilation—most of them are orphans—well, a marital squabble in Larchmont complete with cooks and nannies . . ."

"Yes, I see, but that doesn't make it any less tormenting to
you."

Alex actually laughed and said, "Slightly less tormenting. I
mean, luxury can be a consolation."

"Did you see this coming?"

"He was staying away one or two nights a week. When I
went to St. Barts, he extended his stay at the Pierre by quite a
bit despite his hotel phobia."

Jack rolled his eyes. "The hotel phobia . . ."

Alex said, "He knows I'm here with you and thinks it's a
good thing. He says he knows I'm the one who needs a friend."

Jack liked Alex so much. He'd always admired her, and now
he enjoyed sitting across from her in this chic little restaurant that
smelled so good—the smell of Alex's quiche and his own nava-
rin with the small pieces of lamb and the little green peas and
potatoes chopped fine, all in a smooth mahogany sauce. The
table lamps under yellow shades and the cornucopia of fruits
and vegetables on a central table joined forces to war against the
gloomy day. He liked the way Alex was wearing a black skirt
and a cardigan sweater and around her neck a shiny gold ceru-
lean scarf.

"Is that scarf Indian?"

"It's sort of cheap, but I think it's pretty." She looked down
at it with a derisive smile. "By the way, I saw you the other night
at that benefit dinner for Skowhegan. I wanted to get over to
kiss you, but I never found the right moment. You were at the
very best table, Jack Holmes, right next to Alice Tully."

"She's a sweetie," Jack said. Then, out of the blue, he asked, "If you could save the life of a child or a dog, which would it be?"

"Is this a trick question?" Alex asked. "Both. I'm sure both. Or whichever one I knew better."

"So length of association counts?"

She said, suddenly serious, "It counts for a lot." She thought for a moment. "I thought gay men were usually closer to the wife than to the husband."

Jack felt awkward and said, "You and I are plenty close."

He felt afraid, but of what exactly? Was he guilty about sheltering Will during his vacation from life—from Alex? Or was he afraid Will would run off to some Mexican beach town with Amy and sleep his life away with her in a double hammock and eat tortillas and drink tequila and never be heard from again? Alex would fall apart and start drinking too, and her children would be sent off to her mother's house to live. Jack was afraid that he would end up alone and their cartel of friendship would break down into its individual entities, that their molecule would revert back to freely circling rogue atoms.

Amy's mother, who was only four or five years older than Will, cleverly took her off to Europe for a three-month trip. At first Amy sent Will letters, then postcards, then nothing. She and her mother, who was an art historian in Washington, settled in Paris, where they were taken up by the museum crowd. Amy fell for a young French curator of Kufic script and Islamic manuscripts, who wasn't an Arab or even a Muslim. She decided to do the big, cattle-car Sorbonne course on French civilization, and every day she attended language classes as well. She bought black clothes and avoided the sun and had her hair cut like a boy's. Soon she'd moved in with Cyril, though by that time Will had lost interest in her and stopped writing her back.

Once Amy defected, Jack had less of a reason to barricade himself in his room with Rupert. He spent more and more time with Will, and even Rupert could see he was besotted with his old friend. Rupert knew the words to "My Old Flame" and often sang them to infuriate Jack. Jack maintained his rule of not fraternizing with Rupert on the job.

As a result Jack and Rupert spent less and less time together, except in bed, and even there they were less and less compatible. Rupert was tired of being buggered nightly, as he put it, and wanted to dominate Jack at least once in a while. Most of the young men who circulated through Jack's apartment were so awed by Jack's penis, so insecure about their own dimensions, and so overwhelmed by Jack's sexual authority that they submitted to him with passionate enthusiasm.

But none had been permitted to hang around long enough to feel restless in that role. At first Rupert gloried in all the attentions that Jack lavished on his body, and what might have appeared to be passivity he experienced as narcissism richly gratified. But as the weeks wore on and Jack became much less tender but no less lusty, Rupert rebelled. Again he said he wanted to fuck Jack.

"Don't be absurd," Jack said. "Look at our age difference! Even the visual would be ridiculous. Pretty Boy Mounts Old Goat. Ganymede with Average Meat Rogers the Hung Eagle!"

"The truth isn't all in the captions," Rupert said. "At first I was overwhelmed by . . . It. But now I've regained my confidence, and I want to be the eagle at least one night out of three and try my wings."

"That's grotesque," Jack said. "Shut up and assume the position."

This kind of rough talk had always worked in the past with other men. Rupert, however, was offended and got up and dressed. "I do have my own apartment," he said.

"That dirty little room in Brooklyn? You're not comfortable there. Stay here and we'll jerk off together."

"I can do that alone." Rupert was pulling on his sweater. "We need a break. You're living in an earlier decade—in love with a straight man, closeted at work, rigidly macho in bed."

"That's cruel of you—to take the things I've confided in you and turn them against me."

"So . . . but you haven't told me these things; I've observed them."

For so many years Jack had known nothing but men who worshipped him as Priapus, and he was astounded by someone who sought the active role, especially such a flaxen-haired, plush-bottomed little guy, someone so mouthwateringly fuckable. Now Jack understood why so often you met older gay couples who were looking to put together a threesome with someone passive. They might have started out fighting to get to the bottom, but mostly because whoever played the bottom didn't usually have performance anxiety. When the anxiety eventually melted away, in the affirmation of a secure, long-lasting relationship, a latent male urge to dominate rose to the surface.

If Will had moved out too, Jack might have mourned Rupert, but since now it was just Jack and Will, Jack was free to give all his attention to his friend. Rupert found a new job as a cultural reporter for the *Christian Science Monitor*. Will asked Jack where they'd gone wrong with their young lovers.

"Young people change entirely every six months," Jack said. "Every brain cell is replaced twice a year. Our only mistake was to become too involved with them."

Will seemed more inclined than previously to listen to Jack's opinions. In the past Will had been not only straight but also married. Now they were both single and on the prowl.

"My rule before Rupert," Jack said, "was never to see anyone more than three times, no matter how well it was going. Mind you, that's harder for a straight guy to pull off, to maintain a strict statute of limitations, since women want to date before they put out and want to marry as soon as they start fucking. It will be even worse now that you're ostensibly single."

"How do you enforce that rule of yours?"

"You say any malarkey, make any promise, in order to bed them. Then after three dates, no matter how hot the sex is or how simpatico the talk—crunch!"

And Jack mimed a guillotine blade falling.

"Ouch," Will said, delighted, "you're cruel."

"You have to be cruel if you want to be a libertine. They were right in the eighteenth century when they—"

"Is that what we are: libertines?"

"It's what I am," Jack said, "and what you aspire to be."

"What would be my first step toward full membership?"

"You'd return to your orgy club."

Will's eyes tightened, then he smiled.

Curiously, Will hadn't quizzed Jack about his lunch with Alex, nor did he speak of her often. Was he really that indifferent? Or did he feel so responsible for his family that his truancy didn't bear talking about?

Once Alex telephoned in a panic because Palmer was gasping with such urgency that she feared he might die. Will called for a Larchmont ambulance and rushed out in a taxi to the hospital, where he met Alex and Palmer in the emergency room. Will didn't come back to Manhattan for two days, but when he returned it was with suitcases full of his clothes.

Will's mother called and apparently was very severe with her son. She told him that he was guilty of criminal negligence and couldn't reproach his wife with a single fault.

That evening Will drank almost a fifth of scotch in glass after glass that he poured and swallowed rapidly. " 'Not a single fault,' she said. And I had to agree with her." Will poured Jack a drink. "Alex is perfect but not the usual icy perfection you see so often in our world. She's a good guy too."

"Did your mother ask you what was driving you apart?"

"Oh, hell yes, she kept hammering away at that. She wondered if I was sleeping with you, and I told her"—here Will interrupted himself, calmed his indignation, and nearly whispered—"no. Then she wondered if I was ashamed to take Alex's family money, and I said, 'Mother, I'm a Wright, and we've been living off women for centuries.' That, actually, made her laugh. Then she asked me if my business was failing."

"Is it?"

"It's not exactly in brilliant health. She asked me if there was another woman. I said that there had been, but that was over. Like a good novelist I simplified my two affairs into one."

"Did she ever ask you for your own thoughts about your midlife crisis?"

"All I could say—all I could think, to be honest—is that I'm bored with my life to a nearly terminal degree, that I hate my work because it's so demeaning and trivial, that I don't think it's fair that Alex had a few affairs before we married, but I just had those sordid tussles in the backseat of my Ford, that I feel my novel failed because I hadn't experienced anything, and that now I want to catch up while I'm still sort of young and sort of vigorous."

"You said all that?"

"I thought it all and said half."

Jack moved over next to Will on the couch and said, "I wish you'd repeat all that to Alex. I think she'd understand everything and even sympathize with most of it. She wants you to write. She can't bear the possibility that she and the children have made you give it up."

Will was now very drunk. He looked at Jack strangely (or was it admiringly?) and said, "You figure people out quick, Jack. You're never at a loss. Why is that? Is it because you've been shrunk?"

"I'm not even sure it's true."

"Hell yes, it's true," Will said vehemently. "Want to hear my theory?"

"Sure."

"I think gay guys are surrounded by enemies. Not really, but anyone could turn on you. So you gotta be alert. You can't ever let your guard down. So you get real good at figuring people out. Other people. You pick up on every little signal no matter how faint. Whereas we straight guys are just smiling all the time from ear to ear like, 'What? Me worry?'"

Five days later Will went to another orgy, and when he returned home at three in the morning, Jack snapped on the light in his bedroom so that Will would feel free to come in. He did, very stoned, smiling broadly, his limbs so loose that he reminded

Jack of pulled taffy. He looked handsome under the harsh overhead light, which made his deep-set eyes disappear and turned
his hair into glowing filaments.

"How was it?" Jack asked.

"Great! Lots of people, maybe twenty. Almost all the women
were really attractive, and the two that weren't—what do the
French say?—had a certain charm."

"Did you participate?"

Will sat down on the edge of Jack's bed.

"God, you sound prim. Yes, I 'participated' with three ladies. Good ones, lusty ones."

"And the cocks-and-balls problem?"

"No one bothered me, but I decided to watch, overcame my
squeamishness, and picked up a couple of pointers. Straight men
don't get the chance to learn technique by observing other men
unless it's in porno or an orgy, and I've never had the stomach for
porn."

"Did you have a rematch with Beatrice?"

"Did I ever! But she's so popular that I had to be assertive to
get my turn with her."

"Glad you went?"

"And how, though of course, an evening of pure pleasure is
always melancholy. But I'll have lots of mental movies to replay
for nights to come."

"Did you talk to anyone?"

"Wyatt. He's a hell of a nice guy, really. When it was very
late and even Beatrice had fallen asleep but right there next to
us, he and I were sitting around in our underwear, out of our
gourds, jabbering like crazy. He told me all about life in Lubbock, Texas, and his father the doctor, and how when his father

told his mother that he was keeping another woman on the side, his mother said, 'That's okay, sugar, jus' buy me a mink.' And the son of a bitch did!"

"I'd come to the next orgy," Jack said, "since I'm built like a horse, but I wouldn't really get excited over the little ladies."

And you, Will, would be intensely embarrassed, Jack thought but didn't say.

"Like a horse, huh?" Almost involuntarily Will stood and headed for the door. "You and Wyatt could compete in the size department. I'm off to bed. Thank god tomorrow's Saturday and I can sleep in."

"Tomorrow is Sunday," Jack said, but Will didn't hear him.

Will turned off the light and closed the door behind him. Jack was so excited that he jerked off twice, though the second time he was only half hard and sore.

3.

ALEX CALLED JACK at work on Monday.

"I don't think I can go on like this. I twisted my ankle just getting out of the car, no good reason, and now I'm on crutches and my foot is all bound up in an elastic bandage, and I can't drive because I have a stick shift and it's my right foot, and Margaret has started mocking me, and yesterday when I told her she couldn't take flamenco classes until she got her grades up, and besides she was a little tubby for Spanish dance, she put both her hands on the dinner table and got halfway up out of her chair and stared me right in the eye and said, 'I hate you!'"

"No, no," Jack protested.

"That's exactly what she said. 'I hate you.' She looked like a gargoyle. Her face was hideous. Of course, I should never have said that about her being tubby. Poor little Palmer was so upset that Ghislaine had to take him off for a walk, but there are some paths here that are so overgrown they're impassable. I feel like taking a chain saw to the whole thing."

"The whole thing?"

"The garden and the house . . . and the children. Palmer has turned into a sort of drag queen. He's always in my clothes. I want a vacation from my life too, which hasn't really worked out, has it? I was so smug. I thought, my husband might not have made Ivy, but that was okay; he was a modest, soft-spoken, true-blue knight, a knight of the Round Table, and I his Guinevere . . ."

At this point Jack could sense a smile creeping into her voice before disappearing again behind a mountain of self-pity.

"We've run out of money, or rather I had to call my mother to get Daddy to put some money in my account—and so I had to tell Mummy the whole sad story, and I was so ashamed and she was so alarmed, and she made Will's defection sound even worse than it is or at least more definite. Daddy called in his highest dudgeon and wants us to get a lawyer. He is a lawyer, so that's his solution to *every*—I should get a lawyer and have him sort of—it would freak Will out."

She paused, then went on. "I guess I'm calling to tell him I'm on crutches and my daughter hates me and my son is a transvestite and I'm going somewhere, maybe Rio, for a vacation from my life, and if Will cares about the children, he'd better do something about them, because they are no longer my responsibility."

"Sure."

"He won't return my calls."

And she hung up.

Jack thought that Will's children were going to end up having the sort of precarious childhood that he, Jack, had had. Everything had looked so ideal for Palmer and Peggy, with the nanny and the private school and the beautiful rich parents, but chaos was always lurking just behind these arrangements like the flooding ocean just beyond the seawall and the houses raised prudently on stilts and the dunes intelligently replanted in grass.

Although Alex had sounded mostly sad and discouraged, just

before she'd hung up the surf had risen above the wall. She'd been sputtering with rage.

Not telling Will at all was a thought that crossed Jack's mind, but he knew that the instant Alex caught Will on the phone, they'd put their heads together and they'd detect Jack's treachery in a minute, and they might even sacrifice Jack's friendship on the altar of their renewed love. And what would happen to the children?

As Jack walked crosstown to his apartment, he dodged one person after another. No one stepped aside to accommodate him. If he didn't flinch they'd run smack into him. He said to himself that living in New York was no better than residing in the Grand Bazaar—everything for sale and everyone a merchant. No trees. No fountains. Only slivers of sky. Throngs of people all shoving each other out of the way.

When he saw Will that night, he reported everything Alex had said in a neutral voice. He didn't want to interpret her words.

Will said nothing, but he winced and feinted and punched the air as if he were shadowboxing. "Damn!" he said, and turned to look Jack in the eye, as if he'd had a revelation. Then he repeated, "Damn!" as though that word clarified everything.

Jack could see that Will was drinking colossal amounts from the empties that lined the kitchen floor. Obviously Will was someone who'd always had people to pick up after him; he probably assumed that trash disappeared on its own.

One morning when Jack arrived late, at eleven, to his office, Alex was already sitting in the chair facing his desk. She was wearing a dark suit with a Louis XVI knot of pale gold and dark gold on the lapel—a 1940s clip. She stood and embraced him.

He said, "Alex, you've been drinking."

She said, "I was just so happy to see you, so I started celebrating early."

Then she buried her face in her hands, and he saw that her nails were dirty.

When she looked up again she said, "I hate you, Jack. You've stolen my husband away from me. I hope you rot in hell."

She got up and seemed to be concentrating on not weaving as she opened the door and stumbled down the corridor toward the elevator. She still had an Ace bandage around her foot from her injury.

Jack thought, To hell with both of them! I don't give a shit about either of them. They're not friends, they don't care about me, and they never have. I never sucked Will's cock—hell, I've never even seen his flabby body naked. Now he's too old and I don't care. What did I do? I've done nothing to wreck their frigid, unworkable marriage. My only mistake was introducing them to each other. No wonder their kid is asthmatic with a smothering mother and a father who's only good at disappearing. No wonder Margaret hates her iceberg mother.

I know Will thinks I introduced the worm into the apple when I brought Pia out to Larchmont. Actually I invited her to go with me as protection. I didn't want to be their little capon they could coo over, the sensitive, sad, sweet little faggot they could pity. I wanted to bring a fascinating, sexy, European woman into their little suburban House of Usher—and if she wrecked their marriage, she just had to give a little push to a structure already hollowed out and ready to topple.

And I didn't, honestly didn't, give Will shelter because I wanted—oh, come on, Jack, face it: you did want him to live with you, if only for a month, if only for a week. You love him, though he's as stiff as a scarecrow and about as human. He's a talentless writer. I've done a little snooping around, and I know his business is about to go under. He's turning into a drunk; he's a heartless father and a faithless husband married to a maniac.

But I do love him. He's as attached to me in his way as I am to him. We belong together. We could grow into two old libertines together, beauty patches on our zinc-oxided cheeks, pitiless in destroying young lives, as devoted to each other as two alligators dozing in the mud.

When Jack told him about Alex's terrifying visit to his office, Will said, "This time she's gone too far." And Will called the house and got Ghislaine on the phone. She said that Madame was *un peu folle* and that she cried all the time but hadn't abandoned them yet.

Will told her to hold on, that he'd be back soon—he was sitting right next to Jack, and Jack was able to piece together the whole conversation from Will's end.

The next morning Will came into Jack's room in just his underwear.

"Can I show you something?"

"What?"

"Look." And, unbelievably, he pulled down his underpants and showed Jack his penis and a drop of white pus gathering at the slit.

"And the front of my underpants is stiff—see? And it burns like hell to piss."

"You've got the clap," Jack said. "Don't worry. Go to the doctor and he'll give you a big shot of penicillin, and by tomorrow it will be gone."

"But how on earth?"

"One of your little ladies from the orgy, no doubt. Unless there's someone you haven't mentioned."

"No, no, there's no one else. But this is disgusting."

Will went off to wash his hands with soap.

"It's the spoils of gallantry," Jack called after him, "the white badge of courage. Today, my son, you are a man." He waited for Will to come back.

"Has it ever happened to you?"

"Three times. But only three times out of three thousand fucks."

"And syphilis?"

"Do you have a chancre on your penis? A sore? I didn't see one. In any event Dr. Siegal will run a routine blood test for the syph. And if you have it, the penicillin for the clap will probably produce a Herxheimer reaction."

"A what?"

"You'll run a sudden fever and sweat and get the shakes overnight. By tomorrow it will all be gone."

"Have you had that one?"

"Just once."

When Will had gone to shower before heading off to the doctor's office, Jack lay back and closed his eyes and thought, So I've finally seen it. I might have even been able to take it into my hand. It looked warm, resting like a wounded Tristan, suffering but still royal. It was like that one time I saw my father's dick. What do the Freudians call the little one's glimpse of the parents going at it? The primal scene. Today, this was my primal scene and all accomplished with a breathtaking simplicity and directness, like a star athlete showing his swollen balls to the man who has spent a hundred sleepless nights coveting him: "Hey, Coach, look at this. What the hell's going on? Is this a football injury or what?" "Come a little closer. I gotta take a closer look at it." If Will hadn't been in a medical panic, he would never have shown me his dick. Nice shape. Looks like the circumcision was botched, with that extra dewlap of flesh hanging down on one side. Milk white skin with that ropy blue vein rushing down the shaft. Neither big nor little. Just big enough to satisfy anyone. Long straight hairs disguising its full size; it looks like one of those mad medieval Japanese heroines in the movies with their pale faces drowned in hair pushed forward.

When Jack came home from work, he found Will smoking, something he almost never did, though Amy had filled the place with her smoke. Will sat on the couch with his tie at half-mast but hadn't taken off his suit jacket. He had a tumbler half full in front of him.

"What did he say?"

"You'd better come in and sit down for this one."

"What is it?" Jack asked, thinking the doctor had found a suspicious lump, there would have to be tests—and Jack could scarcely bear the idea of any harm coming to Will. Before a word was said, Jack had resolved to take care of him, to see him through.

Will said that there had been a rapid inspection and a swab dipped in the discharge and streaked across a slide that Siegal had examined then and there.

"He said it was the clap, and he took a blood sample for a Wassermann test—that's for syphilis, right? And then he slapped my butt hard and gave me a big penicillin shot, big enough for a horse. Only a gay doctor would dare to slap a guy's ass like that, but it worked. I didn't even feel the needle going in."

"So where's the problem?" Jack asked, about to run off to piss.

"Come right back."

What could it be, Jack wondered as he urinated, other than something much more dire to do with Will's health.

When he came back in, Will didn't even look up. He was concentrating on his cigarette as if he didn't recognize it, as if someone had just put this strange object between his fingers.

"I'm all ears," Jack said, flashing a smile that got no response.

"He told me about this new disease they call—here. I wrote it down."

He pulled a slip of paper out of his pocket.

"GRID—gay-related immune deficiency. He said fifty men have already died of it and many more are sick. So far they're all gay, but the doc thinks it's going to spread and affect whole populations—and millions of straight people too. It's sexually transmitted."

He looked at Jack and added, "There's no treatment."

"Oh, but there are always new horror shows like this—and if they're sexual, the doctors exaggerate them to scare us. They all want us to be faithful to just one person—to have the same dull lives they lead."

"Why would a gay doctor take that stand, someone who looks like a rogue to me with his mustache and grabby hands?"

They talked about it for hours. Will was completely shaken, maybe because the clap had already depressed him, maybe because he feared that this new disease would stalk him like the Stone Guest, taking revenge for all his excesses.

When Jack awakened the next morning, Will had left with his suitcases.

His note said, "I've gone back to Alex. I called her, and she said she'd take me back. I would suggest you find one person who's clean and hunker down with him for the duration. Our libertine days are over."

Epilogue

The day before Palmer's seventeenth birthday, I told him I'd take him to Brooks Brothers to buy him two new sports jackets and four pairs of trousers. He wasn't too thrilled since, as he said, those clothes weren't stylish. That was the word he used, "stylish," one of his mother's words. I told him he should say, "What guys are wearing," or "trendy," but he just flicked his long blond forelock away from his head and stared off into space four inches to the right of my ear.

I knew he was mad, but only because I was used to him. Anyone else would have said he was lost in thought.

"Come on," I said, "it's your birthday," and I put an arm around him and pulled him to me, which I never did. I never touched him. He seemed to like it in his embarrassed way, though it was sort of awkward since he was two inches taller than me, and I felt odd because he was so beautiful with his long straight hair and very full lips and his mother's small nose and ears and his flame red cheeks. The color swam over his high cheekbones, gathered in his cheeks, and bled down toward his chin line, almost as if an actor applying theatrical makeup had overdone it so it would "read" in the top balcony. That Palmer's features were so delicate and that he was often in a rage made him all the more striking, as if boiling water had just been poured into the finest bone china. It was translucent and it was steaming. Maybe he thought being hugged in public made him look like a little kid.

He said, "My birthday, big deal."

When I glanced over at him, he gave me a shy grin and actually leaned into me. We were in the shirt department on the main floor of Brooks, and an old lady customer looked at me with blazing eyes, probably indignant that I was hugging my underage lover. I was still good-looking, maybe more so than when I was younger, since my skin had gradually cleared up and my hair was coming in silver, so much better than its original mousy brown. I suppose we would have made a plausible couple, Palmer and I.

"We can go anywhere you like," I said. "You're the one who has to wear the damn clothes."

Palmer's face flushed an even darker red from the capillary crisis of having to express an opinion.

"It's okay, Dad, I'd like to buy some things here. I need them for dress-up occasions, and I don't want to be too punked out at church or whatever. It's just I'd like to eventually, you know, be able to get some, well, like Doc Martens boots and some camouflage shirts and safari stuff."

"I still have my safari clothes from the Serengeti."

"Dad!"

"Okay, okay."

Just as we were about to go up the carpeted staircase, Jack came down it, talking to a portly older man who was bald and had a radio announcer's voice and had stopped on the stairs to make a point, which obviously required a raised eyebrow and the positioning in midair of stubby fingers freighted with gold seal rings.

"Hey, Jack!" I said, after I realized he'd already seen me and there was no escaping.

"Will! Is that you under all that—" Then he broke off, mid-joke, and said, "And hey, is that you, Palmer? A regular young man. How many years is it since I saw you last?"

I couldn't help noticing how Jack, without showing an improper interest, was spontaneously drawn to my kid.

Over the years I'd seen Jack's picture on the society page from time to time, at some benefit or wedding, usually in the back row or dancing with some bigger, older matron. He'd finally become friends with our ballet friend Sofia Phipps, who spoke about him often and with great enthusiasm. She said that Jack was the most agreeable man about town, cultured and always *serviable*.

He said to Palmer, "You probably don't remember me. I'm Jack Holmes, an old friend of your parents from the seventies and even earlier, right, Will?"

Palmer turned a bright red—I knew it was just from being scrutinized by a stranger, but I was afraid Jack would think it was from embarrassment at talking to someone "notorious."

In point of fact Alex and I never mentioned Jack.

"This is my partner, Harry Diamondstein. Harry, this is Will Wright and his son, Palmer."

Harry and I shook hands. I made certain not to be too hearty lest I hurt him, so bedizened was his hand.

"Harry, what line of work are you in?" I asked, and immediately regretted my rudeness.

Jack looked astonished and said, as if I'd not heard correctly,

"Harry Diamondstein, the theater director. *The Hamlet Affair*—you've heard of that surely? The Met's new production of *Andrea Chénier*?

I looked up and saw the same disapproving woman studying us—three older fags preying on an innocent boy. Harry's flashing rings and gestures only confirmed her suspicions.

"Shouldn't we go somewhere nearby for a cup of coffee or something? Get out of the way and off the staircase?" I said.

Ordinarily, I knew, Palmer would bitterly resent any time spent with people his father's age, but today he'd heard "theater director." Palmer hoped to be an actor.

When we started out together for the coffee shop, Jack and Harry led the way. Palmer and I followed in silence for half a block until he bubbled over.

"How come you never mentioned these guys? I mean, with my career and all. They're *rad*."

"I only know Jack."

Palmer said, "It's not exactly like any of us—you or me or Peggy or Mom—has that many friends. And no really cool ones like them. Actually we just have each other. That guy Harry is famous."

I smiled at him.

"At your age it's hard to believe, but you'll find out that in the end that's all anyone has, family."

Palmer said, "That's the most depressing thing you've ever said."

He put his arm around me and gave me a big squeeze and grinned. Another first.

"You walk with Harry and let me talk to Jack," I said.

"Dad!"

"Do it!" I ordered. "It's for your career."

We were headed to an Italian coffee shop five blocks away that Jack knew about. I thought, I realize it's hard for you to walk with Harry Diamondstein, Palmer, old man, but think of it as your first audition.

Jack looked young still but lined, as if the pottery had been fired too hot and had broken into a fine crackling just below the smooth porcelain surface. He moved with such energy that I wondered if he was nervous.

"So Harry's your partner?" I asked, not sure if he'd meant business partner or mate.

"Yes, we met very soon after you went back to Alex. I took seriously what you said about settling down. I thought, Enough kids! I should find a nice older guy, someone who would be capable of fidelity. So I went to a great piano bar, and there I met Harry. He's not exactly my type, I know, but we hit it off right away. We talked for hours and hours. He's the most interesting man alive. We have sex at a nice regular clip, three times a week. Like clockwork. He loves that, and I like our life together. He's enormously successful—he has two hits on Broadway right now, I can get you guys house seats—and we have a house in Amagansett and a wonderful, rambling prewar apartment on Central Park West."

"Still at *Newsweek*?"

"Lord, no. Harry made me give up journalism so I could devote myself full-time to our AIDS charity, which preserves the texts and images of thousands of gay writers and painters who have died during the plague. It's very exciting—we're about to join forces with Princess Di and Marguerite Littman. And then we travel a lot. We were just in Gstaad, where we rented a chalet. We saw a lot of Valentino and Liz Taylor and of course Amin Aga Khan."

"And your own health?"

Jack lowered his voice. "Never quote me on this, but tops don't get it. Tops? The active partners? Oh, I know they do in Africa, but that must be for some other reason. And heterosexuals—non-drug-taking white American heterosexual men—don't get it either, though don't quote me. So," he went on and smiled, "we both gave up sex for no good reason, though I must say I'm glad I changed my life. It was so empty before."

"What about Rupert?" I said. "Ever get any news—"

"Dead," Jack said tonelessly. "He's dead."

We walked a block in silence.

"And Pia?"

"She lives mostly in Rome. She drinks a lot and has put on a few pounds. She's helped us a lot with our charity—she knows everyone. Charity work is very, very social, as you must know. I love that aspect of it. I've always liked little old ladies, but when I was a libertine, I scarcely had time to meet any."

Then he looked over at me. "How's Larchmont? Your work?"

"Well," I said, "when I moved back in with Alex, she made me promise I'd stop seeing you, and I made her promise we'd move into New York and have a bedroom of our own far from Palmer's. By the way, he's outgrown his asthma. We live twenty blocks north of here in the East Sixties. I'm like you: I don't work anymore. My business went belly-up. Alex's father died and left us some money. I'm in the charity business too. We have a foundation to protect those wild white horses in the Camargue."

"Where?"

"In the South of France."

"Oh."

"And I published a second novel."

Jack said, "Hey! But oh, I'm sorry I—"

"Never heard of it? Join the crowd. It was called *The Camargue*, though it had nothing to do with the region. It was another fantasy deal, more mimsy-whimsy, and it didn't get reviewed. It sold five hundred copies, and the other fifteen hundred were pulped."

"You'll have to give me one. I'd love to read it."

I said, "Sure. There is one novel I'd love to write, but you'd never give me the necessary lowdown—the story of your childhood."

Jack smiled and said, "No one writes Gothic horror stories anymore. But tell me before we get to the restaurant: is Palmer gay?"

"Wouldn't that be premature to say? For god's sake, he's only seventeen. But yeah. Is it that obvious?"

"What a beauty. Listen—if he ever has any questions about AIDS, send him to me."

"Sure. He wants to be an actor. I may send him to Harry and you both for advice on that."

"You'd better check that out with Alex first."

We had our coffee together. I was proud of the way Palmer opened up around them. I knew he was excited about meeting two gay friends of mine, one of them a famous director.

When we all said good-bye, I took Jack's hand in both of mine and held it for a moment, but then Harry raised an eyebrow and said in his booming, trained voice, "Oh for Chrissake, Jack, we're late for our meeting with Cecilia. She's pledged a million to the AIDS Archive, and we can't keep her waiting, can we?"

Harry made a fuss over Palmer and handed him his card, saying, "You must promise me you'll call."

"Deal," Palmer said. "And thanks, Mr. Diamondstein."

"Harry. Call me Harry."

I watched Jack button up Harry's jacket with a proprietary air. Jack seemed so relentlessly animated now, as though he'd been entirely absorbed by his role as a "social" maven. And as the younger partner to a famous man. Jack was no longer the mysterious sleepwalker from the Midwest nor the shy boy who'd been in love with me—nor the sleek libertine of the 1970s. Now he was smiling and nodding as they walked down the street but toward no one in particular.

ACKNOWLEDGMENTS

I want to thank my friends Rick Whitaker and Greg Pierce for reading every word of this book and suggesting significant changes. John Irving and I started new novels and finished them at the same time and encouraged each other all along the way; his energy and enthusiasm are unique. My partner, Michael Carroll, did a careful first edit and has encouraged me at every moment, day in and day out—without him, nothing. He was the one who suggested to me a new way of writing a novel. My agent, Amanda Urban, remains my friend and protector; her energy and loyalty and acumen helped me through a very difficult moment with this book. Anton Mueller is my brilliant and totally reasonable editor; his final edit helped me give the novel more coherence. Beatrice von Rezzori opened her house in Tuscany to me—the ultimate paradise for a writer. For a month I was a resident of Bogliasco, near Genoa. Joyce Carol Oates was a first and invaluable reader. George Pitcher, Will Evans, Yaron Aronowicz, and David Russell sustained me and advised me while I worked on this book. David Ebershoff has always urged me on to write it. Paul Muldoon, the director of the Lewis Center for the Arts at Princeton, graciously gave me leave from my teaching duties, which allowed me to pursue this project.

Keith McDermott and Zachary Pace typed the manuscript and made many suggestions along the way. Gary Mantello corrected a few mistakes I made about foxhunting, though I alone am responsible for any that remain. Bill Tucker helped me out with medical information.

A NOTE ON THE AUTHOR

An esteemed novelist and cultural critic, Edmund White is the author of many books including the autobiographical novel *A Boy's Own Story*; *The Flâneur*; a biography of the poet Arthur Rimbaud; *Hotel de Dream*, a novel; and two memoirs *My Lives* and *City Boy*. Edmund White lives in New York City and teaches writing at Princeton University. He is an Officier of the Ordre des Arts et des Lettres and a recipient of the Award for Literature from the American Academy of Arts and Letters.